WHAT KATHLEEN DID

WHAT KATHLEEN DID

Jill McRae-Spencer

T

Troubador Publishing Ltd
Unit E2 Airfield Business Park,
Harrison Road, Market Harborough,
Leicestershire. LE16 7UL
Tel: 0116 2792299
Email: books@troubador.co.uk
Web: www.troubador.co.uk

ISBN 978 1805145 356

British Library Cataloguing in Publication Data.
A catalogue record for this book is available from the British Library.

Printed and bound in Great Britain by 4edge Limited
Typeset in 11pt Minion Pro by Troubador Publishing Ltd, Leicester, UK

All my love and many thanks to Alison and Duncan for their support and encouragement

CHAPTER 1

August 1929

In the dream, the man has his back to her. It isn't her father; she can tell from the line of his head and shoulder. She calls out to him, although she doesn't know his name, and he turns to face her. Everything is still a blur; she cannot make out his features, yet he seems to be smiling at her. A rattle and a clank, and her heart starts to pound, and a familiar voice, a girl's voice, is saying that they are only five minutes late...

Kathleen woke up to find that she was still on the train, and opened her eyes in time to see Alice, the owner of the voice, reaching for a suitcase from the rack as the train gave a final shudder and ground to a halt. With a shriek Alice toppled over and landed on the seat beside her.

"I wish they wouldn't do that," Alice complained. She took a deep breath to retrieve her dignity, and reached again for the suitcase.

Kathleen's mouth felt all furred up and her shoulder numb where she'd leaned against the window, and the dream had left a tight feeling in her chest. She rubbed her shoulder and tried unsuccessfully to stifle a yawn. Gathering herself together, she stood up, wiggled her hips to shake the creases from the skirt of her lemon-and-white polka-dot dress, and gazed out the window. The flower bed of Ivybridge Station in South Devon, overflowing with asters and sweet alyssum, entertained a host of bees and red admiral butterflies in the afternoon sun. Drunk on nectar, legs heavy with pollen, a bumblebee, mistaking a woman's hat for a gigantic lavender bloom, buzzed around her head. The woman screamed, fending it off with an arm, and the man beside her flapped a newspaper until the bee flew away. Kathleen smiled to herself and yawned again.

"We'll need porters." Alice's voice sounded firm.

"Of course," agreed Kathleen. She opened the door of their compartment in the first-class carriage and scanned the scene. Farmers, tradesmen and families back from a day out poured like a flood towards the barrier, obscuring her view.

Further up the carriage, another door opened, but Kathleen never saw the young man in a double-breasted navy jacket who stepped onto the platform. And he never glanced in her direction. She failed even to catch a glimpse of him as he strode towards the exit, where the stationmaster raised a hand in salute and exchanged a brief word. Nor did she observe him hand in his ticket, make straight for the only taxi and climb in. If she had, or if he had glanced in her direction, their story might have been different; very different.

Doors slammed; the guard's whistle blew. The engine let out a hoot and a hiss of steam. Smoke filled the platform, engulfing the girls marooned beside a mountain of suitcases, bags and boxes, but as the air cleared Kathleen realised that their plight had been spotted by two porters, racing to offer assistance.

"Porter, madam?" asked the first, an eager grin on his face.

"I'm sure we'll need both of you," Kathleen replied. "We do have rather a lot of luggage, I'm afraid."

"No trouble, no trouble at all," said the second porter, already loading suitcases onto his trolley.

Arm in arm with Alice, Kathleen strolled to the barrier and looked around.

"No taxis?" Alice spun round to face her. "What are we going to do?"

"No taxis? Huh. Where's the stationmaster?" Kathleen stepped smartly back onto the platform. "Excuse me!" she called out.

The stationmaster stopped in his tracks. He turned, a weary look clouding his features.

"I'd like to know where I can find a taxi." Kathleen's tone was polite yet firm. "When we left Paddington this morning, they said all stations had taxis."

"I'm sorry, madam," he replied. "There was a taxi, but Mr Neville took it."

"When will it be back?"

"Difficult to say, madam." He consulted his pocket watch. "All local trains till five o'clock. I'm sure Mr Neville would send it straight back, if he knew."

"Well, what do you propose, seeing that Mr Neville, whoever he is, *doesn't* know?" Kathleen met the stationmaster's gaze.

He glanced away, looking up the track, seeking inspiration. "Where exactly are you heading?" he enquired.

"The London Hotel."

"If you wouldn't mind the walk, the porters could take your luggage."

"Is it far to the hotel?" asked Alice.

"About quarter of a mile – all downhill." The stationmaster raised one eyebrow in a hopeful expression.

Alice rewarded him with a smile. "I'm sure we'll manage very well."

As the trolleys trundled across the humpbacked bridge spanning the River Erme, Kathleen took off her hat and shook her head, flicking hair the colour of rich chocolate from cheek to cheek.

"You're so lucky, having straight hair," complained Alice. "It's impossible to have a bob if you don't have straight hair."

"Oh, Alice, don't worry." Kathleen put an arm round her shoulder. "The next thing will be waves. You'll see. Everyone will want waves and you'll be the height of fashion."

The procession halted outside the hotel's main entrance. Kathleen took two half-crowns from her purse and gave one to each porter. Grinning at one another, the men pocketed the coins.

"Much obliged. Thank you, madam." Each touched his cap in turn.

The London Hotel, once an old coaching inn, now had aspirations for the modern era, but its clientele did not always recognise this fact. A scrawny man with thin grey hair, a racking cough, and stooping shoulders appeared, and identified himself as the hotel's 'boy'. He unloaded the trolleys and staggered with the suitcases through the

4

entrance into the lobby, which was cool and dim, with a slightly musty smell caused by the collection of stuffed animals and birds that inhabited it. A couple of stags' heads glowered at each other; a fox, its mouth open, stood poised for flight on a plinth near the window; an array of buzzards, skylarks and hooded crows occupied the top of a bookcase.

At the reception desk a balding clerk, attired in black except for a white wing-collared shirt, stood up to greet them. The dark oak desk was cramped and curved, so that the little man gave the impression of a mole rising from a molehill. "Good afternoon." He peered through round-rimmed spectacles with pebble lenses.

"Miss Wyndham and Miss Fitzgerald," said Kathleen. "I believe you have a letter from my father concerning the arrangements for our stay."

The clerk bent down, burrowed among a mass of correspondence, and dug out a letter. "Yes, of course, madam." He held it close, eyes straining to decipher the contents. "You are staying with us for seven nights, I see." He looked up. "If you'd just sign the visitors' book." He indicated a leather-bound volume.

Formalities completed, he led the way up the stairs, along a corridor where the floor sloped to one side, and stopped opposite an oil painting of a racehorse with an impossibly small head and thin legs.

"Your room, mesdames," he said, placing the key in the lock and opening the door. "The ladies' bathroom is at the end of the corridor." He indicated with a hand. "Oh, I nearly forgot to tell you. I do apologise. Your bicycles – the railway people delivered them yesterday. May I wish you a very pleasant holiday?" He smiled and gave a little bow.

The moment they were alone, Kathleen looked at Alice. "Do you think we've come to the right place? It's not quite what I expected. The way Marjorie Thompson went on about it: how perfect; how much her family enjoyed their holiday…"

"I don't know," said Alice. "Anyway, we're going to be out most of the time, aren't we? I'm sure it'll be fine."

After breakfast the following morning, they made arrangements for a picnic lunch, then wandered over to the reception desk, where the little mole-man greeted them. In a rack on the counter sat postcards with views of Ivybridge in sepia tints. Kathleen bought one with a picture of the ivy-clad bridge that spanned the river, and Alice chose one of the main street. Then they retired to the lounge, where pens, ink and blotting paper for the use of residents were set out on tables.

Kathleen dipped a pen in the inkwell and wrote:

Dear Mummy and Daddy,
Arrived safely, as did the bicycles. Going on a picnic. Weather hot.
Lots of love,
Kathleen

When the postcard arrived tomorrow during breakfast, her father would seize it off the silver tray brought by Elsie, their maid. He'd be smiling and pleased that everything was well, and he'd hand the card to Kathleen's mother. And her mother would sigh and take it from him with a look that said she was bored. She'd glance at it, put it to one

6

side, then reach for her cigarette case and insert the first one of the day into her cigarette holder. More than likely she'd toss the postcard into the wastepaper basket before the week was out.

A kitchen maid arrived with their picnic lunches, and the mole-man escorted them to the old stables where the bicycles were housed. They set off, the sun hot and strong on their backs. Kathleen should have been happy, because they'd planned this holiday for almost a year – their last year together at Chiltern Ladies' College – and they were following in the steps of Marjorie Thompson, their old head girl. Kathleen had once had a bit of a crush on Marjorie – she admitted as much – but then, so had a lot of the other girls. Marjorie inspired them; told them that girls could do anything they wanted these days, didn't have to marry the first young man who came along, and that she herself had no intention of marrying. Kathleen believed her. After all, Marjorie had declared that she was going into public life and would one day stand for Parliament. Now that women had the vote at twenty-one, the same as men, there would be more and more women MPs. Although Kathleen was sure that she too wanted to 'do' something, the 'something' she was destined to do obstinately refused to reveal itself to her.

The slopes of Dartmoor rose, slate blue and smooth, above the patchwork of grazing meadows, cornfields and blackberry hedges that was the Yeo valley. As they paused for a moment to hang over a gate and catch their breath, Alice asked if that was where they were heading, nodding at the moor, and Kathleen said yes, because if they reached it they would have a terrific view.

7

A mile or so further on they came to Southwood village. The road opened out into a square, where a cross carved from granite and mounted on octagonal steps recorded lives lost in the Great War. Boys in short trousers and scuffed shoes shouted and chased one another up and down the steps, oblivious to the monument's solemn warning. To one side of the square, substantial white-painted gates suggested a residence of substance lay just out of sight. On a bench outside the blacksmith's forge a couple of old men sat gossiping, heads inclined towards one another, caps pulled down to shade their eyes from the sun's glare. Kathleen asked them where the road led, and whether it was possible to reach the open moor. The first man looked amused at her question and said he presumed they weren't from round these parts. The second added that if they turned left about half a mile further on and kept going, eventually they'd come to Moor Gate.

Following those instructions, they found the hedges growing ever higher and the gradient steeper, until they came to a fork in the road and wondered which way to go. The moor was still some distance away, but if they took the track to their right the ground flattened out. Kathleen screwed up her eyes against the sun and surveyed the valley. Past midday, and heat lay on the hillside and wooded valley, swathing fields, farms and cottages in a blue-grey mantle. Her eyes followed the line of the river, meandering south towards the sea; hill after hill, each paler than the one before, fading into far-distant haze, so that it became impossible to say where the earth ended and the sky began. Sweat trickled down the back of her neck and stood in beads on her forehead.

"Must be time for our picnic," Alice said.

"Let's see if we can find some shade." Kathleen had spotted a gate a few yards further on. "How about this field?"

But the instant they reached the gate, she realised they were not alone. Two shire horses, driven by a man, pulled a machine that cut the ripe stalks of grain, binding them together in sheaves, then spewing them out onto the stubble. Following in its wake, three more men gathered the sheaves and arranged them in stooks. The driver lifted a lever so that the machine stopped working, and he began to drive the horses towards an ancient oak offering a pool of green shade in the hot stillness of the midday hour. The men took this as a sign that their morning's labour was over, and made for the shelter too.

The farmer began to walk towards the gate. He must have seen the girls, because he was beckoning to them. Kathleen could hear her heart beating as he came nearer. His hands, face and neck, exposed to sun and wind, glowed like mahogany. Only a few feet from her, he put up an arm to wipe a forehead shining with sweat, and his shirt – collarless, buttons undone at the neck – revealed the pale skin of his chest. As she looked up to meet his gaze, something in the pit of her stomach curled up and twisted itself into a knot.

He smiled. "Jim Wilcox," he said, offering a hand. "You visiting these parts? Come and join us – we're stopping for our dinner."

"Yes, we are. I'm Kathleen Wyndham." She dared not trust herself to meet his gaze again. "And this is Alice Fitzgerald," she remembered to say just in time.

"Come down to the shade. Room enough for a couple more." He nodded towards the oak tree.

"What are you harvesting, Mr Wilcox?" Alice enquired.

"This here's barley," he replied. "And you can call me Jim."

Kathleen stole a glance as Jim ran a hand through his dark, unruly hair. Behind his ears, it curled like feathers in a duck's tail.

"We'll get the reaping done by tonight," he continued. "We'll need to make a rick when the grain's dried out." Setting down his jacket on the dusty ground, he invited them to sit on it.

From her saddlebag Kathleen took a bottle of lemonade and a packet of sandwiches. Although she chewed and chewed, the bread stuck in her mouth and refused to go down her throat. Even though she took gulp after gulp of lemonade, the sandwich lay unfinished in her hand when the bottle was drained. "Not as hungry as I thought," she said, giving Alice a weak smile.

"Like a sip of this?" Suddenly, Jim was there, an earthenware bottle in his hand. "Been in the stream all morning – cold as a body could wish for."

"What is it?" Kathleen glanced up as she spoke. His eyes were blue; a piercing blue. Her heart began to thump against her ribs; it must surely give her away.

"Cider," he said. "Do you good. I can see the heat o' the day's getting to you."

As she took the bottle from him, the back of his hand brushed hers in a careless gesture, and a blistering current shot up her arm. She almost dropped the bottle. Had he meant to touch her? Surely he must realise what he'd done. Yet without a backward glance, Jim joined the men, who were laughing and joking as they sprawled on dusty, dried-out earth around the tree roots.

Hands trembling, Kathleen put the bottle to her lips and took a long draught. The taste was strong and mellow, the icy contents slipping down her parched throat. She wiped the bottle with a clean handkerchief and offered it – more from politeness than anything – to Alice, but to her surprise Alice took the bottle from her.

"Well, just a sip. Don't want to get tipsy. And you must promise not to tell. Mummy would be horrified if she knew I'd broken the pledge." Alice giggled. She swallowed twice and handed it back.

"Don't worry – no chance of me telling your mother." Kathleen drained the bottle. Then she lay on her back, head on the jacket, and gazed into the gnarled branches above, where flashes of gold danced among leathery green leaves. Sweat and straw and dirt – the smell of Jim lingered on the jacket's lining. Turning onto one side, she stuffed a sleeve under her head for a pillow. Sounds and images swam in profusion as she drifted in a delicious, cider-induced stupor.

"Sleeping beauty, if ever I saw one." Jim was standing over her. "Stay right there and take a nap, if you've a mind."

Back stiff and hip sore, Kathleen sat up and rubbed her eyes. A short distance away Alice was picking up sheaves, struggling to stack them together in a stook.

"Like to help?" Jim enquired.

"Yes." Kathleen scrambled to her feet and followed him.

"Like this," he said, reaching for a sheaf. "One under each arm and one in each hand."

But however hard Kathleen tried, the sheaves lodged under her arms fell down every time she went to pick up the third, and the straw scratched her skin and left red weals.

"No, no. Not like that." His arms encircled her, guiding her. His hair flopped forward, brushing her ear, and his breath was moist on the back of her neck. "See? Now you know how to do it," he said, straightening up. Then he was gone, and she stood alone, staring after him and wondering how she could feel so bemused.

She worked on, arms aching, back aching, but never mastered carrying four sheaves at a time. Whenever she glanced up to see where Jim was, his attention was always on the horses or the men; she might just as well not have been there. She tried to think what it was – something about his face, his touch, his voice – that drew her to him; that unsettled her. Somewhere towards the back of her mind, a warning voice told her he was dangerous; that she should be on her guard; that she was playing with fire. But she pushed the thought away and it lay unheeded where it fell.

Alice was sitting under the oak when Kathleen wandered over and slumped down beside her. "It's been fun but we've quite a way to cycle back," Alice reminded her.

"Yes, time we were going." Kathleen yawned, pushing her fringe off her forehead with dusty palms.

"Gosh, if you could see yourself." Alice smirked.

"Why? What's so funny?"

"You've just put dirty marks all over—"

"Just wait till *you* look in the mirror." Kathleen burst into a fit of giggles.

"Now then, ladies, I expect you'll want to get along. 'Twas most kind of you to lend a hand." Suddenly, Jim was there, looking down at Kathleen, and the thudding in her heart started up all over again.

"Jolly good fun, but we'd better be off now," said Alice. "Wait a moment – let me take a photo." She went to fetch the Box Brownie camera from her saddlebag.

Kathleen stood beside Jim, they turned to face Alice, and Jim placed a hand on Kathleen's shoulder.

"Now then – smile, please." The shutter snapped. "Got it." Alice wound the film on.

"We'll be rick-making on Thursday," Jim said, releasing Kathleen's shoulder. "If you've a mind, come along – we'd appreciate the extra help." His smile was gentle, coaxing.

"I think we might manage that," replied Kathleen, failing utterly to notice the dismay on Alice's face.

That evening, whenever she had a moment to herself, Kathleen would conjure up an image of Jim, allowing it to linger in her head. She indulged herself in recalling sensations, new and raw, fermenting within her, and told herself she could walk the tightrope and not fall off. She was so unusually quiet, and must have appeared so out of sorts, that Alice asked if she were unwell, and Kathleen replied, "Awfully tired, but I wouldn't have missed it for the world. I'm really looking forward to going back", and gave a quick smile.

"Are you mad?" Alice stared at her. "We're on holiday; we're not here to work like peasants in a barley field."

Kathleen's reply came as a silent stare.

"No, Kathleen, no."

"I want to help Jim." Kathleen stuck out her jaw. "Besides, I rather like him." There – she'd said it, and as she spoke, colour flooded her cheeks.

"You can't – you don't know anything about him. It could never go anywhere."

To her annoyance, Kathleen found her whole body shaking in defiance.

"Well, it's true," Alice insisted.

"Do what you want, Alice. I'm going back to the farm on Thursday. I'm going to help Jim." Kathleen saw Alice's hurt expression and wished she could take the words back, but discord hung in the air between them like a stale odour.

CHAPTER 2

Kathleen surfaced from a restless sleep as the grey light of dawn crept between curtain and wall. She wondered if Jim was awake too, and if he was, whether he was thinking of her. Yesterday at this time she had known nothing of him, had not known that he even existed, but today she could picture him in the barley field, coal-black hair curling over his collar, the merest hint of a smile as he spoke, and the very direct way he looked at her. Outside in the yard someone started clanking dustbins, while on the other side of the room Alice stirred, turned over, and opened bleary eyes. Kathleen decided it would be best to say nothing more to Alice about yesterday or Jim. She went to the window, drew back the curtains, and remarked on how fortunate they were to have such glorious weather. It was then that she noticed a car parked on the far side of the courtyard.

"Oh my goodness, look at this, Alice!" she exclaimed. "It wasn't there yesterday." What a bit of luck, having something new to talk about. Guilt still gnawed away as she recalled what had passed between them last night. But Alice had no idea how it felt; she just didn't understand. How could she?

"What are you talking about?" Rubbing her eyes, Alice stumbled over to join her. "I say, what a marvellous colour. I do so adore bright blue."

"I wonder who it belongs to?" said Kathleen. "Whoever they are, they must be staying here, mustn't they?"

It was when they were finishing breakfast and talking about what they might do that day that Kathleen looked up and saw a young man approaching. He was round-shouldered, thin as a beanpole, and with an eager expression that was mildly irritating. She would have liked to ignore him, but to her surprise Alice jumped up and greeted him with delight.

"Binkey, fancy seeing you here. Kathleen, let me introduce Bertram Arbuthnot."

"Please, call me Binkey, everyone does." The young man chortled nervously and held out a limp hand. "Saw you come in yesterday. I was in the lounge with the parents."

"How do you do?" Kathleen rose from her seat, grasped the flabby extension, and shook it briefly.

Binkey had large ears that stuck out beneath a shock of coarse, mousy-coloured hair that refused to submit to the Brylcreem lavished on it. "We're off to see the Nevilles today," he volunteered. "D'you know the Nevilles?"

Kathleen shook her head, although the name sounded familiar.

"Live at Alston Hall, in Southwood."

An image of the white gates in the village square formed in Kathleen's mind.

"Lord Neville invited us over for the day," Binkey continued. "Robert – that's his son – used to be at school with my brother, so I sort of know him. Might get in a spot of golf, I dare say."

Of course – the man who'd taken the only taxi at the station the day they'd arrived was called Neville, but before Kathleen could say anything disparaging about the Nevilles, a kitchen maid arrived with the picnic lunches they'd ordered. As Kathleen was about to give Alice a let's-be-on-our-way look, an image of the blue car leaped into her mind, and curiosity overcame her. "Is the car in the courtyard yours?" she asked.

"Yes," said Binkey. "Like to see it?"

They followed him across the cobbles to where the car basked in full sun. Binkey showed off, patting and smoothing down the vehicle's hood with obvious affection and telling them it was a Morris Cowley, seated four, and his father had bought it for touring.

"Do you drive it, Binkey?" Alice gave him an admiring glance.

"The pater says I'm not to," said Binkey. "Not till I've learned properly. Says he doesn't want me bashing it up before he's had a chance to enjoy it." He chortled again.

Alice remarked that Kathleen's father had taught her to drive, which surprised Binkey no end. His obvious reluctance to acknowledge that a mere girl could master such a difficult art Kathleen found annoying, and deliberately she let it drop that she would most likely be getting a car for her twenty-first. She even specified the model – an Austin 7 – just to show she knew what she was talking about.

"Well, we'd better be off now," she said. Binkey's attempts to be friendly were turning his face into a perpetual smirk and getting on her nerves. "Come on, Alice, let's fetch the bicycles." Kathleen, with Alice in pursuit, fetched the bicycles from the shed.

"Bye. Have a nice picnic." Binkey waved an arm as they set off.

"Enjoy your golf." Alice waved back, then pedalled furiously after Kathleen. "I say, wait a moment. What's the rush?"

"Just want to get away from Binkey. He's a drip."

"How can you say such a thing, Kathleen? Such a nice young man, and I'm sure he's from a good family."

"Alice, you are no judge of men," Kathleen said. "All that time at Chiltern Ladies' College, surrounded by girls and female teachers, has wilted your brain."

"You were there as long as I was." Alice drew level with her. "What about you, then?"

"All I'm saying is that I'm just not prepared to settle for someone ordinary." Kathleen said this because she wanted Alice to think that she'd no intention of taking Jim seriously, despite what she'd said about liking him. "I'd rather *do* something. Do you realise girls can do anything these days? Girls don't just drive cars; some girls fly aeroplanes, you know."

"You're so brave, Kathleen. I could never do anything like that."

"It's all in the mind, Alice. You can do anything if you want to – *really* want to."

"Anyway, where are we going – now, I mean?" Alice called after her. "We're following the same road as yesterday, and I thought we'd decided to head for Grimstone Down today."

They had come too far, Kathleen agreed, and needed to retrace their steps, but at that moment a noise from behind warned of an approaching vehicle. Within seconds the Arbuthnots' car appeared in a cloud of dust, driven by a man with a thin, lined face and a handlebar moustache. Beside him sat a lady of copious proportions and stoical expression. As a wheel hit a pothole and the car lurched to avoid the cyclists, Binkey waved with one hand and clung on to the back seat with the other. Alice waved back, but Kathleen pretended to have grit in her eye.

Grimstone Down was wonderful: wide tracts of finely cropped grass studded with tiny yellow flowers, occasional clumps of sweet-smelling heather, and swathes of bracken as high as a man's shoulder. At the highest point of the down, from where you could see for miles, someone had once had the foresight to plant a clump of trees, and here they sat in the shade to eat their picnic, and wondered whether the blue haze in the far distance really was the sea. It occurred to Kathleen that Jim might be thinking of her as often as she was of him. She pictured him standing there in front of her this very minute, smiling.

"What are you smiling at?" asked Alice, catching her off guard.

"Nothing really; it's just such a perfect day, isn't it?" It wasn't quite a lie, but she couldn't tell Alice the truth, could she?

Kathleen was all for planning their next excursion as they sat in the lounge that evening drinking coffee, so when she spotted Binkey approaching, she groaned inwardly – he was making straight for them. She could have done without his eager enthusiasm, but Alice appeared pleased to see him.

"I say, I had a marvellous day at the Nevilles," he began, grinning from ear to ear. "You girls have a good time?" Scarcely waiting for a reply, he continued, beaming with pride, "I told Robert about you, and he's asked me to invite you over on Wednesday. Said he'd pick us up and take us all to Alston Hall – you two and me. You will come, won't you?" His eyes fixed on Alice as he spoke.

"I'd love to come," she replied. And, turning to Kathleen, "It *would* be marvellous, wouldn't it? Do say yes."

"Yes, we'd love to come." Kathleen drew back the corners of her mouth in an expression that resembled a smile.

The weather held and the days passed in cycling expeditions and picnics, and always the thought of seeing Jim again and wondering if there might be some excuse for him to put an arm around her shoulder, or skim the back of his hand across hers, remained an absorbing pastime for Kathleen. However, as time drew on the visit to Alston Hall and meeting the man who'd bagged the only taxi without a thought for anyone else also became an intriguing proposition. She rehearsed in her mind the things she might say to Robert Neville, and decided she'd be magnanimous when he apologised for his loutish behaviour in leaving two young ladies stranded in unfamiliar surroundings. So when, on Wednesday morning, having spent some considerable time deciding what to wear, she and Alice waited among the stuffed animals of the lobby, it was with genuine pleasure that she greeted Binkey.

"I'm most awfully sorry." Binkey's features drooped, like those of a bearer of bad tidings who is praying that the messenger will not be shot.

"Whatever's the matter?" asked Alice.

"Just had a telephone message from Alston Hall." Binkey looked pale and nervous. "Robert's asked if we'd mind putting off the visit till tomorrow. Their groom's been kicked by a horse – broken rib, they think – and Robert's taking him to hospital."

"How awful," said Alice. "Poor man."

"So you don't mind if we go tomorrow instead?" Colour flooded back into Binkey's cheeks. "I'll telephone and leave a message for Robert." He looked as if he could have hugged her. "Thank you for being such a sport about it."

"You've forgotten something," hissed Kathleen, when Binkey was scarcely out of earshot. "We're going back to the farm to help with the harvest. We can't go to Alston Hall." Her heart began pumping hard and her face flushed with colour.

"Kathleen, you're being silly again." Alice stared at her. "I thought you'd got over all that. You haven't said anything about it for days."

Kathleen hated arguing with Alice. She found herself trembling with embarrassment, but the confrontation had sprung without warning from Binkey's message and ambushed her when she was least expecting it. "Do what you want, Alice. I'm going to the farm. I'm going to keep my promise." She saw the hurt expression on Alice's face, but there was no way back – unless, of course, she gave up for good the idea of seeing Jim again.

Alice combed sandy-coloured hair away from her eyes and scrutinised her dress in the wardrobe mirror. She twirled around, making the floral-patterned skirt flare out. It was the following morning and they were getting ready to go out.

"When you do that, your stocking tops show," observed Kathleen.

Alice ignored the remark. "I think the waterfall frill on the shoulder is just perfect," she said, flicking it back with a careless gesture. "What I can't decide is whether to wear a hat. I suppose one should. Mummy always says you can tell if a girl's been brought up properly by what she puts on her head."

"If you must wear a hat, it's got to be the blue cloche with the yellow band. You've got the bag that matches," Kathleen advised.

"What are you wearing? If you don't get a move on, we'll be late."

"Navy shorts and cream blouse," Kathleen replied.

"You can't possibly wear shorts to meet the Nevilles. Don't be ridiculous."

"You've forgotten – I'm going to help Jim with the harvest." Kathleen stood, hands on hips, defying Alice to contradict her. "In fact, I'd better get dressed right away and be off, or he'll think I'm not coming."

She pulled on her clothes, hands trembling, and scampered down the stairs with Alice's voice begging her to come back ringing in her ears. As she flew through the lobby, she glanced into the lounge where Binkey was deep in conversation with his parents, and a pang of remorse shot through her. It had been kind of him to get them an invitation to Alston Hall. She was already on her bicycle and well away from the hotel when she realised, too late, that she'd come without food or drink.

As she reached Southwood, the great white gates of Alston Hall were opened by a boy from the lodge. A car – she recognised it as a Bentley – was driven into the square by a man in his twenties. Now that had to be Robert Neville: clean-shaven, tanned face, fairish hair, good-looking and probably knew it. What a pity to miss the opportunity to tell him what she thought of him.

The air grew sultry and hotter than ever, although the sun was hidden by a thin veil of cloud, softening the shadows. She pressed on, reaching the field all hot and sticky, and hung her arms over the gate. A horse-drawn wagon piled high with sheaves came towards her. In its wake a flock of rooks scavenged for grain, bobbing and strutting among the putty-coloured stubble that had been cleared of stooks. A half-built rick sat within yards of the gate with Jim standing on the top, but the moment he spotted Kathleen he jumped down. Her heart gave a sudden lurch as he strode towards her.

"Where's your friend?" he asked.

"Alice has gone to Alston Hall."

"Why aren't you there? Aren't you good enough for the likes o' them?" His forehead furrowed in a deep line between the brows.

"I was invited, but I said I'd promised to help you with the harvest."

"You said that?" He threw back his head and let out a roar. "What a maid. Telling the gentry folk you're coming here 'stead of going there. Well, my handsome, let's see what we can give you to do." He took her bicycle and propped it against the hedge. "Know much about horses? How about taking over the wagon?"

When she nodded he placed an arm around her shoulder and led her towards the wagon, and it was so delicious to have him touch her again that she almost forgot to breathe.

"You can pitch a few sheaves," he told the driver. "The maid's taking over the wagon."

The driver, a swarthy man with sinuous arms, got down and grasped the fork Jim offered.

Jim raised his eyebrows at Kathleen and nodded in the direction of the narrow driving bench, and she scrambled up. He squashed in beside her, his thigh pressed against hers. Almost delirious with joy, she had to force herself to concentrate, because she didn't want to end up looking a complete fool. He demonstrated the turns and commands until she was beside herself with impatience and almost snatched the reins from him. He patted her on the back, jumped down, and strode back to the rick. Now she was in charge, doing a real job, a job Jim trusted her to do. She drove carefully, stopping only long enough for the men to throw the sheaves onto the wagon, then returning to the rick for unloading. Work was relentless until the final sheaf was placed and a tarpaulin hauled over and secured. Only then did she glance at her watch – gone two o'clock.

"Well, my flower, we couldn't have done it without you." Jim stood beside the wagon, sweat trickling down his face and neck. "Now, how about something to eat and drink?" His arm went round her waist, lifting her down, and her heart was racing in a frenzy of delight and pride. "See that basket over there?" He pointed to a wicker basket covered with a white cloth. "'Tis full – two loaves, butter, cheese, slices of ham. Put it all out on the cloth. Cut slices of bread an' butter, and we'll help ourselves." He turned to the man next to him. "Go down to the stream and fetch us back the cider. We deserve it today and no mistake."

Kathleen cut slice after slice with the carving knife she'd found at the bottom of the basket, buttering the bread as she did so, while earthenware cider bottles were handed round.

"Here, take some ham for your bread." Jim was leaning over her. "And see this bottle? I kept it special for you; no one's drunk from it. 'Tis yours."

The chill stone cooled her hands and the cider slipped down her throat. She nibbled at bread and ham, then gulped more cider until she'd almost finished the bottle.

"Won't be long now, I reckon." Jim cast an eye towards dark, towering clouds. Flurries of dust and straw rose from the ground, lifted by a swirling wind. Scarcely had he finished speaking when a fork of brilliance rent the gloom, followed by the crack and boom of thunder. Unsettled, the rooks cried out and took to the air in unison.

"Hitch the horse," Jim commanded one of the men. "Best get home soon as us can." Kathleen felt his hand on her shoulder. "Come back to the farm," he begged. "Wait till the storm's over. You'll get soaked if you try to get back to Ivybridge now."

"What about my bicycle?" She struggled to her feet and almost keeled over.

"Steady on, my handsome. Cider gone to your head, I shouldn't wonder. Don't worry now – bicycle can go on the wagon." He lifted her onto the seat, clambered up beside her and took the reins. "Ho, there," he shouted, and the horse lumbered into action, through the gateway and down the hill, the men ahead making for home as fast as they could.

Just as the wagon turned into the farm lane, a dazzling flash and a clap of thunder overhead made Kathleen jump. Great drops the size of pennies plopped down and the air took on a sharp freshness. The horse broke into a slow jog, reaching the yard as the clouds opened and rain like stair rods hissed down on the cobbles. Jim lifted Kathleen down from the wagon and her arms closed around his neck. He carried her into the barn and gently put her down. Her head swam; she clutched at the wall and stood shivering, rain dripping from her hair, nose and cheeks, her blouse clinging to her shoulders.

As soon as he'd seen to the horse, Jim was back. "'Tis a darn sight more cosy up here," he said, taking her hand and leading her towards a ladder at the back of the barn. "Up you go – I'm right behind you."

She grasped the rungs of the ladder and climbed, one careful foot at a time, into the loft, where hay lay several feet deep. He fetched a blanket hanging on a rafter, shook it out, and spread it over a hollow. Gently he pushed her shoulders and she sank down. Whether she was drunk on love or on cider, she could not tell.

He knelt beside her. "You'm cold, my flower. Here, let me give you some warmth."

His hand reached out and turned her face to his. And when his lips brushed hers, she thought her heart would burst. She opened her eyes to look at him, but the loft seemed to be in motion, so she shut them again and sank back.

"Liked that, didn't you, my lovely one? See what you think of this, then."

He ran a finger down the back of her ear, her neck, down her blouse. A moan escaped her. He undid the buttons, one by one; she did nothing to stop him. Her body was paralysed with delight: never had anything felt so beautiful.

"Jim, Jim, what are you doing?"

"Making a woman of you, my lovely one."

His lips pressed down on hers, his tongue finding its way into her mouth. His hand moved over her body. She gave in; she could resist him no longer.

"There, there, my beauty. Have no one done that for you before?"

Then it was all over and he rolled off. Unable to speak, she turned to him, clasping his shoulder and burying her head in his chest as he pulled the blanket around them.

CHAPTER 3

"Jim? Jim!" The voice was a woman's; an older woman's, quavering on the high notes.

Kathleen opened her eyes to see Jim sitting up, forefinger to his lips, giving her a look which said, *Don't say a word.*

"What's the matter, Mother?" he shouted.

"'Tis the cows at the field gate. They'm getting restless. 'Tis past milking."

"I'm seeing to it, Mother. Go back inside and make yourself a cup of tea. I'm seeing to the beasts, soon as I'm finished up here."

He dressed quickly, then helped Kathleen to her feet and told her to get her clothes on, because the storm had passed. The swirling in her head had become a dull ache, but her befuddled brain began to ask questions. What had he done to her? What had she let him do?

"Must see to the milking – cows won't wait," he said. But all the same he drew her to him, his grip so tight she could scarcely breathe, and kissed her. "You'm a real beauty, but I must let you go. Careful now – I'll help you down."

He fetched her bicycle and pushed it for her as she walked beside him to the yard gate. "Staying long at Ivybridge?" he enquired.

"Catching the train back tomorrow."

He studied his boots and sighed. "That's a shame... can't be helped, I suppose. You've got your own folk." He turned on his heel and trudged back to the yard.

She pushed the bicycle down the lane through muddy rivulets. She didn't look back because it would be undignified to look back. Mist rose from the valley and lingered on the hillside; ferns, grasses, nettles and docks, laden with droplets, hung from the hedgerows.

What had she done? She had done *it*. She had done *it* with Jim. Well, what was so terrible about that? "You should save yourself for your husband; no man wants to marry a girl who isn't pure." Everyone at school had said things like that. But who would know she wasn't pure? If she didn't tell anyone, who would ever know? She shut her eyes and trembled. Never had she imagined... She gripped the handlebars to steady herself. A breath of wind swayed a hazel branch overhead. She cried out as the shower soaked her hair and trickled down her neck. Just as well she was going home tomorrow, out of harm's way, because if she was alone with Jim again... Oh heavens, what he did to her... she'd never be able to stop him; she'd want him too much.

The rain started again, soft, gentle drops, as she freewheeled down to Southwood. No one about; windows and doors all shut against the storm. She pushed on, but mile or so before Ivybridge the distinctive chug of a car engine made her stop and move over to let it pass. However, the car slowed and came to a halt.

"Kathleen, Kathleen!" The car was the Bentley she'd seen earlier, and there was Alice sitting in the back with Binkey.

The driver climbed out, ran round to the front of the car, and extended a hand. "Sorry, we've not been properly introduced – Robert Neville," he said. "Here, let me help you." He propped Kathleen's bicycle against the hedge and opened the passenger door. "Please, get in."

She glanced at her bicycle and hesitated.

"Don't worry, we won't leave it behind," Robert said.

"All right, thank you." She slid onto the front passenger seat – soft grey leather. "So very kind of you to give me a lift."

Robert stowed the bicycle away in the boot, and returned to the driver's seat. "Pleased to be of service," he said. His eyes flashed and his smile had a hint of the mischievous. "I understand you were none too pleased when you arrived last week to find I'd taken the taxi. Perhaps you'll allow me to make up for my transgressions and take you back to your hotel?"

"You're very kind," she said, looking down at her hands.

"And would you allow me to fetch you and Alice from the hotel tomorrow and take you to the station?"

"Really, you don't need to go to all that trouble, but thank you all the same." She glanced up.

"Oh, but it would be my pleasure, and enable me to make amends for my churlish behaviour at the same time."

"It's very kind of Robert," Alice broke in.

Kathleen managed a faint smile. "We'll be happy to accept your offer, I'm sure."

The instant they were back in their room, Kathleen grabbed her washbag and towel. "I've just got to have a bath and wash my hair, Alice. You cannot imagine how dusty it was in the barley field."

"What on earth did you do when the thunder started?"

"Went back to the farm and sheltered till it was over." Kathleen was acutely aware that the smell of Jim lingered on her, the odour so overwhelming she half-expected Alice to make some remark. "Must dash." She scurried down the corridor to the bathroom, locked the door behind her, and prepared to wash away every last trace of that afternoon.

By eight o'clock, when it was time to go down to dinner, she was almost her old self: her hair was as sleek as usual, and she was wearing her favourite evening dress – sleeveless peach lace with a low scooped neck. A long look in the wardrobe mirror was reassuring: deep brown eyes with heavy lashes looked back at her from under thin, arching eyebrows. The only thing she'd change, she mused, would be her nose. It was straight, which was good, but just a bit longer than she'd have liked. She pursed her mouth and was kissing the air when she became aware of Alice's reflection in the mirror, staring at her. Feeling stupid, she wheeled round and remarked, "Really suits you, that colour blue."

"Thank you."

"Ready?" Kathleen felt the flush in her cheeks, and hoped Alice hadn't noticed.

As they passed through the lounge, Binkey waylaid them. "I say, you two. Gosh, you look simply wonderful."

"Thank you, Binkey," said Kathleen, but he wasn't looking at her; he was looking at Alice.

"Would you care to meet the pater and mater?" The

nervous excitement in his voice showed. "They're dying to be introduced to you."

"I'm sure we would," Kathleen said, although it was clear by now that the real object of Binkey's attention was Alice.

"Come on," said Binkey, "they're just over here."

Grinning like the Cheshire cat, he led them to where his mother was sipping a gin and tonic and his father nursing a glass of Scotch in one hand and a cigar in the other. They looked up and rose to their feet as the girls approached. Colonel Arbuthnot had an earnest countenance that gave the impression that he expected disaster to strike at any moment, and that when it did, he would be ready for it.

Mrs Arbuthnot smiled warmly at the girls. "So pleased to meet you," she said as Alice and Kathleen were introduced.

"Damn shame about the weather breaking," said Colonel Arbuthnot. "Heard you got caught out." His eyes flashed at Kathleen from under bushy brows.

Her heart lurched, but she steadied herself; there was no way he could know what had happened. "Yes, got rather wet. Never mind, I'm fine now."

"I understand you're going home tomorrow," said Mrs Arbuthnot.

"That's right," said Alice. "Robert's very kindly offered to take us to the station."

"Oh, Robert – such a nice young man," Mrs Arbuthnot mused. "I'm sure it's a great comfort to Frederick to have Robert at home."

"Frederick's not the man he was." Colonel Arbuthnot took a sip from his glass. "Failing, if you ask me. May not have long. Damn bad luck, Wilfred getting killed like that, so late in the war." He leaned back. "Wilfred was his heir, you know. But Robert will be there to take over now; run the estate for him."

"Are you staying long in Ivybridge?" Kathleen enquired.

"One more day," replied Mrs Arbuthnot. "Then we're taking to the road again."

"Bertram has to be back in the office on Monday," chipped in the colonel, "so we're travelling in the general direction of home."

"What kind of office?" Kathleen turned to Binkey. "What do you do?"

Binkey opened his mouth to respond, but Mrs Arbuthnot sprang in first. "He's going to be a solicitor. The firm he's with, Rawlinson, Ashcroft and Pepperfield, is very well respected in our area, and he's articled to the senior partner. Only two more years and Bertie will be sitting the Law Society's Final Examination." She beamed affectionately at her son, whose pale countenance turned deep red.

"Too many damned examinations, if you ask me," said the colonel. "Don't have all that bookwork in the army. Show 'em what you're made of. He'd have done better if he'd gone in the army like his brother."

"Now you know that's not true, Augustus," Mrs Arbuthnot reprimanded him. "Bertie's very good with his brain; brawn isn't everything. And the way Mr Pepperfield spoke the other day, it sounds as if there'll be an opening for him with the firm when he's qualified."

"Humph. We'll see."

A waiter approached. "Your table is ready, sir, madam." He bowed twice. "If you'd be so kind as to come this way…"

The next day was fresher as the wind had gone round to the north-west and blown away the intolerable heat of the previous week. Robert arrived with commendable punctuality and insisted on overseeing the handling of the luggage. Even the hotel boy appeared revived by the change in the weather, whistling to himself through cracked teeth as he went about his duties. At the reception desk Kathleen cast an eye down the bill and, satisfied, completed her father's cheque, filling in the amount.

"Thank you, madam. I do hope you enjoyed your stay. The railway people collected your bicycles while you were at breakfast," said the mole-man.

Outside, Binkey was talking to Alice and Robert. As soon as he saw Kathleen, Robert left them and came over.

"How are you? Are you completely recovered?"

"I'm perfectly all right again." But the dark rings under her eyes told a different tale. "It's sweet of you to be so concerned."

Robert consulted his watch. "We'd better get you and Alice to the station. Don't want you missing your train, do we?"

Things happened when it was known that Robert was at the station. The stationmaster saluted, porters sprang into action, and the booking clerk allowed him in without a platform ticket. The porters staggered across the bridge carrying the luggage and stood ready on the up-line platform. Robert slipped each a coin and glanced at his watch. Kathleen looked down the track, thinking to spot the train in the distance, but all at once became aware of Robert standing close, observing her.

"You look absolutely wonderful," he said. "I hope you don't mind my saying so."

She found the self-assured confidence he radiated attractive, but wondered all the same how he could pay her such a compliment when she knew she looked all washed out.

"I'm coming up to town next Friday," he went on. "I wonder whether you and Alice would care to have lunch with me?"

The invitation was so unexpected it stunned her, and Alice had to reply for the two of them.

"That's very kind of you," Alice said. "We'd love to, wouldn't we, Kathleen?"

"Yes. Oh yes, very kind of you, Robert. We'd love to."

"Can you find your way to the Savoy? One o'clock? I'll look forward to seeing you then," he said.

As the train pulled away, Kathleen rested her head against the seat and stifled a yawn. An ever-changing scene rolled past the carriage window: fields, trees, houses, church spires, towns. The rolling, rocking train dulled her senses; her eyelids drooped and her thoughts wandered. Images of home, the avenue of trees, and the respectable neighbours whose names she hardly knew floated around in her brain. Alice lived only two streets away but they'd met as boarders at Chiltern Ladies' College and discovered that they came from the same part of Wimbledon. Alice's father worked in the City, like Kathleen's own. Her father was a stockbroker; Alice's something to do with insurance. The two men had been catching the same train every morning for years and had never spoken to each other until Kathleen and Alice had brought them together.

She imagined how it would be at Paddington: Daddy holding out his arms to greet her. She'd rush to meet him, and he'd hug her and tell her how much he'd missed her. He'd ask whether they'd had a good time, if the weather had been as hot as it had at home, whether they'd done much cycling, if the hotel had been up to scratch, and whether they'd bumped into anyone they knew. He'd be as excited to see her as she was to see him. And when they reached home Mummy would say something like, she hoped all the fuss had been worthwhile and now that Kathleen had had her cycling holiday, perhaps she'd start thinking seriously about what she was going to do? Finishing school would be the sensible choice, but Kathleen had never been sensible, so why should she start now? Mummy's eyes would flash and her cheeks would colour in annoyance. Kathleen knew how it would be. She drew in a deep breath and exhaled slowly. For a few minutes she drifted, allowing the perpetual roll and clunk of the train to cloud her consciousness.

The next thing she knew, Alice was saying that they were in Berkshire, and that that was where the Arbuthnots lived.

"Hmm," replied Kathleen, opening one eye fleetingly.

"Binkey's asked me to meet him the first Saturday in September at Oxford Circus. He says we can have lunch at Lyons, Corner House. It's so exciting."

"Really?" Kathleen opened both eyes and sat up.

"Oh yes," Alice said, "but I need your help."

"Why? What do you want me to do?"

"I want you to come with me."

"What on earth for?"

"Because if Mummy thought I was meeting a boy on my own, she'd have a fit. She wouldn't let me go. But if we catch the train up together, she'll think we're just going shopping and she'll be all right about it."

Alice wanted her rendezvous with a respectable young man in the middle of London to be kept hidden from her mother. Kathleen almost laughed because suddenly she felt immensely superior. Jim had made a woman of her, while Alice was still a mere girl.

"What is it, Kathleen? Have I said something funny? You will come, won't you?"

"I'll come. Don't worry, I'll come."

But first, there was lunch with Robert at the Savoy on Friday. Already Kathleen was beginning to look forward to that.

Kathleen studied her watch. *He's late*, she thought, and leaving her chair strolled towards the Savoy's reception desk; she was not sure why, but doing something always made her feel better than doing nothing. Turning on her heel, she meandered through the chairs back towards Alice, idly thumping a fist in her palm. Then a voice called her name and she spun round to see Robert hurrying to greet her, a hand smoothing down his hair.

"Hello, Kathleen, Alice – my apologies. Couldn't find a taxi, and then the traffic was terrible coming out of Paddington."

"So you know what it feels like, not being able to find a taxi when you really need one." Kathleen couldn't resist the jibe.

"You know we've forgiven Robert. You really mustn't go on about it," said Alice with a touch of embarrassment.

"Sorry, Robert, I'm afraid I tend to speak first and think later," said Kathleen.

"Forgiven and forgotten already." He met her eyes, the gaze lingering a second or two longer than she was expecting, and she looked away. "Now, may I escort you two delightful young ladies to the luncheon table?" he asked.

During the next couple of hours, Kathleen had ample time to observe Robert. He behaved in a most gracious manner, ordering whatever they desired and attending to their every need. His eyes were a greyish kind of blue and he had freckles over his nose.

"What brings you to London, Robert?" she asked.

"An appointment with the family solicitors in Lincoln's Inn."

"Sorry, I didn't mean to pry."

"It's not going to be private much longer. Father insists the Alston Estate is resettled on me. Says it will give him peace of mind, now his health is failing."

"Your father's not well?"

"He's been in poor health for a while now, and he has turned seventy. Never really got over Wilfred being killed in the war. Mother dying so soon after was the last straw."

"Wilfred was your brother. Binkey's father mentioned him."

Robert nodded grimly. "Three years older than me."

"Robert's sister, Florence, runs the household," Alice explained. "We met her that day at Alston Hall. You'd have met her too if... She's absolutely marvellous; so brave. Never got the chance to marry; her sweetheart Jack's buried in France too. She showed me the citation: 'An officer of the most brilliant promise,' it reads. She's so proud of him, but it's so very sad, don't you think?"

"Thousands – hundreds of thousands – like Wilfred and Jack," said Kathleen, "and what was it all for?"

"To make sure it never, ever happens again, of course," replied Alice. "You must believe that, surely."

Kathleen fiddled with her napkin and said nothing.

"Keeps saying he wants to see me settled – Father, that is." Robert's voice filled the void. "By that I expect he means he wants to see me married to a good woman who will give me an heir." He caught Kathleen's eye and held her gaze a moment too long.

"I imagine your father wants you to learn how to run the estate," said Alice.

Robert nodded. "I know most of the tenants. Some families have farmed on the estate for generations. You've met one already – Jim Wilcox, Higher Haydn Farm. Wasn't long back from the war when his father died and he took over."

Mention of the name startled Kathleen.

"Some tales told in the village about him." Robert tried to suppress a grin.

Alice's eyes opened wide. "Oh, go on, Robert, you can't stop now."

"I'm not sure I should say anything in front of innocent young ladies."

"You're teasing, Robert. You must say what you mean. Don't leave us in suspense," implored Alice.

An icy chill, a sense of foreboding, gripped Kathleen.

Robert was looking at her in a curious manner. "I won't go on, if you'd rather I didn't."

"Oh no, it's absolutely fine," she said. "You mustn't leave Alice in suspense."

"If you're sure…?"

"Yes, yes."

Robert hunched his shoulders and lowered his voice. "There are stories told about Jim Wilcox and a secret love nest in his hayloft."

A wave of dismay swept over Kathleen.

"They say," continued Robert, leaning forward, "he sometimes invites a girl from the village for a night of love, then sends her home in the morning." His eyes took on a conspiratorial gleam. "And it's a different girl each time."

"Oh my giddy aunt, such goings-on." Alice's hands flew to her mouth and she gasped in horrified delight. "Kathleen, are you unwell?"

"I just feel a little odd," said Kathleen, brushing it off. "I can't think why."

"Here, try some water," suggested Robert.

She drank from the glass he offered and managed a weak smile. What a fool, almost betraying herself. "There, I'm fine now," she said.

After that, Kathleen succeeded in banishing all thoughts of Jim until she was home, alone in her room. It wasn't true, what Robert had said; it was gossip, that's all it was. But the blanket hanging over the beam; the blanket he'd spread on the hay – was that left over from the last time he'd had a girl in the loft? Was she just the latest in a long line? It was maddening, absolutely maddening, to think that she'd been so naive, so stupid as to have been taken in by him, to have thought she was in love with him, to have thought he felt the same about her. She flopped down, angry tears welling up as she pummelled the pillow with her fists.

"Kathleen?" her mother called. "What are you doing?"

"Just coming," Kathleen called back, blowing her nose and wiping her eyes. "Won't be a moment." She went to the washbasin and splashed cold water over her face, patting it dry with a towel. She looked in the mirror. Creases showed in her dress where she'd lain on the bed, but never mind; there were plenty more in the wardrobe. She selected a fresh dress and put it on, pulled a comb through her hair and went downstairs.

"Tell me about Robert – the Honourable Robert Neville." Her mother was beside herself with curiosity. "What's he like?"

"Tall, fair hair, that sort of thing," said Kathleen. "Anyway, you'll see for yourself soon. I'm meeting him for tea next Saturday and he's asked me to the theatre. He's getting tickets for *Bitter Sweet*."

CHAPTER 4

Kathleen's mother, Alexandra, was in rapture. "Robert's taking you to see *Bitter Sweet*? How absolutely marvellous. Which theatre did you say?"

"His Majesty's."

"His Majesty's... such atmosphere. I adored that theatre." Alexandra clasped her hands in a pose of veneration, almost exaltation. Bright red varnish that matched her lipstick adorned long, oval nails in immaculate condition.

"What were you in?" Kathleen asked.

Alexandra took a deep breath and exhaled slowly. "I never actually played there, but it would have been wonderful, I know it would. Your father used to take me to the theatre every week when we were first married."

"Daddy came to see you in the theatre, night after night. That's how he fell in love with you, isn't it? Is it true that he took you out to supper and showered you with bouquets of roses until you promised to marry him?"

"In a way... that sort of thing."

"Which theatre was it?"

"You don't really want to know."

Why wouldn't she say? As soon as Kathleen asked,

Mummy always clammed up. "I'd really like to know. It's a wonderful story," she encouraged.

Alexandra's hand reached up and closed around the string of pearls at her throat. "I hadn't quite made it to the West End when I met your father." Her fingers toyed with the necklace. "I was still playing at Wilton's Music Hall."

"Wilton's Music Hall?! Where on earth's that?"

"Enough!" Alexandra laughed and held up both hands. "You'd better ask him."

It was Saturday, a week later, and Kathleen was going up to town with Alice. "For a shopping spree, and then in the afternoon I'm meeting Robert for tea," she explained to her parents, mentioning nothing of Alice's proposed tryst with Binkey at Lyons' Corner House.

Alexandra tended to have a rather short temper and a scathing tongue – artistic temperament, probably – but the topic of Robert had created such good humour in her that Kathleen was astonished. Today she was encouragement itself, lending face powder and lipstick and supervising its application, almost like a kindly older sister. And most amazing of all, she agreed as entirely suitable the blue dress that Kathleen decided to wear.

It wasn't far to Alice's home, and as Kathleen strolled beneath the canopy of plane trees lining the avenue, her mind drifted back to the first time she'd taken this route, when the two of them had returned home for the holidays after meeting at boarding school. Then, Daddy had walked beside her. To his surprise, he'd recognised Alice's father, Will Fitzgerald, as the man who sat opposite him on the train every day, reading *The Telegraph*. After that, Will Fitzgerald and Ray Wyndham had got on so well that they regularly played golf together. From the start, Kathleen had been wary of Ethel, Alice's mother – a staunch Methodist of modest appearance and frugal appetites, quick to give her opinion, whether or not her views were sought. Alice had a big sister who looked in many ways like a younger version of their mother. Hair ruthlessly scraped back to the nape of her neck and worn in a bun, she appeared the archetypical schoolmarm. From sheer force of character she'd battled her way to Oxford, studied history and, after obtaining a first-class honours degree, secured a place at a minor public school by the age of twenty-eight. Kathleen rarely saw her now, unless it was the school holidays, when she came home because she had nowhere else to lodge. Alice's brother still lived at home – a bigoted creep who, Kathleen hoped fervently, would one day get his comeuppance. She loathed his round, podgy face and sneering mouth as he talked down to her as if she were an imbecile without a mind of her own. Following in his father's footsteps, he travelled each day to the City to work for an insurance company. Kathleen had never been sufficiently interested to ask which one.

"You will be careful not to let on?" whispered Alice when she arrived, letting her in. "We'll have to buy a few things otherwise she'll get suspicious."

Alice looked so furtive Kathleen suppressed a giggle as she entered the hall. "Don't worry," she whispered back. "Your mother does know you'll be coming home on your own, doesn't she?"

"Yes, but—"

Mrs Fitzgerald materialised as if from thin air, and immediately Alice clammed up. "Good morning, Kathleen. I hear your young man is taking you for tea at the Ritz."

"Yes, that's right. I'm hoping he'll be able to tell me he's got tickets for *Bitter Sweet* at His Majesty's Theatre... marvellous reviews, you know." Kathleen produced her most angelic smile, but the old bat was having none of it.

Mrs Fitzgerald folded her arms and stood her ground. "Well, your mother knows what she's doing, I suppose. I'll say no more." Her mouth had a grim expression; her voice a touch of acidity.

Kathleen attempted to renew the smile but it faded on her lips. "Better be off, then. Goodbye, Mrs Fitzgerald," she said with forced cheerfulness. Turning on her heel, she flounced out through the front door, while Alice kissed her mother and hurried after.

They bought tickets for Piccadilly Circus and emerged into the daylight with no clear plan of what to do. After some discussion, they decided to look in at Swan & Edgar, where they tried on hats until the assistant began to give them odd looks. Then they moved on to lingerie, where Alice bought a camisole and Kathleen a pair of silk knickers.

"You don't want me hanging around while you and Binkey gaze into each other's eyes, do you?" asked Kathleen as they strolled up Regent Street.

"I'd rather meet him alone, if you don't mind." A look of embarrassed pleading flickered across Alice's face.

"Don't worry. I'm not very hungry. I'll get a milkshake or something in that little café we saw down the side street."

"You're sure you really don't mind?"

The look was so pathetic – like a naughty puppy – that Kathleen burst out laughing. "For goodness' sake, Alice – go, will you? Just go." Truth be told, she was glad to be on her own. The endless commentary on Binkey and his family was wearing. Maybe she shouldn't blame Alice. Maybe the heat was getting to her; it was ridiculously warm for September.

Sitting quietly in the café, gazing through the window at the stream of passers-by, Kathleen sipped a milkshake and felt better. There was a tap-tap-tapping sound and into view shuffled a man, hunched over, white stick moving from side to side in front of him. On his threadbare jacket a row of medals glinted in the sun. He was missing an arm and someone had pinned the empty sleeve to his pocket to stop it flopping about. Four girls – Kathleen guessed in their late twenties – burst into the café giggling and chattering. They were all as skinny as each other in faded cotton dresses a little too long to be fashionable. They ordered the cheapest items on the menu, counting out coins from worn purses as they exchanged tales of the office. The fair-haired, large-mouthed girl proposed they go window shopping in Regent Street until it was time for the tea dance at a place Kathleen had never heard of. A mere handful of the million surplus women trying to make the best of it, and all because young men had gone to war and few – so very few – had come home again.

By four o'clock she was waiting for Robert in the lounge of the Ritz Hotel. It was true that he occupied her thoughts frequently these days; she found him extremely attractive.

But her mother acted as if an engagement would be announced at any moment, which was ridiculous because Kathleen had only known him a couple of weeks or so. It wasn't that she hadn't thought about marriage to Robert in a sort of abstract way, but the idea was not appealing. He was very gracious and charming and all that, and absolutely loaded with money, but he treated her like a china doll without any opinions of her own. Besides, she wasn't ready to settle down; she hadn't done anything yet. However, what it was she was going to do was still a mystery. She could take a secretarial course, but she wouldn't want to end up like those sad girls in the café. No good thinking of becoming a stockbroker like her father; they didn't allow women on the floor of the Stock Exchange. At the back of her mind lurked the vague notion that women were allowed to be lawyers, but it took years of training and passing exams, and she didn't much care for exams or being surrounded by young men like Binkey. Something wildly exciting, something that would show that she was a woman to be reckoned with; that's what was needed. A stream of possibilities floated before her, then her mind seized and settled upon an idea so outrageous it nearly took her breath away: she'd learn to fly, that's what she'd do. There was that woman at the London Flying Club – what was her name? Amy... Amy... Johnson? She'd got her pilot's licence only a few weeks ago. It'd been all over the papers. They said her father was going to help her buy an aeroplane.

"Looks as if you're miles away." Robert was standing beside her. "How are you?"

"I'm very well, thank you," Kathleen replied as he took the chair opposite. "I was just wondering what I was going to do," she continued. "You know, what I should do with my life."

"You're not one of those girls with an insane craze for independence, are you? Don't tell me you want equal rights." Robert's face creased with amusement. "It's well known that deep down every girl, even if she tries to pretend otherwise, wants a husband, a home and children." He was waving a forefinger as he made his speech.

Kathleen said nothing and gritted her teeth, although she knew she ought to say something, have it out with him, because otherwise he'd take her silence to be agreement.

"Well now, let's see about some tea," he said, oblivious to the icy resentment growing within her. He looked so nonchalant, so at ease, as he raised a hand and snapped his fingers, and a waiter moved speedily in their direction. "We'd like the full tea," Robert announced. "Sandwiches, cakes – everything you've got." He smiled at Kathleen. "I wouldn't want you to go hungry." He could have asked, but instead he behaved as if he knew what she wanted better than she did herself.

The waiter bowed. "Certainly, sir. At once."

As it happened, she was ravenous, because the only thing she'd had since breakfast was the milkshake, but Robert wasn't to know that, and she wasn't going to let him off so lightly. "I was just thinking I'd ask Daddy to let me get my pilot's licence."

"Why on earth would you want to do that?" He searched for a hint that she might be teasing.

She tossed her hair in defiance. "I could start up an air taxi business or something like that." She said it as if it was the most normal thing in the world.

"You don't mean… you're not serious… you can't be." His face contorted into a crooked smile that betrayed his discomfort. "Ah, here's tea." He rubbed his hands together and displayed exaggerated pleasure at the arrival of the waiter.

An uneasy quiet hung over the table as the waiter's immaculate, white-gloved hands displayed a practised dexterity, arranging the silver tea service and the porcelain cups, saucers and plates. With silver tongs he served wafer-thin ham sandwiches, and in silence they watched him.

When the waiter had left, Robert said, "I've got the tickets. Couldn't get them for next Saturday, I'm afraid – fortnight today all right?" He glanced up to see her reaction. "You do still want to come?"

"I'm looking forward to it," she said demurely.

"That's all right, then." His relief was clear to see. "I was afraid you might've changed your mind."

"No, why should I? You asked me whether I'd like to go and I said yes."

After that Robert was a little wary, but they parted on good terms and in the intervening days he telephoned from Alston Hall on numerous occasions, which must have run up the most frightful bill.

Two weeks later, on the Saturday, Kathleen went round to see Alice to ask her advice on what to wear for the theatre that evening, and to hear the latest on Binkey.

"Could we possibly go back to your place?" whispered Alice. "I can't talk here, with Mummy around all the time." Her voice resumed its normal volume. "I'd love to see what you're going to wear tonight."

"I'm torn between the silver and the peach," replied Kathleen, giving Alice a wink. "I'd really appreciate your help."

"Mummy, I'm just going—"

"Yes, I heard," said Mrs Fitzgerald. "I trust you will have an enjoyable evening, Kathleen." Sheer hypocrisy – she meant nothing of the kind.

"Thank you, Mrs Fitzgerald. I'm sure I will," said Kathleen in measured tones, and walked towards the front door, conscious of the pale blue eyes scrutinising her back. Suddenly, the hall was suffocating and she needed to escape, yet even the pavement dust had a peculiar smell, and it gave her a slightly nauseous feeling. The sensation passed and she linked arms with Alice, ambling along, exchanging giggles.

"Now, what do you think of this?" asked Kathleen, holding the silver silk dress in front of her and giving a twirl. "It's got the tiniest stain, just here." She indicated a mark. "But it won't show if I wear this sash."

"What about the peach?" asked Alice. "You always look terrific in that. Robert hasn't seen it, has he?"

"He hasn't seen either of them. Oh, I can't decide." Kathleen flopped down on the bed.

"You're getting really keen on Robert, aren't you?"

"You mean he's keen on me."

Alice looked puzzled. "But I thought... you look so good together, as if you were made for each other, and you've introduced him to your parents. Has he said anything yet?"

"Such as?"

"Kathleen, you can be so irritating sometimes." Alice preened herself in the wardrobe mirror, trying to straighten a defiant curl. "He's given some inkling, surely. Hardly lets you alone for more than two minutes and he obviously thinks you're the bee's knees."

"I don't know what you mean."

"If you're going to be disagreeable and pretend you don't know what I'm talking about, I think I should go." Alice stuck her nose in the air. "I was going to tell you all about Binkey…"

"I'm sorry," said Kathleen. "It's just that I don't want people marrying me off to Robert before I've had a proper chance to think about it myself. Heavens, I'm not sure I want to marry anyone. I haven't done anything yet." She sat on the edge of the bed and patted the counterpane. "Do tell me about Binkey – all the things you didn't want your mother to hear."

Alice let out a snort of mirth, half-stifled by a hand over her mouth. "You're jolly well not going to believe this."

At seven o'clock Kathleen was in the drawing room with her parents. She'd settled on the silver dress. It showed off to wonderful effect the diamond necklace and matching bracelet her mother had insisted she borrow. When the front doorbell rang Ray disappeared into the hall to answer it and returned a few moments later with Robert. Impeccably clad in evening dress and white scarf, Robert enquired first after Alexandra's health, then took Kathleen's gloved hand in his and raised it to his lips.

"You look absolutely exquisite. Here, let me help you with your stole," he said.

She let him gaze deep into her eyes. "Thank you, Robert."

"Now, look after her and bring her back safely," said Ray.

"I will, sir. You can count on me." Robert shook Ray's hand.

Alexandra was smiling, a bright, satisfied smile, long fingers clasping an elegant cigarette holder. A cocktail glass stood empty on the cabinet beside her. "I'm sure you will, Robert," she added.

The heat had gone from the day, the crowds had thinned, and in the dusk of early evening an air of expectancy hung over London's West End as buildings began to take on a different character: clubs, restaurants and theatres opened their doors and pools of light fell across dusky pavements. The taxi turned into Haymarket and drew up at the kerb outside the theatre. Robert helped Kathleen out, paid the driver, and as they stood on the pavement he looked at her, not saying a word.

"What is it?" she asked. "Is something the matter?"

"I'm sorry to stare. It's just... you look so beautiful." He reached out and placed his hand under her elbow, the warmth of him penetrating the fabric of her glove. "You do realise how much you mean to me, don't you?"

Suddenly, a group of revellers, laughing and loud-mouthed, swaggered past, engulfing them and marooning them on a private island of intimacy. A loutish youth barged so close that Kathleen let out a shriek and grabbed

Robert's arm, and they were thrown together. Without a backward glance the revellers careered on, while Robert held her close, his breath warm on her face.

"Are you all right? I thought they were going to knock you over."

"Lucky I had you around to protect me."

She offered him an arm. Robert squeezed it gently and led her into the foyer, and after that the evening passed in an unspoken understanding and a gentleness that was new, and she felt fortunate to know him and grateful to be with him.

Robert hummed one of the songs under his breath as they left their seats in the stalls and shuffled towards the exit at the end of the performance.

"Difficult to get it out of your head, isn't it? Such a catchy tune," she said.

"But so sad at the same time," he replied. "Love lost is so sad, don't you think?"

The theatre was packed and the way out jammed full of hot, perspiring, jostling bodies. The crowd had used up all the air, leaving behind a foul-smelling odour. Kathleen's vision blurred and she gasped and clutched at Robert's arm.

"Kathleen? Kathleen!"

His voice drifted into her half-conscious brain and a low moan escaped her. She felt dreadfully sick.

"Make way! Stand back there; give her some room."

The mass of bodies parted, like a rolling back of the waters, and she found herself half-propelled, half-carried through the foyer and into the blessed coolness of the night air.

"Breathe, Kathleen." The voice was Robert's. "Deep breaths, my darling." Only his arm around her waist kept her from falling. A chair was brought and Robert eased her onto the seat. "Lean forward. Keep taking deep breaths." Crouching beside her, he held her safe.

"Shall I send for a doctor, sir?" a man asked.

"Thank you, no," Robert answered. "She's recovering."

Kathleen pulled herself up, resting her back against the hard wooden slats. She was tired, so very tired. "Please take me home, Robert. I don't feel at all well."

Amid the staring crowd of onlookers, someone called for a taxi. When it arrived, the cab door was opened, and Robert was there, helping her onto the back seat, and she was saying that she had no idea what had come over her, and that she'd be perfectly all right soon. He slipped an arm around her and insisted that if she wasn't entirely well by the morning her mother must call the doctor.

CHAPTER 5

"Your young man's telephoned already," announced Alexandra, putting the tray on the stool by the dressing table. She pulled back the curtains and light flowed over the limed-oak bedroom suite, rose-coloured carpet, and satin eiderdown.

Kathleen rolled over, sat up, and pushed the hair out of her face.

"He's charming, perfectly charming," Alexandra continued, adding that the holiday in Devon had been such a good idea, that Kathleen had done the right thing getting herself introduced to the Honourable Robert Neville, and that he'd probably ask her to marry him before the year was out if she played her cards right.

On the tray was a silver teapot, a milk jug, buttered toast and a boiled egg. Kathleen took one look, threw back the covers, and made for the washbasin. She retched, bringing up nothing, but her eyes watered and a horrid cramp gripped her stomach. She hugged herself, retreated to bed, and wiped her eyes on the sheet, feeling too ill to do anything except pull the covers over her head.

"Kathleen, sit up," Alexandra demanded.

"Take it away. That's what's making me feel sick. I don't want it."

"Don't be so ridiculous. I never heard anything…"

The silence lasted so long that Kathleen peeped out from under the sheet. Her mother was staring down at her, a cold, hard stare. What was it? Why wouldn't Mummy say anything? What had she done? Why was Mummy looking at her like that?

"What have I done?" Kathleen asked.

"Done? You tell me."

"I don't know what it is I'm supposed to have done." Kathleen could hold back the tears no longer; they trickled down and fell onto the sheet.

"No good playing the innocent with me," Alexandra shouted, trembling with rage as she dumped the tray on the end of the bed. Hands on hips, cheeks burning with indignation, she glowered at Kathleen.

Ray's head appeared around the door and enquired as to whether they were having a row. When she saw him, Kathleen flung back the covers, dashed across the room and propelled herself into his arms.

"Daddy, I don't know what it is I've done to upset Mummy."

"Well, Alex, what is it she's supposed to have done?" Ray asked.

"She knows what she's done all right. She's let Robert have his way with her and now she's going to have his child. I knew we should never have let her go to Devon. I said it all along; I said—"

"But he hasn't, he hasn't. It's not true," Kathleen protested though her tears.

"Struck me as the perfect gentleman," said Ray. "What makes you think he's seduced her, for heaven's sake?"

"You mark my words," retorted Alexandra, "that girl is with child."

Daddy held Kathleen at arm's length, waiting for an explanation, yet all she could do was stare back at him through wet lashes, because suddenly the truth struck her like a bolt of lightning.

"Look at her – *look* at her! You can see I'm right." Alexandra was triumphant.

"Oh no – could I really be having a baby?" Kathleen whispered.

"You said you hadn't let Robert have his way with you, so how can you be going to have a baby?" Alexandra's tone was sarcastic now.

"Not... Robert," Kathleen murmured.

"And who the hell is the father if it's not Robert?" Alexandra screamed.

Kathleen could scarcely get the name out, but eventually she managed to say, "Jim", and tell them that he was a farmer – one of Robert's tenants – and that she and Alice had met him when they'd helped with the harvest.

"What were you damn well thinking about? A farmer – a bloody farmer?!" Alexandra was incredulous. "How could he possibly have done anything to you with Alice there?"

But Alice wasn't there, Kathleen explained, at least not the second time, because Alice had gone to Alston Hall with Binkey to meet Robert. Alexandra yelled that surely there must have been other people around, working in the field.

"Of course there were other people." Fresh tears welled up at every accusation. "After we'd eaten… the storm came on… and we went back to the farm."

"You stupid girl. If you had to have a man, why couldn't it have been Robert? Fancy, a mere farmer is good enough for you."

Ray tried to calm things down, telling Alexandra that she'd said enough, but Alexandra retorted that she hadn't even started; that Kathleen was a silly little bitch and should at least have asked how to avoid getting into trouble, but no, she'd gone her own way as usual.

Kathleen clung to her father, her breath coming in great gulps.

"He's got to marry her; he's got to – just think of the scandal." Alexandra glared at Ray.

"Well, let's hope he wants to," Ray replied. "But shouting at her isn't going to help." He stroked Kathleen's hair, took a clean white handkerchief from his pocket, and gave it to her. He suggested she went back to bed and snuggled down for a bit, while he and her mother talked things over.

Kathleen dived under the covers and wept into the handkerchief. She couldn't have got caught out; surely she couldn't. It wasn't the right time of the month. The girls at school had said it couldn't happen unless… Oh, damn and blast! What did it matter now what they'd said? She thought of Robert; kind, considerate Robert. She'd betrayed him even before she'd known him, and now it was too late.

Her mother and father were having a terrible row on the landing. Alexandra was shrieking at the top of her voice that Kathleen would do as she was told, and Ray was insisting that they must ask Kathleen how she felt and what it was she wanted to do.

"What *she* wants?" Alexandra's voice cracked in rage. "Ask *her*? After what she's done?"

"You're a fine one to talk. No one forced you to marry me when you were expecting her."

"Keep your voice down, Ray. I don't want her to know."

"Better to be honest… anyway, we've done all right, haven't we? But we must ask her. This is about her life, not ours. Let me talk to her; find out how she feels about this fellow, Jim."

Her father's footsteps came back into Kathleen's room and made their way across the floor. The bed went down where he sat on it, and his hand came over and rested on her shoulder.

"Could you be happy with him – with Jim?" he asked her.

Until that moment she'd never given marrying Jim the slightest thought, and the very idea felt strange to her. After a while she turned and looked up at her father, and asked whether what she'd heard was true: that she'd been on the way when he'd married Mummy. And he stroked her hair and said that having Kathleen was the best thing that had ever happened to him, and kissed her on the forehead.

"Why is Mummy so sure I'm going to have a baby?" she asked.

"She knows the signs."

"But she might be wrong; I could just be ill." She said it more as an afterthought than with any hope that it might be true; yet it was a relief to hear her father agree, and promise to send for the doctor first thing Monday morning. It was a reprieve, at least for the moment, and perhaps everything would be all right, but it was difficult to keep her spirits up, especially because from time to time the nausea would well up and she'd gag, and run to the nearest basin with a hand over her mouth.

About three o'clock in the afternoon, while Ray and Alexandra were in the sun lounge, Kathleen answered a ring at the front door and found Alice flushed with excitement. It seemed that Alice's parents were to be introduced to Binkey next month at a 'do' her cousin was organising. You'd have thought Binkey was the most exciting man who'd ever walked the earth, the ridiculous way Alice was going on about it.

"You're looking a bit off colour," Alice observed. "Are you feeling all right?"

Kathleen gave an unconvincing smile.

"How did it go last night? Were you out late?" Alice enquired.

Kathleen could not speak. She studied the pattern in the carpet, blinking hard, until, unable to stifle the tears any longer, she looked at Alice with moist, red eyes.

"Whatever's the matter? Have you two broken up?" Alice asked.

"I'm not supposed to say," Kathleen confided in a broken whisper. "Anyhow, you'll be so shocked you'll never want to speak to me again. It's just too awful."

"What? What's too awful?"

"Alice, if I tell you... please will you promise still to be my friend?"

"You can't have done anything *really* bad, Kathleen. I don't believe it."

Kathleen couldn't even lift her eyes as she said the words. "I'm going to have a baby."

The chill, intense hush that followed seemed to last forever.

"There – I knew you'd be shocked."

"Oh crikey, oh golly gosh! How could Robert do that to you? He's such a gentleman."

Kathleen gazed past Alice to the oak panels of the front door. This was hard; it was so very hard. "It isn't Robert's."

"But it has to be Robert's. There isn't anyone else…" Then the look on Alice's face said it all. "Kathleen, no. Oh no, it can't be… tell me it can't be."

Unable to look at her friend for shame and embarrassment, Kathleen nodded, and after a long pause she sighed and said in a wobbly voice, "It may be all right. I may not be expecting. The doctor's coming in the morning."

"But if you did it with Jim," said Alice, "you'll have to marry him. You can't possibly marry Robert now."

Just then, the doorbell rang again. Kathleen took a quick peep from behind the lace curtains and saw that the new arrival was Robert. It was all too much. She made for the stairs, scuttling up as fast as she could, leaving Alice stranded in the hall. From her vantage point on the landing she peeped through the banisters and saw her mother answer the door. She heard Robert enquiring as to whether Kathleen was quite recovered, and her mother inviting him in, putting on her sweetest tones and explaining that unfortunately Kathleen was still rather unwell, and they would be calling the doctor in the morning if there was no improvement. After a few further polite exchanges, Robert departed.

Alexandra watched as he walked down the drive, then she shut the door and her voice took on a resentful, ill-tempered quality as she turned to Alice. "I suppose she's told you. Stupid girl, getting herself into trouble like that."

First thing in the morning the doctor was summoned, and he arrived with his Gladstone bag a little before one o'clock. He examined Kathleen, pushing her tummy here and there, asking a few questions. She was to wait another two or three weeks, he advised, and if she missed a second period she was pregnant. He was so matter-of-fact about it all.

In the days that followed the sickness got worse; she ate scarcely anything because all food tasted odd and different. At night she lay awake, unable to reconcile herself to the brutal fact that confronted her whichever way she turned: that a tiny pinhead of humanity was growing inside her, and one day it would become a baby. The enormity of what she had done was all-consuming. Whenever Robert turned up she refused to see him, and eventually he stopped coming and she guessed he'd gone home. Alexandra scarcely spoke to her without resentment or recrimination. Ray would put on his solemn look to enquire how things were, and Kathleen would shake her head. He'd draw her to him and give her a hug and a kiss her forehead, just as he'd always done. Then one day in early October, he sat down beside her on the sofa in the drawing room and suggested it was time for a serious talk.

"Tell me about Jim," he said. "Do you like him?"

The late afternoon sun streamed in at the window, reaching as far as the magazines on the side table. Everything was familiar and normal, yet a chasm was opening up in Kathleen's life; so wide, so deep she could not close it down: she must choose which side to take. In her imagination she recreated the barley field, and Jim working and laughing with the men, and what it felt like when he touched her.

"I liked him very much," she replied.

"Enough to marry him?"

She thought about the stories of girls in the hayloft, and it seemed unlikely that Jim would want a wife.

"How would it be if I wrote and asked him?" Ray continued.

There was no harm in asking, so she nodded.

"You know," Ray said, "Mummy and I didn't have much when we started out. She was only sixteen when she had you."

"Was Mummy cross about me? About having to give up her career? She said you saw her at Wilton's Music Hall but she never said why you were there."

"We grew up only a stone's throw from each other," Ray said. "The East End was my home as well as hers, but she pretends not to remember things as they were back then. The very first time I saw her was when she won a beauty contest at the Cambridge Music Hall in Spitalfields. Couldn't take my eyes off her, and I followed her home afterwards to see where she lived."

"But I thought she was an actress."

"A dancer – when she was thirteen."

"Really?"

"You wouldn't remember when we lived near the market," he said. "No, you'd be far too young."

"I don't remember anything much before that house near the park."

"Bethnal Green," he said. "During the war, that's when we moved there."

"And what—" she began.

"We're not talking about me and your mother," he interrupted. "We're talking about you and whether you care for your farmer enough to marry him. You've a home here, whatever your mother may say. But you must realise, life's not good to a girl with an illegitimate child."

If Daddy hadn't married Mummy, Kathleen would be illegitimate.

"If he's got ambition, wants to get on and buy his own farm, I dare say I could help," suggested Ray.

"You'd lend him money?"

"No, I was thinking of a wedding present," he said.

The reply from Jim came quickly, almost by return of post, and was surprisingly positive. Within the week Kathleen found herself staying, with Ray and Alexandra, at the Grand Hotel on Plymouth Hoe. Alexandra had insisted on a hotel in the city because, as she explained, she found the countryside strange and most unnerving.

The morning after their arrival, Kathleen stood at her bedroom window, gazing out over Plymouth Sound in the early light, only half-watching as a ship cast a V-shaped trail over tranquil grey water. The heavy burden of decision-making was almost upon her, because within hours they'd be on their way to the farm and Jim. Her previous encounter with him had thrilled and delighted her, and set her on fire. Once she was over this dreadful sickness, it could be like it was again, couldn't it? It was bumping into Robert that worried her more than anything, and she wondered how she could ever face him. She had allowed him to take her out, and all the time she had another man's child growing inside her. Guilt lay like a dead weight, forever reminding her of what she had done.

The drive to Higher Haydn Farm seemed interminable. She sat in the taxi between her mother and father and no one uttered a word of the least significance.

The taxi drew up outside the farmyard. Ray got out, and gave Kathleen a pat on the shoulder. "I'll come and fetch you if things go well," he said.

Time dragged on and Alexandra lit cigarette after cigarette, and still Ray did not return. The air became so full of stale smoke and Alexandra's resentment that Kathleen could stand it no longer.

"I'm just going to walk a little way down the lane," she said, opening the door.

"You can't possibly," shrieked Alexandra. "Look at the mud. You'll ruin your shoes."

"I don't care." If she married Jim, she'd be free of Mummy telling her what she must or must not do, or think, or say. That had to be an advantage, surely. She picked her way down a lane oozing with mud that seeped into the stitching of her soft leather shoes, and her feet grew chill and damp. Shrivelled bracken, withering grass and balding nettles in the hedgerow showed how the optimism of summer had given way to the melancholy of autumn. The harshness of winter was still to come.

She glanced up to see her father returning, and walking beside him was Jim. Hurrying towards them, she tried to read the expression on Jim's face. He didn't look in the least put out; in fact, he was grinning.

"What I want to know," he said, "is whether you're of a mind to marry me or whether 'tis other folks that have put the notion in your head."

Kathleen took a deep breath and summoned up the courage to look directly at him. "You know I'm going to have your child. Daddy has told you, hasn't he?" There was a terrible shame in saying it, as if it was all her fault and Jim had had nothing to do with it.

He nodded. "'Tis no bad thing, having a child. Another pair of hands on the farm, especially if 'tis a son, would be welcome. And your father's offering a fair bit of money to buy a farm. I doubt the Alston Estate'll sell this one but there are others. We could move away."

His eyes told her that he wanted her still, and she remembered now what it was that had drawn her back to the barley field in the heat of the August haze.

That evening Kathleen sat in the hotel lounge and wrote to Alice, saying that she was to marry Jim, and that they were staying on for a few days to make arrangements for the wedding to take place in October at Southwood church. She hoped that Alice would be able to come. It was rather a vain hope, she acknowledged, but she had at least to go through the pretence that Alice would have a choice in the matter.

Alexandra stood by the window in one of her favourite

poses – cocktail glass in her hand, looking out to sea – and observed that it was so much more agreeable the last time she was here.

"You've been here before?" asked Kathleen.

"You remember, when Daddy took me on that cruise to New York? We were waiting for the *Île de France*... June, I think. Yes, it was definitely June, two years ago. The decor on that liner – oh, it was the very height of fashion... so *moderne*." Alexandra raised her free hand in mock amazement as she pronounced the final word in French. "And such a thoroughly nice class of people you meet on a cruise like that." She caught her reflection in the mirror above the fireplace; she put up a hand and touched her hair, then her face. "I half-expected to be discovered and invited to Hollywood," she simpered.

Alice's reply came by return of post, saying that she would not be able to come to the wedding because her mother had discovered that Kathleen had gone off the rails, and had forbidden any further contact.

Apparently, Robert had contacted Binkey, imploring him to find out from Alice what was wrong and what he could have done to offend Kathleen. Mrs Fitzgerald had spotted Alice's reply to Binkey, and had demanded to read its contents. Even this letter Alice was writing now needed to be smuggled out of the house. She finished by assuring Kathleen of her continued friendship – which, given the ferocity of the old dragon breathing down her back, was a very brave thing to do.

So, Robert knew, and there was nothing more that could be said.

CHAPTER 6

Kathleen arrived at St Michael and All Angels, Southwood, accompanied by Ray and Alexandra, a little before twelve o'clock on Saturday 26th October. The day was kind – mild, almost balmy – but the year had turned and drifts of dried-up leaves gathering in the churchyard gave the lie to the sun's belated efforts.

Alexandra had complained bitterly about the lack of suitable bridal gowns at this time of year, and declared that nothing truly fashionable could be found. In the end she'd chosen for Kathleen a loose-fitting cream silk dress embroidered with tiny pearls, and Kathleen was grateful for its long sleeves.

Clutching a bouquet of pink carnations with trailing asparagus fern, Kathleen held her father's arm, and listened to her mother totter on high heels all the way down the aisle to a pew at the front. When she had taken her seat, the two of them walked together in silence through the Gothic archway, and Ray gave Kathleen's arm a little squeeze of encouragement. A chill penetrated the soles of her satin shoes and a musty odour rose from the ancient tombstones set in the floor; their inscriptions worn away by the footfall of years. From the east window, where St Michael in billowing robes lifted his sword to slay a cowering Satan, sunlight swelled through the stained glass, drifted over the altar, and flowed across the chancel tiles to where Jim was waiting.

The moment he heard them, Jim stood up and looked around. In the pew behind him sat a woman who'd clearly made an effort to dress up for the occasion, yet her hat and her coat with leg-of-mutton sleeves had all the hallmarks of an earlier era. She would be Jim's mother, Kathleen thought. Even in his robes the vicar, bald except for a skirting of grey hair and a neat moustache, was a most unprepossessing man. Eyes dim from reading in poor light, he peered through horn-rimmed spectacles as bride and father approached, clearing his throat and producing an unconvincing smile as they halted in front of him. A couple of strides and Jim was standing by Kathleen's side, and his presence lent a warmth that was reassuring.

The vicar intoned the opening words of the marriage service: why the congregation were gathered here today; that it was to join the two of them in the bonds of holy matrimony. Kathleen stole a glance at Jim and her thoughts drifted back to the first time she'd seen him. In her imagination she conjured up the heat of the day, the dust, the taste of cider.

The vicar's voice droned on. He was telling them now that marriage was ordained for the increase of mankind and the bringing up of children. Children? There'd be children all right. She was feeling better now, a lot better, and there was pleasure to be found in allowing her mind to float in a sea of delicious memories. Sometimes she even allowed herself to relive the time in the hayloft.

Then came the challenge: was there any man able to show just cause as to why they should not be joined in matrimony? "… Let him speak now," came the command, "or else hereafter forever hold his peace." Time came to a halt as the little congregation waited in silence for the voice that would never come. No one would speak up and stop this wedding. Kathleen would be bound to Jim for life, and from that there would be no escape.

The vicar proceeded to ask Jim if he would take Kathleen as his wife. For an instant she wondered whether he might regret his promise and refuse to have her, but the answer came loud and strong. There was no doubt. Then the vicar turned to Kathleen. A brief look, then, eyes down, he read from the page, asking her if she would have this man as her husband. She thought of Jim and what it felt like to be with him. And then came the most important words of all: forsaking all other men, would she keep herself only for him, as long as they both lived? And she heard her voice answer with a strength that surprised her as it echoed from the vaulted ceiling, saying that she would indeed.

The vicar turned to her father and asked who was giving her to be married to this man. She caught her father's eye and saw his face crease into a smile. She felt him squeeze her arm again, then give her a little pat on the hand. She'd never loved him more than at this moment, when he was giving her away to another.

The pledges and promises were made: for better, for worse, for richer, for poorer; the plighting of troths; and the ring placed on her finger. Within no time at all the vicar was pronouncing that those who had been joined together no man should put asunder, and that they were man and wife together.

So it was done – the knot was tied. No one, not even Robert, could come between them now. Robert? Why on earth had she thought of Robert?

The wedding breakfast had been arranged at Southwood Inn, in a private room upstairs, hired for the occasion. The innkeeper greeted them with a nod of the head and a wink for Jim as he led them through the oak doorway and up the stairs, the old boards squeaking and groaning at each step, to a room that had been laid out with care. A circular table, covered by a white linen cloth, boasted a magnificent arrangement of golden chrysanthemums in a silver bowl at its centre. Around this, five places had been set: bone-handled cutlery, large white table napkins, drinking glasses. The afternoon sun exuded a warm, mellow atmosphere as Kathleen, holding her husband's hand, entered the room. Alexandra followed with a flourish, looked round and made a sound that might have been dubious approval, while Ray offered his arm to Jim's mother, who had been introduced as Edith, and escorted her up the stairs and into the dining room.

"Ready for me to serve now, sir?" the innkeeper asked Ray.

"Well, let's see if anyone would like a sherry or an aperitif," said Ray, looking around. "Edith, how about you?"

Edith shook her head and would not be persuaded to take anything alcoholic, while Alexandra declared that if she didn't get a gin and tonic right away she'd die of thirst. Jim said that cider would suit him just fine, while Kathleen asked for a lemonade shandy. After Ray had given the order for drinks, they all stood around, trying not to look at one another. It went on for such a long time that Kathleen wondered whether it was up to her to say something, but Ray got in first, asking Jim about the harvest and what prices were like, and whether on the whole this had been a good year on the farm. Alexandra, on the other hand, stood by the window, gazing out, looking her most bored.

Kathleen felt obliged at least to attempt to engage her mother-in-law in conversation. She took a few steps towards Edith, who was looking as uncomfortable as a fish out of water. "We'll need to get to know one another," Kathleen began. "Especially with both of us living in the same house."

"'Twill be difficult for you. You've a lot to learn." Edith's face had disapproval written all over it.

"I shall rely on you, then, to put me right," replied Kathleen, summoning up her most diplomatic manner.

Edith looked her up and down. "We'll see how you gets on when you've taken all they fine clothes off and put on something more sensible."

"I'll try my best. I don't mind hard work. I helped with the harvest and Jim said I did really well."

"He did, did he?" The way Edith looked at her, she must have guessed about the hayloft.

The roast beef and parsnips the landlord served were excellent, and so was the Eve's pudding accompanied by ample quantities of clotted cream. During the meal the conversation wandered here and there with no particular sense of direction. Ray and Jim got on well enough, debating the merits of wine, beer and cider, but Alexandra and Edith said scarcely a word to one another, so that Kathleen felt obliged to spend equal time talking to one and then the other. She was extremely relieved when the time came for the speeches. Ray wished both of them happiness in their life together. Jim replied, and thanked him and Alexandra for the fine meal they had all just eaten.

Two taxis had been hired and were waiting outside the inn. The driver of one opened the door and Kathleen, Jim and Edith climbed in. Ray and Alexandra waved them off and got into the second. Kathleen turned in her seat, looked out of the back window, waved them goodbye, and wondered what this life – the life of a farmer's wife – would be like. The taxi drove up the lane to Higher Haydn, and came to a halt in the farmyard. The driver opened the door for Edith to get out. She stepped carefully into the mud and, without a backward glance, made her way across the yard and disappeared into the farmhouse.

Jim looked at the yard, and he looked at Kathleen's satin shoes. "Nothing for it; I'll have to carry you. Not that you'll be wanting those shoes again in a hurry, far as I can see."

He lifted her up, her arm went round his neck, and she leaned into him as he carried her over cobbles hidden by mud and cow muck, away from the yard and through a stone archway into the farmhouse. Once inside his arm relaxed and he set her down on uneven flagstones in a gloomy, damp passage.

"Sooner you get into something more suitable the better," he said, casting an eye over her bridal outfit.

Holding her hand, he led her to the place where they would be man and wife together, and she told herself that there would be no need for girls in the hayloft now, because he had her, and that would be enough for him. He opened their bedroom door and ushered her into a great cavern of a place, the ceiling as high as any she'd ever seen. She guessed that the last time it had been decorated, Victoria was still on the throne. Sepia wallpaper displayed clusters of fruit: grapes, pears and peaches; chipped brown paint on the skirting and window frame hadn't been touched for years; crimson velvet curtains, faded in the folds, reached the floorboards. On the dressing table stood a blue-and-white Willow-pattern washbasin and jug, and on the mantelpiece a pair of brass candlesticks. The most imposing feature of the room was an enormous brass-knobbed bed with a multicoloured patchwork quilt spread over the blankets.

"There's your luggage." Jim pointed to the dark leather suitcases, embossed with the initials 'KW'. "Must get on with the milking – cows won't wait." He began to take off his clothes, tugging at his tie and struggling with the top button of his shirt. "Darn it, can't abide these things." He paused to look at her. "Well, aren't you getting changed too?"

"I suppose so," she replied. "I'll have to unpack first. I don't know where anything is."

"Well, when you're done, come back down to the kitchen."

About an hour later, after she'd sorted out her clothes, stowed most of them in the wardrobe, and found a home for other things in the dressing table, Kathleen decided that the most suitable thing to wear for the afternoon would be her beige wool-crepe dress. So she put it on and went downstairs, wondering what on earth she needed to do to get on with her mother-in-law.

As she entered the kitchen Edith was tending to the range, putting a couple of logs on the fire and swinging a soot-encrusted kettle, suspended from a hook, over the flames. Above the hiss and crackle of burning wood came the loud ticking of a grandfather clock in one corner of the room. On its face stood a lion in a field of improbably coloured flowers, the creature's beady eyes moving from side to side in time with every passing second.

Edith turned and greeted her. "Come in, come in, my dear. I want you to get the idea about the way us does things – just so as you'll know what to expect. I am sure you'm wanting to please your new husband. And there are a lot of things I need to tell you about the house as well as the farm."

The list seemed endless. Milk that wasn't taken to the dairy in Southwood was scalded for cream, but when the milk was rich in the spring and summer there was butter to be made, and cheese; and after a pig was killed, puddings and hams were to be hung in the larder. It was women's work to look after the hens, collect the eggs and get them ready for market. Apart from this, there was bread to be baked, rabbits to be skinned, and jams and preserves to be made when the fruit was ripe. On Mondays the washing was done, and that meant lighting a fire under the copper in the scullery and swirling the clothes around in the boiling water. After this they were to be put through a mangle and rinsed in a galvanised iron bath. And all this happened without the benefit of electricity, gas or mains water. Kathleen had hoped that there'd be a daily help, and possibly even a maid for the dairy. There had been a girl until last week, Edith said, but now Kathleen had come to the farm, what need was there for hired help?

Kathleen gave her a doubtful glance. "There's an awful lot to remember. I'm not sure—"

"Don't worry. I'll show you what to do. Oh, and I'd better show you the privy." Edith took Kathleen to what she called 'the front door', which was merely a door opening onto a garden. She pointed to a path leading to a wooden shed behind blackcurrant bushes. "There 'tis – down yonder. Chamber pot's under the bed for the night, of course."

Kathleen only nodded, because she could not think of anything worth saying in reply.

By the time Jim returned from milking the light was fading; the red glow of the fire the only thing that gave form to the furniture and the other things inhabiting the kitchen. Edith lit a candle set in a blue enamel holder. Grease from previous burnings had run in a cascade down one side and gathered in a pool at the base. She placed it on the sideboard, then turned her attention to two well-polished brass paraffin lamps at either end of the mantelpiece, next to the white china dogs. When the lamps were lit too, the room took on a more comfortable, homely look. Edith waved aside Kathleen's offer of help and spread a damask cloth over the kitchen table's oilskin cover. She took out cups, saucers and plates – rose-patterned, the gilded edges worn away in places, with a milk jug and sugar basin to match. The brown earthenware teapot she put to warm on the range. From the dresser she took an old biscuit tin, the seams rusty and the paper surround so worn that the make of biscuit was no longer decipherable. However, as the tin was no longer used for biscuits, this was of little consequence. Reaching inside, she brought out a rich-looking fruit cake, studded on the top with almonds, and set this on a doily-covered plate.

"'Twill do well enough for supper," she said. "Fine dinner your parents laid on for us." And for the first time she smiled at Kathleen.

Although Jim removed his boots at the back door and put on slippers, the smell of cow hung about him, but Kathleen did not protest as he took her hand and led her to the settle. He sat her down next to the fire with himself beside her. As soon as supper was over, Edith made an excuse to leave them alone.

"Well, my lovely one, what do you think to us being wed?" Jim asked.

It was the moment Kathleen had been waiting for: just her and Jim – alone. And as she murmured a reply, she felt an arm slip round her waist and pull her close, and his hand slide across her belly, feeling for the slight thickening that told of the unborn child.

"Let's hope 'twill be a boy," he said. "We could do with a strong son to help on the farm." His hand moved higher and stroked her breast. "I think it might be time for us to go to bed, don't you?"

While she waited on the settle, he reached up and turned down each lamp until the flame was extinguished, and from the wicks acrid-smelling smoke spiralled up to dissolve in the shadows. The one remaining light – the candle on the sideboard – he held high in the air to light them up the stairs and into the bedroom. The single flame shed an eerie light and sometimes it was difficult to see the way, but after the bedroom door was closed and the candle put on the dressing table, a quiet glow spread around the room.

Kathleen undressed, facing away from him, although why she should be so modest in the presence of the man who'd fathered her child she didn't know. About to put on her new nightdress, she felt Jim beside her, his arm slipping round her waist, drawing her towards him. Her skin tingled at his touch and her body trembled at his closeness. He kissed her, and the kiss was long and full of memories. And then she was lying on the bed between the white sheets, and he was kissing her. She lost herself in him so completely and utterly that nothing else mattered anymore.

When she awoke, it was daylight and the bed beside her was empty. She got up right away, went to the washstand, splashed some water on her face, and brushed her hair. Pulling on the clothes she'd worn yesterday, she hurried downstairs. Jim and Edith were in the kitchen talking, unaware of her standing in the doorway.

"She's a lot to learn, son," Edith was saying. "Hard to tell whether she's going to cost you more than you bargained for."

"Don't fret yourself, Mother," he replied. "The price I got her father to promise for taking her off his hands will be enough to see us settled on a farm of our own."

CHAPTER 7

Stunned by what she had overheard, Kathleen retreated to the staircase and stood there, uncertain of what to do. It wasn't right, what she had heard, it couldn't be. There must be some mistake, surely. A deep breath, and she marched into the kitchen where Jim and Edith were still deep in conversation. The instant they saw her they broke off, and Edith's face clouded with guilt. She melted away towards the scullery, muttering about something she needed to do, but Jim stood his ground. He looked directly at Kathleen, a creeping smile overtook his blank expression, and he opened his arms, entreating her to come.

"'Tis true your father wanted you off his hands. Saw you were damaged goods, he did, and wanted a good settlement for you."

Kathleen stared, open-mouthed. How dare he presume to know what her father thought? Anyway, it was outrageous, regarding her as no more than goods, a mere possession, something to strike a bargain over.

Again he raised his arms, inviting her to come. "You're lucky I married you. Now your child won't be a bastard; he'll be my son."

Blind fury overcame her and she ran at him, thumping him hard on the chest with her fists. "Who got me like this? Who did this to me? It's as much your fault as mine. How dare you say things like that about my father? He's giving us a wedding present – both of us. It's for both of us, not just you."

Jim's arms encircled her, binding her to him so that she couldn't move, but she felt his body shaking. He was laughing – laughing at her.

"Don't you want this baby?" she blurted out, stiffening in defiance under his iron grip. "Because if you don't, perhaps I should get rid of it."

He stroked her hair with a tenderness so unexpected that the resistance drained from her and tears blurred her sight. "You'm a fine young woman. I knew that from the moment I saw you," he said. "I wanted you from that first sight. But wasn't just me, was it? We're well suited, thee and me. Both like a bit of coupling, don't us? 'Tis true."

"Love at first sight? Was it like that for you too?"

"Call it what you like," he said. "You can well satisfy me, my dear, and I don't think I'm saying anything amiss when I says you enjoys it too."

She rested against him, already starting to forgive his outrageous comments of a moment ago.

"This child is good for us," he went on. "So don't you go doing anything daft, because 'tis the reason us is wed. And when that money comes through from your father we can buy ourselves a farm, just like we said."

In the days that followed Jim was particularly attentive and Edith bore the brunt of the work around the house.

Kathleen tried her best to be a farmer's wife. She collected and cleaned the eggs, which was not difficult; she scalded milk for cream, which was more difficult, because it had to be judged just right or the milk would boil and the cream would be ruined. In the larder, hams, sides of bacon and puddings – black and white – hung from hooks on the ceiling, amid bunches of dried sage and strings of onions. They'd killed a pig round Michaelmas, Edith said, and Kathleen was thankful to have missed the event.

A brief letter arrived from her father saying he hoped she was well and sending his good wishes to Jim, but making no mention of the money. A couple of weeks later Kathleen was pleasantly surprised to receive another letter, this time from Alice.

Dear Kathleen,

I'm so sorry I couldn't come to your wedding but Mummy was totally unforgiving and forbade it. I won't tell you all the horrible things she said. But if anyone asks me, I tell them you're so brave you'll make a go of things whatever you're faced with.

Please write to me c/o Binkey – address at bottom of page. This is the only way we can stay in touch, because if you send anything to me at home, Mummy will immediately pounce on it and tear it up.

You remember I told you about my cousin? It was at my cousin's tennis party that Binkey and I met. She's been absolutely marvellous, inviting both of us to every kind of social event. Otherwise I don't think we'd be able to see each other with Mummy doing her beastly guard dog impression.

I do hope you're keeping well, Kathleen. Write and tell me what life on the farm is like. And is Jim really a wonderful lover?

Your dearest friend,
Alice

An address in Berkshire followed her signature.

The days grew darker; the rain more incessant. Muck from boots and shoes invaded the house, and however hard Kathleen tried to keep it out, washing down the flagstones every day, it returned like a bad dream. Sometimes she felt the farm mocking her, telling her she wasn't strong enough, wasn't game enough to take it on, but Alice's letter had given her hope.

One evening, when she knew Jim would be late back from the market, she sat at the kitchen table and, by the light of the paraffin lamps, penned her reply.

My dear Alice,

It was wonderful to get your letter and to know we're still friends. The weather here is so dreary I cannot believe it will ever get any better. It seems so long since we sweltered in the August heat.

I'm sorry it's such a drag for you and Binkey under your mother's eagle eye. And it's all my fault, I suppose. Your mother can't have anything against such a well-behaved young man as Binkey, virtually TT, who's going to become a solicitor.

You ask what life on the farm is like. Well, in a couple of words: hard work. I'm lucky that Jim's mother does most of it at the moment, but when the baby is born I'm sure I'll have to do more – a lot more.

I hadn't realised how cruel life on a farm can be. We keep cats to catch mice in the barns, and the other day one of them got a paw caught in a gin trap. The poor animal dragged itself home and Jim released the trap but he wouldn't let me tend the cat. He said the leg wouldn't mend and a lame cat was no use, so he took it into the field and shot it. I cried, but he just laughed and said I had to learn.

We're hoping soon to hear from Daddy with the money he promised, and then we can think of buying a farm and moving away from Southwood and the Alston Estate. I haven't seen Robert, but our paths must cross at some point, and I'm not looking forward to it.

As to Jim as a lover – I'll just say we're very happy together and leave you to draw your own conclusions.

Dear Alice, thank you so much for keeping in touch. It means such a lot to me.

Your loving friend,
Kathleen

On the shortest day of the year, Jim cut a bough of holly and dragged it into the scullery where Kathleen was busy cleaning eggs at the sink. He made the observation that having a bit of holly about the place made it more festive, and then disappeared again. A few berries rolled onto the floor and some stuck to the mud left by his boots.

Kathleen scrutinised the offering. She bent down, snapped off twigs with berries clustered round the stem, and carried armfuls of holly to the kitchen, ignoring the scratches and weals on her hands.

At the table Edith was kneading dough, and she looked up as Kathleen came in. "I was just thinking Jim was leaving it late. Anyhow, 'tis done now and we can brighten the place up."

Kathleen looked round for the best places to put the holly.

"Top of the clock, mantelpiece and sideboard," said Edith, pointing a forefinger at each as she spoke. "And then put a few bits in the parlour."

"In the parlour?" echoed Kathleen. "No one ever goes there, it's so cold."

"We've folks coming on Boxing Day."

"A party on Boxing Day? Who's coming?"

"Don't know as it's grand enough to be called a party," replied Edith. "Leastways, not the sort you'm used to. Just neighbours and their wives – a sort of thank-you for help during the year."

Having decided to begin with the kitchen, Kathleen pulled a chair towards the clock, put a foot on the seat, and heaved herself up. She placed a sprig behind each finial and then adjusted the first one to make it match the other. The faintest sensation – a kind of wriggle, just as she was about to step down – made her freeze.

"What's the matter?" Edith was staring at her. "Is something amiss? Let me help you down." She wiped her hands. "Careful now, don't want no accidents."

"I'm all right, really I am." Kathleen sat on the chair and placed a hand where the wriggle had been. "I think I felt the baby move."

"That's just as it should be," replied Edith in a satisfied tone. "Once I've got these in the oven," she indicated the loaves, "I'll put the kettle on."

"I could do that," suggested Kathleen.

"No, no. You just sit there quiet for a while."

When Jim came in, he surveyed the holly-decked kitchen with approval and asked whether she'd done the parlour as well. He announced, as he took his seat at the table, that they'd be eating chicken for Christmas dinner. Kathleen thought no more about it, but the next morning, when she was again working at the trough in the scullery, Jim appeared at the back door. In his hands was the brown-feathered body of a plump hen; legs stiff, neck flopping down over his arm.

"Here you are – good fat bird," he said. "'Twill do nicely." He thrust the hen at her.

The body was still warm, blood dripped from the beak, and as she took it from him a wing jerked. She shrieked and the hen landed with a soft thud on the stone floor.

"It's still alive!" she screamed.

"No 'tisn't. Twitch sometimes after they'm dead." He turned away, but stopped and looked back. "'Tis no good. You got to get used to these things."

How could she possibly deal with the dead hen? She felt so fragile, so useless, even touching it revolted her.

Edith must have heard the commotion. "You wanting some help there, my dear?"

"Oh, please… I've no idea what to do with this hen."

"Needs its innards drawn and its feathers plucked. Shall I do it for you?"

"Yes… oh no… I don't know," Kathleen stuttered, her eyes full of misgiving. "I've got to learn, Edith, I've got to learn." They had become friends, something Kathleen had never experienced with her own mother, and Edith was happy with the arrangement.

"Well then, I'll show you, and us can do it together."

While the two of them were working – at least, Edith was working on the bird while Kathleen was watching – there was a loud knock.

"Better go and see who 'tis," said Edith, with a nod in the direction of the scullery door. "My hands are all in a mess with this creature's innards."

Kathleen lifted the latch and pulled back the door, thinking it would probably be the cattle feed merchant who called each month, but stamping his feet in the cold, holding a basket of oranges topped by a bottle of brandy, was Robert.

"Good morning, Mrs Wilcox," he said, raising his hat and speaking with forced cheerfulness. "I hope I find you well."

There was a sharp intake of breath as Kathleen stared at him. It could only have been for a split second, yet it seemed an age. Then her gaze fell on the presents he was carrying and settled there. "Yes, I'm very well, Mr Neville, thank you," she managed to say, not daring to raise her head again.

"I'm visiting all the tenants to wish them a merry Christmas and a prosperous New Year," he said. "Is Mr Wilcox about?"

"Who is it, Kathleen?" Edith called.

"It's Mr Neville come to wish us a merry Christmas."

"Mr Neville? Bring him in, bring him in, Kathleen, and see if you can find Jim."

"Come in, Mr Neville, please come in." Kathleen took a few steps back.

Robert removed his hat, ducked under the lintel and came into the scullery.

"Good day to you, Mr Neville." Edith nodded respectfully, washing blood from her hands in the stone sink. "Take Mr Neville through to the kitchen, my dear."

Kathleen could feel Robert's eyes watching her as she led the way. The skin on the back of her neck tingled and a flush of embarrassment rose all the way to the top of her head. "Please take a seat, Mr Neville," she said. "I'll just go into the yard and look for Mr Wilcox. I'm sure he'd like to see you." She said this without any real conviction, but down the passage and out into the yard she scuttled, forgetting even to grab a coat to fling over her shoulders. "Jim, Jim, where are you? Mr Neville's here to wish us merry Christmas. He's brought presents for us."

The yard was silent except for a black hen scratching and clucking to herself. Kathleen waited and shouted again, her voice echoing round deserted walls, and there she stayed in the stillness, feet as cold as ice, arms covered with goosebumps. One of the farm dogs ran from the barn, dancing around with excitement, pushing his wet nose into her hand. She made a fuss of him, patting his head then sending him away, before coming back in and closing the door behind her. Unsure what to do or say, she walked slowly down the passage to the kitchen where Robert waited.

Edith was talking to him. "Still, we mustn't complain," she was saying. "Harvest was fair enough, all considered, though the price of wheat and most everything's down again on last year."

"I'm so sorry, Mr Neville, I can't find Mr Wilcox," Kathleen said, unable to find it within her to say, 'my husband'. She stole a glance and wished she hadn't. Although he was trying hard, Robert's expression could not disguise his bewilderment.

"Never mind," he said, almost casually. "Please convey my regards to him." He rose, gave a short bow in turn to Kathleen and Edith, retrieved his hat from the settle, and took his leave.

In a state of confusion, Kathleen watched him go. "I can't imagine where Jim is," she said to Edith. "I thought he was mending the manger in the shippon this morning."

Edith shrugged. "Could be he's gone to the village with a few presents of his own," she said.

"You'd think Robert would have seen him… I mean, wouldn't Mr Neville have come across Jim if he'd been going to the village?" Caught off guard, Kathleen felt herself blush, but Edith seemed not to notice. And the question of who Jim might be visiting and why was never asked.

Before Christmas Day a box of chocolates and a greetings card arrived from Kathleen's parents. Written in her mother's untidy hand, it made no mention of the wedding present.

Alice included with her card the snap she had taken of Kathleen and Jim together in the barley field, and a long letter remembering the old times at school. It was this that sparked in Kathleen nostalgia for Christmases of long ago, when she was still a little girl. She recalled her father taking her up to town on the Saturday before Christmas – just the two of them. They'd go to Gamages Christmas Bazaar, and she'd wander from one room to another, down passages, up ramps. And Daddy would buy her the toy she wanted most and the shop assistant would wrap it up in a brown paper parcel, and often they'd struggle to get it home on the train. More mysteriously, a lot of other things that took her fancy – things they didn't buy – found their way to the foot of her bed on Christmas morning. She smiled to herself and sighed, and placed a hand where the baby had wriggled.

On Christmas Eve, Jim stacked up logs on either side of the enormous grate in the parlour and Kathleen placed cards on the mantelpiece, bookcase and shelves. Early on Christmas morning Edith lit the fire and coaxed it into life with the leather bellows that hung from a brass hook on the wall, and the whole room took on a different character. They still ate dinner at the kitchen table, but in between times Kathleen learned that it was possible to sit back and savour the quiet luxury of doing nothing. Of course, Jim had to leave the fireside to see to the milking in the afternoon, but on his return he poured himself a handsome measure of the brandy that was Robert's gift, and Kathleen shared with Edith the chocolates her mother had sent.

When Boxing Day arrived, Edith took down a ham that hung from the ceiling in the larder and put it to simmer in an immense copper pot on the range. After two or three hours she heaved it out and left it resting on a willow-patterned serving dish. Towards evening she warmed up a large quantity of cider and poured it into a silver punch bowl and added brandy, herbs and spices. It came almost as a surprise to Kathleen that being entrusted to set the table in the parlour could be a pleasant experience. As she arranged the punch bowl, the ham with its carving knife and fork, bread, pickled onions, red cabbage and apple chutney, and hot mustard, she pictured her father standing there, smiling at her efforts, and she fancied she heard him say that he was proud of her.

The guests arrived and Jim took obvious pleasure in introducing Kathleen as his wife. She could scarcely remember which name belonged to which face as they gathered round the great mahogany table. Candle flame reflected from the punch bowl shone on faces unable to hide their curiosity. Jim sat at the head of the table and Edith at the foot – just as she'd always done.

"That's right, my handsome," Jim said to Kathleen. "Sit here beside me. I want everyone to see my lovely wife and know that she's expecting my child. Raise a glass, all of you, and drink to the birth of my son."

Kathleen blushed as, one after another, the guests fixed their eyes on the swelling where her waist should have been. "You don't know it's a boy," she whispered, but Jim took no notice and filled his glass once more.

Though the days grew longer, the rain still fell – except, that is, when the wind came laden with snow, dusting the bleak fields and piling up in drifts under the hedgerows. One day towards the end of February, Edith answered a knock at the scullery door and let out a cry when she saw who it was. Kathleen dropped what she was doing and rushed to see a terrified Edith transfixed by the piece of paper in her hand.

"'Tis a telegram," Edith managed to say. "Nothing good ever comes by telegram. Here, you take it. 'Tis addressed to you."

Kathleen took the envelope from Edith's shaking hand, ripped it open and read:

COME AT ONCE STOP FATHER DEAD STOP MUMMY

Although her eyes scanned the words, her mind refused to make sense of them. How could her father be dead? He wasn't even ill.

"Is there a reply?" asked the telegram boy. He took out notebook and pencil and stood poised, ready to record her message.

"Coming at once – stop – Kathleen," she said. Then everything about her went cold and numb, there was no longer any air in her lungs, and the telegram boy faded and disappeared from sight.

CHAPTER 8

Even though she repeated it to herself time and again, Kathleen could not believe it. That telegram, two days ago, had to be a dreadful mistake. There was no reason for her father to die – unless of course there'd been an accident, but the telegram hadn't said anything about an accident. Perhaps he'd been struck down with influenza, but wouldn't she have been sent for if he'd been gravely ill?

Earlier Jim had rolled out of bed and she'd heard him pull on his clothes and shuffle off to do the morning milking. She'd turned over and tried to sleep, but now, wide awake, she slid from the covers and immediately the cold engulfed her. She knew for certain that behind the heavy curtains, frost-fern patterns covered the windowpane.

Today she was going home – she still thought of it as home – to find out what had happened, how it had happened, and why it had happened at all. She shivered, gathered up her clothes together with soap, flannel and comb from the washstand, and crept downstairs to the kitchen to dress.

In the darkness, the moon, full and bright, cast a pale, hard light across the room, making shadows in peculiar places. The embers in the range still had some warmth to them, so she riddled the grate to get the ash out and added a handful of chopped sticks. With a match held to the kindling, flames were soon leaping up the chimney, and the kettle, filled with water from the scullery, was beginning to sing. And there she sat and wondered what was wrong with her because she had not wept for her father. But the truth was that grief had stunned her, and bound her so tight she could not see his long, icy tentacles clutching at her heart and could not yet grasp the bitter gift he brought.

While she washed and dressed she glanced through the window at the icicles hanging from the water chute, and the withered spikes of grass coated in hoar frost that stood erect like miniature daggers in the moonlight. And it seemed to her as if everything was cold and frozen, and that she was cold and frozen too. She suspected Jim did not understand at all how she was feeling. "'Tis the way of things," he'd said, on hearing the news of her father's death. "Of course you must go," he'd added, and straight away that afternoon he had gone to Ivybridge to enquire about the times of trains, but the truth was, he cared more about whether his breakfast was ready when the milking was over.

By the time she heard him come in at the yard door she'd washed, dressed, lit the lamps, put the kettle on again, and had a cup of tea waiting for him.

"That's a welcome sight." Jim took it from her, wrapping his fingers around the cup. "Now I know you're grieving for your father." He sat down, placing the cup on the table, and rubbed his hands together, blowing into them, warming flesh raw with cold. "But it wouldn't go amiss to find out what's happened 'bout the money."

It was a while before she spoke. "I'll find out what I can. I'm sure if Daddy intended us to have it he'll have found a way."

The sun had risen above the horizon when Kathleen took her seat beside Jim on the wagon, but the temperature remained below freezing. Although she was wearing her wool coat, she was grateful when Edith fetched an old tartan travelling rug to tuck around her legs. The horse lumbered into action the moment Jim flicked the reins, steam from its back and nostrils billowing in the frosty air.

On Ivybridge Station people stamped their feet and flung their arms about to keep warm. Jim helped Kathleen down, beckoned the stationmaster's boy over, and gave him a penny to hold the horse.

"Now, you'll be all right, won't you?" he said, and carried the suitcase as they made for the booking office. "Come back soon as you can. Bed'll seem empty without you."

"I'll miss you too, Jim." She put her arms around him and rested her cheek against his.

"And mind – find out what's happened 'bout the money."

She drew away from him. "I'll try."

"Write and let me know when you're coming home." He held her at arm's length and looked into her eyes.

In the distance a toy-sized train puffed its way across the western viaduct and struggled up the incline towards Ivybridge, growing larger with every passing second. It clattered and chugged to a halt beside them and let out a hiss of steam. Jim opened a door in third class, helped

Kathleen in, and put the suitcase on the floor beside her. He embraced her, kissed her full on the mouth – luckily there was no one else in the compartment – and then he was gone, shutting the door and waving from the platform as the train pulled out.

After she'd changed at Exeter – not bothering with a porter because she didn't have much money and the case wasn't heavy – the constant rattling of wheels on track dulled her senses, lulling her into a state of such torpor that she scarcely realised the passing of time until the express hurtled into the outskirts of London and she found that the clear blue sky had been replaced by endless grey cloud blanketing the flat landscape. So much had changed since August when she'd made the same journey back from Devon. Then it had been hot and sunny and she'd flung herself into her father's arms, eager to tell him about the holiday and glad to be there. Now it was dreary, oh so dreary, everywhere she looked, and he was no longer there to meet her.

At Paddington a cold draught blew along the platform and porters rushed to attend to the first-class passengers. Picking up her suitcase, Kathleen began the long walk to the Underground, where she stood and waited for the train to Wimbledon, and fancied that all the people on the District Line looked surly, as if nothing pleasant had ever happened to them.

By the time she reached home it was late afternoon. Gaunt, lifeless-looking trees lined the avenue and a handful of leaves lingered in a pile by the front gate. Ringing the front doorbell felt very odd, as if she was a stranger who had no right to be there.

Footsteps came and her mother opened the door. "You took your time getting here. I was expecting you yesterday. The telegram said you were coming at once."

"I came as soon as I could."

"Well, you'd better come in now you're here." Her mother stood to one side.

"Can you take my case, or get Elsie to do it?" Kathleen looked around. "Where is she?"

"Elsie? Elsie?" Alexandra called out, as if she were asking a question.

"Coming, ma'am." Elsie's face lit up when she saw Kathleen. "It's so good to see you, miss. Oh, I do beg your pardon – ma'am. It's Mrs Wilcox now, isn't it? I'm so sorry about your poor father – tragic, it is."

"Take Mrs Wilcox's suitcase to her room, please, Elsie," ordered Alexandra. "Then you can bring us tea."

Kathleen followed her mother into the drawing room. "Why didn't you let me know Daddy was ill?"

"He wasn't ill. There wasn't anything to tell." Alexandra walked across the room and stood by the window, looking out, as if there was something significant to see in the garden.

"Well, what was it, then? Did he have an accident?"

Alexandra swung round and looked directly at Kathleen, eyes flaming. "Stupid man, dying like that. Just like him, not thinking of anyone else."

"What on earth are you talking about?"

Alexandra glared back. "Hush, be quiet." She put a finger to bright red lips.

Elsie was walking through the hall, carrying the tea tray. Kathleen looked down at her hands and waited as

96

Elsie arranged cups, saucers and plates on the table and set out egg and cress sandwiches, and a sponge cake filled with raspberry jam.

"How did he die?" she asked in a hoarse whisper the instant Elsie left the room.

"That's the problem – nobody knows." Alexandra lit a cigarette, and let the smoke drift in trails from her nostrils. "There's got to be a post-mortem."

"Post-mortem? What for?"

"To find out what he died of, and because the doctor's refusing to sign a death certificate. It will delay the funeral – that's what the undertaker fellow said." Alexandra took a deep drag, and stared at Kathleen through the haze that followed.

"Have you no idea at all? Where was he when he died?" asked Kathleen.

"He went to bed last Saturday, when I was out shopping, and when I got back, there he was – dead."

"So he *was* feeling unwell?"

Alexandra balanced the cigarette holder on an ashtray and the smoke spiralled up. She began pouring milk into the teacups. "Rather a lot of sleeping mixture had gone from the bottle, so the doctor said."

"Sleeping mixture… in the day? Why would… Daddy always sleeps like a log."

"Not any more. Not since… he'd been worried about… things."

"What things? What are you talking about?" Kathleen's brow furrowed.

"Don't you ever hear any news down in Devon?" asked Alexandra. "Haven't you heard about America, about the stock market, about the crash?"

"No, nothing. Nobody's said anything about… but what's it got to do with Daddy?"

"Wall Street – he should never have got mixed up with it," Alexandra hissed back.

"I still don't see… Daddy buys and sells shares in London," Kathleen realised she was speaking about him as if he were still alive, "not in America. It doesn't make sense."

"I blame that Mr Cougar. I wish we'd never met him."

"In heaven's name, who is Mr Cougar?"

"He's the big boss at Cougar Incorporated. I'd string him up if I'd half a chance," retorted Alexandra. She picked up the teapot and poured straight into a cup, forgetting to use the strainer. "Damn and blast. Now there're leaves floating in your tea."

"Never mind. I'll pick them out with the spoon. How did you get to know him?"

"Who?"

"This Mr Cougar."

"On the cruise. You remember – the cruise to New York, on the *Île de France*."

"That's where you met him?"

"You'd think that anyone you met on a cruise like that… Huh!" Alexandra leaned forward, picked up the cigarette holder and took a deep draught. "He told Ray you could make a fortune on Wall Street; 'Beyond your wildest dreams,' he said. All you needed was a small down payment and a broker who'd let you buy on tick – and most of them would, with the right introduction. And he – this Cougar man – said he knew just the right broker for Ray and he'd set him up the moment we docked."

"Is that what he did?"

"Worse than that. Your stupid father even borrowed the money for the down payment, and then bought Cougar shares because of the fabulous returns the corporation was making, and because everyone said this Mr Cougar was a financial genius."

"What went wrong, then?" Kathleen scooped out three or four tea leaves floating on the surface of her cup.

"At the end of October the share price plummeted. Everything did – for a few days. Then the market shot up, but it didn't last. It crashed again, sliding so fast you didn't even know the price you were going to get until hours after the Stock Exchange closed, Ray said. That's when the broker Cougar had fixed for him asked your father to pay what he owed. And of course he couldn't. And even when the shares were sold, he still owed them a massive amount."

"Couldn't Daddy have borrowed money here in London? I thought he knew lots of important people – the kind of people who'd help him."

"He raised what money he could and he mortgaged this house – my home." Alexandra's eyes were wild. "And now I'm to be turned out of it – ruined."

"Daddy wouldn't have left you destitute, surely."

"Apparently, there is a life insurance policy. Mr Fitzgerald got him to take it out ages ago. He's Ray's executor, and he's looking into it for me."

Scarcely had Alexandra finished speaking when there was a ring at the front door. Elsie answered it, and within a couple of minutes William Fitzgerald was shown into the drawing room.

"I am so sorry to hear of your loss, Kathleen," he said, and held out a hand. "Please accept my sincere condolences."

Kathleen took his hand and felt it squeeze her own. "Thank you, Mr Fitzgerald."

"Do sit down, William. Here, take a seat." Alexandra indicated the easy chair on the other side of the fireplace. "Would you like tea? Elsie? Elsie?"

"No, thank you," said William. "I've had tea at home."

Elsie appeared in the doorway and was waved away by Alexandra.

"No need, no need, Mr Fitzgerald's already had tea. Any news?" Alexandra asked William.

"Yes. Fairly good news, as a matter of fact," he replied. "Your husband took out a policy with the Providential Assurance Company some years ago. The sum assured is twenty thousand pounds, and this is held in trust for the two of you in equal shares."

"In equal shares? Why should Kathleen have anything? I was his wife. Anyway, Kathleen's a husband of her own now. It's up to him to look after her."

"As I said, the trust was set up years ago. It can't be altered." William turned to Kathleen. "Your father must have wanted you to have the money. The document's quite clear."

Alexandra looked livid and glowered at Kathleen. "There's nothing else for it. You'll just have to give me your share when you get it. Your father wouldn't have wanted me to be left penniless."

Kathleen did not reply.

"I'll do what I can to get the Providential to pay you as soon as possible." William looked from one to the other and, getting no response, rose to his feet. "Well, I'll be on my way – Alexandra, Kathleen." He gave a little nod to each as he said their names and, without looking back, walked from the room.

There was nothing more Kathleen could do, except go back to Jim and wait for news. She wrote, telling him about the mystery of her father's death and which train she'd be on, and he was there with the wagon to meet her at Ivybridge Station.

"Wasn't a wasted trip," he remarked, as he helped her up and she wrapped the rug that Edith had sent around her legs. "You said something about an insurance policy in your letter."

"I can only tell you what Mr Fitzgerald said. He's handling all Daddy's affairs." She swallowed hard and her voice became husky. "He said that even though Daddy was bankrupt when he died, the creditors can't get their hands on the insurance money because it's in a trust for me and Mummy." Her voice trembled and she struggled to finish the sentence.

"There, there, my lovely one." His arms surrounded her.

Clinging to him, burying her face in him, she sobbed and sobbed, weeping all the tears she'd kept for this moment.

When they reached Higher Haydn, Edith had the kettle boiling and the teapot warming. "'Tis good to see you back, my dear," she said. "Come and sit yourself down. You'll be tired after that long journey. Shame they haven't let you bury your father. Jim says you'll have to go back later."

Kathleen looked at Edith and gave a watery smile. "Yes," she said, her voice still shaky. "We don't know how long it's going to be – with the post-mortem."

"Good thing is, Mother," said Jim, dropping the suitcase in the hall and coming into the kitchen, "Kathleen's father did right by her. Saw to it that the money he promised when us wed is coming at last. When I say, 'the money he promised', fact is, 'tis a lot more than that. I'd say 'tis enough to make us part of the gentry."

Edith gave him a reproachful look. "Now, son, can't you see the poor maid's all cut up with losing him?" She put a hand on Kathleen's shoulder. "I've made a few scones and opened a pot of last year's strawberry jam. Help yourself to cream, my dear."

Kathleen sat down and wound the lace edge of the tablecloth around a finger, wondering how she was going to say what her mother had told her to say. She had to do it before her courage deserted her. "Mummy's going to lose the house. The people Daddy owed money to are going to turn her out and sell it and she says I should…" her voice almost petered out, "…should give her my share."

The only sound to be heard was the steady *tick-tock* of the lion's eyes in the grandfather clock.

"There's no way that mother of yours is getting more than she's owed." Jim's eyes narrowed to mere slits and he raised a finger at Kathleen to make sure she understood. "Your father promised me five thousand pounds to wed you, and it's only right we should keep this money, even if 'tis more than I reckoned on at the start."

"But Mummy says she won't even have a roof over her head. And what she'll live on, she's no idea."

"She'll have the same as us, damn it! If that bloody woman can't live on what the three of us – and a child – can live on, she didn't oughter bother living at all."

"Jim, I'll ask you not to use such language in my kitchen!" Edith exclaimed.

The following week, when Kathleen was in the dairy cleaning out the butter churns, because it would not be long now before the spring grass came on and they'd be up to their eyes in butter-making, the postman arrived with a letter addressed to her in a familiar untidy hand. She wiped her palms on her apron, took the letter through to the kitchen, and sat on the settle. The letter contained no surprises: her mother was begging for help in her hour of need and pointing out all she had done for Kathleen when she was a girl. It was pathetic and stupid to feel she owed her mother anything. Jim was right to say that her father must have wanted her to have the money; otherwise he wouldn't have set up the trust in the way he had. Yet she felt compelled to confront Jim once more and plead her mother's case.

A noise at the yard door – it was Jim, kicking off his boots and coming in for his elevenses. Kathleen took a deep breath and braced herself.

"It's not like we would need to go without anything," she told him. "We could give her *half* my share and we'd still have money to buy a farm."

Jim glared at her and thumped his fist on the table with such force that the cups rattled on their saucers. "Listen here, woman. That mother of yours is getting not a penny of what's due to us. And there's an end to it."

A week later, another letter from her mother arrived. This time she put it in her apron pocket, and it was some time before she'd the courage to open it. Alexandra threatened that she'd never speak to Kathleen again if she didn't help her. Furthermore, she blamed Kathleen entirely, because if she hadn't got into trouble and had to marry that farmer she'd still be living at home, and there'd be no problem because they'd be able to buy the house and have enough left over for the two of them to live on.

Kathleen left the letter on the table, where Jim could not help but see it at dinner time. As soon as his eyes fell on it his body stiffened and his mouth contorted in an expression of outrage. He read it slowly, shaking his head, while Kathleen studied the flagstone by the dresser and waited for what she knew must come.

Jim exploded with fury, tearing the letter into pieces and throwing it on the fire. "You'll do as your husband tells you. I don't want to hear another word. Your mother's not getting my money."

CHAPTER 9

Another letter arrived from Kathleen's mother, short and to the point: the post-mortem had shown the cause of death to be an excessive dose of sleeping mixture. It also said that her father's funeral would be held on Monday 17th March, and Kathleen's presence was required.

To have her father's death confirmed as an overdose raised more questions than it answered. Was it an accident, or had he meant to kill himself? Why would he do such a thing?

The afternoon before the funeral, Kathleen stood in the drawing room of her old home and looked around, wondering if this might be the last time she'd ever see it. Her mother had sacked Elsie and the daily help and hadn't bothered to pick up a duster herself. A grey film lay everywhere and the very soul had gone out of the place.

Kathleen shut her eyes and pictured her father walking through the doorway, standing just inside, calling her name. The vision was so strong that she half-expected to see him there when she opened her eyes, but the empty space rebuked her for being a fool. She sat on the arm of his chair by the fire where they'd shared secrets and laughed together, but now the chair was vacant, and he was no longer there to put his arm around her. When was the last time she'd seen him in this room? Reason told her that it must have been before they'd left for Devon and her wedding; yet that memory was mixed up with memories of all the other times they'd been here together and it was impossible to know which was which. Supposing she'd known then that it would be the last time? That was too dreadful to contemplate.

Her reflections were interrupted by the sound of china smashing on the kitchen floor and Alexandra swearing and screaming that life wasn't fair.

The front doorbell rang, and Kathleen waddled into the hall, only to see that her mother had got there first and was dealing with the cab driver.

"Taxi, madam? You ordered a taxi for two o'clock?"

"Yes, yes, that's right. Our suitcases, if you don't mind." There was more than a hint of annoyance in her mother's voice as she pointed a gloved finger at the luggage.

"I don't know why we couldn't have had your father's funeral here," said Alexandra when they were on the train. "But your Uncle Charlie said the family wanted it back in Spitalfields, and as he's paying for everything, there wasn't a lot I could do."

"I think I can remember Uncle Charlie," said Kathleen. "He's a bit younger than Daddy, isn't he?"

"Yes."

"We haven't seen Uncle Charlie for a very long time, have we?" Kathleen shuffled about and eased her ankles.

"No, we haven't."

"What does he do for a living?"

"Bus driver."

"We used to live near him, didn't we? I think Uncle Charlie and Auntie Mary lived just a bit further up the street."

"Hmm." Alexandra was not in a talkative mood.

Uncle Charlie met them at Waterloo. He stared at Kathleen, and flung his arms around her. "My, my, you ain't 'alf grown, girl," he said. "Should never have recognised you, 'cept you've got your mother's eyes and your father's smile. And you a married woman and expecting." A grin spread across his face.

"Yes, she can't stand around, Charlie." Alexandra started walking towards the taxi rank.

"No need for that – borrowed the van off of Albert," declared Charlie. "Got his own shop now, down Whitechapel Road. Doing very nicely, is Albert."

He bundled them out of the station and led them towards a bottle-green van on which the words 'Albert Wyndham, Fruit & Veg' were painted, together with a garish-looking carrot and a bunch of bright green leaves that might have been either a lettuce or a cabbage.

"Are you expecting me to ride in that?" The expression on Alexandra's face showed utter disgust.

"It ain't that bad; I put a load of clean sacks in the back. You can sit on 'em, if you like."

"Why can't I sit in the front, beside you?" Alexandra was clearly affronted.

"'Cause that's where Kathleen's going. Can't expect her to sit in the back in her condition." Charlie shook his

107

head in mock astonishment, put an arm around Kathleen's shoulder, and winked. "Got to look after you, my dear, 'aven't we?"

Alexandra hitched up her skirt and put a foot on the van floor. "Charlie, what on earth's Albert had in here? Smells like a load of cabbage someone forgot to take off the boil till it was too late."

Charlie gave his hand to Alexandra and helped her up. "There you go." A howl of outrage followed as he slung the two suitcases in after her and slammed the doors shut.

Kathleen climbed into the passenger seat and gave Charlie a grateful smile. During the journey she glanced at him from time to time. In many ways he looked like her father – same large nose and deep-set eyes – yet Charlie was leaner than Ray. His hair had receded, and he was showing the beginnings of a bald patch on the crown of his head. Life had etched deep worry lines into his forehead just above his nose, and if you'd seen them together you might even say her father was the younger.

Charlie knew all the backstreets but Kathleen had little idea where they were going until the van turned into a dingy little row of terraced houses with smoking chimneys and front doors opening directly onto the street.

"I remember this." Her face lit up in recognition. "That's where we used to live. And that's your house down there, Uncle Charlie, isn't it?"

A loud sniff came from the back of the van, followed by a noise that sounded as if something had stuck in Alexandra's throat.

Charlie grinned. "Spot on, girl. You was born here. It's where you belong and don't let no one tell you different."

Within seconds of the van drawing up, the front door opened and there was Auntie Mary waiting to welcome them. She was a good-looking woman in her mid forties, greying a little at the temples. Her honest smile made up for the rather plain dress and drab cardigan she wore. "Aw, lovely to see you – been too long. Cor, you expecting an' all." Auntie Mary's hug was warm and sympathetic. As she was about to take Kathleen inside, a cacophony of fist-thumping and yells from the back of the van made her stop in her tracks. "Dear days, Charlie. Sounds like Her Ladyship's playing up. You gonna let her out?"

Charlie nodded and opened the rear doors of the van, removed the suitcases, and helped Alexandra to the ground. If looks could kill, Charlie would have dropped dead. Alexandra stuck her nose in the air, mustered all the dignity she was able, and tottered on elegant heels towards Mary and Kathleen.

"So good of you to put us up for the night, Mary," Alexandra said, eyes flashing, voice icy.

Charlie put his head inside the front door, cupped his hands and yelled, "Oi, Rose, come 'ere."

A plump girl with kind brown eyes appeared and grinned good-naturedly at Alexandra and Kathleen.

"Rose, this 'ere's your Auntie Alex and your cousin, Kathleen, Ray's daughter," said Charlie.

Rose eyed Kathleen up and down. "Not far off your time," she observed.

"No, not long now – about two months."

"Now then, take 'em upstairs and show 'em where they'll be sleeping," Charlie instructed. "'Fraid we only got the one bed, so you'll have to snuggle up." He picked up the suitcases and ushered them in as he spoke.

"Now, 'ow about a nice cuppa?" said Mary. "Come straight down again and we can talk about Ray's funeral and what we've got laid on."

The living room was cosy and Kathleen sat beside Alexandra on the sofa; brown moquette frayed in places, despite the linen armrests and antimacassar. Charlie, proud of the arrangements he'd put in place, sat next to them in the armchair and explained all the details, and waited for Alexandra to sniff here and criticise there. Mary knelt on the rug in front of the coal fire, sticking slices of bread on a long fork and making the toast. Rose handed round china plates – white with a gold rim, slightly faded – and from the kitchen she fetched butter wrapped in greaseproof paper and jam the colour of Alexandra's nails.

"'Ere we are," she said, bringing in the teapot, milk, sugar, cups and saucers on a tray. "Tea's nicely brewed."

When they'd eaten, Kathleen looked around the room and a photograph in a wooden frame hanging on the wall caught her eye. It was of her father in army uniform. She rose slowly to her feet and went for a closer look. "When was this taken, Uncle Charlie?"

"Reckon that must've been early 1915, when Ray joined up," he replied. "We'd all been told the war was only gonna last till Christmas, but when it didn't Ray thought he'd better do his bit for king and country so he joined the Army Service Corps. That's when he handed over the barrow to Albert." Charlie rubbed his chin thoughtfully. "Your dad was bloomin' marvellous at making the barrow pay its way. Got a good nose for a bargain, had Ray. He could forage about and find things others couldn't and get them at the right price too. Blimey, he was quick with his figures. Could work out anything in seconds, he could. No surprise that after he joined up, his talents was spotted pretty quick. Given the job of batman to Colonel Marshall and posted to northern France. Got quite a reputation, Ray did, for doing deals and finding anything that needed to be found. Colonel got all the credit, of course, but it was Ray what ran the show for 'im."

"Was Colonel Marshall the man he went into business with when the war was over?" Kathleen asked.

"You bet he was," replied Charlie. "He was Brigadier Marshall by then, he'd been promoted so many times. Had connections amongst the rich and powerful, but it was Ray who knew how to clinch a bargain." He tapped a forefinger against his nose as he spoke. "The brigadier had the money, but Ray knew how to make the profits."

"Did pretty well for himself, did Ray," said Mary. "Within a year he'd bought that house down by the park."

Ray's coffin, topped with wreaths of white lilies, lay in a glass-sided hearse pulled by two ebony horses, their plumes nodding as they stepped out, following the black-suited men in top hats with solemn faces who led the procession. Charlie offered Kathleen one arm, Alexandra the other, and they set off behind the coffin at a slow and sombre pace. Bystanders stopped and bowed their heads as the hearse passed, while others joined the throng of mourners and followed at a respectful distance.

The cortège passed down Commercial Street, holding up all the traffic, and reached Spitalfields Market – the place where Ray had first found work as a youngster. It came to a halt on the other side of the road, where the pavement was wide and steps led up to the open doors of Christ Church. Charlie ushered them down the aisle and Kathleen was astonished to see the pews on either side filled with men in Sunday suits and women in black hats and dark coats. To her they were strangers, but Charlie looked around and acknowledged this one and that with a nod of the head and a grim smile.

"They'll have lost a day's wages to come and pay their respects," said Charlie, as they took their seats at the front. "Your dad was well liked round here. Always came up with something from the barrow for the poor so-and-sos who didn't have two ha'pennies to rub together."

The rector's voice rang out, the funeral service started, and the coffin was carried down the aisle by six strong-armed men.

"One at the front, on the right, that's your Uncle Albert," whispered Charlie.

Tears flowed down Kathleen's cheeks. She rose to her feet, because everyone was standing and singing 'Abide with Me', but her voice turned weak and husky and cracked on the high notes. The singing stopped and she sank down onto the pew. Uncle Charlie's hand found hers and held it tight; he was weeping too. The rest of the service was a blur – reading, singing, prayers, more singing, and the rector, who'd never known Ray, telling everyone who did know him how he'd lived and what he'd done.

After the service, when they stood outside, ready to move off to the burial ground, Charlie patted Kathleen's hand and told her she had to look after herself. He took out a large handkerchief, blew his nose and cleared his throat a couple of times. "Ray wouldn't want you making yourself ill on his account," he said. "We've clubbed together for a bit of a knees-up in The Ten Bells to give your old dad a proper send-off." He nodded in the direction of the pub just across the street, then scanned the crowd. "Rose, Rose – here, girl. I want you to take your cousin over the road to the pub and look after her," said Charlie, patting Kathleen on the shoulder.

"Right you are." Rose wound her arm around Kathleen's. "C'mon now. Time to get you in the warm."

The Ten Bells reeked of sawdust, stale beer, and smoke. The barmaid – a handsome, big-bosomed woman with rouged cheeks – greeted them with a broad smile.

"This 'ere's my cousin, Kathleen," Rose announced. "We've just had her dad's funeral and the others are up the cemetery now, burying him. My dad says you've got a bit of a do laid on for us and the others'll be along soon as they can."

"You sit over 'ere," said the barmaid, pointing to a drink-stained table near the window, "and I'll see if I can get you a couple on the 'ouse."

Kathleen sipped a lemonade shandy while Rose downed half of the best bitter, and because they were getting on so well, Kathleen decided to venture a few questions. "Not sure I can remember you, Rose, when we used to live round here," she said. "Are you younger than me?"

"Couple of years or so."

"It's strange our families never kept in touch."

Rose's brows furrowed and she gave Kathleen a

doubtful look. "Mean to say you don't know? You really don't know?"

Kathleen stared blankly. "No, I've no idea…"

"No love lost between me dad and your mother. You can see that for yourself. What it came down to was this. Uncle Ray had to choose between 'em and – not surprising, really – he chose your mother. Just as well for you he did."

Kathleen ignored the implication as Rose picked up her glass and downed the last few mouthfuls. "So why's your dad organising everything and paying for the funeral? Of course, it's very kind of him," she added quickly.

"Well, it's like this, see. When your dad was ruined and your mother was givin' him grief, he came back to see me dad. Said what a fool he'd been, listening to that American – what's his name? Kruger?"

"Cougar."

"Well, don't matter what he's called. Thing is, Uncle Ray was taken for a right ride by that crook. Hurt his pride like nothing else ever could. He'd built his reputation on being as cunning as a fox – no one ever got the better of Uncle Ray. He could charm the hind legs off a donkey. Then this Couger chap does it – takes him for all he's got *and* some. Couldn't go on after that. Topped hisself, I reckon."

Before Kathleen could ask any more questions, the door was yanked open and in came Charlie, stamping his feet and thumping his ribs. "Cor blimey. It ain't 'alf cold in cemeteries." Standing beside him was a younger, slightly taller version of himself. "This 'ere's your Uncle Albert," he said.

"Good to see you, girl – been a long time," said Albert, and shook Kathleen's hand. "Rose looking after you all right, is she?"

"We're getting on just fine," replied Kathleen.

"Now, how about a bite to eat?" said Charlie, marching up to the bar.

The barmaid greeted him. "Charlie, d'you want the pies and eels now?"

Charlie nodded, and the barmaid yelled to someone in the back to bring the food out and be quick about it.

The rest of the mourners poured through the door and stood around as plates of pie and mash and jellied eels were brought out and handed round, and the barmaid pulled pint after pint of beer with amazing speed.

"Here's to Ray," said Uncle Charlie, lifting his tankard. "No better man in the whole of the East End."

A murmur and muttering of consent rolled around the room. "Salt of the earth," someone shouted.

The gathering appeared to have divided into two, Kathleen noticed. On one side stood Uncle Charlie, Auntie Mary, and an assortment of men and women she took to be Wyndhams. On the other was a slightly smaller group to which her mother had attached herself. From behind Alexandra's shoulder came the sound of harsh laughter and a voice said, "Always knew how to look after his own, if that's what you mean."

Charlie scowled at the man; a nasty-looking piece of work. "You don't want to say things like that. It ain't no good digging up the past. What's done's done."

The man stared back at Uncle Charlie, defiant.

Rose nudged Kathleen in the ribs. "Don't want to

get 'em going," she whispered in her ear. "Ain't no telling where it can lead."

"Now, come on, drink up, everyone," said a Wyndham voice, and the tension eased.

"What's it all about?" Kathleen whispered to Rose. "You said my mother didn't get on with your dad, but…?"

"You ain't heard how the Wyndhams and the Dobbins hate each other?"

Kathleen shook her head emphatically. "Who're the Dobbins?" she asked.

Rose's face grew purple with pent-up mirth. "Ain't no one told you, then? Dobbin's your mother's name."

"No it isn't!" exclaimed Kathleen.

"Oh yes it is," Rose insisted. "Your mother's a Dobbin all right – Amy Dobbin. That's her real name. Her mouth dropped open in disbelief.

"Mummy's name is Alexandra," replied Kathleen in astonishment. "And before she married Daddy she was called Devereaux."

At this, Rose fell about laughing until the tears rolled down her cheeks. "You really didn't know?"

"But why…?"

"Alexandra Devereaux was her stage name. How far d'you think she'd have got with a name like Amy Dobbin?" Rose wiped away the tears with the back of her hand. "Not that she got very far anyway. If it wasn't for your dad, she'd still be kicking her legs in the chorus line."

"She was a dancer when she started, but I thought she became an actress. She always says—"

A series of shouts and jeers from a group standing near the bar interrupted the conversation. An argument had blown up between a Wyndham and a Dobbin, each hemmed in by members of their own family.

"Cor, look at that."

Kathleen felt Rose's elbow again. A woman on the Dobbin side had broken ranks and marched up to confront Charlie.

"What d'you want, then?" Charlie stood his ground.

"You take back what you said 'bout my sister." The woman nodded her head briefly in Alexandra's direction.

"That's your aunt," Rose whispered loudly.

Kathleen stared. The woman looked so common: henna-tinted hair and hard-lined face. The forefinger pointing at Charlie was badly stained with nicotine.

"There's no need for this," replied Charlie. "Today is Ray's send-off. And that's his daughter over there." He flicked his head in Kathleen's direction.

The woman was like a terrier with a bone and, for a minute, Kathleen thought she might even hit Uncle Charlie "You're a bleedin' liar, Charlie Wyndham," she yelled at him. "Amy ain't ever looked at anyone 'cept your Ray once she knew he was after her."

Kathleen felt her throat tighten with anger and disgust. She clung on to the sides of the table and rose to her feet. "How dare you carry on like this?" she shouted at the two factions eyeing each other up. "I don't care what the feud's about and I don't want to know. My father's only just been laid to rest. Have some respect, can't you?" She glared at the perpetrators and the room fell silent.

CHAPTER 10

The journey back to Devon was uncomfortable and tedious and Kathleen was glad when the train reached Ivybridge and she found Jim waiting for her. He was in a particularly good mood, wrapping his arms around her and kissing her in front of everyone.

"Missed you too," she said. "And I've got so much to tell you."

Ignoring the remark, he picked up her suitcase and made for the barrier.

"What is it, Jim? What's the hurry?"

"Just wait till you hear what I've done." He helped her onto the cart, untied the horse tethered to the railings, and climbed up beside her.

"What is it? What have you done?"

"Well, the next time I come here to the station, or Ivybridge Market, I shan't be coming with the horse and cart." A self-congratulatory smirk spread over his face. "I've bought a motor vehicle." He looked at her to see the effect of his pronouncement.

"You've bought a car?"

"No, not a car – 'tis like a small lorry, with a cab and an open back. Ivybridge garage man called it a Morris Commercial. 'Tis the thing all go-ahead farmers are getting these days. Asking two hundred pounds for it, he was. Said I'd give him 195 'cause I don't like people thinking they can take advantage of me. Anyhow, I'm picking it up tomorrow. Said he'd show me how to drive it and I've been and got my licence, so it's all legal, like."

"Have you ever driven a car… or any other motor vehicle?"

"No, but it can't be that difficult," he replied. "You see people driving all the time nowadays."

"It might take you a little while to learn."

The seriousness in her voice surprised him. "What would a woman know about such things?" he scoffed.

"Daddy taught me to drive. I can drive a car, though I've never driven a lorry."

"You know how to drive? Well, I'm blessed." He paused for a moment to digest the information.

"I hope the man at the garage is going to explain it all to you," she said.

"Can't be that difficult, if you can manage it. Anyway, if he shows me how to start and stop the engine and where the brake is, I shall get along just fine."

"The gears are the difficult bit. You've got to get the gears right – know how to change from one to the other – or else you damage the engine."

"Don't you tell me what I need to do, woman."

She sighed and left it at that.

"'Tis a long way for you to travel in your condition," said Edith, ushering Kathleen into the kitchen. "Now come in and sit down and I'll make us all a nice cup of tea. Jim, see to her suitcase."

"Yes, Mother."

The kettle was already singing as Kathleen eased herself into a chair and Edith took cups and saucers from the dresser and warmed the teapot.

"Gave your father a good send-off?" Edith enquired.

"Yes... but it was so sad, and it's not as if it's all over, even now."

"Not over?"

"There's got to be an inquest, because the doctors can't say whether he meant to take all the sleeping mixture that killed him."

"Oh, you mean... Oh, I see." Anxious to steer the conversation onto a different track, Edith said, "Jim says you met relations you didn't know you had."

"They were so kind; I really took to them." Kathleen told her all about the Wyndhams, while skirting round the more unsavoury characters on her mother's side.

"What's your Uncle Charlie do for a living?" Edith asked.

"Bus driver. And he's a union leader: shop steward for the Transport and General Workers' Union."

"Suppose that means he's one of those layabouts always coming out on strike and making life miserable for everybody else," said Jim, who'd just returned.

"It doesn't mean anything of the kind," flared Kathleen. "The drivers only strike if there's a grievance, or one of them is victimised. Last year, when everyone else was taking big pay cuts, bus drivers' pay went down by only a farthing an hour."

"No one keeps prices up for farmers. Don't see why bus drivers should be any different," grumbled Jim.

"And your cousin?" asked Edith. "What's her job?"

"She works in a soap factory, on the packing line: wrapping toilet soap and putting it in boxes. Smells a treat, she says, but it's hard on your back and legs, all that standing. She's allowed to buy soap cheap, and she let me have some. I'd like you to have it."

"Oh no, I couldn't possibly—"

"But I insist." Kathleen stroked the back of Edith's hand. "I'd really like you to have it."

Next morning Jim set off for Ivybridge to pick up his purchase, taking one of the farmhands with him in the wagon, and planning how he was going to use the truck to take stock to market. But as Kathleen remarked to Edith, it wasn't just animals that could be loaded on board: they'd be able to take cheeses, butter, cream and hams to market as well, and maybe they could even have a stall with the farm name on it. Edith pointed out that Kathleen wouldn't be doing anything like that for a while yet. Her mouth was set firm so Kathleen knew better than to argue with her, but it didn't stop her mulling over what she might do after the baby was born. At the back of her mind there was a slight, niggling doubt as to how Jim had come by the money to buy the truck, but she shrugged it off and told herself he'd probably saved up for it.

The farmhand returned with the wagon, unhitched the horse, and got on with his work. Dinner time came and still there was no sign of Jim, but shortly before two o'clock the sound of a vehicle chugging along in low gear made Kathleen stop what she was doing and hurry to the yard. A dark green truck crawled into view. The engine stalled and it came to a shuddering halt.

Livid with frustration, Jim climbed from the cab. "Sold it to me under false pretences, he did. Can't get the damn thing to go properly. 'Tis no faster than a horse and cart."

Snorting like an exasperated pig, he allowed himself to be led away to the kitchen and given his dinner. After he'd calmed down, and with careful questioning, Kathleen was able to deduce that he'd driven all the way home in bottom gear. In sympathetic tones she laid the blame entirely on the garage man for not explaining things properly, and asked in apparent innocence whether Jim thought the gears were similar to those on a car.

"No idea," retorted Jim.

"They might be," she suggested. "If they are, I could explain how they work and then you'd be able to drive a lot faster."

He stared at her, his expression difficult to interpret, and for a moment she wondered whether his simmering antagonism would boil over, but after what seemed an age, and without enthusiasm, he grudgingly agreed. "Save me having to go all the way back to Ivybridge, I suppose," he said.

Most of the time Kathleen was impatient for the birth to be over and longed to hold the baby in her arms, but sometimes fear gripped her and she wondered whether the pain would be too much to bear, and whether she'd die trying. When she asked Jim about having a doctor to attend her, he told her bluntly that Meg Blackler cost a deal less than a doctor, and it was Meg Blackler who would be sent for when the time came.

Seeing Kathleen's obvious shock, Edith attempted to reassure her. "No doctor ever knew as much about giving birth as Meg Blackler," she said. "You've no need to worry on that score." Kathleen still looked hesitant, so Edith said, "I'll ask her to tea and you can see for yourself. Her mother taught her, and everyone round here knows what a wonder she was. Why, she brought all my children into this world. No one had kinder hands, and I've heard tell Meg's just the same."

"*All* your children? You mean to say Jim isn't your only child?"

"Why, bless you, no." Edith smiled at her. "Four girls, all grown up and gone away into service or married farmers, but my firstborn was a son. We called him Thomas, after his father. Five years older than Jim, he was."

"What happened to him?" asked Kathleen, and immediately wished she hadn't.

"Died in France," said Edith, her voice becoming a little shaky. "Don't know where 'xactly, 'cause they couldn't find his body. Fighting with the Devonshires, he was. Killed same time as the oldest Neville boy."

What was there to say to a mother who'd lost her son, her firstborn child?

"'Tis a terrible thing, war. So many young men got took back then." Edith shook her head slowly. "Best not talk about it."

"I didn't know... I'm so sorry." Words were inadequate. Then an idea struck Kathleen. "Edith, if my baby is a boy, do you think we might call him Thomas? Would you mind?"

"Mind? I wouldn't mind, my dear. Jim always looked up to his brother and took it bad when the news came. Like as not, it'd please him too."

"Of course, it might not be a boy." She didn't want to raise Edith's hopes only to have them dashed.

"Let's see what Meg has to say." Edith took a handkerchief from her apron pocket and blew her nose. "She can tell from the way you'm carrying whether 'tis likely to be a boy or a girl."

Meg Blackler was a cheery soul with iron-grey hair and an abundance of laugh lines around her eyes. "So nice to meet you, my dear," she said on being introduced to Kathleen. "You'm looking in fine fettle. So when d'you reckon the little one's likely to put in an appearance?"

Edith invited Meg to sit down, and fetched the cake tin from the dresser. "You'll have a slice of my raisin and walnut cake, won't you?" she enquired.

"I'd be a fool to say no to a slice of your cake," replied Meg. And to Kathleen she said, "You know, Edith could make a fortune selling cakes. Famous, she is, for her cakes."

"Oh, get along with you; what nonsense," replied Edith, looking pleased all the same.

When they'd finished tea and caught up on all the gossip, Edith asked Meg if she could tell whether the baby was a boy or a girl, and Kathleen had to stand up and walk about while Meg examined her curves. When she pronounced that it would be a boy, Edith's face lit up.

"What's that? A boy, is it?" Jim put his head around the door.

"If Meg's right, what would you think about calling him Thomas?" Kathleen asked.

Jim looked at Edith. "You told her then, Mother?"

"I told her, and 'twas her idea to call the boy Thomas."

"Well, if you two've decided on Thomas, there's not a lot I can do about it." His tone was stern but his face showed obvious pleasure.

The day the baby was due came and went, and it was one morning nearly a week later when the signs appeared, indicating that the birth was imminent. Kathleen woke just as the pale light of dawn appeared above the curtain and began to creep across the ceiling. Outside a blackbird was singing, and beside her slept Jim, his breathing even and deep. Her back felt stiff and the baby began to kick uncomfortably under her ribs. Then the pain started: a mere niggle in her lower back that she rubbed with the heel of her hand. Slipping from the covers, she eased herself into an upright position, reached for her dressing gown and slippers, and crept from the room. She gripped the banister as she made her way slowly downstairs, then shuffled to the kitchen. With fresh kindling on the embers, she struck a match, the fire caught, and within a few minutes the kettle began to sing.

From nowhere a spasm came upon her with such violence that she groaned and sank down on the settle. This must be the baby coming, surely. But the pain passed and everything went back to the way it had been, so she stood up, made herself tea, and sat with the cup at the table. As she sipped, Jim's footsteps sounded on the stairs, and at that moment another pain overtook her. She tried not to tense up, she really tried, because Meg had said to relax, to breathe deeply and slowly, but it was more difficult than she had expected.

"What are you doing down…?" Jim's voice trailed away to nothing. "Started, haven't you?"

"I think so. Had pains for about half an hour now."

"You get back to bed," he told her. "I'll wake Mother and she'll see to you for the time being, and soon as I'm finished with the cows I'll take the churns to Southwood and fetch Meg Blackler."

When Meg arrived she examined Kathleen. "You've a long way to go yet, my dear," she said. "Your baby'll not be here afore supper time, I'm thinking."

And so the tedium of pain after pain continued, until Kathleen became almost used to it. The sun slipped behind the horizon and she longed for the whole thing to be over. She pleaded with Meg to do something, but Meg had nothing to offer but sympathy.

Edith lit candles on the mantelpiece, brought a chair over, and sat beside Kathleen. "Won't be long now, my dear. I wish you'd have something to eat. You must keep your strength up. You're going to need it soon."

Almost immediately, Kathleen felt a searing pain as if someone had thrust a knife deep into her gut and twisted it, tearing her apart. She screamed and gripped Edith's hand.

"Don't push. Not yet." Meg bent over and stroked the hair from her forehead.

The pain subsided but within a couple of minutes it was back, and it was terrifying and worse than anything Kathleen could ever have imagined. *I'm dying*, she thought. *I must be dying and they're not going to tell me. They'll keep me going as long as they can and try to save the baby.* In the agony of the moment, as the next pain tore into her, she caught her breath and her body was pushing, bearing down. Oh God, this was it: this was the baby coming out of her.

Edith wrung out a cold flannel and wiped her forehead, murmuring, "There, there, my dear. Not long now."

As the next pain overtook her, Kathleen gripped Edith's hand hard, screwed her eyes up tight, and pushed with all her strength.

"Good girl – head's out. One more push," Meg encouraged.

"It's coming, it's coming." Kathleen groaned deep in her throat and yelled as the baby slipped from her.

"It's a fine boy you have," said Meg.

"Is he all right?" Kathleen raised herself on one elbow to look, and the baby gave his first cry.

"Just got to clean him up a bit. There, now you can hold him." Meg placed the bundle into Kathleen's arms: a wrinkled red face framed by silky black curls. The baby's eyelids blinked open, and for a moment dark blue eyes looked into hers.

As each day passed, Kathleen fell more and more in love with Tom. She kept the crib beside the bed, and the instant he fussed she'd be awake: tending to him, watching him, stroking his tiny forehead, picking him up and cradling him, sharing the warmth of her body with him. As the sky grew light in the early morning and the baby sucked at her breast, a joy, the like of which she could never have imagined, filled her with a deep calm and a stout determination to protect the little scrap of humanity in her arms. This was her world, hers and Tom's, and she guarded it jealously lest anyone intrude. Jim showed no indication of wanting to participate. He fell into a deep sleep the moment his head hit the pillow and did not surface until it was time to get up the next morning. During the afternoon Kathleen would lie on the bed and doze beside the crib. Sometimes she pretended to talk to her father, telling him about Tom – the colour of his hair and eyes, the shape of his nose, and how he pursed his lips when he was about to feed.

Edith sent a telegram to Alexandra, and about a week or so later a letter arrived in reply, congratulating Kathleen and enclosing a pair of woollen bootees. Doubting that her mother would pass on the news, Kathleen wrote to Alice, and to Uncle Charlie, Auntie Mary and Rose. Alice sent a matinee coat embroidered with blue ribbon. Goodness only knew how she'd managed to smuggle it past the old witch of Wimbledon. Rose sent a teething ring with a handle and a bell on the other end, so that it served as a rattle too.

Kathleen showed Tom each of the presents, and she fancied that he kicked his legs and waved his arms at them. "You really love them, don't you, my darling boy?" she said. "Your grandad would've sent you a present too, I'm sure he would, if only he was still here. I've told him all about you, and sometimes I think he's looking over my shoulder and smiling at you."

It was summer and the farm was exploding in an orgy of growth – young grain swelling, grass nearly ready for the hay cut, lambs fattening, piglets too. In the orchard, apples the size of walnuts, hard and green, grew where blossom had faded and fallen. Higher Haydn's herd of South Devons – sleek, terracotta-coloured cows – consumed the lush grass and gave the richest milk of the year. With the cheese- and butter-making season at its height, Edith suggested they get in help from the village.

"Dolly's a good worker," she said. "I've used her afore, when I've been run off me feet and not known which way to turn. When I go to Southwood this afternoon, I'll call in and see if Dolly fancies a bit o' dairy work. We can't pay much but like as not she'll oblige."

"We must pay her a proper wage," said Kathleen. "Where does Jim take our dairy produce? Are we getting a good price?"

"Ivybridge Market," Edith replied. "He sells it to a stallholder."

"How much does he get?"

"Don't rightly know I can tell you," said Edith. "Jim puts whatever he gets in his pocket and don't say much about it."

"He never gives you anything?"

"Gives me money to pay the dairymaid when we've got one, that's all."

"That's so unfair."

"'Tis the way us have always done things," observed Edith.

Not for much longer, if I've anything to do with it, Kathleen decided.

Jim worked from dawn to dusk. Last thing he would come in, pour himself a tankard of cider from the cask in the scullery, and sit in the kitchen while the shadows lengthened and twilight crept over the hill. He was pleased he had a son, he told Kathleen, and she'd heard that he boasted about it to his cronies in the village. Sometimes he'd muse on how Tom would help on the farm one day, and what a farm they'd have when the insurance money came through.

Kathleen was usually the first to bed, feeding Tom and settling him down for the night, so that by the time Jim came up she was dozing off to sleep. But one night, about a month after Tom had been born, she felt Jim put a hand on her shoulder as he climbed into bed.

"Time we got back to being man and wife," he said.

"But, Jim, I'm still bleeding. I don't think we should; at least, not just yet."

"Oh, I don't mind 'bout that – I still want you."

He lifted her nightdress and, ignoring her protests, clambered on top of her. His mouth covered hers, stifling her cries.

As he took a breath she pleaded, "Please, please, Jim, you're hurting me."

He ignored her pleas, and when he'd got what he wanted he rolled off, turned over, and within seconds he was snoring.

Kathleen lay sobbing silently. The world that she had built – the world that only she and Tom inhabited – had suddenly come to an end.

CHAPTER 11

The next day the bleeding increased and it hurt more than usual to sit on a kitchen chair. She waited until Jim had eaten dinner and Edith was washing dishes in the scullery before she spoke to him.

"Tom's a beautiful boy," she began, "and I really would like to enjoy him. It would be difficult having another baby right away."

"Nothing difficult 'bout bringing children into this world," he retorted.

"Not for you, maybe, but it's not as easy for me. I need to get over this baby before I have the next."

"Nature'll take its course and if other children come along, that's the way of things. Not a lot you can do 'bout it." He fingered his chin, playing with its black stubble as he rose from the table. He stretched his arms above his head, then yawned and scratched a rib with his finger. "Can't hang around. There's work to be done to put food on the table."

"That's another thing I want to talk to you about."

"It'll have to keep till later." He rubbed his eyes and lumbered away.

She sank down on the settle, its padded seat more

comfortable than the chair. He really didn't understand what it was like or he'd be more sympathetic.

When Kathleen asked Edith, in a casual way, how many years had passed between her first and second child, Edith guessed the real question and said that a mother was unlikely to start another baby while she was still breastfeeding. This gave Kathleen some comfort but it was clear that she was going to have to take matters into her own hands.

Every week Edith bought the *South Devon Times* for Jim and a magazine for herself called *Woman's Life*. Kathleen noticed that the latter had a problem page, where readers wrote in seeking advice. Problems suitable for publication, like the best way to protect woollens stored in a chest from the ravages of moths, were fully discussed and the answer given in detail, but others received a very cryptic response, and occasionally a reader was requested to send a stamped, self-addressed envelope for the reply. Clearly, these were questions too intimate, on too delicate a topic, to be published. She recalled her mother shouting at her for being stupid, for allowing herself to get caught. Alexandra had said that there were things you could use to stop yourself having a baby, and why hadn't Kathleen bothered to ask? It was possible that the magazine knew where she could get advice. So one day when Edith was busy with Dolly in the dairy and no one else was around, Kathleen sat down and wrote to the editor of the problem page with her request, pointing out that she was married and had just given birth. She enclosed an envelope, stamped and addressed to herself, and requested that the reply be placed in this.

"Edith, would you mind keeping an ear open for Tom while I go to the village? He's just gone down and he's fast asleep. I'll be about an hour, that's all," Kathleen asked.

"All right, my dear. Nip into the shop for me and pick up the papers, will you?"

"Yes, of course I will."

Slipping out by the yard door, Kathleen retrieved her bicycle from the barn where it had lain unused for months. After a search she found a can of lubricating oil, and worked the oil into the parts that had rusted. The bike felt unfamiliar as she mounted it, the saddle especially hard and unforgiving, but within minutes the strangeness melted away and a glorious freedom opened up. The delicious smell of new-mown hay rose from the field by the river, so she paused a moment by the gate to watch knee-high grasses, red clover, and dog daisies fall in swathes under the blade, while the sun beat down on the team of horses plodding back and forth across the meadow. She was on her own, she was free, and life was filled with the scent of summer. Almost jubilant, she pedalled on to Southwood and the red postbox. The envelope slipped from her fingers through the slot and landed with a muffled thud in the dark interior. It was only a first step, but she was on the way to getting back control over her life.

Every morning she looked for the postman and counted the days since she'd sent her request, and every day there was nothing for her. About four weeks later, when she'd almost given up hope and was in the kitchen ironing a shirt, Jim came in holding an envelope in his hand.

"What's this? 'Tis your handwriting, 'less I'm very much mistaken," he said. He held the letter high and waited for her reply.

Kathleen felt herself blush with embarrassment, while her mind searched frantically for an explanation that would throw him off the scent. "Oh, it must be those recipes I sent for," she lied. "The magazine said you had to enclose a stamped addressed envelope but the recipes are free." She gave what she hoped was a convincing smile.

"Free, are they? That's all right, then." He handed her the envelope and watched while she opened it.

"Oh yes, it's what I was expecting." This time she told the truth.

Satisfied, he sat down on the settle and folded his arms. "Cup of tea and a slice of cake wouldn't go amiss."

She thrust the letter back into the envelope and stuffed it in the pocket of her apron. "Kettle's on the boil," she said brightly, relief flooding through her. "There's bit of your mother's fruit cake left in the tin. Will that do?"

"That'll do nicely, thank'ee." He shut his eyes and leaned back, resting his head, waiting for her to tend to his needs.

When he'd drunk his tea and eaten his cake he lumbered back into life and set off in the direction of the yard. She could hear him pulling on his boots at the door. It would be some time before Edith returned from the dairy, so Kathleen took the envelope from her pocket and opened the letter once more. To her immense delight it gave the name and address of a lady doctor with consulting rooms in Plymouth:

You will need to contact her to make an appointment. Her telephone number is… We are unable to say what fee Doctor will charge for the consultation. This is a matter between you and her, although we understand in cases of great hardship she will offer a reduction.

She folded up the letter, and returned it to the envelope, stuffing it away as she heard Edith approaching. "Thought I'd pop into the village this afternoon," she said in a casual voice. "We're running a bit low on raisins and sultanas, and we could do with some more cinnamon. Jim ate the last of the fruit cake just now."

"Don't you worry 'bout Tom. I'll look after him." Edith had become so fond of Tom that she welcomed any excuse to fuss over him. "There's money here," she added, taking the housekeeping purse from the dresser drawer. "Take it with you."

After dinner, while Edith played with Tom, Kathleen fetched her bike from the barn and cycled to the village. She'd added a few precious pennies of her own to pay for the phone call. Edith would be sure to know exactly how much money the purse contained, and besides, it would be like stealing from Edith to use the housekeeping money. She propped the bicycle against the post office wall and sneaked into the phone kiosk, hoping no one had seen her. The operator connected her and the call was answered at the other end by a female receptionist with a cut-glass accent. Kathleen explained that she'd been given the telephone number by *Woman's Life* and asked for an appointment. The receptionist suggested a day and time, and Kathleen agreed. It was all very simple.

"Very well, Mrs Wilcox, we shall expect you next Thursday afternoon at two o'clock for a consultation," the receptionist said.

"Can you tell me how much the fee will be?"

"The initial fee is two guineas for the consultation itself. If Doctor prescribes a device for you, of course, that will be extra."

"Thank you so much. You've been very helpful."

Kathleen replaced the receiver and wondered how on earth she was going to find that sort of money. Deep in thought, she wandered across the square to the grocery shop and bought the dried fruit and a packet of ground cinnamon. She might as well pick up the newspaper and magazine, so she went to the other shop and asked for *Woman's Life* and the *South Devon Times*. She opened the *Times* out of idle curiosity and flicked through it. The inside pages carried advertisements announcing gigantic price reductions for the first week of the summer sales. The price of household linen in some Plymouth department stores was reduced by as much as a half. As she rode back to the farm, the first hint of a plan began to take shape in her mind.

Kathleen took great trouble over supper, especially with the jam pudding, and even suggested Jim might like a second tankard of cider with his meal. Then, as he mellowed visibly in his favourite chair, she struck up a conversation with Edith. "Have you had a chance to see the paper yet?" she said, opening it to the page where she knew the advert was. "Have you seen this? It says all the bed linen in Spooners' sale is down next week – as low as half price."

"That's a real bargain," replied Edith with genuine interest in her voice. "Spooners is always good quality."

"We could do with some new sheets." Kathleen sneaked a look at Jim as he sat replete by the fire. "The sheets on our bed are so thin it wouldn't take much to stick a foot through."

He might look as if he was asleep, but he was listening all right.

"'Twould be a good time to get sheets," agreed Edith. "Even if the others go on for a month or two, you'd still have to buy more and then you'd be paying full price for 'em."

"You could do with new sheets as well, Edith," Kathleen continued. "And it won't be long before we'll need some for Tom."

"The boy's not going to need sheets for a year or more." Jim opened an eye as he spoke, then closed it again.

"Give her the money, Jim," said Edith. "Heaven knows when there'll be another bargain like this. If you don't, you'll be cutting off your nose to spite your face."

Jim sighed, but his mood had been sweetened by good food and plenty of cider. "Anything for a quiet life," he said. "Money's in the parlour – top drawer of the desk. Take what you need."

"Thank you, Jim," Kathleen said. "I'll go next Thursday – I'll catch the one o'clock bus, if that's all right with you."

However, when Thursday morning came Jim announced that he needed to go to Ivybridge on important business. This came as a blow to Kathleen's plans because he'd promised to run her to Southwood for the one o'clock bus, and meet her on her return from Plymouth with the things she'd bought.

"How am I ever going to carry everything back to the farm on my own?" she complained, frowning at him. "You promised, Jim, you promised," she added, because she wanted him to feel guilty about letting her down.

"You just get yourself to Southwood, and I'll be there when you come back. 'Tis the half past four bus you'm coming back on, isn't it?"

"That's the one." She bit her lip and dared not make a fuss. But why wouldn't he take her to catch the one o'clock bus? What was so important in Ivybridge that he had to go right away?

She ate dinner and fed Tom at the same time, and left him in Edith's capable hands, praying she'd be back before he became desperate with hunger. There was no other way; she had to do this, for his sake almost as much as her own.

Grabbing her bicycle from the barn, she pedalled as fast as she could to Southwood, and propped it against the wall of the grocery shop. Lace-up shoes she exchanged for heels, and with her hat on her head and her gloves in her hand, she put her head round the shop door. "Just off to Plymouth," she called to the woman behind the counter. "Left my bicycle outside. It'll be all right, won't it?"

"I'll see no harm comes to it." The woman smiled. "Off to the sales, are you?"

"Yes. Oh, there's the bus. Must dash."

The bus took her to the very centre of town, to a broad street in front of the Theatre Royal. She asked the conductor for directions to The Crescent (the address she'd been given for the doctor's consulting rooms), and was relieved to be told that it was only a few minutes' walk. The lemon-and-white polka-dot dress felt good on her. She hadn't worn it since last summer, when it'd been the height of fashion. It gave her a feeling of elegance, and she walked with a light step and was quite composed when she rang the bell.

"Mrs Wilcox?" enquired the receptionist.

"Yes, that's me." Kathleen ventured a smile.

"You're ten minutes early." The voice was crisp and cold.

"Sorry. I came by bus, and I didn't know how long it would take to find you."

"Please take a seat. I'll see if Doctor is ready for you."

Kathleen looked around the waiting room, and decided on a leather-upholstered chair near the window. The room was empty, except for a few old magazines on a table. She guessed she was the first patient of the afternoon.

"Doctor will see you now, Mrs Wilcox. Come this way, please."

Kathleen rose and followed the receptionist. She was shown into a room with a large desk at one end, behind which sat a woman with sad, dark eyes, who smiled as she rose to greet Kathleen. If she'd not studied medicine and become a doctor, she'd be one of those kind maiden aunts who looked after other people's children, thought Kathleen, who took to her at once.

"Mrs Wilcox, isn't it? Do come in and make yourself comfortable." The doctor indicated a chair and Kathleen sat down. "Now, I just need to confirm a few details."

The questions were easy to start with, but the one that came right at the end, Kathleen was not prepared for.

"And your husband, Mr Wilcox – he knows you're here and he's happy about it?"

Stunned by the implication, Kathleen hesitated. The way she saw it, it was nobody's business but hers whether she should have more children. Heartbeat rising, she looked the doctor straight in the eye. "Oh yes, he's very happy for me to be here today."

"Very well." The doctor gave an encouraging smile. "I need to examine you and see which size cap to prescribe. Please strip below the waist and lie down on the consulting couch – just over there, behind the curtain."

Kathleen was glad when it was over and she could escape into the warmth of the sun and the noise of traffic. It hadn't been particularly pleasant, having things stuck up inside her, and the doctor had remarked on her tenderness. But she'd got what she'd come for and her concern now was to hide from Jim not only the cap itself, but the amount it had cost.

She retraced her steps to the Theatre Royal and asked directions to Spooners from a woman waiting at the bus stop.

"Go along George Street and turn right into Bedford Street." The woman raised an arm as she spoke, indicating the direction. "It's down the end – Spooners Corner. You can't miss it."

Kathleen thanked her and hurried away. People jostled on crowded pavements. It was thrilling, almost to the point of intoxication, to be a part of life in the city, and she arrived breathless and excited at the Spooners store. Four storeys high, it straddled the corner, just as the woman had said. Marching in through the main entrance, she looked around for the household department and couldn't help noticing that the store had a hairdressing salon on the second floor. How she would love to have her hair cut – restyled, even – and there by the stairs she spotted directions to ladieswear. Stop; she must stop immersing herself in delicious fantasies – there was no time to waste. Sheets were what she'd come to buy, and sheets she must buy, or awkward questions would be asked.

The sales assistant, an older woman impeccably turned out in the store's uniform – black dress with white collar and cuffs – was most helpful. "Very wise choice, madam," she said, as Kathleen selected pure cotton sheets for herself and Jim – two pairs of doubles – and for Edith a pair of singles. "Can I interest madam in anything else? Pillowcases, perhaps?"

"That will be all for now, thank you."

"Is it cash, or on madam's account?"

"Cash."

The sheets were carefully wrapped in two brown paper parcels tied with string. They were top-quality sheets, and to get them at half price was indeed a bargain. Her father would have laughed, patted her on the back, and congratulated her on a job well done.

On the way back she took a shortcut down a street so narrow it looked as if the buses would touch as they passed one another, but of course they never did. She treated herself to an ice-cream cone from a little shop at the end, and rested her parcels on the pavement. In the warm afternoon the ice cream melted quickly and she had to lick her fingers. So full of life, she felt she had the energy to do whatever she wanted, if she wanted it badly enough. In buoyant mood she climbed aboard the bus, and on the journey back to Southwood imagined how it might be if one day she could shop in Plymouth regularly, maybe even once a week. She could look at dresses, coats and hats; lunch in Spooners' restaurant; and have her hair done in the afternoon. What a dream that would be.

Ready to tell Jim all about her shopping expedition (if nothing else), she got off the bus and handed the parcels over to him. He'd spotted her bicycle and had already put it on the back of the truck. She began to speak, but he was not paying attention; he was ignoring her account of the afternoon.

"You wait till you see what I've bought," he boasted. "Handsome, handsome, he is. And I got 'im for a lot less than I would've done if Robert Neville had bid against me. I slipped someone a pound to pass a message that the auction had been delayed. It worked and he missed the sale."

"What have you bought?" she asked quickly.

"A hunter, that's what I've bought – sixteen-hand, four-year-old chestnut gelding; a real beauty. Robert Neville will be livid when he finds out what I've done. Wanted the horse for himself, he did, but I got him." His eyes flashed in triumph, and he threw back his head and laughed. There was a terrible crunching noise as he changed gear at the first corner. "Damn it. Darn thing oughter run smoother than that."

His breath smelt of alcohol. That meant he'd been to The Sportsman's Arms and had a few. She wondered what on earth he was going to do with the horse, and felt a pang of sympathy for Robert.

"I'm going to be hunting him in the autumn." Jim said it with something of a swagger. "And I'll put him in the point-to-point races, and I shouldn't wonder if he'll earn me a pound or two with the bookies."

CHAPTER 12

Jim was full of himself for a day or two, boasting to Kathleen and Edith about how he'd outwitted Robert Neville. "You should have seen the look on his snooty face when he turned up and found the deal done." Jim slapped a hand on his thigh in glee. "Mad, he was. You could near enough see the steam coming out his ears." He collapsed in paroxysms of laughter.

Kathleen felt sorry for Robert, being tricked like that, but what a bit of luck that Jim's attention had been entirely focused on the horse, so that he didn't give a fig about her trip to Plymouth or how much she'd spent. Captain's Orders, the animal was called, and a finer example of horseflesh would have been difficult to find anywhere in the county, it was said. No wonder Robert had been interested in acquiring him.

Jim added *Horse & Hound* to the account at the newsagent. Late into the evening, over a cider or two, he'd flick through the pages, while Kathleen slipped away upstairs to undress and practise getting her cap in the right place. Jim would appear after she'd fed and settled Tom down for the night. Sometimes he'd woo her, and then the lovemaking was exciting and thrilling, just as it had been at the start. But more often than not he'd look merely to relieve himself of the tedium and strain of the day by pulling up her nightdress and clambering on top of her. Within a few minutes he'd gratified his own desire and was snoring beside her, while she lay awake wondering at his lack of affection.

The autumn was cool and wet and the harvest difficult. Jim said it was as well the grass kept growing or they'd be hard put to find fodder for all the beasts, and it was just as well they hadn't planted the usual acreage of wheat, because the price was down on the year about eight shillings, and if beef and mutton prices descended much further it would hardly be worthwhile farming at all. On the other hand, the orchard produced a good crop of cider apples, which cheered him up no end. On the strength of this he went to Ivybridge and bought himself breeches, boots and jacket, together with a bowler hat, ready for the hunting season, and with his attention diverted, he forgot the first anniversary of their wedding in October.

Kathleen was not surprised. She'd grown used to his selfishness and her expectations of married life had shrunk to accommodate the reality. Tom was the true love of her life, and the ties that bound them grew deeper as each day passed. She'd cradle him in her arms, breathing in the scent of him. He'd look at her and gurgle in delight and close his tiny hand around her finger, and she loved him more than anything else in the world. When she was working in the dairy or busy in the kitchen she'd imagine him taking his first step and wonder what his first word would be. She pictured holding his hand as she led him to school, and when she fetched him hearing the teacher say how well he was settling in and how much the other children liked him. She kept these thoughts to herself, never sharing them with Jim, although for his part, he never held back in declaring Tom the apple of his eye and boasting that one day he would have a pony of his own and go hunting with his father like a gentleman. And when the life insurance money came through – and it couldn't be much longer now – they'd be able to buy a farm and Jim looked forward to having his son work it with him, and they'd be men of property.

One bleak, forlorn day in early November, Kathleen received a letter from Mr Fitzgerald. The instant she saw the typewritten envelope her heart missed a beat, because she knew it must contain important news. The letter informed her that the inquest into her father's death had been held and the jury at the Coroner's Court had returned a verdict of suicide by poisoning. Mr Fitzgerald was very sorry to be the bearer of such dreadful tidings and hoped Kathleen would find the strength to overcome this most unfortunate turn of events. He concluded with the advice that the Providential Assurance Company had referred the matter of her father's policy to their legal department on account of the jury's finding of suicide.

Jim became extremely irate on being told the news. "Businessmen in cities don't know how the real world lives," he complained, thumping the kitchen table with his fist. "Damn it, I needs the money now – when 'tis a good time to buy. So long as wheat price is low, land'll be cheap, but the minute things turn, we'll have lost the advantage."

"I'm sure Mr Fitzgerald is doing everything he can," Kathleen said.

"Well, whatever 'tis he's doing, 'tain't good enough." He thumped the table again, his knuckles white with rage.

The wind blew in from the west, ripping every last leaf from tree and hedge, and rain beat down, a relentless deluge day after day. The stream that provided water to the farm overflowed and flooded the lane, wearing away the gravel and gouging out gullies. One afternoon in such a downpour Edith came home from a visit to Lower Haydn Farm soaked to the skin, shivering, and complaining that she'd never known such a time in all her born days. Straight away Kathleen built up the fire and pulled the kettle over. Edith changed her wet clothes for dry and sat on the settle, the tartan rug wrapped around her legs and the tabby cat snoozing on a cushion beside her. Despite Jim's warning that pampering ruined the animal as a mouser, Kathleen had allowed the cat into the kitchen.

"You'm sensible, you are." Edith stroked the tabby's head. "Indoors is better than out in this weather."

The cat stretched out all four legs, stiff as pokers, and arched her back. She blinked at Edith a couple of times, and relaxed into a rhythmic purr of contentment.

"Fancy a piece of walnut cake with your tea?" Kathleen enquired.

"That'd be nice, but it's hot tea I'm needing," Edith replied. "Chilled to the bone, I am."

The following morning when Kathleen was working in the dairy she found that the brass cream skimmer was not in its usual place, and remembered that Edith had been polishing it in the kitchen a couple of days earlier, so she went to see if it was still there. Edith stood at the kitchen table, sleeves rolled up, stirring dried fruit into the Christmas pudding mix. Her cheeks were flushed and her eyes – usually alive and quick to smile – were dull and lifeless. She swayed a little, and put out a hand to hold the edge of the table.

"Whatever is the matter?" Kathleen ran over and put an arm around her.

Edith gave a moan and coughed a few times. "Don't you worry 'bout me; I'll be right as rain d'reckly." She gave a wan smile, but her knees buckled under her and Kathleen struggled to get her to the settle.

"You're very poorly; you should be in bed."

"No time for me to be ill," protested Edith, but she showed no sign of moving from the settle. "There's things as need to be done."

"Sit there for a moment and I'll make you a cup of tea," Kathleen persuaded her.

Between sips of tea Edith was racked by fits of coughing, her fingers grew clammy and cold to the touch, and she began to tremble until her whole body was convulsed by fever. Since she'd come to live at the farm Kathleen had never told Edith what to do; she had always deferred to her and sought her advice, because she recognised that Edith had been mistress of the house since before Kathleen was born. But now things needed to change.

"Edith, you are going to bed," Kathleen said.

Edith tried to protest, and pretended the coughing was just a passing fit.

"The kettle's boiled again and I'm going to fill two stone jars and put them in your bed, because that's where you're going." Kathleen stood firm.

Edith gave in, and allowed herself to be helped up the stairs and taken to her room – a chill, damp little place with faded green curtains and worn furniture. Kathleen glanced at the fireplace. She doubted there'd been a fire in it for years, and there might even be a bird's nest in the chimney. On hands and knees, she put her head into the fireplace and looked up the chimney, and to her relief saw daylight. Edith was in bed by the time Kathleen returned with newspaper, sticks and logs in a bucket. She knelt on the rug in front of the fender, laid the fire, and soon had a blaze going.

"You rest now, Edith," she said. "I'll see to the pudding – you can tell me later how to cook it."

Before Kathleen could tie up the pudding in its cloth, Tom was awake and crying to be fed, and as soon as she'd seen to him, Jim came in from the yard asking where his dinner was.

"Your mother's ill," she told him. "I can't do everything at once. Here, you look after Tom while I get dinner on the table and see what your mother wants."

"Me? Me, look after the baby?"

"If you want your dinner, you're going to have to amuse him," she said in an exasperated voice. "If you don't want to hold him, then prop him up with some cushions and talk to him." She thrust Tom at an astonished Jim, then ran upstairs.

Edith said she couldn't eat a thing but wouldn't mind another cup of tea. She shut her eyes, lay back, and coughed again. Kathleen raced down to the kitchen. Tom was sitting in the armchair, propped up with cushions, a rattle in his hand. Jim was bending over him, looking like a ram in a thorn hedge that knows he's stuck fast.

"You'll get your dinner quicker if you set the table," Kathleen said as she scurried about, making a fresh pot of tea and wiping dribble from Tom's chin.

"Huh – women's work," Jim muttered to himself, but he did as she told him.

The next day Edith was worse: bathed in sweat, cheeks flushed, eyes sunken and dark. It was clear she was running a temperature. She told Kathleen she'd hardly slept at all. "I'm sorry, my dear," she wheezed. "I'll not be a lot of use today."

"I'm worried about you, Edith. I think we should send for the doctor. I'll have a word with Jim."

"There's no need for that; I'll…" Edith began, but a fit of coughing overtook her.

When Kathleen told Jim that Edith needed the doctor, he retorted that his mother would be all right in a day or two, and there was no need to go to the expense of calling out a doctor when she'd get well on her own without one.

"I really think we ought to have the doctor," insisted Kathleen. "Your mother is very poorly."

But Jim merely grunted, turned on his heel, and walked away.

However, by the end of the week Edith's condition was giving cause for even more concern. Kathleen tended to her as best she could, soothing her forehead with a damp flannel, plying her with tea and soup and anything else that would give her strength. Edith refused most things, coughing and turning in her bed and saying she would soon be well, yet the truth was she'd grown pale, wizened, and shockingly frail.

"Jim, she's a lot worse," said Kathleen. "I don't know what else I can do for her. You really ought to send for the doctor.

"She's a tough old bird," he replied.

"You've not been near her for two days. Go and see for yourself."

"Oh, all right, I'll get the doctor if you'll stop going on so," he said, with evident bad humour. "I'll drive down to Southwood and see if I can telephone the doctor. But he'll probably charge me a couple of guineas for nothing."

The doctor looked grave when he saw Edith and said she was suffering from bronchitis. "You've been doing a good job looking after her," he said to Kathleen. "But it will take her a while to recover. I'll prescribe a tonic to buck her up a bit, and in the meantime, try this linctus. It should help with the cough."

Jim complained when the bill arrived in the post. "Told you it would cost me a pretty penny." He waved it under Kathleen's nose.

"But she's your mother, Jim. Surely you care about her?" Kathleen replied.

It was fast approaching Christmas before Edith was well enough to leave her bed. Kathleen lavished care upon her, helping her down the stairs, wrapping a rug around her knees as she sat by the fire, and tempting her to try some scrambled egg or nibble a sponge cake with her tea. And Edith would hold Kathleen's hand, or touch her arm

151

affectionately as the two sat at the kitchen table writing cards.

"Never been so well looked after in all my life," she said. "You're wonderful kind to an old woman, my dear."

Christmas cards began to arrive and Kathleen placed them on the mantelpiece and dresser, so that the kitchen began to take on a festive look. One – addressed to Mr and Mrs Wilcox, with a Wimbledon postmark – was from Alexandra. Kathleen was surprised that, despite her mother's protestations earlier in the year, she'd found a way to keep the house. When Jim read the message – Alexandra hoped they were all well and looking forward to a prosperous New Year – he said it must mean she'd heard something about the insurance company settling the claim, but Kathleen had her doubts and kept quiet.

Alice enclosed a letter with her card in which she wrote that her parents had got on tolerably well with the Arbuthnots when they'd met at her cousin's 'do', although her mother had been astounded at the quantity of spirits Colonel and Mrs Arbuthnot could put away without appearing any the worse for wear. On the other hand, her mother had observed with approval that Binkey drank only orange juice and soda the whole evening.

Charlie and Mary's card contained a letter, written by Rose, with news about members of the Wyndham family. She hoped that Kathleen could come and see them one day and bring young Tom with her. Rose had stuffed a little bar of chocolate in with the letter – a present for Tom – that fell apart as Kathleen undid the wrapper. She presented the fragments to Tom, who reached out for a piece, stuffing it in his mouth with an open palm, spreading chocolate all over his face.

Jim found a high chair in the attic that he and his brother and sisters had once used. He sanded it down, painted it blue, and presented it to Kathleen with a beaming smile on Christmas morning. "There you are – it'll do for the little 'un." He put an arm around her – something he'd not done for a long time – and gave her an affectionate kiss on the cheek.

"He'll love that," she said. "Thank you, Jim."

At dinner, Tom sat in his chair gnawing on a chicken drumstick, looking around at everyone and laughing as if it was all a great joke.

This year there was no party on Boxing Day, because Jim was riding to hounds. He was particularly pleased that they were meeting at Alston Hall, because it gave him an opportunity to show off Captain in front of Robert Neville and rub salt in the old wound.

By New Year it had turned cold; so cold that overnight all the windows iced up on the inside (all, that is, except the kitchen window), and the ice on the water trough in the yard had to be broken every morning. Cows with steaming breath stood around, and hens scratching at the frozen ground found little to eat, and ran to Kathleen the moment she appeared, begging to be fed. Jim rode out with the dogs and brought the sheep down to the fields near the house. Even the hardy black cattle that grazed the moor ran short of fodder. They found their way down to the woods for shelter, and Jim sent the farmhands with precious hay to supplement the meagre grazing the beasts could get from the undergrowth.

As winter gave way to spring and the point-to-point season well underway Jim found a tough young man with a taste for taking risks over fences, who claimed part-Irish ancestry on his mother's side, and set him up with a racing saddle and a jockey's cap. He took to betting heavily and thought nothing of having time off work to attend the races. Captain was generally well placed and even won on a couple of occasions. Jim ignored his losses but spent a fair portion of his winnings buying drinks all round in The Sportsman's Arms in Ivybridge.

With his mind on other things, Jim seemed scarcely aware of anniversaries as they came and went during the early part of the year, but for Kathleen it was different. The day she'd received the telegram saying that her father had died was imprinted on her memory. She relived the journey to London; finding Charlie, Mary and Rose again; the funeral; the scene in the pub afterwards. The anniversary she truly looked forward to with celebration in her heart was that of Tom's birth. He was her delight, her inspiration and sometimes, she thought, her reason for living. By his first birthday Tom would pull himself up from the floor and stagger from chair to chair. He would glance at her and chuckle with delight.

Life settled into a routine; not a lot different from one week to the next. Then, one day in June, Edith came back from Southwood in a state of great excitement. "You'll never guess what I've just heard," she told Kathleen. It couldn't be anything bad because Edith's face was beaming with pleasure. Not even waiting for Kathleen to ask, she blurted out her news. "They say Robert Neville's engaged to be married. What d'you think of that, then?"

The words hit Kathleen like a blow to the stomach. "I don't know," she said. "I suppose it's good news for Lord Neville. He'll want to see his son settled."

"Of course he will. He'll want to know young Mr Neville's going to give him an heir – stands to reason." Edith's voice was bright, almost jubilant, as if the forthcoming wedding was of as much interest to her as it was to the Nevilles.

Kathleen asked herself why it should matter to her that Robert Neville was going to be married. It was absolutely no business of hers. Robert could marry whoever he pleased. "Who's he marrying?" she asked.

"'Tis Miss Sarah Something-or-Other." Edith frowned. "Miss Sarah Fortescue – that's it. Not from round these parts, though." She shook her head slowly. "They say 'tis over Exeter way her family comes from."

"When's the wedding?"

"Sometime in August, I'm led to believe," replied Edith. "I suppose they'm not affected by harvest and suchlike as we folks are."

CHAPTER 13

Robert and Sarah were married in Sarah's parish church and went on honeymoon to Italy, and it was nearly the end of October before Kathleen heard they'd returned to live at Alston Hall, and that Robert's sister, Florence, who used to run the household at the hall, had moved into Glebe House on the outskirts of the village. Curiosity getting the better of her, Kathleen frequently rode her bicycle to the village on the excuse of some errand or another, secretly hoping to catch a glimpse of Mrs Robert Neville being driven in or out of the white gates in the square, but fate made her wait until it was almost Christmas before she saw Robert's bride.

The new village hall, paid for by public subscription and built on land donated by the Alston Estate, was to be opened by Mrs Neville on Saturday 12th December. The occasion for the opening was the Southwood Christmas Market, and Kathleen made sure to book a place for Higher Haydn Farm.

At ten o'clock, when all the stalls were laid out and the stallholders ready inside, a red ribbon was placed across the entrance to the hall, where a crowd had gathered. Kathleen could hear the babble of voices, then a moment's silence. A female voice – the words scarcely audible – was followed by cheers and clapping of hands and someone shouting, "God bless you, Mrs Neville." Her heart gave a funny sort of leap as she spied within the throng Robert and Sarah walking around the hall, talking to a stallholder here, making a purchase there. She checked her own display for the umpteenth time, and when she looked up, only two stalls away, there was Sarah on Robert's arm.

The image of Robert's wife in Kathleen's imagination – slim, beautiful, engaging – crumbled before her eyes. Sarah looked rather plain, her face homely rather than beautiful, eyes small and close together, chin a little too large. In her defence, she'd a pleasant smile and when she moved it was clear from her bearing that she'd been brought up to be a lady.

Mr and Mrs Neville moved on and came to a halt at the Higher Haydn stall.

"That looks absolutely delicious." Sarah indicated a Dundee cake made by Edith.

"My mother-in-law made it; she insists on only the best ingredients." Kathleen smiled and licked her dry lips, stealing only a brief glance at Robert.

"I must have it – it looks absolutely splendid. How much is it?" asked Sarah.

"Two and sixpence, madam."

Sarah took a purse from her bag and counted out the coins. "There, I think that's just right, Mrs…?"

"Mrs Wilcox," said Robert. "Her husband's one of our tenants."

"How marvellous. I do so hope you'll have a merry Christmas, Mrs Wilcox." Sarah moved on to the next stall, Robert by her side, leaving Kathleen staring at his back.

The event unsettled her, although it was hard to admit that the cause of her disquiet was seeing Robert with his wife. She chided herself, because it should be no concern of hers who Robert married, but the image of Robert and Sarah together, laughing and talking, made her wretched. Sometimes in her dreams she would meet Robert, but then Sarah would arrive, and Kathleen would wake up. It gave her a profound sense of desolation, knowing that Sarah had usurped the position she herself had once occupied in Robert's affections. She remarked to Jim how surprised she was that Robert hadn't chosen a better-looking bride.

"He'll not have picked her for her looks," Jim replied. "Like as not, he'll have made sure her comes from good breeding stock."

"That's a terrible thing to say. He must love her, surely."

"Needs an heir, don't he? That's what he'll have been thinking about."

"But love must come into it."

"Can always get that elsewhere, if he's a mind." It sounded uncaring, stony, chilling.

Kathleen worked out when Robert, and probably Sarah too, were likely to show up on the doorstep with the customary Christmas gifts. To have to invite them both into the kitchen and make polite conversation would be so humiliating, she could not face the prospect. She kept a watchful eye on the kitchen window and when, a couple of days before Christmas, two figures walked past, Kathleen left what she was doing and pelted down the passage towards the yard, leaving Edith to answer the knock on the scullery door. She pulled on gumboots, grabbed her coat from its hook and dashed across to the barn, pursued by a flock of hens squawking with excitement at the prospect of some corn. She hid behind the barn door, beneath ancient cobwebs swathed in grime that clung to the beams, and listened.

From somewhere in the distance came the sound of voices: a man's first – that was Robert's – then Edith's, and after that the sounds died away. Edith would have invited the visitors into the warm, and they'd all be standing in the kitchen, talking. Cold from the cobbled floor began to find its way through the soles of Kathleen's boots. If she'd not been in such a stupid panic, she could have pulled on the wool socks she kept on the shelf behind the yard door. More than anyone, she knew how the possibility of changing your mind, the possibility of doing things differently, could go forever in the twinkling of an eye.

After what seemed an age, and when her hands had turned purple with cold, the voices came back. She could make out Robert's, and a woman's voice – that must be Sarah. Then everything fell silent, and the only sound was Captain in the loose box, shuffling around and snorting, so she stole back to the house and crept in.

"There you are!" exclaimed Edith. "You've just missed Mr Neville and that new wife of his."

"What a pity," Kathleen replied, but only because she had to say something.

On Christmas morning Kathleen lit a fire in the parlour first thing, hoping that by the afternoon the room would be warm enough for Tom to play on the floor. As she set the table for dinner in the kitchen, Tom was busy trying to climb up the side of his high chair. She heard footsteps, and looked up to see Jim coming into the room, hiding something behind his back.

"Look what I got for you," he said to Tom, bringing out a parcel. "Look what's inside this, my handsome."

Tom screamed with delight and tore at the paper.

"This is the way to do it, like this." Jim helped Tom tug at the string, and out tumbled a collection of painted wooden farm animals: two cows, three sheep and a pig.

Tom seized the cows, then the pig, only to drop a cow as it tumbled from his grasp.

"Fellow I know down at Alston Mill made 'em for me," Jim said, seeking Kathleen's approval.

"They're lovely," she replied.

Tom disappeared under the table, trying to retrieve his animals, and Jim joined in, scrambling around on hands and knees, hiding them in all sorts of peculiar places and encouraging Tom to find them.

"We'll make a farmer of you yet," he said. Then he eased himself into the armchair and reached for his tankard of cider. "How much longer till dinner? I'm famished."

"Not long now," she said.

"Here's to a merry Christmas." Jim held the tankard high, lowered it to his lips, and took a draught. "And here's to a prosperous New Year." He raised it again. "Let's hope the money gets here soon. It's been a long time a-coming."

The optimism of Christmas became mired in the mud of January, a month that was unusually mild with bands of rain sweeping in from the west, and it became impossible to walk anywhere without the aid of stout boots and a good stick. A rumour went about that Lord Neville was failing. Someone who had seen him in a car driven by Robert remarked how frail the old gentleman looked.

"You mark my words," said Edith, "he's hanging on till he knows Robert has an heir."

But on this Edith was wrong. Towards the end of February, Lord Neville died and his funeral was held at Southwood church. Villagers and tenants lined the route to St Michael's and dropped their heads in respect as the hearse passed. It was a family service because Lord Neville had, on the whole, kept himself to himself, never taking his seat in the House of Lords as he was entitled to do. However, it turned out that Edith's sentiments were not entirely misplaced. Within a short time it became the talk of the village that the new Lady Neville was expecting a child, and it was conjectured that old Lord Neville would have known about this before he'd been laid to rest.

It was soon after Easter that Kathleen received a letter; the handwriting on the envelope instantly recognisable.

"Who's writing to you, then?" asked Edith.

"It's from Alice, my best friend. She says she's getting engaged… she says Binkey – that's not his real name, of course – has passed his final exams and… they're getting engaged now and are going to marry next summer… in July."

"Nice young man, is he?" enquired Edith.

Kathleen thought of the gangly youth Alice had introduced to her at The London Hotel. "He seems to make Alice happy, and I suppose that's what counts," she replied.

"You'll be going to the wedding, will you?" Edith looked at her expectantly.

"No, I don't think so. It's Alice's mother; she's been a bit funny since…"

"Since you got in the family way?"

Kathleen made a face.

"Well, that's how some folks are," said Edith.

Kathleen replied to Alice, telling her the news about Lord Neville and mentioning that Robert and Sarah were expecting a baby. Within a couple of weeks Alice wrote again, saying that she and Binkey were making arrangements to honeymoon in Devon after their wedding:

…and it would be so nice if we could all meet up again. Binkey seems to think it likely that we will be asked to spend a few days at Alston Hall.

Alice was not thinking straight; it was a ridiculous idea. There was no way, absolutely no way that Kathleen and Jim could meet Alice and Binkey at Alston Hall. It would break all the rules of polite society for a tenant and his wife to meet the landlord like that. By the same token, there was no way Kathleen could visit without her husband. She felt cross with Alice for not having seen the implications, and spent some time mulling over the problem before eventually thinking of a solution. When she wrote back she asked whether Alice and Binkey would be staying at a hotel nearby and suggested that she and Jim could meet them there. Alice replied that they probably would, but she wasn't sure, and so arrangements were left in the air for the time being.

On the first Tuesday of every month the cattle feed merchant, Joseph Greenwood, came to take the order for Higher Haydn Farm. He was a tall man with such a thin, lined face that Edith had once remarked that Mr Greenwood looked as if he could do with a good square meal. Kathleen rather liked him and found his manners exemplary. She always made a point of inviting him into the kitchen for a cup of tea and a slice of cake while he took the order. When Mr Greenwood knocked on the scullery door in June it was a beautiful day, dry and sunny, and Jim had just remarked to Kathleen that if it continued this way, they'd be in for the best hay season in years.

"Order's all ready for you," Jim said to Mr Greenwood. "Just ask the wife," he added, and left in a hurry.

"Come into the kitchen, Mr Greenwood, and I'll make you a cup of tea," said Kathleen.

"It's rather awkward, Mrs Wilcox," Mr Greenwood began. "I don't rightly know how to put this."

"Why, whatever is the matter?" she said, thinking how wretchedly uncomfortable the man looked.

"It's about the account," he said, his voice thin and formal as he pronounced the words.

"What about the account?" She gave what she hoped was an encouraging smile. "Do come in and let me make you tea, like I always do."

Mr Greenwood followed her into the kitchen, coughed nervously a couple of times, and sat down at the kitchen table, avoiding her gaze. The worry lines between his brows and around his mouth seemed more pronounced today.

"Now, what is it about the account you need to tell me?" she said, placing a cup of tea in front of him.

At last Mr Greenwood raised his eyes and looked at her. "I'm afraid I'm not able to let you have anything further on credit until the outstanding amount is settled."

"Outstanding amount? What outstanding amount?" She could not imagine how this could be so, but when she looked again it was clear from his expression that he was serious. "How much does Mr Wilcox owe you?"

"I'm afraid the account's six months in arrears." His face said it all – both grave and sad – as he raised a hand to smooth back receding hair.

"Do you mean to say that my husband has paid you *nothing* this year?"

"That is so, Mrs Wilcox."

"There must be some mistake, some oversight, surely."

"I'm afraid not, Mrs Wilcox. I checked the account to make sure before I came out this morning. The last payment Mr Wilcox made was for December."

"Well, thank goodness it's summer and the grazing's good," she remarked, wondering where to take the conversation next. "But Mr Wilcox has indicated here that he needs crushed oats for his horse and I need grain for the hens. Could you see your way to letting me have just these two items, while I sort out why the account hasn't been settled?"

Mr Greenwood shook his head slowly. "I'm very sorry, Mrs Wilcox, but I have to take cash for any order you place. I need the money now." He looked at her expectantly.

"How much would this come to?" she asked.

"Six pounds, thirteen and six," replied Mr Greenwood, after a quick calculation.

"Very well. I'll pay you in cash, and I'll see that the account is settled as soon as possible." She stood up, opened a drawer in the dresser, and took out the housekeeping purse, from which she counted out six pounds, thirteen shillings and sixpence. "There you are, Mr Greenwood. I think that's the correct amount. Perhaps you'd be kind enough to make out a receipt so there can be no doubt that I've paid what I owe."

When Jim came in, Kathleen asked him about the unpaid bills. "I told him I was sure it'd merely been an oversight on your part," she said. "I can't think why you've let it go on so long."

"Don't you speak to me like that," he flared. "'Tis down to you and that father of yours that I'm in the predicament I am."

Her eyes grew bright with indignation. "What? How can you say—"

"If your father'd kept his word and paid what he owed, I'd be able to pay my debts too." He glowered back at her.

"It's nothing to do with my father. It's you – you don't run this farm properly. You can't expect people to give you credit when you don't pay your debts."

"Don't you tell me how to run my farm," he shouted, and stuck his forefinger nearly in her face. "You keep to the kitchen and mind your own business."

"If I'd kept to the kitchen and not made money out of the dairy and the eggs, selling to people around here, I wouldn't have been able to pay for Captain's oats this month."

"Damn and blast! You've shown me up good and proper, you little hussy." He ground his teeth in resentment.

She was stunned into silence because she expected him to thank her for using money that she and Edith had earned to pay for Captain's oats. Then rage and disappointment overcame her and she shouted back, "I told him you'd settle the account because I was sure there'd been some mistake. So you'd better get on and do that if you want any more cattle feed."

"Damn and blast you!" he yelled. "Why don't you write to that Mr Fitzgerald of yours and find out what's happened to the money?"

Within days, Mr Fitzgerald replied to Kathleen's enquiry and the answer made her stomach churn. Lawyers acting for the Providential Asurance Company had advised them not to pay:

...and unfortunately, Kathleen, they appear to think they have a public duty not to pay you and your mother the amount stated in the policy. Regrettably, it is because your father died by his own hand. Under the law, no one may benefit from a crime and, as you are aware, suicide is a criminal offence. I have argued with them that it is not your father but yourself and your mother, innocent beneficiaries, who should be in receipt of the money. Unfortunately, they refuse to see it in that light, and believe that the rule extends to anyone benefiting from the crime of another.

The only way in which we can move the matter forward is to take legal action in the High Court to sue the Providential Assurance Company for breach of contract. I myself am not in a position to finance such a course of action, and I wonder

*whether you or your mother might have sufficient funds to
instruct solicitors.*

Yours truly,
William Fitzgerald

Kathleen sat, head in hands, wondering what was to
be done. She'd have to tell Jim and he'd explode with anger
and recriminations; she knew he would. She guessed it
was better to wait until after Edith had gone to bed and
he'd a tankard of cider in his hand. Even so, she broached
the subject full of foreboding and struggled to find the
right words.

"Well, what're you going to do, seeing as it's your father
who's let me down?" he snarled, thumping his fist down
with a force that made her jump.

"What am *I* going to do?" she shouted. "Where would
I get the money to pay for lawyers?"

"Ask… your… mother." He pronounced each word
slowly through clenched teeth.

"I shouldn't have to rely on my mother. You're my
husband." Bitter resentment welled up in her. "But you
won't be able to help if you owe money left, right and
centre."

The accusation struck a raw chord and Jim's full fury
erupted. He slammed the tankard down, drops of cider
slopping over onto the table. "'Tis not my fault if your
father can't keep a bargain." His eyes bulged above florid
cheeks and the veins on his forehead stood out.

Jim refused to speak of the matter again, but before the
month was out he'd sold Captain, which confirmed

Kathleen's suspicion that he'd borrowed money to buy the horse in the first place. If so, at least that debt could be paid off, and he might even have made a bit, given Captain's success at the races. She wondered how many more debts were yet to make their presence known, and whether he still owed Ivybridge garage for the truck.

Holding out little hope, she wrote to her mother and asked what she intended doing. Alexandra stood to lose just as much as she did, and besides, her mother must have come by some money from somewhere, because she'd kept the house. A few weeks later, not having received a reply, Kathleen decided to try a telephone call.

"You're through," the operator told her.

"Hi there! Who is this?" a man's voice drawled on the other end of the line.

So startled, so taken aback, Kathleen said nothing for a full five seconds.

The man spoke again. "Anybody there?"

"Hello," she said. "May I speak to Mrs Wyndham, please?"

She heard voices in the background and then her mother came to the phone.

"Mummy, is that you?"

"Kathleen." The voice sounded shrill; a little nervous. "What a surprise. Fancy you ringing me."

"Mummy, who is that man?"

"Oh, that's Chuck. He's absolutely marvellous. He's going to take me to Hollywood and get me in the movies."

"Mummy, you can't—"

"Don't talk to me like that, Kathleen. Chuck's been very good to me. Anyway, what was it you wanted to say?"

"I suppose you've heard from Mr Fitzgerald, about the insurance. He says the company won't pay out unless we take them to court, and that means we need money for lawyers."

"Oh, I can't be bothered with any of that," said Alexandra. "I've a new life. You must do as you please. You've a husband; why don't you ask him for the money?"

Kathleen replaced the receiver without another word. She walked slowly back to the farm, sickened and shamed by her mother's behaviour. Her father had taken his life thinking that it was the only thing, the very last thing, he could do for them. And her mother had thrown it back at him. She'd cast aside his sacrifice; rejected it as if it were a mere trifle. Kathleen crept into the kitchen carrying her great burden and sat weeping quietly to herself. She didn't hear the footsteps and was surprised when an arm rested on her shoulder.

"What's so terrible bad, my dear?" Edith said.

Kathleen swallowed hard but the lump in her throat refused to go. Tears crept out from under her closed eyelids and trickled down her face. Between sobs, she went over it all: her father's death; the money not being paid; her mother not caring any longer.

Edith listened, murmuring sympathy from time to time. "'Tis a hard life we have to bear, my dear. Just as well we can't see into the future, or we'd never have the courage to keep going." She stroked Kathleen's hand. "But 'tis never all bad. Why, just this morning when the postman came, he brought news from Alston Hall. Lord and Lady Neville have a son; born yesterday, he was."

Fresh tears welled up and Kathleen's shoulders shook with sobs.

CHAPTER 14

Jim went tight-lipped and morose when she told him what Alexandra had said. He gave her a withering look and went away, muttering about "that bloody woman" and "conniving bastards". He ignored Kathleen for a long while after that, hardly exchanging a civil word, but when he climbed into bed at night, he made sure he got what was due to him.

The autumn was grim and money tight – very tight. Every time Kathleen needed to buy anything, she had to ask Jim. He kept the cash from selling butter and cream in Ivybridge – not that there was a lot, because it was the autumn – so there wasn't much that found its way into the housekeeping purse except for the money she and Edith made from baking and selling dairy and eggs to neighbours. Even the annual pig-killing brought little relief. All the hams, bacon and puddings had to be sold, and Christmas 1932 was a miserable, frugal affair.

At the turn of the year Kathleen resolved that something must be done. "It's so unfair," she complained to Jim. "Edith and I do all the work in the dairy, and you pocket the takings."

"Unfair? Trying to keep your head above water when

people let you down and don't pay you what they should, now *that's* unfair."

She ignored the jibe and kept a cool head. "Why don't you let me take charge of the hens and the dairy? I'm sure I'd make more money than we're getting now."

"You? *You* take charge?" He tossed his head and gave a sarcastic snort.

"Jim, think about it, I'm serious. How much do you think the dairy and the hens should bring in each week?" she asked. "Would you be happy with fifteen shillings?"

"I'd be doing all right if I could get fifteen shillings off you every week for surplus milk during the season and letting you run a few hens."

"You supply me with the same amount of milk as usual – not any less, mind and let me decide how many hens in the flock, and I'll pay you fifteen shillings a week. Any profit goes to me and Edith. Agreed?"

Jim laughed. "You'll not make more than a few pence over fifteen shillings. But try if you like." He laughed again, failing utterly to comprehend her determination.

The following morning Kathleen explained her plan to Edith. "We sell a lot of what we bake. Your fruit cakes are especially popular," she said. "We've got a customer for our cream, butter and cheese, and the other day the Southwood butcher asked me if we could supply chickens for the table."

"We're not doing badly, are we? Got a lot to be thankful for." Edith's lips formed a satisfied smile.

"But we can do better – a great deal better. Jim has agreed that we can keep all the profit we make, so long as we give him fifteen shillings a week for supplying the milk. We've got a good deal, don't you think?"

"Don't know about that. Can't rightly say. 'Tis a lot of money, fifteen shillings."

"I've done the sums and I'm sure we could make double that amount." Kathleen flung her arms wide, flushed with excitement. "And I think we ought to let people know that everything comes from Higher Haydn Farm."

"But they do; course they do," said Edith, puzzled by the suggestion.

"I was thinking of getting labels printed," Kathleen continued, "and seeing if we couldn't get shops in Ivybridge to give us regular orders. And the first thing I'm going to do is tell that stallholder in the market that if he wants our butter, cream and cheese, he'll have to pay a fairer price."

"There's only thee and me," said Edith doubtfully. "And young Tom's getting more of a handful than ever these days. How'd we manage?"

"We can take on more help in the dairy – give Dolly a permanent job."

"Well, let's see how us gets on," replied Edith. "You'm full of good ideas."

Before the week was out Kathleen called at The Southwood Inn, because if anyone knew of a printer, it would be the landlord. He was known for keeping an ear close to the ground and being acquainted with everyone's business better than they were themselves.

"And why might you be wanting a printer, Mrs Wilcox?" he asked with an amused smile. "What's your husband up to now?"

"Nothing, I hope," she replied, ignoring his vaguely facetious tone. "It's me that needs the printer. I was wondering if you might know where I could find one. You're quite renowned as a source of information." She raised her eyebrows in a hopeful expression.

The landlord was a man who jealously guarded his reputation as the fountain of all local knowledge. Besides, a number of patrons in for a dinner-time pint were listening to the conversation. He looked at her and in a loud voice pronounced the name, "Brown & Co." A murmur rippled round the bar, and those who'd been eavesdropping on the conversation raised their tankards for a sip.

"Where would I find them?" Kathleen asked, aware that all eyes were now trained on her.

"You'll find Brown & Co. in Ivybridge."

"Where in Ivybridge?"

"I was coming to that." He appeared irritated by the speed of her interrogation.

She waited while the landlord savoured the moment, dominating his audience.

"You'll find them if you go down Fore Street and turn right just before the ironmongers. Printing works are at the back. You can't miss them – you'll hear the noise long afore you gets there." He tapped the bar with his fingertips and waited for her grateful thanks.

"Thank you so much. You've been very helpful."

"You haven't said why you want to know," he observed.

"Just a little idea I have. You'll see soon enough." She swivelled round to go amid a chorus of good-natured guffaws from his customers.

On the first market day in February she took a lift in the truck to Ivybridge with Jim. It'd turned cold and blustery and the river was brown and swollen with rain. Jim parked the truck on waste ground not far from The London Hotel.

"Mind you'm back here twelve sharp," he said, before wandering off in the direction of the cattle pens. Times were lean and he'd nothing to sell, but he liked to keep an eye on prices and have a chat and a drink in The Sportsman's Arms.

Kathleen carried the dishes of cream she'd brought with her in a wicker basket covered by a white cloth. Her first task was to have it out with the stallholder. She'd no idea how much he paid, because Jim had been more than a little evasive on the point. To give herself a better chance, she took a stroll down Fore Street, stopping to look in windows that interested her. Ivybridge Dairy sold butter, cream and cheeses as well as milk, but she lingered longer outside the bakery, the grocer and particularly the cafés. She jotted down prices in a notebook and, satisfied with her efforts, went off to see the stallholder. Few customers appeared to be attracted to the stalls huddled at the back of the cattle pens. Most stallholders looked glum and resigned as they stood – hands in pockets, shuffling from foot to foot – waiting for trade. The man selling dairy produce had a stall right at the end and about as far away from the footpath as it was possible to get. He looked surprised to see her.

"Where's Mr Wilcox?" he asked, when she introduced herself.

"At the cattle auction by now, I expect," she replied. "He likes to keep an eye on prices."

The stallholder shuffled uncomfortably, as if he had a suspicion that something unpleasant was about to happen.

"The price you give Mr Wilcox for cream – what is it?" she enquired.

The stallholder's eyes narrowed and his voice took on a dubious edge. "Shilling for a large dish," he replied.

"One like this?" She lifted the cloth and held up a dish containing a pound of cream.

The stallholder nodded.

"A shilling a pound for the best clotted cream?"

"Mr Wilcox is happy with the price," said the man defensively.

"Well, I'm not." She turned on her heel and marched off.

"No one else's going to take all that off your hands. You'll be left with it," he shouted after her, and heads turned to see what the commotion was.

But Kathleen didn't care – she had other ideas.

The manageress of The Riverside Café was impressed with the quality of the cream. "Looks wonderfully thick for this time of year," she observed. "Does it taste as good as it looks?"

"Why not take this as a free sample?" suggested Kathleen. "If your customers take to Higher Haydn cream, you could place a regular order."

The manageress took the dish. "That's very civil of you, Mrs…?"

"Wilcox. Mrs Wilcox."

"What would you normally charge for a dish this size?"

Kathleen steadied herself and replied, "Two and sixpence."

"Oh, that's very reasonable – especially for top quality."

Kathleen's heart leaped, but to outward appearances she remained calm. She was on the brink of her first deal. Her father would have been proud. "I'll be in Ivybridge again in two weeks' time," she said, with all the decorum she could muster. "We can discuss the details then, if you like."

The manageress smiled. "Very good, Mrs Wilcox. I look forward to seeing you."

So far, so good. There was still a second dish of cream in the basket. Kathleen paused, deep in thought for a moment, then marched up to The London Hotel. Locating the tradesman's entrance, she went in and asked to see the head chef. After similar exchanges to those she'd had with the manageress of The Riverside Café, the chef took the free sample and agreed to discuss terms with her in a fortnight.

She visited the bakers, a tea shop and a butcher, making enquiries at each, and found them all sufficiently interested to ask the prices of the things she was offering to supply. Flushed with success, her next stop was Brown & Co. and, as the landlord at The Southwood Inn had indicated, she found them easy to track down. A small family business, they were quick to oblige at reasonable rates, offering printed notepaper, cards and labels – in fact, everything she wanted.

Satisfied with her morning's work, Kathleen went back to the truck to wait for Jim. He turned up after about twenty minutes, cheeks red as if he'd had a few in front of the fire at The Sportsman's Arms.

"Get on all right?" he enquired.

"Very well indeed," she replied.

"How much did you get, then?" He knew she'd meant to renegotiate the price with the stallholder in the market.

"I'm sure I'm going to get regular orders from The Riverside Café and The London Hotel."

"How much did you get?"

"Nothing today. I gave them the cream as free samples."

He stared at her in disbelief. "You gave away good cream. What's in that stupid head of yours? I never heard the like." He pressed the starter button and the motor spluttered into action. Muttering about having an idiot for a wife, he crunched into bottom gear and the truck jerked forward.

Brown & Co. were as good as their word, and before long a parcel arrived addressed to Kathleen containing stick-on labels, tags, and price lists of all the things they hoped to sell.

"I never thought that shop in Ivybridge would want to take my fruit cakes," said Edith.

"And they wanted to know if we did pork pies and things like that," said Kathleen.

"You think they'd get them from the bakers," said Edith.

"The bakers don't want to be bothered making a few of this and a few of that. They're interested in making dozens and dozens of the same-sized loaves. And that's where we come in – we could get regular orders for all sorts of things: cakes, pies, cream. The butcher's willing to pay a good price for roasting chickens, and what's more, he's happy to take them live, thank goodness."

"Well, my dear, looks like 'tis all set for us to go into business, and a proper job us'll make of it, I'm sure." Edith gave her an affectionate pat on the shoulder.

Within a month orders were coming in at a steady pace, and Dolly was employed full-time. As soon as she'd finished in the dairy – and there wasn't a great deal to do yet, because the new grass was only just coming in – she helped in the kitchen under Edith's instruction.

Jim annoyingly refused to allow Kathleen to drive the truck, because driving was a man's job. She was forced to make other arrangements for deliveries, and fortunately the carrier in Southwood was an obliging soul. His van was on the small side but he was willing to take Kathleen and the goods to Ivybridge once a week for a reasonable charge. Trips to Southwood she could manage, pushing Tom's pram loaded with cakes and pies for the village shop.

Jim scorned her efforts and was as unaccommodating as possible, but the profits she shared with Edith mounted and at last she had money to call her own. She took Tom shopping in Ivybridge and bought him new shoes and a picture book about a teddy bear. She'd read him the story at bedtime until he knew the tale so well he'd shout out if she got a word wrong.

"You know, Edith, there's something else we could do," said Kathleen when they reviewed their takings one day. "The farm lane doesn't end in the yard, does it? It goes past, into Grendles Wood, and comes out on Haldon Moor."

"Yes, 'tis a footpath, though no one uses it much," replied Edith.

"No wonder. It's inches deep in mud most of the time."

"'Tis the stream, you see," Edith explained. "The drain's broken."

"But it *is* a footpath, so the public can use it, can't they?" Kathleen persisted.

"Shouldn't think they'd want to. Not unless they're wearing gumboots." Jim gave a hollow laugh. He'd come in while they were talking.

"We could fix the drain and maybe put down some gravel and then it would be perfectly all right to walk on"

"Another of your crackpot ideas." He'd never got over her ridiculous behaviour in giving away free samples. "I'm not spending money on mending a drain just so as people can go for a walk in the woods." He gave a snigger and turned to go. "Some of us got work to do."

"We've enough money to employ a man to do the job," Kathleen said, when Jim was out of hearing.

"But why would us want to? Like Jim says, why should us pay to keep people's feet dry?"

"Because we'd sell them teas on the way home."

"Don't know as I could do any more work," complained Edith. "And anyway, who'd want to come all the way up here just to walk in the woods?"

"People from the city would. People would come from Plymouth to walk through the woods and out onto Haldon Moor. Of course they'd want tea on the way home, and we'd sell it to them."

"How would anyone in Plymouth get to hear about a footpath in the woods?"

"We'd let them know," said Kathleen. "We'd advertise."

Fired with enthusiasm and an intense desire to prove Jim wrong, Kathleen put her plan into action. He was livid that she should spend money employing a man to mend the drain but, as she pointed out, it wasn't his money. He mocked her when she insisted that people would love to come for a walk through the woods and, if they did, they'd be prepared to buy tea on the way home. He was opinionated and cantankerous, so she ignored him and went her own way.

The printers produced fifty posters for her and, by the end of March, many were displayed in shop windows around Plymouth. She persuaded the bus company to take a few, and even suggested that they might run excursions to Southwood. With help from Edith and Dolly she spring-cleaned the old barn at the top of the lane that was no longer used. She whitewashed the walls and bought a whole set of tables and chairs for next to nothing from a parish on the other side of Ivybridge, and Edith remembered the trestle table she'd once used for harvest suppers. On Easter Monday they covered it with a large white cloth, and set out a tea urn, cups, saucers and plates, ready for business.

Kathleen was in the kitchen, putting yet another tray of scones into the oven, when Jim sauntered in and sat down. "Don't know who you think's going to eat all those," he said disparagingly. "'Less there's an army on its way, of course." He looked around the room. "Would be nice if somebody had time to make a man a cup of tea."

"I really haven't got time, Jim," she said. "You could always pull the kettle over yourself and make a cup."

He grunted, rose from the settle, and slouched off towards the yard door in high dudgeon.

"I hope he's not right." Kathleen turned to Edith, who was busy putting raspberry, gooseberry and blackcurrant jam into glass dishes. "I'll have wasted an awful lot of our money if this doesn't work."

At that moment, Dolly rushed into the kitchen in a state of high excitement. "I looked out the window and I saw two men and two ladies a-coming up the lane to the farm. Look like townies, they do; I'm sure they were townies."

Kathleen wiped her hands, dashed out the scullery door, and made for the lane. Sure enough, four people were nearing the farm. From their clothes she guessed they were intent on a serious walk.

"Good morning, madam." One of the men hailed her with a walking stick. "Is this where we can get tea?"

"Yes, sir – we're serving teas from three o'clock in the barn, just over there."

"Right, we'll see you then." The man gave a cheery wave and the group proceeded on its way.

About to return to the kitchen, Kathleen spied Nell from Lower Haydn Farm puffing and panting up the lane. "Why, whatever's the matter?" Kathleen said.

"Down there," gasped Nell. "'Tis a charabanc. They'm parked on that bit of spare land down by the bridge. Looks like they're coming this way."

Kathleen's heart began to pound. "How many, Nell?" she asked.

"Can't rightly say – must be at least a couple dozen of 'em."

It was just the start. People flocked to Higher Haydn Farm to take the footpath to the woods and moor, and some days Kathleen even put tables outside. She and Edith could scarcely cope with the baking, and so she paid Nell to bake and serve with them. But Jim was as grumpy as ever and protested that a man should have a bit of peace and quiet on his own farm, and that Kathleen never thought of him when she ran these hare-brained schemes.

In late June two letters arrived in the morning post. One (addressed to Jim) Kathleen placed on the dresser; the other – she recognised Alice's handwriting – she stuffed in her pocket, intending to read it at dinner time. She gave no further thought to the letters until she was collecting eggs, when Jim bore down on her, waving the envelope and shouting that he'd been right all along.

"See this?" he yelled, brandishing the letter above her head. He was breathing heavily and looked fit to burst.

"What is it?"

"'Tis all your fault, you interfering woman." The veins on his neck stood out and he was shaking with rage. "They'm putting the rent up," he snarled, and stuck the letter right under her nose.

She put up a hand and grabbed the letter from him. It was from the steward at Alston Hall:

...and it has come to my attention that you have been using Grendles Wood to generate income. I have to remind you that Grendles Wood is not part of Higher Haydn Farm and therefore not included in your tenancy. As a consequence, assuming you wish to continue with your profit-making activities, it is only fair that you pay a higher

rent. To this end, I have to warn you that a formal notice of increase in rent will be served on you at Michaelmas.

"See what you've done, you bloody stupid woman? Meddling in things you don't understand."

She put down the eggs and ran indoors, still clutching the letter. Upstairs, she scrambled into her best dress, brushed her hair, and put on lipstick, although that was tricky because her hand was shaking so. When she came down, Jim had gone. *Probably drawn a tankard and gone to sulk in the stable*, she thought.

"Edith, I must go to Alston Hall right away – there's been a terrible mistake. Can you keep an eye on Tom?"

"Course I will, but what's it all about? You'm in some state."

"Sorry – must dash," Kathleen called over her shoulder.

Still fuming with indignation, she knocked briskly on the estate office door and, scarcely waiting for a response, burst in. The man at the desk had his back to her.

"What do you mean by this? It's outrageous!" she exclaimed, holding the letter aloft.

As she spoke, the man turned around and she saw that it was Robert.

CHAPTER 15

Robert looked as shocked as she was to find himself face to face with her. "How do you do, Mrs Wilcox? Are you well?" He extended a hand in welcome.

She stood motionless, her mind devoid of any sensible thing to say, but after what seemed an age she lifted her hand and took his. Their fingers touched, and it felt like it always did when they touched. And all the time they hadn't touched, all the time in between, melted away as if it had never been. She swallowed twice. "Quite well, thank you," she replied.

"It's been so long…" His hand still clasped hers. "Whatever's the matter? What's happened?" His other hand covered hers, its warmth melding with her own.

She looked at her hand, squeezed between his. It shouldn't be there; he shouldn't be holding her hand at all. Yet she didn't draw it away and, as in a dream, she waited for something to happen.

He led her to a chair and sat her down. "What's this all about?" he asked.

The words stuck in her throat when she opened her mouth to speak, so she waved the letter and he reached out and took it from her. She watched him read it and wondered if there'd be another chance for their fingers to touch, just for an instant, when he handed it back.

But he didn't hand it back. When he'd finished reading, he looked up. "This is quite wrong," he said. "I never authorised this. I'd no idea... it should never have been sent."

She watched and waited to see what he'd do. His face was grave but his eyes had the same look they used to have.

"I'll speak to the steward," he said.

"You'll make sure the rent doesn't go up?" she asked, and her voice sounded strange and distant, as if she wasn't really there at all and it was just an echo.

"I'll have a word today and tell him that the Alston Estate has no right to demand payment from tenants because people are using a public footpath." And then he rose and held out a hand to her to show that the meeting was at an end.

"I'll leave things with you, then," she said, taking his hand, wanting him to keep hold of it, like he had before. But this time he released his grip, and then she was leaving, walking away, wondering what had happened or whether anything had happened at all.

She stepped out into the bright noonday sun and everywhere was very warm and very alive. Beyond the Yeo valley and Grendles Wood, the moor was dotted with cattle and sheep grazing beneath sweeping cloud shadows. She couldn't recall the sky being so blue in a long while, and all at once the world seemed young again, and she was young with it. She breathed in the scent of summer and it had about it a sweetness she'd long forgotten.

When she got back to the farm, she found Jim in the kitchen waiting for his dinner, a tankard of cider in his hand. Assuming her news would cheer him, she called out, "You'll never guess what I've done – no rent rise. I've spoken to Lord Neville and there'll be no rent rise."

Jim rose and lurched forward on unsteady legs, pushing his face right into hers. "Been interfering in my business again?" he snarled. "How dare you?"

"I thought you'd be pleased. You're not going to have to pay more rent," she replied, her voice faltering.

"If this gets out, what's folks going to say?" His forefinger was raised at her. "I'll be a laughing stock, that's what I'll be. They'll say I send my wife to see the landlord 'cause I can't face up to him myself." He let out a bellow of frustration and staggered off down the passage and out into the sunshine. He crossed the yard, the metal studs in his boots clanking on the cobbles.

Kathleen sighed and looked around the kitchen. The aroma coming from the oven suggested that dinner was almost ready, so she shook out the cloth and began to set the table. In the scullery Tom was chattering away to Edith, but before Kathleen had taken a step in their direction a howl of rage followed by a crash shattered the peace of the yard. Edith dropped what she was doing and the two women raced for the door. Kathleen got there first and found Jim at the foot of the ladder that led to the hayloft, tankard still in hand, its contents splashed all over the dust. Lying on the ground beside him was a broken rung from the top of the ladder.

"Jim, Jim, are you all right?"

"Course I'm not all right. Do I look as if I'm all right? Well, don't just stand there – get me another cider."

"You've had too much already."

"Don't want no lip from you. Do as you're told, woman." With a hand on the ladder, Jim rose unsteadily to his feet. But with his first step, he cried out in pain and clung to the ladder again. "Damn it. Damn it, woman. Come here." His eyes radiated a look of such malice that for a moment she hesitated. "Do what I tell you."

She stepped close to him and allowed him to transfer his weight onto her shoulder, using her as a crutch. Tom, who'd followed them into the yard, began to cry. Edith held him tight, took a handkerchief from her apron pocket and wiped his eyes.

"Now, don't take on so, my little one. Daddy'll be all right d'reckly, you'll see. 'Tis just the shock of it, my handsome. Here, blow your nose." She held the handkerchief to his nose and Tom gave a feeble snort. "There, that's better now," she said.

Little by little Jim struggled across the yard, leaning on Kathleen's shoulder. They made it up the passage to the kitchen, where he subsided into his favourite chair with a groan. Despite his protestations, she unlaced his boot and took it off. The ankle and lower leg, flushed with angry purple bruises, were swelling rapidly.

"Edith, can you look after things here while I go for the doctor?" Kathleen said.

"Yes, my dear," Edith replied. "Tom and me'll look after things – off you go."

Jim sat in the chair all afternoon, muttering and grumbling, and yelled in anticipation if anyone came near his leg. When Kathleen got back from telephoning the doctor, Jim wouldn't let her rest until she'd found one of their labourers – the man who lived down at Bridge

Cottage – to come and do the milking, and with Tom afraid to go near his father, Kathleen and Edith lost an afternoon's baking.

The doctor arrived shortly before tea and without hesitation declared the leg broken in two places. "Clean breaks," he said to Jim. "I'm putting your leg in a splint but you won't be able to walk on it for twelve weeks. You must rest, in bed if possible, for at least the next month."

"I'm a farmer; I can't be resting in bed with the harvest coming on," grumbled Jim.

"You'll not be harvesting anything with a leg like that," replied the doctor. "And if you don't do as I tell you, you'll end up much worse." He supported Jim, groaning and protesting, up the stairs and into the bedroom, where Kathleen undressed him and helped him into bed. "You might want to give him a little of this, if the pain's too much," said the doctor, handing her a small, dark bottle. He closed his bag and was gone.

After Kathleen had taken Jim his tea on a tray, she came downstairs and slumped over the table with a sigh.

"There you are, my dear," said Edith, putting a cup of tea in front of her and cutting a slice of jam sponge. "Need to keep your strength up."

Tom grinned at Kathleen from his high chair. He picked crumbs off his feeder and put them in his mouth. She grinned back.

"I put your letter on the dresser," said Edith.

"Letter? What letter?"

"Fell out your pocket when you took off your apron and went for the doctor."

Kathleen looked at the dresser and then she remembered – Alice's letter. She'd put it in her pocket to read later, when she had a minute.

Alice wrote that she and Binkey were to be married on the 1st July, after which they'd be travelling to Devon and staying at the hotel on Burgh Island:

...an absolutely spiffing place – the very lap of luxury. They say Noël Coward went there for three days and stayed three weeks. And Agatha Christie often stays there when she's writing her murder mystery novels.

Unless you send a message saying it's not convenient, we'll expect you and Jim for tea on Saturday 8th. Looking forward to seeing you.

Yours ever,
Alice

"It's from Alice – you know, Edith; I told you she was getting married. They're honeymooning in Devon and staying at The Burgh Island Hotel. She's invited us – Jim and me – for tea next Saturday. I can't go, of course; not now, with all this happening."

"That's a shame," Edith replied. "I could look after Tom; he's no trouble. I suppose 'twould be difficult to get there on your own without Jim to drive, though."

Jim directed operations as well as he could from his bed. In many ways, the place ran itself; the farmhands knew what to do because they'd been doing it for a very long time. And the man who lived at Bridge Cottage was pleased to earn a bit extra for doing the milking, and took the milk churns by horse and cart to Southwood each morning.

The big difference now was that there was no one to drive the truck to market – or anywhere else, for that matter – and with Jim immobilised, Kathleen took her chance. It wasn't long before she got a feel for the gears and the clutch. She drove to Southwood with cakes and eggs for the shop, and a few chickens in a crate for the butcher. After that she ventured further and took the weekly order to Ivybridge. So when Edith persuaded her that looking after Tom really was no trouble at all, she decided to risk it and go on her own to see Alice and Binkey. She asked directions to Burgh Island from the landlord of Southwood Inn and he raised his eyebrows and asked if she thought it wise for a woman to drive all that way. And she replied that she'd driven at least as far as that on numerous occasions, which was not strictly true, but his arrogance made her all the more determined.

When Jim was dozing she smuggled the clothes she would wear into Edith's room. Shortly after dinner on Saturday afternoon, she put on the lemon-and-white polka-dot dress she'd not worn in ages and chose a pair of shoes that would never survive the farmyard – she'd wear lace-up shoes for driving and change when she got there. Moths had eaten holes in the lemon felt cloche that went with the outfit, so she discarded that and tied her hair back with a length of yellow ribbon.

The landlord's directions she found difficult to follow and it was three o'clock before she arrived in Bigbury and parked at the side of the road near the beach. The tide was coming in and the sea tractor was about to take passengers across to Burgh Island. It was a heavenly day; light dancing on the water and scarcely a cloud in the sky. On the sands, children shrieked in delight and chased one another through gentle waves, and parents dug sandcastles, trying in vain to shore up the sides as the tide swept them away.

Alice and Binkey greeted Kathleen with such obvious pleasure that she felt almost moved to tears by their affection. Alice hugged and kissed her, and a smiling Binkey shook her hand and said how sorry he was to hear of Jim's accident. He seemed to have grown up a lot since their last meeting. No longer a thin, gangly youth, he wore spectacles now and altogether looked more distinguished.

Fashions had changed; she should have known that from reading Edith's magazine. Dresses were longer now, well below the knee, and waists had retreated to their normal place. Acutely embarrassed, Kathleen fidgeted, trying to pull her skirt down so that her knees wouldn't show as they sat and talked in the hotel lounge. Alice's hair had been expertly styled; its natural curl coaxed into waves around her face. Kathleen looked with envy at her well-manicured hands as Alice showed off her sapphire engagement ring. Her own hands were rough and chapped from farm work, and baking and washing, and the dirt that got everywhere. She wanted to hide them, and when she wasn't pulling down her skirt, she sat on them.

At four o'clock, when Binkey had just ordered tea, a clerk came across with a message that more visitors had arrived, and Kathleen looked up to see Robert and Sarah waiting at the reception desk. Binkey stood to greet them, and waved them over. Kathleen stared at the new arrivals, like a rabbit caught in the headlights of a car.

"We hope you don't mind," said Robert, hiding his surprise at finding her there remarkably well. "We were just out for a drive and on the spur of the moment we decided to pop in and see you."

"Yes," said Sarah. "Blame me if you like – it was my idea."

Binkey made the introductions. "Robert, you know Kathleen, of course."

"Yes, Kathleen and I know each other." Robert smiled.

Kathleen's pulse was racing so, she could hear blood pounding in her ears.

"This is Robert's wife, Sarah," said Binkey.

"I'm not sure if we have met before, Kathleen," said Sarah, her expression slightly puzzled, "although I'm sure your face is familiar."

"Kathleen is married to Mr Wilcox of Higher Haydn Farm, my dear," said Robert.

A look of horror spread over Sarah's face. "You mean she is married to one of the tenants?"

"Kathleen is a very old friend of mine," Alice explained hastily. "We used to be at school together – Chiltern Ladies' College."

"Good gracious me." Sarah rolled her eyes. "Now, tell me, Alice," she said. "Tell me all about your house – a wedding present from your parents, I believe."

While Alice told Sarah about the kitchen and the electric cooker, Kathleen could only sit and listen. Alice's dining-room suite had come from Heal's: a limed-oak table that seated eight, and ladder-back chairs with upholstered seats.

"…and the most wonderful sideboard," said Alice enthusiastically. "It even has a cocktail cabinet at one end, although we drink hardly anything. Still, it's nice to have when one's entertaining."

Kathleen thought of the kitchen at the farm: the old dresser that had stood on the flagstones for generations, and the grandfather clock in the corner. She thought of the logs piled up waiting to be put on the range fire, and how tricky it was to get the oven up to just the right temperature. She half-listened to the conversation between Binkey and Robert. It seemed to centre on cars and whether it was better to have a sports car that took two, or a large car like the Bentley that had plenty of room for luggage if you went touring.

She was glad when tea was over. Robert and Sarah left and it was just Kathleen, Alice and Binkey again.

"It's been absolutely marvellous seeing you," said Alice. "This is our address." She handed Kathleen a printed card. "If you ever come up to town, you must call in and see us."

"Thank you, I will," Kathleen said, because there didn't seem to be anything else she could possibly say.

On Monday morning Jim told her that they were already late with the shearing this year and it was time to make haste. They'd need half a dozen new hurdles for penning the sheep and getting them through the dipping trough after they'd been sheared. Kathleen was to go to the estate's sawmill and order the hurdles right away.

It was a fine day, so she decided to walk along the road that followed the river and take the back drive to Alston Hall, where the sawmills were – about halfway along on the left. She'd placed the order and was enquiring about when she might take delivery when a shadow appeared right beside her.

"Might I have a word with you, Mrs Wilcox?" The shadow belonged to Robert.

"Of course," she said, trying to appear calm.

"Somewhere more private, if you don't mind." He began to walk along the back drive in the direction of Gardener's Cottage.

She fell into step and walked beside him. "What is it? It's a problem with the rent after all, isn't it?"

"No, nothing like that. Someone told me your husband's had an accident, broken his leg and can't work. I just wondered how you were managing; whether you needed any help; if I could lend you one of my men." His voice was amiable yet serious.

"It's very kind of you, but I think we can manage," she replied. "I don't think we could afford to pay another wage just at the moment."

"Oh, I didn't mean for you to pay. I was offering to lend you a man," said Robert.

"You can't do that – what would people say if they found out?"

"It wouldn't matter at all what people thought if it helped you," he replied.

They'd almost reached Gardener's Cottage. She looked up, sneaked a glance, wondered what she ought to say and didn't know, so she just went on walking beside him.

His pace slowed and he turned to face her. "Kathleen?" He said it slowly, with an inflection that made her name sound like a question. He placed a hand under her elbow, as if he were going to draw her to him. Then he stopped and let go, and everything went very still and very quiet, and she waited for the moment to pass; for time to move

194

on and reach the point where he would say goodbye and she would walk away. But instead he raised a hand and stroked her cheek with his finger. It was so gentle, so beautiful that she held her breath with the shock of it. His face was close to hers and she put up a hand to stop him, but he took it in his and raised it to his lips.

"No, no." She pulled away from him. "Someone in the cottage might see."

"The cottage is empty. The new gardener doesn't come for another month or more. Look!" He pointed to drawn curtains at the windows.

Relief flooded through her. Thank God they weren't discovered.

"We could sit inside awhile and talk," he said.

She sensed there was still time; still time to walk away and pretend nothing had happened. "Oh, I don't know. I ought to be getting back," she said.

"We've never talked properly since I took you home from the theatre," he said. "Tell me what happened, Kathleen."

She saw the pleading in his eyes and felt that everything was her fault, and that she needed to explain. And if she did, perhaps he'd forgive her and stroke her cheek again.

He led the way round to the back of the cottage, unlocked the door, and pushed it open. Inside it was hot and dry and the air was stale, and she knew it was wrong to be there and that she should make some excuse and go. But he closed the door and came and stood close to her.

"Robert, I was so stupid. I'm so sorry. You've no idea how many times I've wished I could turn the clock back and start again." The words poured out and she buried her head in her hands and could not look at him for shame. She told him about the cider and the thunderstorm and the hayloft, and by the time she'd finished, her body was shaking with sobs.

"Oh, Kathleen, I wish it had been me." He kissed her throat, her mouth; wrapped his arms around her and pulled her close.

Now it was too late; she wanted him so much it was impossible to hold back.

CHAPTER 16

She clung to him and closed her eyes because it was wonderful and frightening all at the same time. As he struggled with his clothes she kissed and hung on to him, afraid to let go; afraid of losing him. She helped him unbutton her blouse and take off her skirt and everything else. She put her hand around the back of his neck and kissed him. He pulled her close to him, and the moment was so exquisite she forgot to breathe. With his arms around her they lay there on the sofa, drifting together, not caring about anything beyond themselves.

Eventually, he raised himself on one elbow and brushed the hair from her face. "Why, oh why didn't you tell me you were in trouble right at the start? All I got were messages telling me to keep away, and I thought, *This girl doesn't care for me one bit.*"

She opened her eyes to look at him. "When I realised I was having a baby, I was so scared I'd no idea what to do." She took his hand, brought it to her lips and kissed it. "I thought you'd never want to speak to me again. You'd think I was terribly fast; not the sort of girl you'd want to have anything to do with."

"How on earth did it happen? You said he gave you cider. Did he force you? Is that how it happened?"

"I'm not sure I can explain it even to myself. I was drunk with the cider, of course, but it was more than that. I wanted to feel what love was like. I don't know what I imagined. I was stupid, so stupid." She buried her face in her hands and felt ashamed all over again, and wondered how it was that he was still there beside her, when he knew what she had done.

He leaned over and kissed her forehead. Then he stroked her hair and ran a finger down her neck and over her shoulder. "You were young and he took advantage of you. He should've known better."

She caught his hand and held it, twining her fingers around his. "You can't imagine how often I wish it'd all been different."

"I think I can… if you'd told them I was the father, it could have been different." He gathered her in his arms and held her close. "I'd have married you. I wouldn't have cared, if only you could've been my wife."

"You'd have married me, even though I was carrying another man's child?" She felt her heart must break, and her voice trembled as she spoke. "I must go. I can't stay any longer; I'll be missed – Jim sent me to order hurdles, and Edith's looking after Tom." She began to pull on her clothes in panic and confusion. "There'll be questions and I shan't know what to say."

"Come back again. Please come back," he pleaded.

"I don't know… I can't say." She buried her face in her hands.

"I'll be here Wednesday, same time. Come if you can. I'll be waiting." He kissed her forehead and let her go.

She ran from him, and wondered why she was running away when what she wanted more than anything was to stay. She hurried along by the river, thankful for the shade of arching branches that shielded her from the scorching sun, and raced up the lane to Higher Haydn, sweat glistening on her forehead.

Jim was fuming, ready to burst into one of his rages. "Took your time, didn't you?" he began.

Her flustered explanation of having to wait at the sawmill and seeing to business of her own in the village met with grudging acceptance, and the moment of danger passed.

While day lasted, she dared not think of what she'd done. The very thought of Robert and her together made her heart race and her mind seize up, and she must surely give herself away if she didn't keep her wits about her. But when it grew dark and she was alone, she sat on the front doorstep and watched the crescent moon and the stars appear one by one. And then she thought of Robert and wondered how life could be so sweet and so terrible all at the same time, and knew she would go to him again if she could.

And she did. Once, sometimes twice a week she'd escape to Gardener's Cottage, driving the truck to the village and leaving it in the square so that people would think she was making a delivery. Then she'd walk across the path fields, and Robert would be waiting for her, and they'd make love and linger for as long as they dared. Everything about her love for Robert felt right, and it amazed her that, knowing what he did, he still loved her. She lived only in the moment and it hardly mattered what had gone before or what might come after, although she knew – they both knew – it must end. But a door had been opened and the light had exposed the ugliness of her marriage. There was no longer anywhere to hide from the truth, and nowhere to flee from it.

Towards the end of August the doctor allowed Jim to hobble about on crutches. His leg was healing well and the splints could come off in a couple of weeks. Meanwhile, Jim insisted on checking every task Kathleen did about the farm. Instead of making a fuss about the truck and forbidding her to use it, he made her drive him everywhere. She found herself taking him to market or The Southwood Inn, and fetching him late in the evening when they turned him out and closed the doors. There was baking still to do and deliveries to be made, and at the weekends the barn café was filled with visitors. It became more and more difficult to get away to Gardener's Cottage.

"Robert," she said one day as he held her close, "I don't think I'm going to be able to come again. I've hardly a moment to myself and Jim watches me like a hawk. He'll suspect very soon."

"I don't want to let you go, ever," Robert said. "If you could get away just once in a while…" His voice drifted off and his eyes looked very bright.

"But where could we meet? You said the new gardener starts at the beginning of September."

Robert held her close and whispered, "You know I love you, Kathleen. If there's any way we can be together, you will get word to me, won't you?"

She nodded, not trusting herself to look into his eyes, because they both knew that this was the last time. It seemed so final, so dreadfully final, yet something deep inside her denied that it was so. How could it be the end if they truly loved each other?

They got dressed slowly and she left the cottage first and walked back by the river, where brambles grew in profusion and the blackberries were ripe and ready for picking. She wondered how she'd manage to live without Robert, knowing that he was there but not seeing him. It couldn't be as it was before, because now she knew that he loved her and that she loved him. There it was: the simple fact that changed everything and yet changed nothing. There was no way back to a different time; a time when the truth was hidden.

She found Jim in a foul temper, probably because he'd not had a woman for a long time. The very idea of him pawing her, his mouth pressed down on hers, the foul, stale smell of cider on his breath, filled her with revulsion. Yet it would not be long until the splints came off and he would demand of her what was due.

The next day, when Kathleen was in the dairy talking to Dolly, a wave of nausea swept over her. The feeling passed and she thought no more about it, but the day after, when Edith put stew on the hob to cook, the smell of the raw meat disgusted her and, hand over mouth, she made a dash for the sink.

"Whatever is it?" Edith asked. "You look as white as a sheet."

"I just feel a bit odd," Kathleen replied, sitting down on

the settle. There was something familiar... it was like this when she was expecting Tom.

"You'm looking none too clever," Edith went on.

"I... I don't feel very well. I think maybe I'm going to have a baby."

"Why, my dear, that's wonderful news!" exclaimed Edith. "I was wondering when you were going to have another little 'un. Tom's gone four – time to be having another." Edith clasped her hands in excitement. "Have you told Jim yet? Does he know?"

"No," said Kathleen. "I've only just this minute realised it myself." Rising from the settle, she steadied herself. "Can you manage on your own for a few minutes while I go and lie down?"

"Of course, my dear, take as long as you need. 'Tis wonderful news. Fancy – another baby round the house come spring."

Kathleen lay on the bed and looked up at the crack in the ceiling that ran all the way to the window, and listened to the sound of her heart beating. When she and Robert had made love she had felt reckless, *been* reckless, because nothing else had mattered. And then it occurred to her that this was what she'd wanted all along: his child; a child conceived in love.

For a brief moment she imagined Sarah finding out about the baby and divorcing Robert. But in the next instant she realised what a forlorn hope that was, because Sarah wouldn't take Kathleen seriously as a rival. She'd dismiss the whole thing as a mere indiscretion by Robert, like getting one of the maids into trouble. But if Jim knew she'd been unfaithful, he would turn her out; send her packing without a penny. Then how would she manage: a woman on her own expecting a baby, with nowhere to live and no money coming in? He must not find out, ever. When she'd been carrying Tom, Jim had treated her well, so the sooner she told him about this baby the better it would be for her. She'd pretend the baby had started before his accident, work out the dates very carefully, and complain about being overdue when she knew she was nothing of the sort.

At dinner time Jim hobbled in, and lowered himself with a grunt onto his usual chair. Edith was flitting about like a sparrow that'd just found a store of crumbs, and kept looking at Kathleen as if expecting every moment to hear the announcement she knew must come.

"For goodness' sake, Mother, sit down and let Kathleen put dinner on the plates. You've been like a cat on hot bricks ever since I come in." He looked from one to the other, seeking an explanation. "Something's going on; something I should know about."

Kathleen stood there, putting stew and dumplings on the plates, feeling his eyes fix on her.

"Well?" he demanded in an exasperated voice.

"I'm expecting," she said, making it sound as normal as possible. "At least, I'm pretty certain I am, although it's early days, of course."

"So you thought you'd tell my mother afore you told me. That's why she's been flapping around."

"'Twasn't like that at all," protested Edith. "The poor girl come over all queer this morning and had to go and lie down. That's how I knows."

Kathleen could feel Jim scrutinising her face.

"You must be near on two months gone," he observed.

"Yes, it must have been about the end of June. Just before you had your accident." She dared to give him a direct look. "It's lucky I haven't felt queasy before now, what with all the extra work."

She hadn't meant it as a criticism, but he took it that way.

"Don't think you did anything special, like. 'Twas an emergency." He glowered at her. "Women's work is in the kitchen and the dairy and don't you forget it."

Her throat tightened in anger, but she bit her lip and said nothing. Let him think what he liked; she didn't care as long as her secret was safe.

Kathleen had been right about one thing: Jim did show consideration to the extent that he went along with her when she said she felt tired or unwell, and didn't make excessive demands on her. No doubt he found his satisfaction elsewhere. Once his leg had mended he'd often go to the village after tea, and sometimes she'd be asleep when he rolled into bed with so much noise and bluster that he'd wake her up. When she couldn't get back to sleep, she'd lie awake pretending it was Robert lying next to her, and that she only had to put out a hand to touch him.

One day in October, when Kathleen was making a delivery to the village, she almost literally bumped into Robert. Caught completely off guard, she stood there, unable to utter a word.

"Good morning, Mrs Wilcox," Robert said. "I hope I find you well?"

"Yes, yes," she replied, still flustered. "And you – are you well?"

He ignored the question. "There's something I need to tell you. We can't talk here. Can you take a walk this afternoon – along by the river?"

"Yes, I suppose so… I might have to bring Tom with me."

"All the better. About three o'clock?"

She nodded.

"Well, good day to you, Mrs Wilcox. So nice to have met you."

The afternoon light was low, filtering through the hazel and alder branches that overhung the river. Bluebottles feasted on watery blackberries and swarms of midges rose and fell in a never-ending dance. And in the distance Kathleen could see Robert walking towards them, and her heart skipped a beat.

"Who's that man, Mummy?" asked Tom, pointing at Robert.

"Don't point, dear. It's rude."

Tom lowered his arm and looked up at her. "Nice man?" he enquired.

Kathleen smiled. "Yes, he's a very nice man. He owns the farm, and he lets us live there if Daddy pays him pennies."

Reassured by her answer, Tom smiled. When Robert reached them, he raised his cap to Kathleen and bent down to shake Tom by the hand.

"Mummy says you're a nice man," announced Tom.

"I'm pleased to hear that," said Robert. "And I hope you take care of her, because she's a very nice lady."

Tom grinned and slipped his hand into Kathleen's.

She looked at Robert and sensed that something had changed; something she could not put a name to. Her mind rippled with possibilities, fantasy chasing fantasy in ever-widening circles. "You wanted to tell me something?" she said.

"I find I cannot live here any more." He gave her a meaningful look. "I find it too painful – the whole thing; longing for what I cannot have." His eyes left hers and he gazed into the distance, where the river flowed into trees that marked the start of the Alston Hall grounds. "There's work to be done and it's my duty to do it. I'll be taking my seat in the House of Lords shortly. As a result," he turned to face her again, "I shall be spending as much time as possible in London."

Although she heard the words, they seemed unreal. How could Robert even think of spending time in London when she was here? He was waiting, waiting for her to reply, yet there was only silence and Tom's hand holding hers.

At length, she spoke. "I hope you'll find life in London more fulfilling." As she said the words it sounded as if there was an edge of bitterness which she hadn't intended. She felt numb, as if she'd just been told that someone she loved had died.

"Don't look like you'm late, my dear," said Meg Blackler, the midwife, running her hands over Kathleen's bulge as she lay on the bed. It was early April and Kathleen had invited Meg to tea at the farm. "Maybe you made a mistake counting the days. I'd say there's a couple of weeks to go afore you'll see this little 'un."

"I'm sure the dates are right," replied Kathleen. "Jim had his accident at the very end of June and was laid up for six weeks with his leg in splints, so it must have happened before then."

Meg shook her head and pursed her lips. "Baby don't seem big enough for that."

Kathleen laughed. "Well, I'm pleased the baby isn't big. Less work for me to do when the time comes."

As April dragged on Kathleen complained about the tedium of waiting for the baby to come, but it wasn't until the 27th of the month that her wish was granted. The birth didn't take as long as Tom's but the pain was just as bad. She'd forgotten just how much it hurt, giving birth. "There'd be far fewer children brought into the world if women remembered what it was like," she remarked to Edith, when it was all over and she cradled her daughter.

"Real picture, she is," said Edith, beaming at the tiny, screwed-up features and wisps of brown hair. "Looks just like her mother, she does."

Kathleen smiled and looked down at the new life in her arms, and all she saw was Robert; not because the baby looked like Robert, but because she *was* Robert's.

She named her Elizabeth, called her Beth for short, whispered to her things that no one else could possibly understand unless they knew the secret, and was grateful that she could lavish all the love and care in the world on Beth without anyone thinking it the least strange. To her immense relief Jim took little interest when the baby turned out to be a girl, leaving Kathleen and Beth to grow close to one another in peace.

She wrote to her mother, Alice, and Rose, telling them about Beth. Her mother sent a postcard from Scarborough some weeks later, congratulating her, but giving no explanation as to why she was in Scarborough. Alice's letter came in a parcel containing a little white cotton dress with smocking, pink embroidery, and puff sleeves.

And I'll be finding out what it's like to be a mother myself pretty soon. I'm expecting a baby in October. The first bit – feeling sick and all that – was pretty ghastly but I'm a lot better now. I expect you'll say there's worse to come, so I shall just enjoy what I can and put up with the rest. I'm not sure whether I'd rather have a boy or a girl. I keep changing my mind!

Your ever-loving friend,
Alice

PS: Binkey sends his regards and says congratulations on the birth of your daughter.

Rose replied within the week, saying how delighted everyone was to hear the news and hoping that all was well with Kathleen and the nipper. She enclosed a teddy she'd bought:

...from one of them stalls down the Lane, 'cause every girl needs something to cuddle, don't she? And this 'un's got a kind face.

And by the way, your Uncle Charlie says mind and get your driving licence made out for all vehicles, not just cars, now you're driving that truck all over the place. He's heard

down the depot they're bringing in driving tests next year,
and if you ain't got your licence by then you'll have to take
the test.

Ta-ta for now.
Love from all of us,
Rose

Kathleen ran a hand over the teddy and stroked his ear. He'd a kind look about him, just like Rose said.

One August afternoon, when there were errands to be done – nothing very much, just picking up a few stamps and some knitting wool that Edith had ordered – Kathleen put Beth in the pram and set off to Southwood. Beth was fast asleep long before they reached the village. Kathleen parked the pram outside the post office and went in. There was a man at the counter, being attended to by the postmistress. A flush of excitement coloured Kathleen's cheeks as she realised that the man was Robert; yet when he turned and saw her the look he gave was that of a stranger – distant and deliberate – and her smile faded.

"I hear congratulations are in order, Mrs Wilcox," he said. "I believe you have a daughter."

"Yes, she's called Beth." Kathleen drew back her lips in a pretence of a smile, acutely aware of the postmistress on the other side of the counter, observing them. "May I show her to you, Lord Neville? She's in the pram outside." She walked with studied nonchalance towards the door, and Robert followed.

"I suppose it's as well for you that you've made things

up with your husband." His voice, although polite, had within it a trace of sarcasm.

Kathleen stared at him in dismay, smarting from the assumption. "No, no, Beth is yours," she said, her voice no more than a whisper.

Stunned into silence, Robert stared at her. "Can you be sure?" he asked, the sharpness all melting away.

She held his gaze. "Completely and utterly sure," she said, and lapsed into silence as a village woman, on her way to the post office, came close. Robert and Kathleen both smiled and greeted her.

"Why on earth didn't you tell me?" hissed Robert when the woman had gone.

"I didn't know I was expecting that last time we were together at Gardener's Cottage," Kathleen answered, keeping her voice low.

"But you must have known later. You must have known when we met by the river." Robert's eyes rested on his daughter as she stirred in her sleep.

"How could it have made any difference if I had told you?" Kathleen was looking at Beth too, not trusting herself to meet his eyes.

"There must be something I can do," he said.

"Such as?" she replied. "Neither of us is free. I can't imagine in my wildest dreams that Sarah would ever divorce you. There is absolutely nowhere we can go, and just think of the repercussions if we were found out! You might survive the scandal but Jim would turn me out. I'd be destitute."

Their conversation was halted once more as an old man hobbled past them. He rested on his stick for a moment and raised a hand to his cap. "Afternoon, Your Lordship. Fine day."

Robert acknowledged the greeting and waited until the fellow had gone. "You'll let me see her? You will let me see Beth, won't you?"

"I'd love to, but it would be difficult at the moment without somebody getting suspicious. Perhaps when she's older..."

"If there's ever a chance..." Robert's voice shook. He turned on his heel and walked away.

She watched him go and gazed at his back all the way to the white gates in the square. If ever there was a chance, one day he might talk to Beth and hold her hand, and the very idea was so beautiful and so precious it hurt Kathleen just to think about it.

CHAPTER 17

April 1937

Kathleen sat at her desk in the parlour and looked out over the garden. When business had expanded she'd decided she needed an office, so a year or more ago she'd bought the desk at an auction sale, and in it she kept accounts in leather-bound journals and money in a cash box locked in one of the drawers.

The books done for the week, she sat back and thought about how time had flown, and how very soon it would be Beth's third birthday. She pictured Beth: dark-haired and brown-eyed, often laughing, sometimes serious, toddling round the farm, asking questions, and scolding the hens or petting the cats as the fancy took her. Next week Kathleen would take the bus to Plymouth and buy a really nice present for Beth – a book of nursery rhymes with lots of coloured pictures, or a doll with eyes that closed and hair she could comb. And she'd make a sponge cake and put raspberry jam between the layers, with icing on the top and three candles… she'd need to put candles and candleholders on the shopping list too.

Only another two years and Beth would be off to school, like Tom. He'd started at Southwood School in the September following his fifth birthday. He could read quite well now and would look at picture books in bed, although he always wanted Kathleen to read the story he'd chosen before he went to sleep. He'd written his name in the last book she'd bought and had shown her the spidery letters with pride.

Business had prospered. She supplied shops in Southwood and Ivybridge with butter, cream, cheese, eggs, roasting chickens, and much more besides. Not that all of it was from the farm itself; a fair amount came from the wives of farmers and smallholders on the Alston Estate. Her standards were high and the produce always commanded a good price. Cakes, pastries, pies and hams, made to Edith's recipes and bearing the Higher Haydn label, had gained a reputation.

Being so well organised now, Kathleen had more time for the children. And when Alice had written to say that her baby had arrived, Kathleen had gone to Plymouth, bought the little boy a romper suit and sent it off, all nicely packaged up with her letter of congratulation.

Edith had more money than she'd ever known in her life but, having little idea what to do with it other than save it, she'd often treat the children to sweets or a toy. Kathleen smiled as she thought of the pleasure that gave Edith. She'd tell her she was spoiling the children, but always said it with laughter in her eyes so that Edith knew it was all right and that Kathleen wasn't really cross.

Jim's accident had been a blessing in more ways than one. Kathleen smiled wryly to herself whenever she thought about it, because since then he'd allowed her use of the truck for deliveries, and she'd heeded Uncle Charlie's warning about her driving licence and had it made out for 'all vehicles'. Mind you, Jim did well out of the arrangement too. He knew that every Monday, when she drove to Ivybridge, she'd fill up with petrol, pay for it herself and save him the expense. It was a tacit agreement between them that a full tank of petrol was her price to pay for using the truck. That scarcely bothered her now that she had money to buy whatever she and the children needed. She'd even gone to town and bought herself an outfit at Spooners department store. It may not have been up to London fashion standards but it was much more becoming than the dungarees she wore every day for work.

Despite all this, a yawning gap had opened up in her life; a space that only Robert could have filled. After their last meeting he was rarely seen in Southwood at all. Rumour had it he was chairing a committee in London that was trying to find ways to help farmers in the slump: falling prices, year after year, in the face of cheap imports. Perhaps he was having some success, because this year the price of grain was up.

Notes and coins accumulated in the cash box; so many that Kathleen wondered whether she'd be able to buy herself an Austin 7 car one day soon. She felt nervous about keeping money like that in the house, although there'd never been a burglary on the Alston Estate. One day she mentioned to Jim that she was thinking of opening a bank account.

"If you trust they bankers with your money, you're a fool," he replied.

"Bankers are highly respectable people," she argued. "You can hardly imagine they'll run off with customers' deposits."

But Jim merely scowled and refused to say anything more on the subject.

Undeterred, she took twenty pounds from the cash box and on her next trip to Ivybridge asked to see the manager of the Provincial Bank.

The manager wanted to know where Mr Wilcox was, and appeared astonished that she should even consider opening a bank account in her own name without her husband. "Most irregular, most irregular," he said, shaking his head. "I cannot understand why your husband would send you here unaccompanied because his consent is required."

"My husband didn't send me here, and frankly there's no reason why he should." Her tone was icy but her eyes full of fire. "The money I wish to deposit is business income – income from *my* business. It has nothing to do with my husband; it's quite separate from the farm."

The manager leaned back in his seat, palms resting on the desk, a condescending smile on his lips. "My dear Mrs... Mrs Wilcox, the bank is not interested in a farmer's wife and her pin money. You cannot have an account in your own name, in any event. If, however, your husband wanted to open an account himself and allow you to draw on it, that would be a different matter. Now, be a good woman and run along. Stop wasting my time."

She ground her teeth in anger at the insolence of the man. That pompous idiot was getting none of her money; she'd never open an account with the Provincial Bank, ever. "You haven't even done me the courtesy of asking the nature of my business." She pronounced each word in a way that would have brought praise from the elocution teacher at Chiltern Ladies' College.

A puzzled look clouded the manager's face and the space between his eyebrows narrowed as he grappled with the notion that the woman before him was something other than a mere farmer's wife with ideas above her station. But before he could recover, Kathleen had turned and was walking swiftly away.

"My dear woman—"

The sound of the door being shut forcefully interrupted the conciliatory speech taking shape in his mind.

Still bristling with indignation, she drove back to the farm. That intolerable, opinionated little man – how dare he treat her as if she existed only as an extension of her husband? She gripped the steering wheel with a fierce determination and clenched her teeth until her jaw ached.

When she reached home, Mr Greenwood's van was parked in the yard and Mr Greenwood himself was sitting in the kitchen, talking to Edith.

"You're early today!" Kathleen exclaimed, returning his smile. "We don't normally see you until the afternoon." She glanced at the clock. "And here it is, only half past eleven."

"I'm afraid I've fewer customers these days," he replied. "The company's reorganised my round and from now on I'll be coming late morning. I hope that's all right with you?"

"Of course, Mr Greenwood, that's quite convenient."

"I've made him a cup of tea and given him a piece of cake for his elevenses," chipped in Edith. "I've given him the list Jim made out, but I couldn't find the money no place."

"How much is it?" Kathleen craned her neck to look at the bill.

"Ten pounds, two and sixpence," replied Mr Greenwood.

Kathleen took the money from her purse and set it down on the table next to the bill. "I expect Jim was intending to sort it out when he came in at dinner time," she said with characteristic stoicism.

"Look what Mr Greenwood's left." Edith held up two small carved wooden figures, each only a couple of inches tall. One was a goat with horns and a beard; the other a bear, lifting its head as if to growl.

"I hope you'll accept these for your children," said Mr Greenwood. "I seem to remember your little girl has a birthday soon."

"That's right: she's three this month."

"My father made them for me when I was a boy but I'm a bit too old for toys now," said Mr Greenwood.

"They're really lovely." Kathleen picked up the figures and examined them closely. "Your father was a very clever man, Mr Greenwood."

"He was a cabinetmaker by trade, but in the winter evenings he would get out his knife and carve things from bits of wood he'd picked up during the summer."

"Where did he carry on business?" She could tell Mr Greenwood wasn't local but couldn't quite place his accent.

"Oh, a long way away," he said. "Not round here. It was a long time ago and much has happened since then."

"Really? Would that be before the war?" she asked. "Oh, I'm sorry; I'm not doubting what you say."

But Mr Greenwood was rising from his chair and nodding to Edith and thanking her for the tea and cake. "Well, I must be on my way," he said, picking up the order and the money from the table.

The sound of his van chugging down the lane had scarcely died away when Jim strolled into the kitchen and slumped down on the settle, saying he thought it must be nearly dinner time.

"What a pity you've just missed Mr Greenwood," said Kathleen, a slightly acerbic quality creeping into her voice. "I've paid the bill for you. It was just over ten pounds." She held out the receipt to him.

"'Bout time you paid for a few things round here. Been far too lenient, I have; I can see that now." He scowled at her and ignored the receipt.

"We have an agreement. You said all you wanted was—"

"I know what I said, woman. You don't have to remind me." The look he gave her implied that she was a complete idiot. "You've no idea, have you? You've no idea how much I'm getting for the beasts at market, have you? And the price of milk – where d'you think that's headed?"

"That's why I think we should make as much as we can out of butter and cream and feed the skim milk to the pigs, and then—"

"So you think you know better than me how to run this farm, is that it?"

"I was only saying—"

"Well, don't. I don't know how any farmer's expected to make a living these days. What us could do with is another war; a damn good war."

"You can't be serious about wanting another war." She stared disapprovingly at him. "Nobody wants another war."

"It'd put prices up, that's what a war'd do. 'Tis the only way us is ever going to get a living wage again."

She did her best to stay calm. "Where would you say the biggest profit comes from?" she asked.

"You take care what you're saying, woman." He was waving a finger at her; something he hadn't done in quite a while. "You keep your mouth shut and don't meddle in things you don't understand. There's a way of doing things round here – I do things the way my father did, and his father before that, and that isn't going to change just 'cause some bossy female comes along and thinks she knows better."

Kathleen sighed, gave up trying to reason with him, and set the table for dinner. It was clear that the more she earned, the more resentful Jim became, but she needed to earn money to buy clothes and shoes for the children and herself.

He'd made no demands on her in the bedroom since Beth's birth, and that at least was something to be grateful for. But that night, as she sat alone by the fire, he came home from Southwood Inn in a foul temper, reeking of cider. He demanded she come to bed, grabbed her hand, and dragged her up the stairs. The thought of him filled her with revulsion but she was too terrified to protest. And what was worse, taken by surprise, she'd had no opportunity to put her cap in place. He shut the bedroom door with such force that the noise might have woken the children. Flinging his jacket on the floor, he fumbled and swore at his belt buckle and tugged and pulled every stitch from his body. She stood trembling as he staggered towards her.

"Whatcher waiting for?" He leered at her. "Don't you want me?" He pawed with drunken fingers at the buttons on her blouse and, awash with frustration, ripped it from her shoulders.

"Jim, please, I'm very tired. My back's aching. I just want to go to sleep."

"You're my wife; I have my rights. Take the rest of your clothes off, or I'll take 'em off for you."

"Please be quiet. You'll wake the children and your mother." Then, hand over mouth, stifling a scream, she backed away, and let her skirt fall to the floor.

"That's more like it," he said.

Shaking with fear, she stood before him. He eyed her up and down for an instant, before grabbing a wrist and dragging her to the bed, where he flung her down. She wanted to cry out, to plead with him not to do it; she opened her mouth but not a sound came out. His hands held her down, his fingers dug into her flesh, and she closed her eyes to blot out the sight of him. He was hot and sweaty, with an odour that disgusted her. She tried to scream but his hand, pressing down on her face, drowned her cries and nearly suffocated her. The throaty yell he gave lasted for several seconds. Triumphant, his body relaxed and he rolled away, turning his back on her. He pulled the covers over his shoulder, sucking in a draught of cold air.

Kathleen lay sobbing quietly to herself, listening to him snore, and praying she would not fall pregnant again.

CHAPTER 18

Sleep eluded Kathleen until the early hours, and even then oblivion brought no relief. In her dreams Jim mocked her when she found she was expecting, saying it was her own fault, and she woke up full of anxiety and apprehension. There was no one she could tell; no one she could confide in. She was alone, utterly alone.

She wondered whether she might have to put up with this every night, and vowed she'd take precautions like she used to, if only it wasn't too late. *Oh, please let it not be too late.* She asked herself if there was a reason for the way he'd behaved. Maybe something had provoked him. Had *she* provoked him? A string of possibilities ran through her exhausted mind as she dressed and went to see to the children.

Tom, who was sitting up in bed thumbing through a book that had pictures of farm trucks and tractors, looked up and grinned as she came in. "Daddy's going to buy one of these," he said, pointing to a shiny red tractor parked in an immaculate farmyard. "He says I can drive it."

"Hmm… that'll be nice," she murmured. "It's time you got up and had some breakfast. You don't want to be late for school." *Where does Jim think he's going to find the money?*

It's too bad of him, leading Tom on like that. Perhaps he was expecting her to pay for the tractor; maybe that was the explanation. She thought about having it out with him, getting things straight. But that would only give him an excuse to punish her, and she knew what the punishment would be, so she kept quiet and said nothing.

In Beth's room she pulled back the curtains and looked at blinking, sleepy eyes gazing up at her. "There – isn't it a lovely day? What do you think we should do today? We could go to the pond this afternoon; see if the tadpoles have grown legs and started turning into frogs. Would you like that?" Chatting all the time about this and that, she dressed Beth, took her by the hand, and led her downstairs. Where Jim had gripped her on the arm a bruise was starting to show, so she pulled her sleeve down, hoping Edith wouldn't notice it.

Edith was talking – something about the dairymaid and having to replace her – and Kathleen answered her, not paying much attention to where the conversation was leading. Saying she'd go and talk to the dairymaid herself, Kathleen left the breakfast table and went off to the dairy. The dairymaid, whose name was Nancy, had only been with them twelve months. Dolly had given up work (because it was all getting a bit too much at her age, she said), and had suggested that Nancy from the village might be willing to take over, and so the change had been made.

In the dairy, Nancy was churning the butter. Her body, silhouetted against the light from the window, told its own story. Kathleen wondered why she hadn't noticed it before. It was so obvious that the girl was expecting; likely to give birth in two or three months. As she entered, Nancy looked up and made an attempt at a smile.

"Just on the turn, ma'am," she said. "I needs to keep going."

While they waited for the churning to be finished, Kathleen pretended to inspect the stores and get ready things needed for delivery that day. And when the butter had come, Nancy stood, hands on hips, her cheeks red with exertion or embarrassment – it was impossible to say which – and waited.

"I can't help noticing you're expecting a baby," Kathleen said.

Nancy refused to raise her eyes. She stared at the flagstones and folded her hands neatly in front of her, making her predicament all the more obvious. "I'm sorry, ma'am. I was going to tell you, quite soon. It's just that I want to go on working as long as I can."

"Have you anyone to support you? Is the father of the baby standing by you?"

Nancy went even redder and muttered that she'd only her mother to care for her. Despite careful questioning, she steadfastly refused to say who the father was; only that he was not in a position to marry her, because he was already married himself.

"I will have to find a new dairymaid," Kathleen said. "Perhaps if I find one fairly soon, you'll be able to show her how we do things here before you leave to have your baby."

Nancy gave a grateful smile. "If it's all the same to you, ma'am, I'd better get on now."

Walking slowly towards the yard door, Kathleen wondered whether Dolly might know of another dairymaid. Then voices coming from outside raised her curiosity, and she hung back in the shadows of the passage to listen.

"This cannot go on, Mr Wilcox – the other tenants are complaining." It was Alston Estate's steward speaking.

A stubborn silence followed, and then Jim said, his voice shaking with barely contained hostility, "I'm not the only one round here got ragwort, you know. Why pick on me?"

"Now don't you take that tone with me, my man. If you'd pulled out the ragwort when it first appeared on Lower Meadow last summer, it wouldn't have seeded and spread to the other farms."

A snort escaped Jim's throat. "Expect me to spot it now, and pull it out, afore it's flowered?"

Silently, Kathleen implored him to hold his tongue, but Jim had the bit between his teeth and his animosity was galloping away with him.

"If you think I'm—"

Seizing the initiative, and before he could say another word, she walked from the shadows into the yard and hailed the steward.

Immediately, his attention was distracted. "Good morning, Mrs Wilcox." He raised his hat.

Jim scowled, while beside him Kathleen chatted about the late spring and how wet it'd been, but at least it was growing warmer now, and perhaps they'd have a better hay cut than you might've thought back at Easter.

At length, the steward doffed his cap to her again, but before he left he turned to Jim. "I shall inspect again in a week's time, and I expect the farm to be clear of ragwort." As he spoke, he raised a forefinger to him.

Jim stared back at the steward in insolent defiance.

Kathleen dared not look; she'd seen it before. His face would be livid, the veins standing out on his forehead, his eyes narrowed to ferocious slits. The steward was out of earshot before she dared speak. "I've a bit of spare time this afternoon. I could check a few hedges for you, if you like."

The look he gave her was nothing but contempt, and she wished she'd kept her mouth shut and hadn't bothered.

Over tea, Edith complained that Jim was wasting money, paying a man to do the milking for him, instead of doing it himself like he used to. She'd grown bold in her old age, altogether more confident since Kathleen had shown her how to make money, and these days she spoke as she found. "You sit on your backside and let others do the work," she reprimanded him. "You've become lazy, relying on your wife to bring in the money."

Edith had gone too far – much too far – this time. Jim slammed his cup down so hard it broke into smithereens and hot tea flowed across the tablecloth. The cream dish, next to the loaf of bread, was the only place Kathleen dared look. She heard him pull back the chair, its legs scraping the flagstones, then toss it to one side and march from the room. Tom watched tea drip silently onto the floor. Beth's face crumpled and she began to cry.

"Hush, hush, little one, it's all right, Mummy's here." Kathleen lifted Beth and cradled her in her arms. "Please don't say things like that to him again, Edith."

Jim would take it out on her for all the insults he'd borne that day, she knew he would, and she was fearful

225

of what the night would bring. Frustration and anger fermented in him, and when he came to bed they exploded with such ferocity she scarcely knew what to say or where to put herself. He took pleasure in taunting her, and laughed in her face when she cowered before him. A gaping void, a black hole had opened up in her life and she teetered on the brink of a chasm. She tried not to look down. *If you look down, you'll feel giddy and fall*, she told herself, so she did her best not to stare into the abyss, and turned her mind to practical things instead, such as not getting in the family way, and finding another dairymaid.

She asked Dolly, she asked around the village, but no one was interested in the job at Higher Haydn Farm. She even mentioned it to Mr Greenwood on his next visit, without any real expectation that he would be able to help, and was surprised to hear him say he'd heard of a farmer's daughter, east of Ivybridge, who was looking for work.

"But she'd never be able to travel all that distance," Kathleen said.

"She wouldn't have to, if she lived here," suggested Mr Greenwood.

Now that was a thought. In days gone by most workers had lived on the farm: men above the barn and stables; women in the house. The girl could be housed above the dairy. It wouldn't take much to feed another mouth, and they'd be able to keep an eye on her. "What a brilliant idea, Mr Greenwood," she said.

"Comes from a hard-working family," he continued.

"Suit you very well, I'd say. I could bring her over to see you, if you like."

"That's very kind of you but I wouldn't want to put you to any trouble."

"It would be my pleasure."

"You're absolutely sure you don't mind? It would be most kind. Now the grass is growing, we've so much milk it's hard to keep up. We could use another pair of hands right away."

Kathleen cleared out the attic above the dairy and whitewashed the walls. It was all settled within the week and the dairymaid, whose name was Annie, moved in. A pleasant girl with round features and straw-coloured hair, Annie had large blue eyes and freckles over a snub nose. Despite her plump appearance, she was as fit as a fiddle, and got on with her work. Nancy took to her right away, and the two of them could be heard chattering and laughing as far away as the kitchen.

"How's the new dairymaid?" enquired Mr Greenwood the following month. "Doing well, I hope."

"Yes, it's all working out very well, thank you," said Kathleen. "You must get to know a lot of people, travelling from farm to farm like you do." She signalled him to sit down at the table while she put the kettle on. "How did you get into the business? Do you come from a family of farmers?"

"No, not farmers – at least, not on my father's side."

"No, of course not. How silly of me; I remember you saying he was a cabinetmaker."

"That's right, but he died many years ago."

"I'm sorry. Did he work around here?"

"No, in London – in a number of places – until he went into partnership and started up business at a place called Bethnal Green."

"Bethnal Green?"

"Why? Have you heard of it?" Mr Greenwood's eyes registered surprise.

"Heard of it? I used to live there," she replied. "I was very young when we left, but I can remember some things, like going down Petticoat Lane for a bargain, and passing the market and smelling all the fruit and vegetables. And your family, they lived in Bethnal Green too?"

"No, no. That's where my father had his workshop. We lived south of the railway in Spitalfields; one of those great tenement buildings."

"Oh yes, I know. My Uncle Charlie still lives in Bethnal Green, in the same house he always used to. And Rose, my cousin, she sent Beth this teddy she bought down the Lane. Teddy's fur's wearing a bit thin, especially the ear she sucks." She picked up the bear and smoothed the threadbare patch. "She won't go to sleep without him, ever."

"Children need to feel safe, don't they?"

"Did you ever go down the Lane for a bargain, Mr Greenwood?"

He shook his head and gave a rueful smile. "We went the other way. Mother was always afraid we'd get run over if we had to cross the main road – all that traffic."

"Your mother, was she from a farming family?"

"Brought up on a smallholding, she was – used to big, open spaces and village life. I don't think she ever got over moving to the city." He glanced at the grandfather clock.

"Is that really the time? I must be off, or I'll be late. Thank you so much for the tea."

June was wonderfully dry. The hay cut was the best for years, but now everywhere needed rain. The sun scorched down from a near cloudless sky and Jim was hard put to find grazing for the herd. Great patches of dust round the roots of the oak trees in Higher Path Field showed where the cows gathered each day, trying to escape the flies.

Kathleen had a few deliveries to make in Ivybridge one morning, and when Jim announced that he was taking a couple of calves to market, she begged a lift from him. The cab was stiflingly hot and she wound down the window and flapped a hand in front of her face for a breeze.

So far that day, nothing had gone right. Tom had complained of a headache and wanted to stay home from school, but she hadn't let him and now she was wondering if she'd been wrong and maybe he was poorly after all. Beth had eaten next to nothing for breakfast, and Edith had said that in her day you'd be made to sit there till you'd finished what was on your plate, but Kathleen had let Beth get down and Edith had sniffed and said she supposed Kathleen knew best.

Jim started the engine and swore as he grasped the steering wheel, saying it was hot enough to take the skin off your hands. He found a bit of sacking and wrapped it round the wheel. Kathleen took a deep breath and waited for him to crunch the truck into action. He'd had a new clutch fitted last year and the man at the garage had said that the gearbox needed replacing, but Jim thought he knew better. *Please don't let it break down today*, she prayed. *I could do without anything else going wrong today.*

When they got to Ivybridge the shop in Fore Street complained that she'd brought the wrong cakes, and the hotel insisted that they'd ordered extra cream, and when would she be delivering it? She laddered a stocking, snagging it on a chair as she left the café. Instead of returning to the searing heat of the truck (parked in full sun), she loitered under the café's red-and-white awning, and waited for Jim to come. Not ten yards away a conversation was taking place among a group of farmers, their voices carrying in the suffocating stillness.

"They say if it wasn't for his wife, Wilcox would be bankrupt," said one.

"'Tis her as keeps him afloat," observed another.

She turned her back on them, and looked through the window into the café at the white tablecloths and silver cruet sets and the customers drinking coffee and tea and eating slices of Edith's cake. Then beside her something moved, and there was Jim with a look like thunder on his face, and she guessed he'd overheard the remarks. Grabbing her by the arm, he propelled her to the truck.

"Get in," he snarled. "How's a man supposed to make a living? Calves should have fetched twice what they did."

She opened the passenger door and climbed in, wound down the window and waited. It was like an oven; the heat unbearable. Jim yanked the choke right out, as far as it would go, and pushed the self-starter. The engine turned over a couple of times, spluttered and died. He tried again and again until it barely responded. He got out, slammed the door behind him, and brought his fist down hard on the bonnet. Leaving her in the truck, he marched off to sit under the shade of a tree near The London Hotel. Kathleen released the choke because she guessed the engine was flooded. After ten minutes or so she tried again, and this time it sparked into life. Jim scowled as he strolled back. Without speaking, he climbed into the driver's seat, and he maintained a sulky silence all the way home.

Resentment smouldered in her, and indignation at the punishment Jim would be sure to mete out to her in the bedroom that night. But as the day wore on, for some reason she couldn't fathom, he seemed to be keeping out of her way. After tea he made some excuse, went out to the yard, and disappeared.

With the children in bed and Edith in her favourite chair, half asleep already, Kathleen sat on the front doorstep, listening to the crickets chirping in the long grass. The sun dipped below the horizon, and the sky turned a dusky peach as the shadows softened and lengthened. She rose to her feet; went through the house and out to the yard, because she needed to shut the hens in for the night.

Scarcely had she put a foot beyond the yard door than two figures emerged from the shadows. She watched as Jim gathered Annie in his arms and kissed her full on the mouth.

"How dare you?! How dare you, Jim?!" Kathleen yelled, and her shriek of outrage roused Edith in the kitchen.

Annie looked like a frightened rabbit, ready to bolt, but Jim held his ground.

"'Tis my farm. I'll do as I please."

"Why the hell don't you go to bed with her, then?"

Kathleen shouted. She stormed back into the house, pushing past Edith, hurtling up the stairs two at a time, and slammed the bedroom door shut.

CHAPTER 19

Kathleen flung herself down on the bed, hot tears of rage falling onto the pillow. How dare he? How dare he insult her like this? All the times he'd humiliated her, all the times he'd sneered at her, crowded into her head until there was no room for anything else. She felt the hurt and the anger of each one all over again, as if they'd never gone away. She'd borne it all and never complained and always hoped that things would get better, yet always they got worse. She wasn't going to fool herself any more. Now she'd admitted that it was never going to get any better, she felt calmer and even strong, because accepting the truth had given her courage. Yet she was a long way from knowing what to do.

In the gathering gloom she lay on the bed, waiting and listening for him coming up the stairs. Part of her wanted him to come, so that she could have it out with him; tell him what she thought of him and the way he'd treated her. Yet she was frightened of his coming, frightened of what he'd do to her, frightened that she wouldn't be able to say the things she needed to say.

She lay and listened and waited and still he did not come. About midnight, she fell into a restless sleep, her clothes still on, and woke when sunlight flooded the room. He wasn't there. All night she'd been alone.

Stiff and exhausted, she splashed cold water on her face, dressed in fresh clothes and opened the bedroom door. Sounds from the kitchen told her that someone was already down and making breakfast. With a heavy heart she went downstairs and found Edith putting tea in the pot. A plate with crumbs, a butter-smeared knife and a jam spoon indicated that Annie had already eaten.

"Said she had to get on this morning," said Edith with a nod of the head in the direction of the dairy. White-faced and expressionless, she busied herself about the kitchen, studiously avoiding Kathleen's eye.

Kathleen waited for her to say something more, something that showed she realised how impossible it was for things to carry on as usual, but she didn't. After a while Kathleen gave up waiting, called out to Tom that it was time to get up, and went to see to Beth. By the time she'd dressed Beth and brought her down, she could hear Jim coming in, whistling as he took off his boots at the yard door.

"Lovely day today," he observed, rubbing the palms of his hands together as he sat down at the table. "I could do with two eggs and plenty of bacon, and it wouldn't go amiss if you popped a slice of bread in the frying pan." He looked her straight in the eye as he spoke, as if nothing had happened; as if life continued to flow in an uninterrupted stream of normality. But his face told her he'd taken her at her word and spent the night in Annie's bed, of that she was sure.

She stared back, her stomach all knotted up with confusion, unable to say what she wanted to say, so she reached for the pan and cooked his breakfast. It wasn't that she wanted him in her bed. She'd longed for him to leave her alone, but now that he had, it was even worse. Besides, she felt responsible for Annie. She'd brought the girl to Higher Haydn Farm and Annie's parents expected their daughter to be properly looked after. She'd long suspected that Jim made free with village girls after he'd been drinking at The Southwood Inn, but to have his mistress on the farm, under their own roof, that was something else. It was embarrassing; it was unbearably degrading. There was nothing for it but to dismiss Annie and send her home; the quicker the better.

As soon as Tom had gone to school and Jim went out to see to the sheep on the moor, Kathleen walked smartly to the dairy, fully determined to put an end to the affair.

Annie was busy weighing butter into half-pound pats, and looked up as she heard Kathleen approach. "Morning, ma'am." She attempted a smile.

"Now, Annie, I know you're a good worker. You've done well since you came here, but you must realise I cannot allow this situation to continue."

Annie said nothing.

"I'm afraid you must leave, Annie. You must go back to your family. I cannot have you under my roof any longer."

Annie was looking at Kathleen in a way that was hard to decipher, as if she hadn't heard properly or didn't understand, and yet there was an air of defiance about her. "The master told me you'd say that, but he said I was to take no notice."

The sheer audacity of it! Kathleen opened her mouth to reply but words failed her. Flames of fury ignited, ready to burst forth, but reason held them back and told her to resort to icy logic. "Who pays you your wages?"

"Oh, I don't trouble too much 'bout that," replied Annie, without a moment's hesitation. "It's comfy here and I gets all my food, and the master said he'd see me all right, so I'm not bothered if you don't pay my wages any longer."

For a moment or two, Kathleen stood dazed in the face of Annie's ill-concealed jubilation. The instant she recovered, she turned on her heel and walked away. The girl was demented if she thought she'd a future with Jim. He'd cast her off as soon as he was tired of her, but until then there was no way she'd trust a word Kathleen said. It was pointless to try to persuade her to leave, because she was so obviously besotted with him. And Jim knew exactly how to charm a girl; Kathleen had learned that the hard way herself.

The task of tackling Jim about Annie was going to be difficult. Kathleen prepared herself for an eruption of anger, but to her astonishment he merely laughed.

"Only did what you told me to do," he said. "You should just be thankful I didn't bother you."

As she waited for him to come to bed that night she wondered if he would teach her a lesson for speaking as she had. But the night wore on and the bed remained empty beside her, and she didn't know whether to be glad or angry.

It was a no man's land she occupied – torn between wanting him to leave her alone and the humiliation of his sleeping with Annie – and it drained her energy and sapped her determination. Edith pretended not to notice what was going on; that Jim had taken to sleeping above the dairy. Kathleen felt she couldn't say anything because Jim was Edith's son, after all, and she wasn't sure how she would take it, but she desperately needed someone to talk to. As she was on the verge of telephoning Alice, it occurred to her that a call from the phone kiosk in Southwood might be the quickest way to spread her private affairs all over the village. Instead, she wrote Alice a letter and waited eagerly for the reply. At the very least, she expected Alice to sympathise, but she was disappointed.

You knew what Jim was like when you married him. I distinctly remember Robert telling us that Jim was notorious for having girls in the hayloft. Anyway, Kathleen, you really must do your best to patch things up and stay with him for the sake of the children.

Alice had no idea, absolutely no idea what it was like being married to Jim.

An uneasy truce lay over the household for the next week or so. Jim made little secret of his lust for Annie, and she not only encouraged him but began to behave as if she'd acquired a new-found status in the household. Surely there must be something she could do, thought Kathleen. People did get divorced these days, but where would she go and how would she manage? Higher Haydn was her home, where her children were. She earned good money, but what would she live on if she left the farm? The dilemma churned endlessly in her head until she felt her brain would burst.

Then one day, at tea, the dark secret that tormented her was out.

"What's a whore, Daddy?" asked Tom, looking up at Jim.

Everything went very quiet and no one moved a muscle.

Jim turned his head slowly and looked down at Tom sitting beside him. "Why d'you ask, son?"

Blithely unaware of the consternation he was creating, Tom's innocent eyes gazed back at his father. "The boys at school say Annie's your whore." He glanced across at her as he said it.

"Ah," said Jim. "Well, son, 'tis like having an extra wife, which is a good thing if the first one you've got don't like you in her bed."

Kathleen heard the words and they sounded like a sick joke. They terrified her, because she had no idea what to do now any more than she had when she'd first found out about Annie. She cried out, pushed her chair back from the table and fled. Up the stairs she pounded, and slammed the bedroom door shut with such force that the key fell from the lock. So everyone in Southwood knew. It was unbearable, just unbearable. Covering her face with her hands, she wept tears of anguish.

That night she lay awake and racked her brains, trying to find a way out of the maze. When Mr Greenwood arrived the next morning, ready to take the monthly order, her face was pale and strained.

"How are you today, Mrs Wilcox?" he asked in his usual affable manner. "It's been good weather for haymaking. Most of yours saved?"

"I really can't say. I'm not sure where we are with the haymaking. Please sit down, Mr Greenwood, and I'll get the order for you." She tried to speak normally, but her voice came out a bit shaky.

"Forgive me, but are you quite well, Mrs Wilcox?"

His concern caught her off guard, and she moved away, pretending to look for the order on the dresser. All along she knew where it was – it was in her apron pocket – but she played for time because her eyes were full of unshed tears.

"Please, come and sit down," he coaxed, still looking for an explanation.

The instant she looked at him she could not say another word, but slumped down at the table, burying her head in her hands, and sobbed.

"Mrs Wilcox, dear lady, please tell me what's troubling you." Mr Greenwood leaned across the table and laid a hand gently on her wrist.

Immediately, she jerked her hand away and sat upright. "I can't stand it any longer, Mr Greenwood. It's a nightmare, a nightmare... and I can't wake up."

"Please tell me what it is," he said. "What distresses you so?" He touched her hand again, so that she'd look at him, and this time she didn't pull it away. So he gave a little pat to the back of her hand and asked again what it was that was troubling her.

When she was calm enough to speak, she told him about Annie and the intolerable humiliation and how it felt, and that she couldn't go on being a laughing stock any longer; that she wanted to divorce Jim and live somewhere else with the children, but she had nowhere to go, and even if she did, she'd have to find a way of earning a living because she'd have no money. And when she'd finished she cried some more because it was so awful to have said it all out loud and yet not be any nearer to knowing what to do to make anything happen.

"I am so sorry, Mrs Wilcox. I had no idea things would turn out this way." Do you have a mother or father who can help?" asked Mr Greenwood.

It sounded so ridiculous, the way he said it, that she gave a watery smile in spite of herself. "Daddy died some time ago," she said, "and I've no idea where my mother is; she hasn't been in touch for ages."

"I'm so sorry to hear that," he said. And, after a little while, "Your family in London, in Bethnal Green – they'd help, wouldn't they?"

"You mean Uncle Charlie and Auntie Mary?" She thought about them. "Yes, they'd take me in, do their best, but I'd be so far away, I'm not sure... it's Tom and Beth, you see. I don't want to be far away. I want to send for them as soon as I can."

"You want a refuge? Somewhere to go while you decide what to do for the best?" he asked.

She took out a handkerchief and blew her nose, and thought about what he'd said. That was what she needed: a refuge, a calm place, somewhere she could think and work out what to do next.

"I could offer you a place to stay," he said, his voice so quiet that at first she believed she hadn't heard him right. "I rent a little house in Totnes," he continued. "It has two bedrooms. You are welcome to stay in one while you sort your affairs out."

"Oh, I couldn't possibly—" she began.

"Just think it over," he interrupted. "I'll call back next week. I'll make some excuse concerning the order."

He rose from the table, but as he was about to leave she caught his wrist and held it.

"I don't need to think, Mr Greenwood," she said. "I'll accept your offer."

"Please, call me Joseph," he said, and his face lit up in pleasant surprise. "There's a bus that leaves Plymouth for Totnes mid afternoon. I could meet you in Totnes at the bus stop when my rounds are finished."

"Tomorrow; I'll do it tomorrow." Her face was bright with determination. A door had been opened, and she had been shown the way to freedom. "You are sure about this, Joseph? Really sure?"

He nodded. "Dear lady, I will be honoured to offer you a place of refuge." He gave a little bow and smiled.

The next morning, Kathleen wrote a note and tucked it under the teapot, where she knew Edith would find it. She tried to explain why she was running away, but it came out all wrong, so she tore it up and tried again, but the second note didn't work either. In the end she stuck to practical things: she'd send for the children as soon as she was settled and would be very grateful if Edith would look after them for now; and the orders for this week were all set out in a list on the desk in the parlour, and perhaps Nell would be the best person to see that they got to Southwood and Ivybridge, because they'd just bought a truck at Lower Haydn. She finished the note:

I'm sorry I have to ask you to do all this, Edith. You've always been good to me, but you know how things are, and I just can't go on any longer.

Give Tom and Beth each a big kiss from me and tell them I love them very much.

Kathleen

She took all the money in her cash box – notes and coins – and stuffed it in a shopping bag under a nightdress, together with spare underwear and a toothbrush. She dared not risk taking more. Heart thumping against her ribs, stomach churning, she glanced around the kitchen for the last time: the uneven flagstones on the floor, the smell of woodsmoke from the range, the incessant ticking of the grandfather clock. Outside, a hen was cackling, squawking, telling the world she'd laid an egg – stupid creature – and in a distant meadow a cow was lowing. She could hear Annie busy in the dairy, singing a saucy song to herself.

"I'm just off to the village, Edith, to buy a few things," Kathleen called out. "Beth's all right with you, isn't she?"

"Don't you worry about little Beth," came the reply. "She's all right."

Kathleen stepped through the granite archway of the yard door into the light and, one step after another, walked away. She heard Beth chuckling in delight as only a young child can, and then Edith saying something in reply, although Kathleen couldn't make out the words. Her throat tightened and she caught her breath as an image of Beth's face swam before her. Her knees grew weak and she drove her body forward only by an effort of will. As soon as she could, she'd send for Beth and Tom. She loved them more than anything in the world. It would be all right; when everything was over and she was settled, it would be all right then. Tears filled her eyes so that the hawkweed in the hedge became mere blurs of yellow among the grass and nettles. *It wasn't meant to be like this, but you've ground me down, Jim, day after day, draining the life out of me, sucking me dry, so that I've nothing left to give.*

She reached Southwood and passed the school where Tom was at lessons. For a brief, dizzy moment, she wondered whether to rush in, make some excuse, and take him with her, but her legs kept on walking and there was the bus waiting in the square; the driver and conductor chatting. She took a seat near the back and a woman, whose face was familiar although Kathleen couldn't remember her name, smiled. She smiled back nervously. Could the woman know what she was doing? Impossible. She tried to breathe deeply, slowly, but her heart refused to be calmed. The engine jerked into action and the bus moved forward. The conductor was standing beside her.

"Where to?"

"Plymouth," she said, offering two shillings. Did the conductor notice how her hand shook?

"Nice day," he replied, giving her change. The bus lumbered round the corner at the bottom of the village and the conductor was almost thrown off balance. "Last bus back tonight is the six o'clock," he said, grabbing hold of the handrail.

"Thank you." She stared at the floor, unable to look at him. By six o'clock she'd be in Totnes, waiting for Joseph.

CHAPTER 20

Kathleen stepped off the bus in Totnes. Unfamiliar streets with unfamiliar shops, houses and people – everything strange. She thought about what she'd done and told herself that she'd done the right thing… but suppose Tom blamed her for what had happened and Beth forgot who she was? Suppose Edith couldn't cope on her own? Suppose Joseph didn't come to meet her?

To calm herself she walked as far as the bridge and stood gazing down at the river slipping past. She thought of the barley field and the first time Jim had touched her, and how they'd made love in the hayloft, and did not understand any of it any more. She blinked hard a few times and wandered back to the bus stop, glancing up and down the street, unsure of the direction from which Joseph would come. Suddenly he was there, striding towards her, jacket flapping in the breeze, face flushed with excitement, and saying he hoped she hadn't been waiting long.

"No, not long," she replied.

"This way – just down here," he said, picking up her bag.

They walked away from the river and along a narrow backstreet where whitewashed cottages snuggled against one another in a winding terrace, and stopped at a pale blue door where Joseph turned the key and invited her to enter.

The cottage smelt stale and airless. Joseph opened a window and apologised for the stuffiness. He showed her the kitchen and opened the back door onto the yard. Then she followed him up the steep wooden staircase with its threadbare carpet to the back bedroom. He opened the window, and the breeze brought with it the scent of honeysuckle from the backyard. This was her new home, and how peculiar, how odd it felt to even think that.

The following morning she was woken by a knock at the bedroom door and Joseph's voice asking if she wanted breakfast. It'd taken her hours to fall asleep. She'd drifted off only to jerk back into consciousness time and again, and once, just for a few seconds, she'd believed she was back at the farm.

"Thank you, Joseph. I won't be long," she called out, rubbing her eyes.

The kitchen table was set for one. On its clean white cloth was an uncut loaf on the breadboard, a pat of butter in a cut-glass dish, two kinds of jam, and a jar of honey. In a tiny earthenware jug, Joseph had put a few sprigs of honeysuckle to give a pleasant fragrance to the room. He gave a welcoming smile as she entered the room.

"I should've asked yesterday whether you prefer coffee or tea for breakfast," he said.

"Oh, tea will be fine."

"I hope you slept well." He glanced at her but did not wait for a reply. "I expect you've a lot to think about today – you'll need this." He put the door key on the table.

"Yes… thank you."

"See you about six, then," he said, slipping on his jacket.

The door clicked shut behind him and she was alone and wondering what on earth she was doing in this strange place. She should be at home, getting Tom ready for school; chatting to Beth. They'd be sure to ask Edith where she was. And what would Edith tell them? She thought about the drawing of a cow standing under a tree in the meadow that Tom had done for her, and wished she'd brought it with her. She pictured it on the dresser, propped up against a pewter tankard. If she was there now, she'd tell Tom how clever he was and his face would light up. She needed Tom and Beth with her more than anything; they were her life.

After breakfast – not that she felt like eating, but it would be churlish not to eat after all the trouble Joseph had taken – she went out into the town and found a telephone kiosk. She asked the operator to put through a call and was relieved to hear Alice's voice at the other end.

"Kathleen, it's lovely to hear you but I can't stay long. I'm just getting ready to go out – I've a meeting of the Women's League of Health and Beauty. I'm on the committee now."

"Alice, I need to talk. I've got to tell someone what's happened."

"Why, what's happened?"

"I've done it. I've left Jim. He's having an affair with the dairymaid."

The pause was so long that Kathleen thought the line had gone dead.

"Alice? Alice, are you there?"

"Yes, I'm still here. My God, Kathleen, what've you done? You should've told the dairymaid to go and then patched things up with Jim."

"I tried, really I did. But I couldn't get rid of her. She just wouldn't go. Anyway, she wasn't the first and I can't stand it any longer." Kathleen's voice was little more than a hoarse whisper, and a tear trickled down one cheek.

"But the children – how could you leave the children? And anyway, where are you now?"

"I'm in Totnes. I'm lodging with Joseph Greenwood. He's been our cattle feed merchant for years. He's been very kind to me."

"Kathleen, you must be crazy – living with another man. What on earth does it look like?"

"I'm not *living with* him. I'm lodging with him."

"Nobody's going to believe that," retorted Alice. "You ought to have knuckled down and got on with it."

"I can't. I can't do it any more." Kathleen's voice cracked and she wiped the tears away with the back of her hand. "I'm going to divorce Jim and get the children."

"Divorce?!" screeched Alice.

"I have to get away. You've no idea... Alice, I need a lawyer."

"I suppose you mean you want to speak to Binkey. You'd better ring back this evening." There was a click as Alice replaced the receiver.

When Kathleen telephoned again in the evening, Binkey answered, his voice deeper and more self-assured than she remembered.

"I gather you're in a spot of bother," he said. "Anything I can do to help?"

Her throat tightened and she tried her utmost not to cry; not to let herself down in front of Binkey. "I've left Jim and I want to divorce him," she managed to get out, and her voice sounded unnaturally calm, almost businesslike. "I have to get away from him, but of course I want the children."

"Big step, Kathleen. Quite sure you want this?"

"Quite sure."

"Alice tells me you're living in Totnes. Is there a hotel – somewhere I could stay?"

Thank goodness Binkey was taking her seriously. "Yes: The Royal Seven Stars, down near the river," she said.

When she met him at the hotel, Binkey's handshake was firm and his eyes full of sympathy. His shoulders were broader than she remembered and his face had filled out. They walked back to her lodgings and she introduced him to Joseph.

"I'm so pleased Kathleen has someone to help her," Joseph said. "She's been badly treated and deserves better." Pretending to have something to do in the town, he left them alone.

"Tell me what's happened, Kathleen," Binkey said. "I need to know everything."

"I don't know where to start. It's just... I couldn't go on any longer." She waited for him to say something, but he didn't. "Jim is sleeping with Annie the dairymaid, and everyone – the whole village – knows it. Even Tom's asking questions. I thought I'd be able to keep an eye on the dairymaid if she lived in. I thought Jim wouldn't dare do anything if she actually lived with us." She kept waiting for him to say something, but he didn't, and so she told him more: about the dairymaid before this one who'd had to leave because she was expecting, and who wouldn't say who the father was, but... She screwed up her face.

"Might have been Jim?" Binkey suggested.

"Yes, but I've no way of proving it."

"But your mother-in-law knows what's going on now, with Annie?"

"Oh yes, she knows all right."

"I'm sorry I have to ask this, Kathleen, but I need to know. Your relations with Jim – has he been in your bed since he took up with Annie?"

"No, and I locked the door, just in case."

"In case what?"

It took some time before she had the courage to reply; it felt so shameful to say it. "In case he raped me," she said softly. "He often used to, before Annie."

"I'm so sorry."

"Can I divorce him for that?"

Binkey shook his head. "When you marry someone, you consent to sexual intercourse." After a pause he asked, "Did he beat you? Was he cruel like that?"

"He bruised my arms sometimes, holding me down."

"Did anyone else see the marks?"

"No – I hid the bruises."

"I ask because we might've alleged cruelty – you can now, under the new law. Never mind; we'll found our petition for divorce on Jim's adultery with Annie. Try not to worry." The smile he gave her contained something of the youthful enthusiasm of the day they'd first met.

It was the following summer, June 1938, before Kathleen's divorce petition was heard in the High Court at Exeter. Jim was stubbornly defending the action and had refused to allow Kathleen to come anywhere near the children in the meantime. But she'd never given up hope, telling herself that it was only a matter of time before they were together again. She had sent cards and birthday presents but heard nothing back, so whether the children had ever received them, she couldn't tell.

On the day of the trial she caught the early train from Totnes to Exeter and met Binkey at the court. As she entered the building she spotted him, a folder under one arm, talking to a man in pinstriped trousers and a black gown. The man had a lean and pallid look and was wearing a wig. She watched as he drew on a cigarette between thin lips, tossed back his head and breathed out the smoke through his nostrils. She guessed he was her barrister, took an instant dislike to him, and steeled herself to meet him. Jim stood in a huddle with his lawyers, some distance away. One looked as if he might be a farmer in his spare time: young, with fair hair and tanned skin – that would be the solicitor. The other, bewigged and gowned, would be Jim's barrister. He had a square head sitting on a rotund body with little evidence of a neck to connect the two, and as she looked he opened his mouth and gave a hearty laugh. She ignored them and hurried on towards Binkey.

"Mrs Wilcox, do come and meet your counsel, Mr Fletcher," said Binkey.

The barrister held out a scrawny hand to grasp hers. "I was just saying to Mr Arbuthnot," he began, "that it would be in our interests to acknowledge your adultery with..." He shuffled through the papers. "Ah yes – with Joseph Greenwood."

"What?" Kathleen's eyes opened wide. "What on earth are you talking about?"

"I understand you've been living with Mr Greenwood ever since you ran away from your husband." He raised an eyebrow.

"Yes, but I'm only lodging with him."

The thin lips twitched into a sarcastic smile. "Come, come, Mrs Wilcox, you can't expect anyone to believe that a young woman like you is living with a man in a state of innocence." He examined her, his eyes wandering up and down. "After all, Mr Greenwood does maintain you, does he not?"

"He's been very good to me," she said. "I've tried to get employment. People don't like taking on a married woman, but I've managed to get a job as a cleaner at the hotel. It's enough to buy food for the household, and I act as Mr Greenwood's housekeeper and cook."

"Dear, dear, Mrs Wilcox, you make it sound so admirable. But my advice is that you make a clean breast of it. Much better to disclose the adultery and ask the court to overlook it; exercise discretion in your favour." He drew on his cigarette. "If it's not disclosed, and the court decides you are indeed living in adultery, you will lose."

That the court could decide that she'd committed adultery was outrageous, beyond comprehension, and she felt herself grow in frustration.

"It's only to safeguard your position," explained Binkey. "It's going to be very difficult to persuade the court that running away with someone you know, and living with him for a year, is merely a form of employment."

She felt sick and confused and afraid. "But it would be a lie, and the court wants the truth."

"Very well. Be it on your own head," said the barrister; then he took a final drag and stubbed out his cigarette as the voice of the usher rang through the lobby, announcing the case.

And all at once things started to happen and Kathleen couldn't remember what she was supposed to do or where she was supposed to go. Then Binkey was at her side, a hand under her elbow, ushering her in, showing her where to sit. She looked around the stale, airless courtroom lit by dim electric light bulbs – a room devoid of life yet potent with power.

"Court rise," the usher commanded.

A shuffling of feet and a scraping of chairs, and from behind a wooden screen the judge, in full wig and robes, appeared. He bowed, and all the lawyers bowed back. Kathleen glanced around at the men who held her fate in their hands. At first she thought she must be the only woman in the room, and then she spotted Edith sitting near the back, shoulders hunched, staring straight ahead. Fervently she prayed that Edith would tell the truth. More than anyone, she knew what Jim was really like. She knew, too, how hard Kathleen had worked to keep them out of debt. Surely Edith wouldn't let her down?

The proceedings moved at a snail's pace and Kathleen became strangely detached from it all, waiting and waiting for it to be over and herself to be free. She pictured herself reunited with Tom and Beth, and wondered how they'd grown and whether they'd be as overjoyed to see her as she'd be to see them.

Then someone was speaking her name and she stood up, heart racing, and was directed to the witness box, where the usher gave her a Bible, and she swore to tell the truth. She looked up to see her barrister on his feet, gaunt features regarding her with professional detachment. Her mouth was parched and her words so quietly spoken that the judge had to ask her to speak up. It wasn't difficult to answer the questions the barrister asked and after a while she felt stronger, but just when she thought the ordeal was over and she would be allowed to leave the witness box, she was told to wait, because Mr Wilcox's counsel had a few questions for her. She took a step back, resumed her position and smiled at him. He gave no response, no acknowledgement; just a glassy stare.

"Now, Mrs Wilcox," he said, peering at his notes, "I want to take you back to the evening when you claim Mr Wilcox first committed adultery with Ann Sercombe, the woman named in your petition."

She waited, wondering what he wanted to know.

"Do you remember going into the yard?"

"Yes."

"And you saw your husband and Miss Sercombe together?"

"Yes."

"And you saw him kiss her?"

"Yes."

"And then you said, 'Why the hell don't you go to bed with her?' Didn't you?"

"Yes, but—" began Kathleen.

"Did you say that or didn't you, Mrs Wilcox? That's all I want to know."

"Well, yes, but—"

"Thank you, Mrs Wilcox."

She wanted to explain. Why wouldn't he let her explain?

"I want to turn to your relationship with Mr Greenwood." He shuffled more papers, and made a note with his pen. "You've known Mr Greenwood for some time, haven't you?"

Kathleen nodded.

"Haven't you?" he said deliberately, and waited for her reply.

"Yes."

"In fact, you have been very friendly with Mr Greenwood for some years now, haven't you?"

"Yes, I suppose so."

"And Mr Greenwood is a single man, isn't he? He has no wife or children of his own?"

"That's true."

"So, if you wanted to run off with Mr Greenwood, it would be very convenient for you to encourage your husband to take Ann Sercombe as his lover."

"That's not true! It wasn't like that at all."

"So, how was it, Mrs Wilcox? I put it to you that you had already decided to desert Mr Wilcox and you found it very convenient that Mr Wilcox appeared to be partial to your dairymaid." He glared at her, waiting for a response.

She felt like screaming at him that Mr Wilcox had certainly had more than one girl, and that Annie was only the latest of a long line. She'd shouted at him in anger and in desperation, and in any event, he'd always done whatever he wanted and didn't need her permission. "No, it wasn't like that at all."

"Thank you, Mrs Wilcox. That will be all."

Jim was next to take the stand. He was asked to describe his relations with his wife. "Well, 'tis like this, you see, My Lord." He addressed the judge. "Mrs Wilcox wasn't up to much in the marriage bed after Beth was born."

"And who is Beth?" asked the judge.

"Beth's my daughter; my second child."

Kathleen cringed as he said the words 'my daughter'. She shut her eyes and gritted her teeth.

"My Lord," said Jim's barrister, "my client admits his adultery, but claims it occurred because his wife refused him the services of a wife. Furthermore, he alleges that Mrs Wilcox connived in his adultery with the dairymaid, Ann Sercombe."

The judge made a note. "Please continue."

"Tell me, Mr Wilcox, what did your wife say when she found you and Ann Sercombe in the yard?"

Jim turned in the witness box to look at Kathleen, his eyes full of malice. "She said, 'Why the hell don't you go to bed with her?' That's what she said."

Kathleen stared blankly at him. Everything was twisted and contorted so that the truth could no longer be seen. Deception, practised on a gigantic scale, was being woven into the very fabric of the evidence.

255

The proceedings dragged on, little by little; every word recorded by the solicitors, the barristers and the judge.

Jim claimed he'd long been suspicious of Joseph Greenwood and Kathleen's feelings for him. "But I am willing to take her back," she heard him say. "I don't bear no ill will toward her, and the children need their mother." Was there no end to these outrageous lies? He wanted her back so that she could earn money and keep the farm afloat – that's why he wanted her back. She listened with growing unease as Jim stuck to his story. Even when cross-examined by Kathleen's barrister he couldn't be shaken: he'd committed adultery with Ann Sercombe because Kathleen had told him to, and he'd been suspicious of Joseph Greenwood for some time.

Poor Edith had to take the stand, her voice trembling and her hand shaking as she took the oath. She did her best to play down the suggestion of any relationship between Kathleen and Joseph Greenwood, but she'd heard the fateful words and confirmed what Kathleen had shouted when she'd come upon Jim and Annie in the yard together. She tried to say that Kathleen's words had been said in anger, that she hadn't meant what she'd said, but by now the judge wasn't listening, and when he began to review the evidence it was obvious that he preferred Jim's version of events.

"It is clear that the wife connived in the husband's adultery," he said, "and the law says that connivance is an absolute bar. I have therefore no alternative but to dismiss this petition for divorce. However, the husband appears to me to be a most reasonable and merciful man. He says he is willing to take his wife back and forgive her adultery with Joseph Greenwood. If she has any sense, she will take him up on his most generous offer.

"As a consequence of the petition being dismissed, there will be no need to consider who should have custody of the children of this marriage. However, I should like it to be put on record that I judge the petitioner to be an unfit person to have custody. It would be entirely unsuitable for the children to be exposed to the moral hazard of living in a household in which their mother is in an adulterous relationship."

Kathleen could no longer breathe; there was no air left in the room. She rose unsteadily to her feet. Energy drained from her fingers and arms, her legs turned to jelly, and her knees buckled under her. The door swung open and she crumpled in a heap on the floor as darkness enveloped her.

CHAPTER 21

Kathleen sat alone in the sitting room of Joseph's little house, more than six months after that dreadful day. She went on sitting there while the thin light of winter drained away, and tried to summon up enough energy to pull the curtains and light the fire. The fire had gone out about an hour ago but the embers were still warm, so it wouldn't take much to get it going again. It was the effort needed to stand up from her seat and do it – that was the difficult part. Joseph would be home soon and he'd expect the sitting room to be warm and the smell of cooking to be coming from the kitchen. He was entitled to expect things, because he paid for the food and everything else since she'd lost her job at the hotel because she couldn't get up in the mornings.

Every minute of every day she thought of Beth and Tom and helplessness gnawed away within her, sapping her strength and dulling her senses. Sometimes, like today, a black fog descended, and when it did she'd be lost, completely lost in it. She'd slip back down into the pit of despair, convinced that she'd never manage to claw her way to the top and escape.

She closed her eyes, and right away she was back in the courtroom, and they were robbing her of her children all over again, those men in suits and wigs, and it was as real as if it was happening for the very first time...

From the darkness she'd struggled into the light, and someone had asked, "Are you all right?" Edith was kneeling beside her, stroking her hair. "My poor dear – he drove you to it; he drove you to it, he did."

Someone else was shouting, "Fetch a doctor."

Kathleen felt weak and sick, and her head was stinging where it had hit the floor. The bruise was beginning to swell. She tried to understand why she was there on the floor, in a place she didn't know. Then Binkey helped her to sit up, and she remembered what had happened, and that was when it felt as if someone had taken a knife and driven it right through her. It was almost impossible to breathe, and she wondered if she was dying, the pain was so terrible. She stood up, managed to walk a few paces and slump down on a bench.

"I'll be all right. Just a minute and I'll be all right," she heard herself say, leaning forward, resting her head in her hands, waiting for the swirling giddiness to stop.

"Come away, Mother."

Kathleen looked up in time to see the smirk on Jim's face. He was revelling in his victory.

"You don't want nothing more to do with her," he said.

That was where it started: the torment, and the slippery descent into the pit from which there was no escape, and the scene that played over and over in her head whether she wanted it to or not.

When she'd recovered enough to stand and walk, Binkey took her to the station and waited with her until the Totnes train pulled in. "I'm sorry, Kathleen. I'm so sorry it didn't go well for you," he said.

She asked if there was anything they could do, and he replied that an appeal would cost hundreds of pounds, and even then there was no way that they could be sure of success. She dissolved into a fresh bout of tears, and Binkey spoke very gently to her and asked if she'd like to stay with him and Alice for a while and think about what to do. She'd promised to think it over, but had never made a decision one way or the other, because she couldn't make decisions any more. Making decisions was too difficult; decisions required too much effort. Instead she'd drifted in the dark fog at the bottom of the pit and let the fog do with her whatever it wanted.

This morning Joseph had made her a cup of tea and called up the stairs before he left for work. She'd put on her dressing gown and descended slowly, step by step, and sat at the kitchen table, head in hands. Later she'd put on some clothes and sat for hours in the living room, staring at the wall, not caring whether she lived or died. Christmas had come and gone – not that it mattered any more, and Joseph didn't bother about Christmas anyway – and now it was a new year. That made no difference either. Nothing had changed because one year had turned into another.

She rose to her feet and caught her reflection in the mirror above the fireplace: dull, sunken eyes in a pinched face. She winced and moved away and wandered into the kitchen. By the time Joseph came in she was still making pastry for the pie, and he had to light the fire in the living room because she'd forgotten about it.

"Tomorrow you must get dressed before you come down to breakfast," he said. The tone was stern, yet she knew he didn't mean anything by it. He was just concerned about her, that was all. "You are so sad, Kathleen. There must be someone you can talk to. At Christmas you got a card from your cousin, I forget her name – the one who lives in London. Did *you* send *her* a card?"

Kathleen shook her head.

"People will be wondering how you are. What about Binkey and Alice? Did you send *them* a card?"

"You're a fine one to talk," she flared. "You didn't send any Christmas cards at all, as far as I could see, so don't you go telling me off."

When he didn't reply she looked up, wondering at his silence.

"I don't send Christmas cards because I am not a Christian," he said.

How stupid she was not to have guessed. All those things he'd said about the old days in Spitalfields should have been enough to tell her. "You're Jewish, aren't you?"

He nodded. "Yes, I am."

"But you don't go to synagogue."

"True, but you don't go to church."

She gave a foolish smile.

"Does it matter to you, now you know?" he asked.

She thought for a moment. "No, because you're still the same person – you're still you, aren't you?"

"Thank you for saying that." He patted the back of her hand that was resting on the table. "And I still think you should write to your cousin and your friends."

Kathleen bought two Christmas cards that were going cheap from the stationer's shop at the bottom end of town. One she sent to Rose, apologising for its lateness and enclosing a letter in which she tried to explain about the children. She asked after Uncle Charlie and Auntie Mary and whether they'd had news of her mother. The other card she sent to Alice and Binkey. She'd quite forgotten that Alice had been expecting her second child in November, and now she wrote saying that she hoped everything had gone according to plan and that mother and baby were doing well. As she held the pen and put the words on the card, she felt an overwhelming rush of jealousy at the thought of Alice and her baby. She shut her eyes to block it out, but a sensation like the scent of newborn baby filled the room, and with it came an overwhelming sense of her own helplessness.

The day grew cold; the wind raw. Rain lashed the pavements and ran in the gutters. It was late afternoon before it stopped and Kathleen ventured out. A weak sun was sinking behind ragged clouds as she locked the door and made for the post office. A few people, heads down, scurried along, and most of the shops showed signs of closing early. Passing the bakers, she was heading up the hill, gusts of wind whistling through the alleyways to either side, when all at once a child's laugh, full of innocence, drifted on the wind. Convinced that it was Beth's laugh, Kathleen spun round. But only an old woman, clutching a shopping bag and hanging on to her hat, struggled up the hill. Heart pounding, Kathleen scanned the street, searching, hoping. But there was no Beth – no one at all except the old woman – and the day seemed darker; the wind fiercer than ever. Lonely and defeated, she plodded on.

The following week, a letter came from Rose. It was full of sympathy and lambasted those 'bloody lawyers' for not having an ounce of common sense and for doing down an honest woman who deserved better. To Kathleen's enormous surprise, Rose wrote that her mother was back on the stage, appearing in music hall and using her old stage name of Alexandra Devereaux. Rumour had it she was somewhere up north at the moment, although she'd been playing in Shoreditch before Christmas, and was doing all right for herself judging by the furs and jewellery she had on.

And me dad's doing ever so well too. Got himself elected to some committee of the Labour Party and they're even saying the union's going to back him for Parliament if he carries on.

Remember you're a Wyndham and keep your pecker up, girl!

Love from us all,
Rose

Before the week was out, Alice had also replied. The baby had arrived in November and was eight weeks old now.

Doesn't time fly? We've decided to call him Anthony – father-in-law's second name, and the old boy is thrilled to bits!

You didn't say how you are, Kathleen, and we do worry about you, you know. Why don't you come and stay with us for a while? Then I can show off little Anthony and you can tell me all your news.

Yours ever,
Alice

Kathleen showed the letter to Joseph when he came in.

"Why not go? It would do you good to go," he said.

"But I can't; I can't possibly go. Alice has a new…" Unable to say the word, she turned away.

"You are sad; so very sad, Kathleen," he said. "I understand."

No, you don't, she felt like shouting; *no one can understand how I feel.* But she didn't trust herself to speak, and clamped her jaw tight shut.

"I'll go to the station," he said. "I can buy a ticket to wherever it is your friends live. Please let me do this for you."

"You can't; you mustn't – I depend on you too much as it is."

"It's only a little thing."

She searched his face and swallowed hard. "All right, if you're sure. I'll pay you back when I can, one day."

She wrote to Alice, asking if it would be all right to stay over Easter, and Alice replied that of course it would, and she could stay as long as she liked. And when Binkey met Kathleen at the station he said that Alice was so looking forward to seeing her that she'd talked about little else all week. He smiled kindly, picked up Kathleen's meagre suitcase, and led her to a smart navy-blue Rover in the station car park and held the passenger door open while she got in.

Half an hour later, they were driving down a gently winding road bordered by grass verges, tall hedges, and the glimpse of a roof here and there. Binkey slowed down and turned into the driveway of a large house with several chimneys. The front door opened and there was Alice to greet them.

"Oh, Alice, it's so good to see you; I can't tell you how much." Kathleen flung herself into Alice's outstretched arms and hugged her.

"Is that all you've brought?" Alice asked, looking at the single suitcase.

"Yes, that's all."

Alice rang the bell, a maid appeared, and Alice asked her to take Kathleen's suitcase to the guest room. "And when you've done that," Alice continued, "you can serve tea in the sunroom. Three, please – Mr Arbuthnot's in for tea today."

The maid nodded obediently. "Yes, of course, madam."

Kathleen sat in the sunroom with Alice and Binkey and admired their beautiful house and garden. Binkey said that Alice was so fond of gardening she'd even get down on her hands and knees to plant things.

"It's true," said Alice, laughing. "But if I'm honest, I couldn't manage without the gardener – only three days a week, but he's invaluable."

Conversation was interrupted by the arrival of the maid, who set out the tea service, a silver teapot, a hot-water jug, and an assortment of sandwiches and cakes. Then Alice poured tea and handed round the cups, starting with Kathleen.

"There you are, Bertie," she said, giving him the next. "We don't use 'Binkey' any more," she explained to

Kathleen. "It was only ever a nickname from school, you know."

Binkey – Bertie – was now a partner in the law firm of Rawlinson, Ashcroft and Pepperfield, so his career and Alice's security were assured. As well as the housemaid, Alice employed a cook and a daily help who came to clean each morning, and a live-in nanny would stay until both boys went away to prep school. Kathleen wondered what on earth Alice did to occupy her time, and found that she'd been accepted into polite society and onto committees engaged in charitable works and earnest endeavours. The respectable wife and mother, Alice had stuck to the rules and won herself a role that she played to perfection. It occurred to Kathleen that a woman who chose her breadwinner with care could live a very comfortable life and want for nothing, and that if only she'd stuck to the rules she'd be married to Robert and living a life of ease.

"We don't dress for dinner; only when we have guests," said Alice. "Oh – I didn't mean that you aren't a guest, Kathleen. I mean, now you're staying for a while, I feel you're part of the family." Her hand went over her mouth, just like it used to in the old times when she'd made a silly mistake.

For the first time in months, Kathleen almost smiled.

After tea, Nanny brought the children in and the older boy shook hands very nicely and asked Kathleen how she did. The baby Alice cradled in her arms, and Kathleen thought how amazingly lucky Alice was, and wondered how she was going to get through the next few minutes without breaking down and making a complete fool of herself in front of the children, but somehow she managed it.

At eight o'clock dinner was served, and Bertie and Alice talked about things Kathleen was only dimly aware of, because so much had passed her by and she had never noticed.

"Bertie's father thinks there's bound to be another war." Alice glanced at Bertie for confirmation. "'Never trust a German,' he says, 'and this Hitler fellow's got shifty eyes. Don't trust him further than you can throw him. Whatever you give the blighter, he'll want more,' that's what the colonel says."

"My brother's out of the army now – gone into the diplomatic service." Bertie picked up his glass and took a sip of water. "He believes there's got to come a point where Hitler feels he's got all he reasonably can, and he won't risk provoking us or France, because he won't want to lose it all by going to war." He opened his palms in a gesture of quiet confidence. "Who in their right mind is ever going to go to war again? We all know what war means."

"What do you think, Kathleen?" Alice asked.

"Well, I… I haven't really thought about it."

"I suppose it's a bit quiet down there in Devon," observed Bertie. "Foreign affairs not really the thing."

It was nearly the end of April before Bertie put Kathleen on the train back to Totnes. She'd grown accustomed to the leisurely pace of Alice's day and the luxury of having cooking, cleaning and laundry all done by someone else. And she'd met people and been taken places, so that she was beginning to feel that she knew who she was again. Yet when she stepped over the threshold of Joseph's front door, it was the same place with the same dark memories.

Her legs became heavy as she climbed the stairs to her room where she'd spent so many hours gazing at nothing. After she had unpacked and come back down to the kitchen, the lump in her throat and the despair in the pit of her stomach returned. She tried telling herself that she shouldn't feel like this; that it was time to look to the future and not dwell on things she couldn't change. But the black fog had been waiting and it ambushed her when she was least expecting it.

In one of those moments, when melancholy enveloped her, Joseph suggested she write to Edith and ask for news of the children. Without much hope, she composed a letter to Edith, suggesting they meet in Plymouth, and was extremely surprised to receive a reply. She tore open the envelope to read that Edith would be waiting for her at Spooners Corner next Thursday morning at eleven o'clock.

Breathless and excited as a schoolgirl, Kathleen caught the bus to town, and there, on the corner at the entrance to Spooners, stood Edith, waiting amid the bustling crowds. They hugged like long-lost friends and Kathleen took Edith by the arm and led her inside and upstairs to the restaurant, where they sat at a little table, half hidden behind a pillar, and ordered tea and cakes.

"I've missed having you round the place," said Edith. "Farm's not the same since you left. That girl Annie didn't last long, you know – had to go soon as he tired of her. I've got a different dairymaid now; someone a bit too long in the tooth for hanky-panky."

"I'm so sorry; I just couldn't stand it any longer." Kathleen rested a hand on Edith's arm.

"I know, my dear, I know," Edith replied. "Like father, like son, they say. I never had the strength to do what you did." Their eyes met, and Edith shook her head. "You're a brave woman, my dear."

A lump in her throat, Kathleen blinked back tears. "You too?" Her voice was thick and unsteady. "You never said."

"Never mind; 'tis all in the past." Edith sighed. "Now, I 'spect you'll be wanting to hear all about the children and what they've been up to, so let's talk 'bout them."

"They'll have grown so I'd scarcely recognise them."

Edith opened her handbag, shuffled around and pulled out an envelope. "There – see what you makes of that." With a flourish, she produced a photograph.

"Tom and Beth... it's Tom and Beth." Kathleen's hand trembled as she held the small black-and-white photograph and stared at the image.

"Master Robert took that, couple of months back," said Edith. "Takes a real interest, does Master Robert."

"Robert? Lord Neville?" The shock of hearing his name sounded in Kathleen's voice.

"Course, I always thinks of him as Master Robert, but you'm right – Lord Neville," went on Edith, unaware of the turmoil her revelation had caused. "He's very good to the children. Tom's only a year older than his own boy, Freddie, and Master Robert makes Tom welcome down at Alston Hall, and when Beth's old enough she can come as well, he says."

Drinking in every detail, Kathleen gazed at the photograph for some minutes before she handed it back.

"Oh no, that's for you to keep." Edith pushed her hand away.

"Oh, thank you, Edith. Thank you so much. You don't know what it means to have this."

"I'll write, send news when I can, but you know how careful I needs to be."

"I know, I know. Just something – anything – will make all the difference."

Kathleen got off the bus in Totnes blissfully happy, humming to herself as she walked to the cottage and let herself in. She'd hardly begun preparing the supper when Joseph arrived.

"By the look on your face, things went well," he said.

"Absolutely wonderful – look, I've even got a photograph." She brought it from the dresser, where she'd pitched it against a mug, to show him.

"I'm so pleased for you."

"You're early. Anything the matter?" she asked.

"No, I just wanted to know how you got on, and I wondered whether I could take you to The Royal Seven Stars to celebrate. We could have dinner in the restaurant."

That evening the waiter showed them to a table by the window that had a silver cruet set, and a red carnation and a sprig of asparagus fern in a little cut-glass vase. Joseph ordered a bottle of wine, and they ate plaice fillet, roast lamb, and baked custard tart. And when they'd finished and Kathleen could hardly remember feeling as good as this in a long while (except possibly once when she'd gone with Alice and Bertie to the theatre), Joseph became serious and said that he'd something to ask her.

"You know how I've always held you in high regard, Kathleen," he began.

She met his eyes, wondering what he meant, but nothing could have prepared her for what came next.

"But it's more than that. The truth is, I love you, Kathleen, and I was wondering if you would consent to live with me as my wife."

Taken by surprise, she stared at him, struck dumb by the suggestion. He was like an uncle to her. Maybe not as old as Uncle Charlie, but definitely a lot older than she was, and the thought of him as a lover had never entered her head.

"I could buy you a wedding ring and you could call yourself Mrs Greenwood."

"I don't know, Joseph. I... I haven't thought of you that way. I mean..."

"Of course, you must have time to think it over," he said. "I don't expect an answer tonight." But his face showed disappointment all the same.

"All right, I promise I'll think about it."

Just when life had taken a turn for the better, here was Joseph saying things she'd rather not hear. Now that he'd said it, there was no going back to the way it had been before. *It's just the way of things, isn't it*, she reasoned, *the way you must expect to live if you're a woman. If a man provides for you, puts a roof over your head and food on the table, he expects something in return.* She knew only too well what that was, and knew too that there was no way she could refuse him. She was to be known as Mrs Greenwood.

CHAPTER 22

"You're a very mysterious man, Joseph," said Kathleen. It was a Sunday in June the following year, 1940, and they were sitting at the kitchen table, eating breakfast. "I know so little about you."

"It doesn't do to make yourself stand out from the crowd," he replied.

"Tell me about your family. I remember your father was a cabinetmaker, but what about your mother, and your brothers and sisters? You never mention them."

When he didn't respond, her smile faded.

"I didn't mean to pry," she began. "I was just asking—"

"I don't talk much about it – the old days."

The silence lasted so long that she pushed her chair back and was on the point of clearing the table when he looked up.

"I'll tell you, if you really want to know," he said.

She sat down again and waited. He picked up his cup and observed the dregs, swilling them round and around, until she wondered if she'd heard him right.

"We got driven out, that's what happened. People went mad and started shouting and screaming and pulling Jews out of their beds and beating them. They set fire to our house and burned it down, and my sister died – we couldn't get her out. We managed it – my brothers and me, and my father and mother – we got out, but she didn't… and there were others who didn't." His eyes went blank, staring into the far distance, seeing only the hell stored in his head.

"Not in London?" she said. "Not London, surely?"

"No, no, not England," he replied. "Austria – the old Austria, before the war. They didn't like Jews even then, you know."

"When?" she asked.

"1903," he said.

"How dreadful – you must've been a boy."

"Thirteen," he said. "I was thirteen when we came to London. There were lots of us: Russians and Poles, Romanians, Lithuanians – all Jews. We'd squabble and shout, but we always made sure no one ever went without something to eat and somewhere to sleep."

Kathleen smiled. "Sounds like a great big family."

"When Mother sent us on errands, she'd say, 'Go to Levy's and get a ha'p'orth of raspberry jam', or, 'Go to Garfinkle's and get two tomato herrings for tea.' We'd take a saucer or a plate, and sometimes we'd have to wait while he opened the jar or broke into the tin."

"Your mother – was she from a large family?"

"Farming family; ten children. Used to big open spaces, she was. Couldn't possibly have imagined what life would be like in a tenement block. I don't think she ever got over moving there." He ran a hand over his hair and gave a slight chuckle. "Everybody had window boxes, you see, and she used to plant potatoes and beans and things like that in hers. And she used to say to me and my brothers, 'Look, they're growing, they're alive.' And you could see from her face just how much it meant to her that the things were growing."

"She died, didn't she? But your brothers, are they still alive?"

"Yes, they live in the same place, but we don't keep in touch. They said I was deserting the family when I got the job and moved down here."

"I'm sorry." She put out a hand and laid it on his. After a while, she gathered up the plates and tipped tea leaves from the pot into the strainer in the corner of the sink. "Thank goodness we don't need coupons for tea, but you just don't know how bad it's going to get, do you? Did I tell you what I heard in the fish shop yesterday?"

"No."

"The man who brought the boxes of fish over from Brixham said some of the trawlers are sailing to Dunkirk to help bring the troops back."

"Brave men."

She thought for a moment. "It's good Mr Churchill's prime minister, isn't it? We know what we've got to do now."

"I was thinking I might join the Local Volunteer Force, or whatever they're called," he said.

She laughed, and he smiled back at her. Then a sharp knock on the door made them both jump.

"Who on earth can that be?" she said, and went to answer it.

Two policemen stood on the pavement.

A sense of unease settled on Kathleen and her mouth suddenly became dry. "Yes? Can I help you?"

"Morning, madam," said one of the policemen, raising a hand towards his helmet. "Sorry to trouble you so early. We've come for Josef Grünwald. We understand he lives here." He glanced down at an official-looking paper.

"Joseph... who?" she managed to say.

"Who is it, Kathleen?" Joseph called from the kitchen. She heard the scraping of chair legs on the floor, and then he was there beside her.

"Josef Wilhelm Grünwald?" asked the first policeman.

Joseph grimaced. "Yes. Who wants to know?"

"I'm arresting you as being of hostile origin under the Defence of the Realm Act." The policeman pronounced the words with great solemnity and went to lay a hand on Joseph's arm.

Kathleen's eyes blazed with fury. "How dare you arrest him? He's not hostile. He's lived here for years and years, since he was a child. England's his home."

"Can't help that, madam. Says here he's of Austrian nationality." The policeman's finger pointed to the form, where 'nationality' had been stamped in black ink.

"Now, if you could show us your papers, sir," chipped in the other. "Show us you're a British subject. Now that would throw a whole new light on the matter."

"I can't," said Joseph, shaking his head in disbelief. "I never thought..."

"What if he's not British?" Kathleen shouted in frustration. "He's Jewish. How could he possibly be a spy, or help the Nazis? It's completely ridiculous."

"That's beside the point, madam. Here's the order to arrest him." The policeman waved the warrant at her.

"I'll go," said Joseph, turning to her. "What else can I do?" His eyes had the look of an animal at bay; a hunted animal with nowhere to run.

They allowed him to pack a few clothes, and then the door closed and Kathleen was alone, utterly alone in the silent house, wondering what was to become of Joseph, and what was to become of her.

First thing the next morning she went to the police station, asked to see the sergeant in charge, and had it out with him. Although she reasoned and pleaded, he had his orders and there was nothing he could do to help, he told her. As far as he knew, Grünwald and the other alien internees were being held at a camp near Paignton. Beyond that, he couldn't say.

She came home, still fuming, and sat in the kitchen trying to gather her thoughts. Joseph was always careful with money, although he had bought a wireless last September when war was declared, so that they'd be sure to hear all the official announcements. In his cash box she found enough to pay the rent and buy food for about three, perhaps four months. She'd have to find a job – that was absolutely clear. But temporary employment here and there, cleaning or serving in a shop when the regular assistant had her days off, was all she could find, and it wasn't enough.

By July, tea was rationed, Germany had invaded the Channel Islands, and the newspaper stand carried headlines: 'First enemy aircraft sighted over Plymouth'. The war had moved a lot nearer.

September came, and still no word from Joseph. However, news from another quarter arrived. Rose wrote to say that she and Uncle Charlie had volunteered under the Air Raid Precautions scheme, and that being an ARP warden was a dodgy business at the best of times:

Last Saturday that bleeding Hitler had the cheek to send his planes over in broad daylight, would you believe? But he must've had a whole lot shot down, because now he sends 'em only after dark – the bastard.

Kathleen felt guilty writing back and telling Rose that she'd seen a few stray planes and the odd dogfight, but nothing serious yet. She added that she'd heard on the wireless that London was having a bad time, and that other cities were likely to catch it from now on, but she'd decided to try her luck in Plymouth because she needed a job. Joseph had been taken away by the police. He'd never bothered to become a British subject, and without him she was running short of money.

The queue for the Plymouth bus was already long when Kathleen arrived at the bus stop the following morning. The service had been reduced – lack of fuel – and people crowded on the instant the last passenger got off. It was hot, stuffy and sweaty, but she scrambled to the front, opened a window, and sat with her handbag and gas mask on her lap. She bought a return and settled down to enjoy the view: a patchwork of fields and hedgerows and, beyond them, purple and hazy in the far distance, the moor. Tom and Beth were safe, out there with Edith. She'd had a letter only last week. You'd scarcely know there was a war on, Edith had written, except that farm prices were getting better and better.

The bus had reached the outskirts of the city where the road followed the railway line when the siren started wailing. Anxious heads turned and peered out as the bus slowed, then came to a halt. Above the Plym Estuary two Hurricanes chased a Heinkel bomber, the three of them climbing and diving like toy planes in the clear sky. All at once they were over the city, coming this way, and the Heinkel was releasing its load. The bombs fell, four of them, drifting down like tiny specks, growing larger and larger as the plane banked steeply and made off across the Channel. Gripping the seat in front of her, Kathleen watched in horrified fascination, willing the bombs to miss the bus. A man's voice shouted to get down, and a child screamed. Kathleen flung herself on the floor and shut her eyes, waiting, waiting, hearing the whistle, then explosion after explosion, and a violent rush of air. The bus shook and rattled; its windows shattered.

A cry of pain, and sobbing, and she looked up to see a woman wiping blood from her forehead. Voices, shouting, and more screaming. Kathleen felt something warm and damp, and looked down to see blood oozing from the back of her hand. As she rose to her feet and stood on unsteady legs, shards of glass fell from her lap. Passengers were scrambling for the exit, crying, shouting encouragement to one another. Kathleen followed, picking her way carefully through the debris. Dust hung above a crater in the road fifty yards away, and a terraced house further on had taken a direct hit. Smoke rose from the wreckage and a thin flame licked at roof timbers strewn over bricks and mortar. The air was thick with the stench of burning fabric, wood and lino, and scorched metal.

Kathleen closed her eyes to the devastation and forced herself to take a few deep breaths. When she opened them people were emerging from houses nearby, staring in silence at the wreckage.

An elderly woman pointed at the ruins. "She went in… I saw her… a moment ago." She made an incoherent noise and covered her eyes with her hands as if to blot out the tragedy.

"Someone's in there under the rubble!" Kathleen yelled, and staggered as swiftly as her shaking legs would allow towards the remains of the house.

A handful of men from the bus caught up with her.

"There's a woman in there. Start lifting these timbers; we've got to get her out!" she cried.

On the other side of the road, from a house with its windows blown in, a young man emerged, dusty and coughing but otherwise unhurt.

"Is there a phone around here?" she asked him.

"Post office, half a mile – got a kiosk there."

"Run – run as fast as you can and telephone for an ambulance. Better get the fire brigade as well," she added, because the flames were beginning to take hold.

Volunteers poured onto the street and a chain of arms removed lumps of concrete and twisted metal and wooden window frames from the pile of rubble that had once been a home. Others fetched buckets of water, and someone brought out a hosepipe and sprayed the flames.

"There she is!" shouted one of the men.

"Yes, I can see her!" called back another.

"Be careful now," Kathleen warned. "Get the timbers off her, but don't move her until we find out how badly she's injured." She knelt beside the woman, oblivious to the danger, and brushed the dust from her face.

The woman groaned and opened her eyes, blinking at the strong light.

"Ambulance is on its way," Kathleen said, taking the woman's hand in her own. "It'll be here soon."

"Who's in charge?"

Kathleen twisted round and squinted at a figure silhouetted against the sun. When she shaded her eyes, she recognised the uniform of the Women's Voluntary Service.

"She's in charge; that lady's in charge," said one of the men who'd helped with the rescue.

The ringing of an ambulance bell grew louder and louder.

"Over here!" The WVS uniform beckoned and the stretcher-bearers hurried to the spot.

"I feel I really must tell you—" began Kathleen, getting to her feet and extending a hand.

"Parker; Lucinda Parker," interrupted the lady from the WVS.

"Kathleen Wyndham."

"Fine job you've done here, Miss Wyndham. Haven't heard your name before. Are you new here?"

"I'm not from around here at all," she replied. "In fact, I was on the bus coming to Plymouth to find work."

"Huh, we could do with someone like you – calm head in troubled times. Go to the Guild of Social Service, Pilgrim House, in Notte Street. I think there's a job coming up that would suit you. Just tell them Mrs Parker sent you."

Pilgrim House was a charming Victorian mansion covered in Virginia creeper; a few scarlet leaves heralding the change of season. Kathleen looked for a bell or knocker on the black-painted door but, finding none, tried the large knob above the keyhole. To her surprise it turned under the pressure of her hand and the door opened a fraction. She pushed cautiously, and it swung back to reveal an entrance hall, cool and serene, with a massive carved staircase leading to a galleried landing. Most of the room doors were closed, but one – bearing a 'Reception' plaque – was open, and through this a shaft of sunlight drifted out onto the polished wood floor of the hall. Voices – female voices, chattering and laughing – were coming from inside the room. Kathleen walked towards the sound, and as she did it went quiet and a head appeared from behind the door.

"Can I help you?" asked a girl.

"I hope so," replied Kathleen. "I'm looking for work and Mrs Parker from the WVS told me to come here."

The girl wore her hair drawn back into a roll around the nape of her neck, which might have made her look severe, but was countered by the welcome in her eyes. "Come about the job, have you? That's funny." She turned to her companion, a woman of more mature years and stouter waistline. "I thought the advert was going in tomorrow. Did it go in early, Doreen?"

"It may have done," replied Doreen, knitting her brows with the effort of remembering. "Anyway, Mrs Parker is right, we are looking for a new member of staff."

"By the way, I'm Stella." The younger woman held out a hand to Kathleen. "You look a bit the worse for wear, if you don't mind me saying."

"Afraid I got caught up in a bit of an air raid just now."

"We heard the siren go off," said Doreen. "Thought it must've been another false alarm – enemy plane spotted out to sea. They always set the siren going, just in case, you know."

"What happened?" said Stella, showing real interest. "Anyone hurt?"

"Woman, badly injured," replied Kathleen. "But we got her out."

"Coo! That must've been exciting."

"Bit frightening, really."

Stella dived into her handbag. "Here, take a look at yourself." She held out a hand mirror to Kathleen. "Looks like you've been in the war, all right."

Kathleen smiled back, held the mirror in one hand, and combed bits of debris from her hair with the other. "Oh, sorry, I'm making a bit of a mess."

"Here, sit down, my love." Doreen got up and offered her chair to Kathleen. "You look just about done in. Must be the shock of it all."

Kathleen rubbed her eyes and yawned. "I do feel rather strange," she admitted as she sat down. She hadn't noticed the man standing in the doorway, watching them.

"Oh, Mr Teddington, I didn't hear you arrive," said Doreen. "This young lady's come about the job." She turned to Kathleen. "Sorry, dear, I didn't catch your name."

"Miss Wyndham; Kathleen Wyndham."

Doreen returned to Mr Teddington. "Says Mrs Parker sent her, but we didn't think the advert was going in the paper till tomorrow. I'm sure I asked them to put it in tomorrow."

"Quite right, Miss Furze, it's tomorrow," said Mr Teddington to Doreen. "So how did you come to hear about the job, Miss Wyndham?"

"It was just that after the air-raid, when I happened to bump into Mrs Parker, and she said to come and ask at Pilgrim House."

"Mrs Parker – a formidable lady indeed," observed Mr Teddington. "You look a bit shaken. Are you all right, Miss Wyndham?"

"I'm sure I shall be fine – no bones broken." She managed a weak smile.

"I tell you what," he said. "Why don't you come up to my office and I'll give you an application form now – save you sending for one?"

It was the middle of October before Kathleen received a letter calling her for an interview. By the time she reached Pilgrim House her hands felt sticky and her heart was pounding uncomfortably. The application form for the job had been rather vague as to the exact duties to be performed, and she was left with the distinct impression that a lot needed to be discussed afterwards with the successful candidate. One statement in particular had intrigued her: 'Driving licence essential.'

Stella recognised Kathleen the instant she walked in, and gave a friendly wink. "Miss Wyndham, over here, please." She directed Kathleen to a row of chairs, two of which were already occupied: one by a timid-looking girl with blonde hair; the other by a thin, smartly turned out, but rather older woman. Both stared at Kathleen and then looked away as she took her seat.

When Kathleen was called, she climbed the great staircase and entered the committee room, where the air was chill, and a host of faces turned to greet her. Mr Teddington smiled, asked her to take a seat, and introduced the five men and seven women of the emergency committee seated to either side of him. In her confusion, she remembered none of their names, except Mrs Parker, who appeared to recognise her, and an imposing woman wearing a fox fur and an indomitable expression, who was introduced as Lady Astor, Member of Parliament for Plymouth.

"Who'd like to ask Miss Wyndham a question?" said Mr Teddington.

An elderly man, his face consisting mainly of wrinkles beneath a smooth, bald scalp, raised a finger, and Mr Teddington nodded. "Tell us your typing and shorthand speeds, Miss Wyndham," the man demanded.

"I'm afraid I don't do shorthand or typing," Kathleen said.

The man stared at her and then turned to Mr Teddington. "Thought this job was about being your assistant, Henry? How the devil can she do that if she can't type?"

"Emergency coordinator – that's what the job is."

"Humph!"

"Anybody else?" Mr Teddington leaned forward and looked down the line to either side.

"I'd like to ask Miss Wyndham what experience she has of organising; getting things done."

Kathleen looked to see who had spoken, and realised that it was Lady Astor who had asked the question. "I started a café and also ran a business for many years, selling farm produce to hotels, shops and restaurants," she replied.

"So you're used to dealing with people and money?"

"Oh yes. You have to look after those working for you, and if you're not up to scratch, customers soon let you know. I know how to budget and keep the books; I always made a good profit."

Lady Astor made a note on the pad in front of her, looked up and smiled. "Thank you, Miss Wyndham."

The interview progressed until each member of the committee had asked Kathleen at least one question; a laborious process of dubious efficiency.

"Just one final thing," said Mr Teddington. "You indicated on your application that you hold a valid driving licence. Would that be to drive a car?"

"All vehicles," Kathleen replied. "Not just cars."

A murmur ran up and down the table and the expressions on several faces changed from bored indifference to authentic interest.

"But have you actually *driven* some other vehicle – like a truck, for instance?"

"Oh yes. I used a truck to make deliveries."

"Thank you, Miss Wyndham. That will be all." Mr Teddington was smiling broadly as she left the room.

Two days later Kathleen received a letter on Guild of Social Service notepaper offering her the post of emergency coordinator, asking for a reply by return of post, and requesting she start work at her earliest possible convenience. The salary was enough to rent a modest flat in Plymouth.

Before she left Totnes, a letter from Joseph arrived. He was being held at an internment camp. He was being treated well, and rumours were circulating that they might be sent to the Isle of Man. He ended by saying that he loved her and begging her to wait for him. She replied saying that she was pleased no harm had come to him, but carefully avoided any mention of her affections.

CHAPTER 23

"I'm really glad you got the job," said Stella. "I didn't take to the others; especially that one that looked like she'd just sucked on a lemon. Not that you can get lemons these days."

"Thank you, Stella," replied Kathleen. "I'm pleased you think I'm the best of a bad bunch."

"Oh, I didn't mean it like that. I'm sure you'll do a wonderful job and fit in here really well. Anyway, Mr Teddington said to send you up to see him as soon as you arrived. Top of the stairs and turn right – but of course you know that; silly me."

"Better get on, then. Don't want to be late for the boss on my first day, do I?"

Mr Teddington's room was reached through a small anteroom occupied by Doreen, who returned Kathleen's smile and immediately left her typewriter to knock on his door. "Miss Wyndham's arrived," she announced.

Kathleen pulled herself up, took a deep breath and walked into the room. Behind a large mahogany desk, looking out over files of various hues piled in neat stacks, sat Mr Teddington. The bay window behind him was framed by a pelmet and maroon velvet curtains reaching to the floor. A curl of smoke rose from a cherrywood pipe resting in the ashtray beside the telephone.

"I trust I find you well, Miss Wyndham, and ready to take up the task of emergency coordinator." Taking off horn-rimmed spectacles, he rose to greet her, offering his hand.

"I'm looking forward to it, Mr Teddington," she replied, shaking his hand. "Although I'm not entirely sure what the job entails."

"Please, take a seat."

She slipped onto the leather-covered chair that faced him across the desk and waited.

"Cigarette?" he enquired, producing a packet of Craven 'A'.

She shook her head. "No thanks, I don't."

"Well, the job may consist of a lot of things over time." He picked up the pipe, stuck it between his teeth, and drew in a couple of times. "It all depends on what's needed, you see." Smoke billowed from his mouth in tiny clouds as he spoke. "The first thing is to set up something called a Citizens Advice Bureau – a place where people can get advice on anything. No money, of course, so it'll all have to be done with volunteers." He caught her gaze and held it. "Think you can do it?"

"I'll certainly give it a jolly good try. Will the bureau be based here?"

"No, no, can't have it here, not enough room. Miss Clarke at reception tries to deal with queries at the moment but what's needed is something on a much grander scale." He flung his arms wide.

For an instant Kathleen wondered who Miss Clarke was, and then realised he must mean Stella.

"In any event, as I'm sure she'll tell you, Miss Clarke's engaged to be married and when that happens she'll be leaving."

"Surely she'll want to stay on for a while, with all the uncertainty of the war and everything?"

He shook his head slowly. "Whether she does or not isn't up to her. We don't employ married women here."

"Very well, Mr Teddington. I'd better make a start." She looked away, not trusting herself to meet his eyes. "I suppose the first thing is to find a home for the bureau," she said brightly.

"You might try the technical college, and be sure to mention my name to the principal." He took a file from the pile next to him and opened it.

Kathleen took this as a signal that the meeting was over, and decided that the other questions still forming themselves in her head could be left until a later date.

Stella was hovering about in the hall and wanted to know right away how Kathleen had got on, which was a tricky question to answer, because Kathleen herself had only a vague idea of what the Citizens Advice Bureau was all about.

"And I haven't any premises, or any volunteers, or any money. On the other hand, you might be able to tell me where the truck is, but I suppose it's too much to ask if there's any petrol in it." She thumped her forehead with the palm of a hand, while they both struggled to stifle gales of laughter. "On a lighter note, I hear you're engaged to be married soon."

Stella grinned. "Next April – the 19th." She held out her hand for Kathleen to admire the engagement ring: a square-cut sapphire with a diamond to either side.

"What's his name?"

"Ken. He's in the RAF – Bomber Command. Don't see a lot of each other just now, of course, because he's based somewhere on the east coast."

The principal of the technical college was most helpful and agreed to lend Kathleen two large classrooms at the front of the building. To her surprise, he also offered a number of trestle tables, wooden chairs, and strong-armed students to arrange them in lines down the rooms; an arrangement that gave no privacy at all, and she hoped the citizens seeking advice wouldn't mind.

Mr Teddington hadn't been quite accurate when he'd said that there was no money in the kitty. Stella said there was sufficient in the emergency fund to place advertisements in the *Evening Herald* asking for volunteers, and to set up a telephone and a typewriter in each of the rooms. By the time of Kathleen's next meeting with Mr Teddington, replies had flooded in, especially from married women eager to help and offering two or three hours a week.

"You don't have to worry about the volunteers being married," he said, with a dismissive wave of the hand, when Kathleen explained. "The rule's only there to make sure the real jobs are given to those who need them – like men and single girls."

Kathleen gave him a bright smile through gritted teeth.

The bureau became an instant success; the number of enquiries growing every week from people with questions about rationing, war damage, prices, travelling in wartime, evacuation, resettlement – the list was endless.

One afternoon, when she was in deep conversation with a room supervisor, Kathleen felt a tap on her shoulder. She swivelled round to find herself face to face with Lady Astor.

"I've heard through the grapevine what a marvellous job you're doing, Miss Wyndham. I felt I had to come and offer you my congratulations in person. I knew you were the right person."

"Thank you, Lady Astor. It's very kind of you to say so."

"Well, keep up the good work, my dear. If there's anything I can do, just let me know." She offered Kathleen her hand.

"There is something, if you could spare a moment."

"Of course, my dear. What is it?" Lady Astor asked.

"You know what happened a few months ago – how people were rounded up and interned because they had come here often long ago, but had never taken British citizenship?"

Lady Astor nodded. "What of it?"

"Did you know that some of them came to England in the first place to escape persecution? I know of someone who came with his family in 1903, when he was thirteen. I think it's utterly stupid to lock them up; they could be helping the war effort."

"Absurd, quite absurd," said Lady Astor. "It's totally ridiculous to lock up people who have lived here most of their lives. You're quite right. Questions need to be asked." She gave a mischievous chuckle. "I've quite a reputation for making a nuisance of myself, you know."

December, and the weather was remorseless, with gale after gale sweeping in from the sea and dark, ragged clouds flooding the western sky. But one evening when Kathleen left Pilgrim House the air was still and cold, and a nearly full moon was creeping above the city rooftops. Head down, she hurried through the park, where the bare branches of trees cast gloomy shadows onto paths that were already showing the first signs of frost.

She had left the park and was crossing the road when the siren sounded. Behind her, footsteps pounded the pavement and someone, overtaking her, shouted that the shelter was over here, and to get inside. Driven by panic, she chased after the voice until, stumbling, breathless and shaking, she came to a halt, unable to make out where she was. From the darkness an arm reached out, clutched the belt of her mackintosh, and pulled her into the shelter. The door slammed shut, and someone switched on a torch. The dozen or so people crammed into the dingy space glanced at one another, ashen-faced. No one moved, but everyone listened. A little girl with frightened eyes, clutching a teddy bereft of fur, clung to her mother's coat. Kathleen managed a feeble smile for her.

Within minutes the drone of approaching aircraft became impossible to ignore. In a corner of the shelter a lone boy, about Tom's age, abandoned any pretence of bravery and started to cry. Kathleen shuffled her way through the crowd until she stood beside him. She put an arm around his shoulder and he huddled up to her, his body racked with sobs. Thuds, wallops and bangs sounded in the distance, but the cacophony of destruction grew louder and louder until it was possible to hear the whistle of the bombs before they exploded.

"Mummy, Mummy, I don't like it." The teddy fell from the girl's clasp as she buried her face in her mother's thigh.

There was the whistle, an agonising pause for the merest fraction of a second, and an ear-splitting detonation. Instinctively, everyone crumpled to the floor, hands on heads. Then the most violent explosion of all: the *whoomph* of the blast and the air sucked back in again as chunks of concrete and dust fell from the shelter ceiling. Kathleen coughed and spluttered and gasped, and everything went very quiet and still and dark around her.

A light – a warm, rosy glow of a light – suffused Kathleen's consciousness. She tried to open her eyes. Everything felt very strange, as if she didn't quite belong in her own head, and when she tried to move a great weight held her back.

"In here!" someone called out. "Look, it's all right – there's a space where she is."

Kathleen's mind moved lazily, recognising the timbre, the resonance of a familiar voice she hadn't heard for a long time. She floated on the tide of memory, and then there was a sudden lurch, like waking from a dream, because she knew that the voice was Robert's. She blinked and stared, trying to make out his face in the erratic light of a torch. "Robert," she tried to say, but her throat was all husky and dry, and straight away she fell into a fit of coughing.

"Steady now – don't try to move. Hold on; we'll soon have you out." He hadn't heard her try to speak; he didn't know who she was. He was shouting, calling for her to be taken to hospital.

They placed her on a stretcher and loaded it into an ambulance. Again she tried to speak, but the words stuck in her throat and her head started spinning. Her legs and arms were weak and useless and her mouth still full of dust. The ambulance doors slammed shut and the vehicle pulled away slowly. Her shoulder ached – strange how she hadn't noticed that before – and a patch on her face was starting to sting. She stared into the blackness that surrounded her and wondered whether the voice – Robert's voice – had been nothing more than a dream after all.

Inside the blacked-out windows of the hospital, the light dazed her befuddled brain even more, and the pain in her shoulder was growing worse by the second. Calm, steady hands felt down her neck and upper arm, and around her shoulder – a quick jerk, and she screamed in agony.

"Dislocated – nothing more to worry about now." The voice of the doctor was deep; reassuring. "Nurse will give you something to help you sleep."

Kathleen groaned and fell into another fit of coughing; the tenderness of her shoulder was excruciating.

"Don't you worry now, my dear. Just going to give you an injection to take the pain away and make you sleep." The nurse's voice – kindly; reassuring – came from the other side of the bed.

Kathleen tried to open her eyes to see who had spoken.

"Just as well your young man can't see you," the nurse continued. "You're not a pretty sight. But not to worry – only a few scratches and bruises. They'll be gone soon enough."

Kathleen drifted off into a deep sleep, aware of nothing until the clatter of cups and saucers roused her, and a cheerful voice announced that it was six o'clock and time to wake up. Trying to make sense of what had happened last night, she recalled, as if through a fog, the sound of Robert's voice giving orders. But it couldn't have been him. There was no reason for him to be there. And what about the others in the shelter? The boy and the little girl – were they dead?

"No serious casualties," replied the nurse, when Kathleen asked. "You were the one we were most concerned about. The children? Just cuts and bruises, but the little girl was terribly upset about her teddy. Couldn't find him – got left behind in the rubble, I suppose. She was crying her eyes out, poor little mite."

"Hmm... they can get so attached to a special toy."

"Know a kiddie like that, do you?" asked the nurse, and Kathleen could manage only a wan smile in reply.

At 8.30 the doctor allowed her to leave, and she walked towards the hospital gates, stiff and still a little bemused. In the early morning light she could make out an open-topped army car parked beyond the row of ambulances near the exit, and as she drew near a man got out of the driving seat.

"Kathleen! Kathleen – over here." Robert, in army uniform, waved an arm and ran towards her.

"Oh dear God, Robert, I wasn't hallucinating. It *was* you. What on earth are you doing here?"

"I've come to take you home – wherever that is." He went to put an arm around her shoulder, but instinctively she jumped away.

"Oh, I'm sorry; I didn't mean to... sorry. It was presumptuous of me."

"It's my shoulder I didn't want you to touch. It's so sore – it was dislocated."

"Oh, that's all right, then. Oh no… I'm sorry. I didn't mean that either."

He looked so crestfallen that she giggled. It was good to laugh, except that the bruise on her cheek ached, but even that couldn't diminish the surge of joy she felt. After all this time Robert was here, and he was offering to take her home. He opened the door of the car and she settled herself in the passenger seat.

"Where's home?" he asked.

"One of those avenues off Lipson Road – I've got a flat."

Robert started the engine and they moved off, pausing at the gates for a red bus to pass. "We should have a reasonably clear run," he said. "After yours, there weren't any further casualties at this end of the city."

"I want to ask you about that. What on earth were you doing there last night?"

"Let's get you home safely; then I'll tell you everything."

It wasn't far from the hospital to Kathleen's flat. Robert stopped the car by the kerb, opened the door, and escorted her up the steps to where a cluster of milk bottles waited by the front door.

"One's mine," she said.

"Of course," he replied, then bent down and picked up the nearest bottle. "Here, give me the key. You don't want to use that arm."

She let him unlock the door and usher her into the hall. "Upstairs," she said, leading the way.

The flat (which consisted of a bed-sitting room, a kitchen, and a half-share of a bathroom) was at the back of the house in a tenement that looked south over the city to Plymouth Sound. The kitchen was very small, so that the space between the gas stove and the table was limited. Kathleen squeezed onto one of a pair of chairs while Robert filled the kettle and put it on to boil.

"There's a loaf in the bread bin," she said.

He cut a few slices and put them to toast under the grill. Under her instructions he found butter, marmalade and tea; then he sat down on the other chair and looked at her. That great gulf, all the years that had divided them, had shrunk to such a little space. It was no more than the distance of his hand from hers across the table. They both looked at their hands resting on the table before he reached out and let his fingers touch hers. It felt exquisitely beautiful; like coming home after a long time away. She guessed he felt the same, because he stroked the back of her hand very gently.

A smell of burning made them both start.

"Quick!" she cried.

"It'll be all right," he said, turning the slices over. "Just needs a bit of a scrape."

They both laughed – the careless laugh of children at play.

He poured the kettle to make the tea, and she managed to take the top off the milk with her good hand and tip it into a jug. When he'd scraped and buttered the toast and cut it up for her, they sat and looked at one another again and she wondered at her good fortune in finding him, and couldn't quite believe it even then.

"I can see you're wearing army uniform," she said. "But what are you doing here in Plymouth? And why were you around last night during the air raid?"

Robert raised his eyebrows in an expression of amusement. "I could ask you exactly the same."

"But I asked first." She held up her forefinger at him, but let her lips curve into a smile so that he'd know she wasn't cross.

"The army's lent me to Civil Defence, just for the time being: a sort of special coordinator until things are running smoothly. I arrange action parties – rescue squads; ambulances – and report damage; that sort of thing." He tried unsuccessfully to stifle a yawn, and blinked red-rimmed eyes at her. "Sorry... been on duty all night."

"You poor thing. You need to get some sleep." She laid a hand on his arm.

He looked at it, and placed his hand over hers. "You haven't told me about you."

"I've got a job with the Guild of Social Service – emergency coordinator." Her heart was pumping faster as she watched the next question form in his eyes.

"Why did you leave the farm? There've been all sorts of rumours."

An awkward pause followed.

"What did they say? Blamed me, I expect." Much to her annoyance, she found herself trembling.

"They said you ran off with the cattle feed merchant... what's his name – Greenwood?"

"He offered me lodgings when I told him I wanted to divorce Jim, that's all. It was so humiliating: Jim and the dairymaid sleeping together, quite openly. Everyone in the village knew. Even Tom came home with things the other boys had said."

"I knew it had to be his fault." Robert thumped the table with the palm of his hand. "The bastard."

She gave him a watery smile. "I mustn't think about it too much, especially not about the children, or I get into a bit of a state."

He held her hand for a long time and stroked her face with his finger. "My poor darling," he said at length. "You've been through so much."

"I've found you again."

"That's true." He produced a broad grin. "And I'm off on Friday night. How about coming to the pictures with me? I've heard *Rebecca* is on at the Royal. We could get something to eat at Genoni's first."

CHAPTER 24

The days dragged by, but now it was Friday afternoon and soon she'd be seeing Robert again. The first cold snap of winter had grown more severe, and she hurried home from the office past trees in the park, stark and skeletal in the frosty air.

She put the key in the lock and paused on the doorstep, imagining the scene in an hour or so, when Robert would be ringing the doorbell. He'd be standing right here, a smile on his face, and she'd ask him in. He'd enquire how her shoulder was, and she'd reply that it was still sore but a lot better.

Although she really couldn't afford it, she'd bought a new dress and had gone without lunch all week to pay for it. The dress was woollen, deep mustard, very stylish, and when she looked in the mirror she knew it was worth every penny. A dress like that needed high-heeled shoes despite the fact that they might draw attention to the ladder in her stocking. She'd mended it last night but the darn showed at the knee when she sat down. On the other hand, if she kept her legs well hidden under the table at Genoni's, no one would notice. The bruise on her cheek had faded to a greenish hue and she managed to hide it with a heavy application of foundation, but the scab on her nose she could do little about. In a spirit of defiance, she found her brightest lipstick and applied it lavishly.

The doorbell rang. A glance at her watch, and she hurried downstairs. The woman from the ground-floor flat, clad in rose-patterned overall and fawn slippers, was there ahead of her, hand poised to open the door.

"It's for me. I'm sure it's for me." Kathleen gave her a meaningful look, hoping she'd go away, but the woman stood her ground, cigarette between forefinger and thumb, smoke spiralling into nicotine-stained hair protruding from her headscarf.

The bell rang a second time. Kathleen reached for the handle and opened the door, and there was Robert, smiling, just as she'd imagined.

He leaned forward and kissed her on the cheek. "You look absolutely stunning," he murmured in her ear.

The woman from downstairs gave a disapproving grunt, turned, and waddled back to her flat.

"She's such a nosy old thing," Kathleen confided. "But I don't care – not tonight, anyway."

"How is it?" asked Robert, closing the front door and putting a gentle hand on her shoulder.

"Still a bit sore but all right if I'm careful. Look, I need to get my coat. Will you come up for a moment?"

As soon as they were inside the flat he kissed her, and his kisses were full of warmth and passion, just like they used to be. And they kissed for such a long time that all her lipstick disappeared and she had to open her handbag, find the stick, and put more on.

Genoni's was never more welcoming than on that evening. In the restaurant's dim light, couples talked in low, earnest whispers and surreptitiously touched fingers beneath the folds of the tablecloths.

"How Genoni manages to conjure up dishes like this with all the shortages is a total mystery," said Robert as they scanned the menu.

"Absolutely amazing," she agreed.

After they'd chosen and Robert had placed the order, she said, "Tell me about the job and why you're in Plymouth." What she really meant was, *What's happened to you and Sarah, and why aren't you living at home?*

"I was trying to think what I should do – you know, to help the war effort – and was just on the point of joining up. We went to a dinner party, and Nancy – that's Lady Astor – mentioned the Civil Defence in Plymouth. She said she had asked the army if they could borrow an officer with local knowledge, and would I be interested? And I said, 'Yes, very interested.' It's only temporary – just while they're getting the system up and running. I have to report back to the controller and tell him if we can make improvements."

'*We*', Kathleen thought. *That means he hasn't left Sarah.* "Is there anything in this city that Lady Astor doesn't know about?" she said brightly.

"What makes you say that?"

"She was on the committee that gave me my job."

Robert threw back his head and laughed. "She knows everything and everybody. Unless I'm very much mistaken, she'll take a personal interest in you."

"She has already; she's been to tell me she thinks I'm doing a marvellous job."

A little before seven, Robert paid the bill and they crossed the road to the Royal Cinema. All the queues had vanished and the programme was about to start.

"Very popular, *Rebecca*," said the girl in the kiosk. "Not sure I've got two seats left – not together, that is."

Kathleen's heart sank.

"Oh yes, there we are – circle, near the back. That'll be three shillings, please."

Robert grabbed the tickets and they hurried up the stairs, past photos of Joan Fontaine and Laurence Olivier set against towering cliffs and ragged skies. They dashed through the upper foyer full of plush red decor and high wall panels with gold motifs and made for the swing doors. The auditorium was packed, and when the usherette showed them to their seats they had to disturb a whole row of sailors to sidle their way through. They'd hardly settled when the lights went down and music blared. Diaphanous drapes of palest gold, decorated with giant multicoloured butterflies, parted to reveal the screen. Robert's hand found Kathleen's and closed around her fingers.

He bought ice creams during the interval, and then *Rebecca* started and the lights went off again. He rested an arm on the back of Kathleen's seat and ran a finger up her neck so softly that her skin tingled under his touch. She gripped his hand when that awful Mrs Danvers went crazy, and when everything turned out all right her eyes became misty and she had to sniff a few times, and Robert noticed and gave her his handkerchief, and she blew her nose as quietly as she could.

From the cinema to the car was only a short walk but it

felt like heaven – Robert's arm around her waist, and hers slipped casually around his.

"Would you like to come in?" she asked when he'd driven her home.

"Are you sure it'll be all right?" he whispered.

"You mean the old dragon?" she whispered back.

"Yes – I wouldn't want to cause any trouble."

"I don't think she's particularly friendly with the landlady. If we're as quiet as mice she probably won't notice."

Kathleen put the key in the lock and turned it. *Click.* She pushed at the door and it opened slowly. Then just as she stepped over the threshold, the hinges gave a long, high-pitched wail. Robert followed her into the hall. She closed the door and they tiptoed upstairs in the dark. They'd reached the top when a light was switched on down below.

"Is that you, Miss Wyndham?"

Kathleen bundled Robert through into the flat. "Yes, it's only me… nothing to worry about," she replied in a light-hearted way. Then she slipped smartly inside, and shut the door.

"You're *sure* it's all right, my being here?" he asked.

He looked so serious that she had to try hard to stifle a laugh. "It's absolutely wonderful, your being here."

"Well, in that case…"

"Such luxury. I feel quite guilty." Kathleen splashed water over her knees and smiled at Robert through the steamy atmosphere of the cramped bathroom.

"Let me wash your back. I promise I'll be gentle with your shoulder." He knelt on the bath mat and reached out for the soap. "I'm afraid I'll have to leave after breakfast. I don't want to but I haven't much choice."

"Why? Why do you have to go?" Kathleen asked.

"I'm off duty for a couple more nights and I'm expected back at Southwood."

Her heart sank; that meant he was going back to Sarah. "How are things?" she asked, her voice a little too animated, a little too loud.

"We don't live in Alston Hall any longer. About six months ago it was requisitioned as a military hospital. I've taken a lease of the Old Rectory and we've moved in there. Sarah's quite involved with the hospital – the welfare side, you know. She writes letters and makes telephone calls to the relatives of injured soldiers."

"When will you be back?" Kathleen blurted out, almost panic-stricken. He had to come back to her; he *had* to.

"I'm back on duty next Tuesday. Can I leave a message for you at Pilgrim House?"

"Only if you leave it with Stella – Miss Clarke – at reception."

It was then that he saw the real question in her eyes. He turned her face gently towards his and kissed her forehead. "You are my love; my one true love," he said.

In the time left before Christmas, Robert was not on duty all the time, and when he wasn't he'd take Kathleen to places she'd never dreamed existed. He knew funny little streets down near the Barbican with bars and late-night cafés. Once he knocked on a door that looked as if it was the entrance to a warehouse, and a big, burly man let them in when he saw it was Robert. He held her hand and she followed him downstairs, where people were drinking round a bar and a band was playing in the smoke-laden atmosphere.

"How do you know all these places?" she asked, sitting down at a table he'd found.

"Put it down to a misspent youth," he replied, and grinned at her.

The band was playing Gershwin and then moved on to Cole Porter, and Kathleen sipped at the gin and tonic Robert had bought her and looked around. Couples were talking, laughing, dancing, and the air was full of heat and sweat, and all at once she felt free and very full of life. They started playing 'Night and Day' and Robert held out his hand to her. She rose from her seat and he pulled her close. His arms encircled her, slid gently down her back and pressed her body against his, and she could feel him singing the song as they shuffled round the crowded floor. It was bliss beyond imagining. Even if she was killed in a raid tomorrow it would have been worth living just to have shared this moment with him.

The parting over Christmas, when Robert left for Southwood, was painful and the hours without him long, dark and lonely.

Christmas cards started to arrive. Rose enclosed a letter in her card, with a message from Uncle Charlie to join the Transport and General Workers' Union, because Kathleen's job involved driving a truck. She had to smile as in her head she heard Uncle Charlie dictating the words and Rose writing them down. She would join, just to please him, though what possible use it would ever be, she couldn't imagine.

Stella's family invited her for Christmas dinner and she had to hear about all the preparations for the wedding. It was very kind of them, but it made Robert's absence seem worse than ever. Stella's mother did a marvellous job getting food on the table, and naturally Kathleen gave her some coupons of her own to help out.

On a table in the corner of the dining room, she noticed a typewriter. "I wish I knew how to type," she confided to Stella.

"It's not difficult," Stella replied. "Just a matter of practice. I could teach you if you'd like."

"Really? Would you?"

"Come on, let's start now," said Stella. "No time like the present."

Before the New Year arrived Robert was back and sent word that he'd call for Kathleen on the Monday evening. She was listening out for the bell and got there first, despite the old girl in the bottom flat, who grunted and retreated to her lair as soon as she saw it was Kathleen.

"You'll never guess what," Kathleen said, after Robert had kissed her and asked how she was. "Stella's teaching me to type. I learned quite a lot over Christmas."

"Over Christmas... as quickly as that? You're an amazing woman."

"I'm still a bit on the slow side, but Stella knows where there's a spare typewriter I can have at Pilgrim House, and I'm going to practise."

Then Robert looked serious and said he'd like to take her to Genoni's restaurant, because it was quieter than a bar or club and he'd something to tell her. So she grabbed her coat, and tried not to think what it might be, in case it was something alarming.

"I did the usual round of the estate before Christmas," he said, as they sat at their favourite table. "Although of course, there aren't any oranges to be had these days."

She blushed slightly as she recalled her first Christmas at Higher Haydn.

"Jim complains bitterly about being told what to grow by the Ministry, but secretly he's as pleased as punch with the massive increase in prices. Edith tells me they've a pair of land girls lodging at the farm." He was looking at her to gauge her reaction.

She shrugged. "The children? Did you see the children?"

"Yes." The pause that followed lasted too long.

"What's wrong? Has something happened?" Something stirred in her, and she grabbed his wrist.

"Tom told me his mother had died," Robert said. "He looked very solemn when he said it. Beth was there too, and she told me that Mummy had gone to heaven."

Kathleen's heart was thumping so hard it felt as if it was trying to escape. "What on earth did you say?"

"When I was alone with Mrs Wilcox, I asked her whether it was true. She looked extremely uncomfortable and said she couldn't say, and that I'd better have a word with Mr Wilcox."

"How extraordinary… why would Jim tell them I was dead?"

"I can't say." Robert put his hand on hers. "Tom seemed upset when he told me. I think Beth finds it difficult to remember you; she was so little when you left."

"I never left *them*... I didn't... I wanted to have them with me as soon as I could, when I'd divorced him." Her voice broke and she couldn't say another word.

"Maybe we can sort things out, when the war is over," he said. "Things are going to change. Things *have to* change: they can't go on as they are."

Every day brought fresh news of defeat, loss and tragedy. Kathleen read in the newspaper that Amy Johnson, driven off course by bad weather, had ditched her aircraft in the Thames and drowned. She felt a profound sense of grief and shock that a woman who'd faced so much danger, and who'd lived such a charmed life in the public eye, had finally met her end this way.

In Plymouth the bombing intensified, and so many people were searching for relatives lost in the chaos that the Citizens Advice Bureau was almost overwhelmed. Kathleen advertised for even more volunteers and set up what she called the 'Searchers' Service' in one of the rooms lent by the technical college.

One Monday in March, when she was at her desk in Pilgrim House, there was a knock on the door. Almost immediately, without waiting for a reply, the door opened and Kathleen looked up to see an animated Lady Astor.

"I couldn't say before – security, you know – but two very important people will be visiting us on Thursday," announced Lady Astor. "I want as many of your volunteers as possible on the Hoe. Let's hope it's fine."

When Kathleen got home she put a ring around the date on the calendar in the kitchen: 20th March. When Robert came around that evening she pointed it out to him.

"What's it for?" he asked.

"Not exactly sure," she replied. "Important visitors coming, Lady Astor said."

"You'll have to wait till Friday to tell me all about it," he replied, trying hard not to smile. "Remember I'm on duty Thursday night."

"You know who it is, don't you?" She stared hard at him.

"Can't say. Sorry!" But he couldn't help himself; he was grinning from ear to ear.

The king and queen arrived by train. The king was whisked off somewhere while the queen was taken to the Hoe to be introduced to row upon row of volunteers, and various organisations. It was a fine, windy day; the sea brilliant as a thousand diamonds and the air clear enough to see the Eddystone Lighthouse. Presented to the queen by Lady Astor and complimented on the work she was doing, Kathleen was bursting so with pride, she could hardly wait to tell Robert.

It was about six o'clock in the evening when the royal visitors left Plymouth, and Kathleen was in such high spirits, she didn't feel like going home. Stella and Doreen suggested they snatch a bite to eat at one of those little cafés in George Street. It seemed a good idea, because after all, there was much to celebrate. But it was about half past eight, when the three of them were giggling and laughing and recounting tales of the day, that the siren wailed.

"Oh my God!" Stella's face turned pale.

"There aren't any shelters round here!" exclaimed Kathleen.

"Prudential; top of George Street – it's got a basement," suggested Doreen.

They hurried into the street to be met by the deafening, groaning roar of Pathfinder aircraft and a night sky already illuminated by flares and silver barrage balloons. Even as they ran, the first incendiaries hit their targets and burst into flames. Dark figures poured from buildings and raced along glass-strewn pavements as the first small yellow tongues of fire licked at roofs and window frames. Someone barged into Kathleen, and she cried out as she fell, sprawling on the ground.

When she looked up Doreen and Stella had melted away among the stampeding herd of refugees. Breathless, desperate and alone, she scrambled to her feet as the first high explosives came down: *screech... thud... thump... whoomph*. Dust and rubble hit the ground in front of her and the flames sprang up. She let out a scream, darted to one side, and cowered in the doorway of a shop. The heat scorched her hair and her skin felt as if it was on fire. Unable to tell pavement from road, she made a dash for it – the Prudential Building was still there, stark against an apricot sky. Another explosion behind her, and the upper storey of a shop collapsed, sending burning debris scudding along the ground. Fire ran down the wall to Kathleen's right, licked around the door, and swept across the pavement towards her. Streaks of flame bellowed from windowless caverns, whipping the fire into an all-consuming frenzied arc above her head. Fear lent her strength and she bolted up George Street, her only thought to reach the refuge at the end.

With a final effort she made it and, gasping for breath, joined the bodies jostling against one another as they poured into the Prudential Building. Eyes glistening with terror looked out from faces white as sheets as Kathleen hustled and elbowed her way down to the basement restaurant, cramming in among the startled diners. A few yards from her a man groaned and crumpled to the floor, clutching at his chest. Someone loosened his collar, and shouted for a doctor. People stood around and stared at one another, faces blank with disbelief, unable to comprehend the horror engulfing their city.

It was then that Kathleen remembered that Robert was on duty – out there in that hellish firestorm, doing his job. *Please let him be safe, let him be safe, let him come back to me*, she prayed over and over again. She could feel her strength draining away, her knees growing weak, every movement becoming an effort. Tucked away in a corner, she slumped to the floor and stayed there a long time, hands over her head, unable to summon up the energy to move even an inch.

It was towards midnight before she began searching for the others. Stella she found squatting on the Prudential Building's stairs, but of Doreen there was no sign.

Dawn crept over a city shrouded in a pall of foul-smelling smog. One by one traumatised survivors ventured out to survey a scene of utter destruction: their refuge the only building standing amid a pile of rubble. Kathleen and Stella picked their way past firemen hosing down smouldering ruins. They clambered over twisted girders and charred beams, and avoided burst water mains. The disgusting stench made them want to retch, and their eyes, tired and bloodshot, stung and watered in the acrid air.

When they reached Pilgrim House they found rumour running riot: who'd been hit, where the worst casualties were, how many had been killed. Someone told Kathleen that the Civil Defence Headquarters in the Guildhall had taken a hit, and someone else said that Captain Neville was among the casualties. Kathleen sat in Stella's office, put her head in her hands and sobbed. The thought of Robert's body lying somewhere among the rubble was too much to bear.

CHAPTER 25

By mid morning few had turned up for work at Pilgrim House. Kathleen and Stella, bleary-eyed and yawning, hardly knew where to start, and Mr Teddington scuttled about asking if anyone had seen Miss Furze, because he was lost without her. Kathleen left Stella to tell Mr Teddington what they knew about Doreen, which wasn't much, and picked her way through rubble-strewn streets to see how the Searchers' Service was coping.

It was unnaturally quiet as she approached the searchers' room. Her pace slowed and she entered cautiously, uncertain of what she'd find. Hollow-eyed, haggard faces stared back at her; several desks were unoccupied. Kathleen thanked the volunteers for coming in when she knew that they'd probably not had a wink of sleep.

"Can't let those blighters think they've won," a man said. "Just got to get on with it, haven't we?"

Kathleen attempted a smile, and asked if there was any information on casualties, which there wasn't, because the phone lines were down, and someone pointed out that The Royal Hotel had got a direct hit so all their records would have gone up in flames.

"We'd better start with the hospitals," suggested Kathleen. "I'll use the truck and go to the hospitals; get lists of names."

As she was speaking, an old woman carrying a wicker shopping basket wandered in and stood eyeing the scene. "Is this where you come to make enquiries when you're looking for someone who's missing?" she asked nervously.

Kathleen assured her that it was and that they'd do their best to help, although things were a bit difficult after last night. She led the woman to a chair and sat her down. "Now, this lady will take your details and see if we've any information on the person you're looking for."

As more searchers arrived, Kathleen slipped away, leaving the volunteers to offer what help they could. *Please, please let me find Robert safe and well*, she prayed silently over and over again as she made her way back to Pilgrim House, angry tears clouding her vision. The fire brigades were still hard at work, finding bodies among the twisted girders and the grime and the still-hot embers. *Oh, please let Robert not be there.* She followed a route that led her down Old Town Street (scarcely recognisable), and came to a halt outside Spooners – the place where she'd come on shopping trips, where she'd met Edith, where they'd talked and sipped tea. It was a burned-out shell, like all the other shops in Bedford Street; familiar names reduced to blackened caverns. Only yesterday there'd been talking, laughter, people, where now there were only ruins. This war, this blasted war – it was so unfair. She stumbled on, blinded by tears she couldn't quell, and reached Pilgrim House.

Still no news of Doreen, Stella told her. Mr Teddington had been to Doreen's home, where she lived with her elderly mother, and all he had learned was that Doreen had left for work yesterday morning and never come home. So it looked like Kathleen and Stella were the last ones to see her. Secretly, Kathleen was hoping she'd find Doreen's name on a list of casualties; that she'd just been injured and they could visit her later, but at another level she feared the worst, and the closeness of that possibility made her feel cold all over. The truck, thank goodness, was still in one piece and had petrol in it. She took deep breaths, trying to fill her lungs to ward off the exhaustion creeping into every fibre of her body, but the disgusting reek of death and destruction lingering on the air made her want to cough and retch.

The hospital staff were run off their feet; casualties lay on stretchers in corridors and entrance halls, waiting to be seen. Feeling like an intruder, Kathleen apologised for being there as she asked for news on the injured and the dead. A kind lady in admissions was very helpful; she sat Kathleen down and gave her a cup of tea and a bun, because it was nearly one o'clock, and went to see what she could find out. When she returned with a list Kathleen took it from her, thanked her for her trouble, and glanced down the roll of casualties, because she had to know if Robert's name was there, and when she couldn't find it her heart leaped in gratitude. But on a second, more careful examination of the list, she spotted Doreen's name among the dead, and had to blow her nose several times, and the admissions lady guessed that she'd found the name of someone she knew and let her sit there a bit longer. But there were others desperate for information, Kathleen told herself, and she'd better get back with the names, because that was her job and it was about time she got on with it.

So she delivered the list to the Searchers' Service and drove back to Pilgrim House (round all sorts of funny little backstreets, because the main roads were still blocked), and told Stella and Mr Teddington about Doreen. Stella burst into tears, and Mr Teddington went very pale and left at once to break the news to Doreen's mother.

At the end of an agonising day Kathleen trudged to Robert's digs, hoping that his landlady might have some news.

"Captain Neville? No, dear, he was on duty last night – I do know that. But he never came back this morning. And you're not the first to be asking, by any means." Robert's landlady folded her arms under an ample bosom and looked Kathleen up and down. "Friend of yours, was he?"

"Yes, he was an old friend," said Kathleen. My God – she was speaking about him in the past tense. Yet there was no way she'd believe that Robert was dead until she knew for certain. Why, anything might have happened, and in all the confusion, mistakes were bound to be made.

She went home and flung herself down on the bed. Fatigue overwhelmed her, and within seconds she drifted into a deep sleep where the air-raid siren whined and hideous dreams lurked, waiting to torment her.

She woke with a start to find the night sky burning with flares and light streaming in at the window. It was no dream – the horror was starting all over again. Struggling into a coat, she slipped on shoes and pounded down the stairs, her heart racing at the sudden exertion. The first thuds and bangs sounded before she reached the shelter and yanked the door open, trying to see through the darkness. A torch was switched on to guide her and a murmur of voices expressed relief that she'd made it.

When the door was shut against the night, the nosy woman from downstairs took a box of matches from her pocket and lit an oil lamp on a table in the corner. "Same time as yesterday," she observed. "Well-organised blighters, I'll give 'em that."

The family from the upstairs flat at the front of the house was there too, and the father tried to make conversation, asking whether it was true that Kathleen worked for "the Social Service people", as he called them, and whether her young man was in the army, all the time trying to sound normal, as if they'd met casually in the street. Kathleen, too tired to weep, too tired to think, replied in a voice that was flat and heavy, and let him ask whatever he wanted to, and when he had finished she sat as still as a statue, and closed her eyes and didn't care about anything any more.

The next day she trudged into work, shivering from sheer exhaustion, her coat drawn tightly about her. Stella had the kettle on and was handing round cups of tea when she arrived.

"I can't believe it," Stella said. "They say Guildhall Square got it last night and St Andrew's Church is just a blackened, burned-out shell."

"I can't believe we won't see Doreen again," said someone. "I keep thinking she'll walk in and we'll all be back to normal."

"Will it ever be normal again?" asked Kathleen. "It's all gone; everything's gone."

"*Almost* everything," observed Stella. "Genoni's is still there but Goodbody's Restaurant's gone."

"Goodbody's?"

"We were going to have our wedding reception there." Stella gave a long sigh. "We can still get married, but it won't be the same."

A dart of jealousy struck Kathleen. Stella still had Ken – he was alive and he'd be coming home to marry her next month. Stella had no right to moan about a stupid restaurant being bombed.

As the days passed with no news of Robert, nothing made sense any more, and the longer it went on and she heard nothing, the more Kathleen tried to reconcile herself to the inevitable. Then one day in early April, she received a note from the Searchers' Service to say that Captain Neville had been badly injured in the March raids and taken to the Royal Naval Hospital in Devonport. Faint with relief, Kathleen clutched the edge of the table and read the note again, and wondered at her own stupidity in having forgotten about the military hospitals. If the information was true, Robert was alive and a mere bus ride away. After tea she made up her face and put on a dress he especially liked, but her heart raced when she allowed herself to think about what she might discover, and tried to prepare for the possibility that Robert might have been injured so badly that she might not recognise him.

At the hospital she enquired after Captain Neville and was directed to a ward on the first floor. Robert was sitting up in bed, talking to a visitor – Sarah. Kathleen stopped, stood completely still and watched them, wondering if she was a mere spectator at a reconciliation scene. Too far away to hear their conversation, she observed the space between them, the way they moved, and the way they looked at one another. Sarah was sitting on a chair at the far side of the bed, clutching the strap of a handbag resting in her lap. Robert kept looking down at the sheet as he spoke, smoothing the hem with his hands. Scarcely thinking about what she was doing, Kathleen retraced her steps until she found herself at the hospital entrance, grateful that her worst fears for Robert's injuries had not materialised, yet trying to remain calm in the face of Sarah's presence at his bedside. She sat on a chair in reception, pretending to read yesterday's newspaper, trying to work out what to do, and wondering whether if she stayed long enough Sarah would go and she'd be able to slip in and take her place.

With only minutes to spare until the end of visiting time, Kathleen glanced up and there was Sarah walking towards the exit. The instant she was out of sight, Kathleen folded the newspaper casually, and made a dash for the stairs. Robert was gazing out of the window as she came into the ward, and didn't notice her until she'd nearly reached the bed.

"Thank God you're alive, Robert," she blurted out. "No one could tell me what'd happened to you." She placed a hand on his shoulder, and there was such joy in touching him again, feeling him warm and alive under her fingers, and such joy when he returned her kiss.

"Kathleen. Oh, Kathleen, you're alive – you're all right." His hand grasped hers. "I heard you were with the others, in the restaurant and so many people never got out, I thought you must be dead."

"And I kept hoping and hoping you weren't dead." She smiled through her tears at the blurred image of him. "One of my friends, Doreen, didn't make it."

"I'm so thankful you did," he said, and squeezed her hand till it hurt.

"Poor Robert," she said, pulling the chair close and sitting down beside him. "Tell me what happened."

"I don't remember much. I remember going on duty, hearing the sirens and seeing everything lit up by flares. After that it gets a bit muddled, and the next thing I knew I was in hospital." He gave a rueful smile. "They told me I'd been knocked out for a bit."

She asked if he was badly injured, and Robert said that it was his leg (broken at the thigh), and a few ribs bruised. And scarcely had he finished telling her than a bell rang and a nurse announced that visiting time was over.

"I'll come again tomorrow evening," Kathleen said, giving Robert a quick kiss on the cheek.

"No, you can't." Robert held her wrist. "They need the bed. Tomorrow they're sending me to Alston Hall to convalesce."

"Oh no... no, they mustn't."

"Come along now. All visitors must leave immediately." The nurse had Kathleen in her sight and was walking directly towards them.

"Don't worry," hissed Robert. "I'll be in touch – somehow. Stay at the same address."

The nurse was standing at the foot of the bed, glowering at them.

"All right, all right, I'm just going," Kathleen said, and gave Robert's hand a quick squeeze.

Stella married Ken a few days later and Kathleen tried to feel happy for them, but envy crept up on her at unexpected moments. She would find herself agreeing that Stella looked absolutely radiant and Ken wonderfully handsome in his RAF uniform, and then a voice in her head would ask why they should be the lucky ones, while others – she meant herself – always had to struggle and never had it easy. And then she'd feel guilty and wonder at her own selfishness, because Stella and her family had been so kind.

"Ken's only got four days' leave, so we're not going far: just down to Newquay for the honeymoon," Stella explained to a cousin.

"Back at work next week, then?" asked the cousin.

Stella made a face. "'Fraid not. At our place you're asked to leave if you get married."

"Has anyone actually *told* you to leave?" asked Kathleen, who'd been listening.

"No," said Stella, "not actually told me, but everyone knows the rules."

"When you get back," said Kathleen, "why not turn up for work, same as usual, and see what happens? We all want you to stay. It's only old Teddington who'd make a fuss."

"Ooh, do you think I should?"

"Definitely – I'll make sure everyone stands up for you. We'll say the rules should be changed and you've got to be allowed to go on working."

Over the next few days, Kathleen canvassed support among the women at Pilgrim House. They were unanimous: everyone wanted Stella back and everyone thought the rule was unfair. Kathleen wondered whether Stella's nerve would hold and whether she'd turn up, but she needn't have worried. By the time Mr Teddington arrived, Stella was in her usual place, dealing with enquiries.

"My dear Mrs... Mrs Goodwin," he stuttered. "This is most irregular. You know the rules. As a married woman you are not eligible for employment here. You must leave straight away."

Kathleen confronted him. "Well, we all think she should stay and that you need to change the rules."

He blanched and took a step or two backwards. "Some kind of joke, is it?" he said, with a nervous laugh. "You can't do this, you know; you can't interfere with the rules."

"Why not? We all work here and we want Stella to stay."

As Kathleen spoke, doors opened and secretaries and typists emerged from their offices and flowed silently across the polished wooden floor to stand by Stella.

"There you are – I told you so," Kathleen said triumphantly.

"This is ridiculous," retorted Mr Teddington. "Get back to your work at once, girls."

"Action!" shouted Kathleen.

All the women sat down on the floor and trained their eyes on Mr Teddington.

"We're on strike," Kathleen informed him. "We'll go back to work only if you say that Stella – Mrs Goodwin – can have her job back."

Mr Teddington had a stupefied look on his face, as if he didn't quite believe what was happening. "I'll think about your request," he said. "Now, for goodness' sake, run along and stop wasting my time." He waved them away with a hand.

No one moved an inch.

"I'm afraid that's not good enough," Kathleen informed him. "You have to say that Mrs Goodwin is reinstated as our receptionist, otherwise we're staying on strike."

"Oh, very well, she can stay," he muttered.

"That's very sensible of you, Mr Teddington," said Kathleen. "Stella, please give him the letter to sign, saying that you're employed on the same terms as before you got married."

"That won't be necessary," said Mr Teddington. "I'm sure we all know where we stand."

"It'll be even plainer when you've signed the letter." Kathleen smiled sweetly as she handed it to him.

He had the blank stare of one defeated, who knows he's met his match. Without another word he took a fountain pen from an inside pocket, scribbled his signature and returned the letter, with the ink still wet, to Stella.

"Thank you," said Kathleen. "Now that's settled, we can all get on with our work."

A letter arrived from Rose, saying she'd heard that they'd 'had a bit of a do' in Plymouth recently and hoped Kathleen was safe. Everyone up there was saying things had to change, had to be different when all this was over. Uncle Charlie reckoned working people needed a better deal, and the mess the country had got itself into was all down to the posh folk at the top. She finished with news of Kathleen's mother:

You'll never guess what – only the other day we bumped into your mother. She was on the arm of a man – quite good-looking – and she was boasting that this man could get anything you wanted on the black market. Said she was never short of cigarettes or nylons, and even gave me a tin of pineapple to prove it.

Ta-ta for now,
Rose

Waiting to hear from Robert kept Kathleen on edge, and when news came, it was not good. Complications had set in and he needed another operation. It would be several weeks before he could get back to Plymouth. Kathleen missed him dreadfully but there was nothing for it except to buckle down and press on.

Spring melded into summer, the days grew warm, and still there was no news of when Robert might leave Alston Hall. An oppressive day in July, and a rumble of thunder made Kathleen reach for her umbrella as she left work. By the time she reached home the rain was coming down in sheets and she was scarcely able to see where she was going. She fumbled for her key and dashed up the steps to her front door. Glancing up, she was surprised to see a man standing there, the collar of his coat turned up and a brown trilby, dripping with rain, obscuring his face.

"Hello, Kathleen."

She gasped, because the man on her doorstep was Joseph.

"Aren't you pleased to see me?"

She stood there, staring at him, for several seconds.

"Aren't you going to ask me in, Kathleen?"

The rain came down even harder and Joseph stepped to one side as she put the key in the lock and turned it.

"You'd better come in," she said, and led the way upstairs.

"They've started letting people out – people who aren't going to do any harm."

"I know," she said, as they reached the kitchen. "Questions were asked in Parliament about you and the others. It was so unfair."

"You did that for me?"

"Someone needed to speak up for you. It was just so stupid; so unfair."

He sat down and rested an arm on the table.

"How did you find me?" she asked as she put the kettle on to boil.

"Searchers' Service," he replied. "They gave me your address as soon as I said the name Wyndham. Of course it took me a while to work that one out; I tried the others first." He made a move towards her, as if to embrace her, but she put up a hand to stop him, and his face took on the expression of a chastised puppy, his eyes sad and doleful. "What is the matter? I thought you'd be pleased to see me."

"I am, I am, but things have changed, Joseph. This is my home now. I earn my own living, and I must be honest with you: I'm not going to pretend to be Mrs Greenwood again."

Joseph's brow furrowed. "I don't understand."

"Look at me, Joseph. I have a job; an important job. I'm independent and I'm not going to give that up."

"And what will you do when it comes to an end; when the war's over? You'll need a man to support you then."

"Never!" She surprised even herself with the vehemence of her response. "I'm going to keep my independence."

"There won't be jobs for women after the war," he observed.

"Things are going to change," she insisted.

He got up to leave.

"Where will you go?" she asked.

"Back to London, probably. I saw my brother last week after the tribunal let me out."

She heard his feet thumping down the stairs and the front door close behind him. Joseph had a point, she had to admit. What *would* she do when the war was over?

CHAPTER 26

April 1944

Kathleen sat in her office at Pilgrim House and her thoughts drifted back to a time when she'd felt invincible; a time when she'd believed that she could do anything in the world. She recalled her idea of getting a pilot's licence and flying clients all over the country, and thought what a ridiculous notion that had been. On the other hand, some women did succeed in leading interesting lives, and there was no need to look very far – one lived in Plymouth. But Lady Astor had a husband who encouraged her, and she was fabulously wealthy. Perhaps it would be worthwhile having a word with Lady Astor next time she saw her and seeking her advice. She was always popping in, asking how things were going and what needed to be done next.

The following week, when Kathleen was at the Citizens Advice Bureau, Lady Astor swept into the room unannounced. Her usual chatty self, she talked incessantly, telling everyone what a marvellous job they were doing and how Plymouth couldn't do without them, and as she was leaving, Kathleen asked if she could spare a moment.

"Of course, my dear. Of course I can spare you a moment. Now, what is it you want to ask me?"

"I'd really appreciate your advice, Lady Astor," said Kathleen. "I know it's early days to be thinking about this, but I'm wondering what I'll do for a job when the war's over."

"I don't think you'll have to concern yourself just yet; we've a long way to go. But with your abilities, my dear, you won't need to worry." Lady Astor gave her an encouraging smile. "You're so good at organising things; you're an absolute marvel. And everybody loves working with you; they're always telling me how wonderful Miss Wyndham is. You really should think of going into public life. Have you ever thought about politics? How about standing for the city council?"

"There's nothing I'd like better, but unfortunately I've no independent means. I do need to earn my living."

"That's a shame, because you'd do so well." Lady Astor's eyes twinkled. "Perhaps you'd better stand for Parliament – MPs get paid, you know." She patted Kathleen on the shoulder. "I'm afraid I really must go – luncheon appointment."

Kathleen pushed the conversation to the back of her mind, because there was so much to do and most evenings she returned home exhausted, but one day, in the not-too-distant future, she would have to give the problem serious consideration.

Out of the blue a letter from Alice arrived, asking Kathleen how things were in Plymouth, and complaining about the time it took Bertie to get home when he had leave. He'd volunteered for the Ordnance Corps and been sent all over the place, she wrote:

...and I can't tell you how hard I work these days. Just when we put half the ornamental garden down to fruit and vegetables, the gardener was called up. I've managed to find an old man who likes to earn a bit to supplement his pension. But he's very slow, so I have to do a lot myself. Sometimes I think I'm even beginning to look like a peasant.

You mentioned in your last letter that you'd seen Robert; that he was working in Plymouth, but you didn't say how you met him. Was it just by chance, or did your paths cross in the line of work?

Please let me know how life is treating you.

Your dear friend,

Alice

Since his recovery and return to service, Robert had been deployed on a number of different jobs by the army, and now had the task of liaising with American forces pouring into the locality. Everyone knew that an invasion of France was coming, but no one dared guess when it would be. "You know I can't say." He pressed a finger to his lips and looked serious. "Got to keep mum."

"You can't fool me," she said. "All the top brass you've been entertaining – I hardly get a look-in these days. And there's something going on around Slapton Sands. Everybody knows the Yanks are there, thousands of them, and you can't get anywhere near the village, let alone the beach."

The look on his face told her she was near the mark.

"Do you know what I think? I think—"

"Don't say it. Don't say what you think. I mean it."

The smile faded and she looked at him, acutely aware she'd gone too far.

"Now, what I want to know is whether you'd like to go to a dance the Yanks are putting on," he said, deliberately changing the subject.

"When?"

"Saturday," he replied.

"Fine with me. Hope it's as good as the last one." She rose from the kitchen table and looked around for her handbag and gloves. "Now I really must be going or I'll be late."

He held her wrist and looked up at her, and his eyes were laughing. "Not till you've given me a kiss," he said.

The dance hall was awash with military uniforms and women in short-skirted dresses and bare legs. Robert held her hand as they threaded their way through the crowd of gyrating bodies to a space near the band, who were playing Glenn Miller numbers; the noise deafening. Talking being totally out of the question, Kathleen flung herself into the dance until beads of perspiration stood out on her forehead and her breath came in gasps.

"I... need... a... rest," she said, when the tune changed.

"How about a drink?" panted Robert, his face as red and sweaty as hers. "Coca-Cola?"

She nodded and they jostled their way to the bar, and after what seemed an age Robert managed to get the bartender's attention and bought two Coca-Colas that fizzed so much the straws nearly fell out.

"There's something I want to tell you," he said, kissing her on the neck. "Shall we take these outside?"

The look on his face was so serious, a shiver of alarm ran through her. "Why? What is it, Robert?" The band stopped playing and in the yawning silence she could hear her heart racing.

"Don't worry." He kissed her again. "I want to tell you about Sarah," he said as they walked through the doorway.

Oh God – this was it. He'd brought her here to tell her it was all over – he was going back to Sarah. Her throat tightened in anticipation. How could he have carried on, pretending everything was normal?

"Sarah's become very friendly with a colonel at Alston Hall and she's told me she wants a divorce so she can marry him," Robert said.

The words flowed over Kathleen and she stood there, unable to make sense of them.

"And I've agreed. I've said yes, I'll divorce her."

The silence lasted for such a while that Robert had to tell her again.

"I've said yes, I'll divorce her."

This time, somewhere in the layers of consciousness tumbling over themselves in her head, the message reached her brain. "You're going to get divorced?" she said.

Robert nodded. "Seems they'll be living somewhere in Surrey," he continued. "As you know, Freddie's thirteen now – well, almost. Most of the time he's at boarding school, and Sarah's agreed he can spend half the holidays with me at Southwood and the other half with her in Surrey."

Kathleen wanted to laugh, because it wasn't what she'd been expecting to hear at all. Spending so much energy preparing for the worst, telling herself that things weren't going to get any better, and then to find that they had, just like that, filled her with elation. She'd never thought this far ahead. She'd never thought, except possibly in her wildest dreams, she'd hear Robert say what he'd just said. It seemed so remarkably simple; so civilised. Robert would have to pretend to be the injured party, but the divorce would go through because Sarah and the colonel wouldn't fight it.

"Why not see if Jim will divorce you?" Robert ran a forefinger gently down her arm and slipped his hand over hers.

The band started up again, and the noise meant she had to stand closer to hear what he was saying.

"I want to marry you, Kathleen." He leaned forward and kissed her on the tip of the nose. "I want to look after you." Another kiss. "I don't want you to worry ever again."

"You really are serious, aren't you?"

"Yes, I am. We should have married long ago, you and me. Don't let's waste any more time."

She looked at his face and it felt like she was seeing it for the first time, or in a new way, she wasn't sure. Everything felt tender and beautiful and she was different to the person she'd been only a moment ago. Then she remembered Jim, and the fact that she was still shackled to him. Yet so much had changed – perhaps Jim had changed too; perhaps he'd let her go at last. "I'll ask him," she said.

In her letter to Jim Kathleen didn't say specifically why she wanted to see him. Maybe it was the ambiguity of the situation that attracted him, because within the week, he'd replied saying that he would meet her in Ivybridge at The Coach and Horses.

The bus dropped her at the bit of waste ground near The London Hotel. She wondered whether she'd bump into anyone she knew and what she'd say if she did, but in the once-familiar streets of Ivybridge no one recognised her. She waited until the exact time Jim had given, gathered her thoughts together, and walked into the public bar of The Coach and Horses. In the smoke-filled room, heads turned to look at the woman who dared invade the men's precinct. She ignored them and walked with a deliberate air to the snug at the end of the bar. At a table stained by drink sat a man gazing out the window; in front of him a glass of cider, half consumed; a greasy tweed cap lying to one side. Legs apart, the man's hands rested on his thighs, calloused fingers encrusted with dirt. Beneath florid, jowly cheeks his neck bulged over the collar of his shirt, and grey hair curled around his ears. She didn't recognise him at first; then he turned to look at her and she realised that the man was Jim.

"Sit down," he commanded. "Wondered how long it would take afore you came to your senses."

She did as he said, not because his words had power over her any longer, but because she was startled to see the man her husband had become. Time had taken its toll and wrought its revenge on the handsome young man who'd greeted her in the barley field and stolen her heart.

Taking her compliance as a sign of obedience, he smirked in satisfaction. "Well? What have you to say for yourself?" Bloodshot eyes under wrinkled lids looked into hers.

"I came to ask for a civilised end to our marriage."

His eyes narrowed in suspicion and he said nothing, so she continued.

"We've been apart for so long you could divorce me for desertion. It would be so easy." She sensed him sizing her up, and a shiver ran down her spine. In her mind she flinched, waiting for the blow that must surely come.

Having observed her for a full thirty seconds, he drew a deep breath. "It's like this, here," he said. "Can't see nothing in it for me 'cept expensive lawyers." He frowned and leaned towards her. "Tell me one good reason why I'd want to divorce you."

"It would mean we could both have a fresh start." It sounded pathetic, the way she said it, and her resolve began to falter.

"Can't say I want a 'fresh start', as you call it. A woman belongs to her husband and it's him she should obey." He lifted a forefinger to her, just like he used to.

She felt blood rush to her cheeks as he spoke, and the old anger began to ferment deep within her.

"Backalong at that other do, I learned a thing or two from they lawyers. Said that if I divorced you for going off with that man – that Greenwood fellow – I could claim damages for adultery. Turned out he weren't worth suing. Didn't have enough money to pay me what I wanted, you see, otherwise he could've had you."

She clenched her teeth and glared at him, trembling with suppressed rage through a long, stony silence.

He sat back in his seat, pleased at the effect his speech had created. Then he leaned forward, arms on the table, for a final thrust of argument. "Now, you find yourself a man worth suing and I'll divorce you for adultery and claim my money. Money that was owed me long ago; money I never got."

Blind wrath, violent as a volcanic eruption, exploded within her. She rose to her feet, picked up the cider glass and threw the contents at the red face and the bulging eyes. "You know what you can do with that suggestion!" she yelled as he sat there, blinking in astonishment, droplets of cider clinging to his eyelashes. "Excuse me, excuse me." She barged her way through the crowd of men who'd gathered at the entrance to the snug, jostling for a view of the entertainment.

"She got you there, Jimmy," shouted a man. Raucous laughter from his companions followed the observation.

Without a backward glance, Kathleen marched through the bar and out into the street, still shaking with anger. It wasn't time for the bus, so she went to the café in Fore Street that used to buy Higher Haydn cream and cakes, and had a cup of tea and a toasted teacake in an effort to calm down. The manageress had changed and no one there recognised her.

Robert was waiting at the bus stop in Plymouth. The moment she got off, his arms encircled her and he kissed her forehead. "How did it go?" he asked.

"Can we go somewhere and talk?" She was still bristling with indignation.

"How about the Hoe?" he replied. "We could go for a walk."

They marched side by side in silence until they came to the highest point, where they could look out across the water to the breakwater and beyond.

"Clear enough to see the Eddystone Lighthouse today," Robert observed.

"Yes," she agreed, her voice flat as she fought to control the feelings bubbling away below a calm exterior.

"Well?" he asked.

"He says he'll divorce me if I find a man rich enough to pay him damages for adultery."

She waited, expecting Robert to be as outraged as she was, and was irritated when he didn't respond immediately.

"Kathleen, dearest, I know you're very, very cross about all this, and I can understand that. But if he divorced you because of me, you would be free – we could get married. I'd be able to take care of you and there is so much we could do together." He put his hands on her shoulders and turned her gently towards him, holding her at arm's length. "I love you so much it would be a price worth paying. I don't care how much he wants; there isn't anything I wouldn't give for you."

Hot, angry tears flowed down her cheeks. "Robert, how could you? You're as bad as he is. I'm not a possession, I'm not property to be bought and sold, and I thought you knew that. I will not be owned by you or anyone else."

CHAPTER 27

In the heat of the moment she'd told Robert she didn't want to see him; that there was no future for them if that was how he felt about her. Yet in her loneliness she regretted her hasty words and longed for his love and for his touch. Days, weeks passed and still no word came. She half-expected he'd write or be there when she left work, or she'd find him on her doorstep one evening.

"Where's that young man of yours?" enquired the woman from the ground-floor flat. "Had a tiff, have you?"

Kathleen detected a trace of derision in her voice. "None of your business!" She slammed the front door behind her and went out into the street.

It was cold; quite blustery for the start of June. She walked swiftly through the park, past the bombed-out church and the rows of Nissen huts used as shops, and arrived at Pilgrim House.

"Morning," said Stella. "Anything I can do for you?"

"What are you so cheerful about?"

"Nothing special – just got this feeling." Stella hummed to herself as she bashed away at the old Olivetti typewriter.

Kathleen took the key for the truck off the wall. "I

need to make a few deliveries this morning – blankets and things. I'll be back about lunchtime if anyone asks."

It took longer than she'd planned and it was nearly two o'clock before she was back at Pilgrim House. The front door was ajar and she could hear voices inside. Everyone was gathered in the hall, faces flushed, talking in excited whispers, while Mr Teddington stood on the bottom stair, about to make an announcement.

"Just in time, Miss Wyndham." He beckoned. "Come in, do come in."

She came in, stood beside Stella, and waited.

"It's official – I've heard it myself." Mr Teddington beamed at them. "D-Day's come – John Snagge made the announcement on the BBC news. Everything's going to plan, it seems."

They all shouted and cheered, and Mr Teddington suggested an extra biscuit with their tea to celebrate. Kathleen cheered with the rest, but the news came as a stark reminder that soon her job would end. She must find other work; if not in Plymouth, then elsewhere.

One dull July afternoon, when she sat at her desk checking the latest leaflets, Mr Teddington called her to his office.

"Please sit down, Miss Wyndham," he said. He seemed relaxed, almost jolly; pleased with himself, like a schoolboy who's just been told he's won a prize.

She sat down and gave him her full attention.

"Miss Wyndham, I've always had a high regard for you," he began. "You've done a marvellous job during these difficult years and have supported the volunteers when the going was tough." He regarded her over the top of his spectacles, his hands resting on the desk, the fingers forming a steeple. "We'll forget the little incident concerning Mrs Goodwin." He flicked a hand to one side, as if dismissing it as a minor irritation, and then resumed his former pose.

Why was Mr Teddington saying all this? He was obviously building up to something. Perhaps he was about to dismiss her. A feeling like panic rose in her throat and she gripped the sides of the chair, ready for the punch to fall.

"I thought it only fair to tell you, Miss Wyndham, that I shall be leaving in the not-too-distant future." He tried unsuccessfully to keep his face in a sombre expression, but his eyes creased along their laugh lines and he couldn't stop his lips twisting up at the corners.

It was Mr Teddington who was leaving, not her. He was the one who was going, and relief flooded through her. "May I ask where you're going, Mr Teddington?" she enquired.

"You may recall that I was off for a day or so last week," he said, the smile becoming more and more apparent. "Well, I've been offered a post in Birmingham. It's a big step up, you know." The smile spread right across his face; he was grinning from ear to ear.

"Why, that's absolutely wonderful. Congratulations, Mr Teddington."

"Thank you. Thank you, my dear." He smoothed the desk with the palms of his hands and looked around the room in satisfaction. "They were most impressed with the work we've done here; especially the Citizens Advice Bureau and the Searchers' Service. That's what got me the post, I'm sure."

So he had taken the credit for all the work she had done. Kathleen's jaw dropped and she stared at him, but he seemed not to notice and carried on talking.

"Of course, I'll be sad to leave. I've met some wonderful people doing this job. But things move on and there's work still to be done."

She rose to go, and Mr Teddington held out a hand to her.

"May I wish you every success, Miss Wyndham? I'm sure your talents will take you a long way, and if ever you need a reference I shall be happy to oblige."

She wanted to say something witty and sarcastic, but in the heat of the moment her brain seized up, so instead she shook the hand he offered and gave him a bright, false smile. He hadn't said when he was going – probably didn't know himself yet – but it was as clear as day that the post of emergency coordinator was coming to an end very soon.

"Whatever's the matter with you? You look as if you've seen a ghost," said Stella as Kathleen descended the great staircase.

That evening Kathleen wrote a long letter to Rose, asking whether there were any jobs to be had in London. Rose replied that there was bound to be something going, and that Auntie Mary said that when she got the push Kathleen ought to come and stay for a few days and see for herself.

Still wondering whether she should pre-empt her dismissal by handing in her notice, she was called in again by Mr Teddington to be told that the emergency coordinator post was terminating at the end of the year.

Immediately, she wrote to Auntie Mary asking if she could stay for a few days in early November.

Rose penned Mary's reply and it was typically blunt and to the point. Although they'd be delighted to see Kathleen, the trip wouldn't be without danger.

Got to warn you, but I 'spect you'll have heard anyway: that bleeding Hitler's sending flying bombs over now – doodlebugs, we call 'em. As if he ain't done enough damage already! And your Uncle Charlie says it's because he's a bad loser and just doing it out of spite. Long as you don't mind, we'll be happy to see you.

Kathleen smiled as she read the letter. Of course, everyone thought they'd had the worst of the Blitz, and she didn't mind sharing a bit more with them. She was due some leave, so she'd be able to manage a few days with the family and look for a job at the same time.

On a wet, windy morning early in November she walked to the station and caught the express to Paddington. Thick cloud enveloped the hills and rain lashed the carriage window, and she thought of the other times she'd made the journey, and how different things were now. When they got near London everything grew dark and dismal, and just before the train reached Paddington it started to rain again. She took the Tube to Liverpool Street and walked the rest of the way. There were glaring great gaps where buildings should have been, and scrubby buddleia had taken root among piles of rubble still waiting to be cleared.

"Good to see you!" Auntie Mary wrapped her arms around Kathleen in a warm embrace.

"How's Uncle Charlie? Busy as ever, I expect."

"Rose never told you, then?"

"Told me what?"

"In that case, I'd better say no more for the time being."

When Rose came home from work, she was as reticent as Mary, so Kathleen had to wait for Charlie himself to appear. It was close on seven o'clock when she heard the handle of the front door turn.

"Where's my favourite niece, then? Got here all right, has she?"

"I'm here, Uncle Charlie." Kathleen rushed into the passage and flung herself into Charlie's outstretched arms.

"Tea ready?" Charlie asked over her shoulder.

Mary nodded. "Course it is. We're all waiting for you, you daft thing."

They sat round the kitchen table and Mary served up stew with a bit of mutton in it, and dumplings, and for afters there was potato cake with sultanas.

"They're both being very mysterious." Kathleen glanced at Mary and Rose, who beamed back at her. "Tell me, Uncle Charlie, I'm dying to know. What's so special that you have to tell me yourself?"

Charlie puffed out his chest, an unmistakable look of pride on his face. "I've given up working on the buses."

"Really?"

"Got a full-time job working for the party."

"The Labour Party?"

"That Herbert Morrison's a clever so-and-so." Charlie winked at Kathleen. "He's got funds from the Transport and General Workers' Union flowing into the London Labour Party. There're Labour Party offices being set up in every constituency – well, the ones that matter. Tories won't know what's hit 'em when the election comes." A smile started on his lips, then spread to the rest of his face.

"What's your job, then?" Kathleen asked.

"Setting up the constituency organisations, in the first place. But it gets even better." Almost beside himself with self-congratulatory adulation, he paused for maximum effect and silence filled the room. "I've been and gone and got myself selected as the prospective parliamentary candidate for Spitalfields. What d'you think of that, then? Charlie Wyndham, the Labour candidate."

"Wonderful! I'm so pleased, Uncle Charlie. You're sure to get in. Well, I mean, in Spitalfields no one will have a hope except the Labour candidate, will they? Member of Parliament for Spitalfields, how marvellous."

"Now, girl, Rose tells me you're looking for a job."

"Thought I might look around and see what there is – mine's going in the New Year."

"By all accounts you're a dab hand at organising and getting people to volunteer. It's what you've been up to in Plymouth, ain't it?"

"Hmm... Yes."

"We're looking for someone like that in Spitalfields."

"I need a permanent job, Uncle Charlie. And besides, I'm not a party member."

"Course you are," he replied. "You're a member of the union, aren't you? That means you're affiliated. And the job what's on offer is full-time. The agent's got to be there to run the constituency office when I'm elected MP."

"I can't wait till then."

"For goodness' sake, girl – you ain't been listening. They're appointing agents now. Look here – I got the application form for you." He jumped up from the table, took a sheaf of papers from the dresser and, with a flourish, whipped out the form and waved it in front of her.

"You think I could do it? Really?" She felt stirred up, nervous and thrilled, all at the same time.

Uncle Charlie nodded. "Here's where you have to send it," he said as he handed it across the table. "You can do it, girl, I know you can."

Sleep eluded Kathleen for much of the night. If she got the job, she'd be returning to her roots, where the Wyndhams came from and where many of them still lived. And more than that, there'd be work; the kind of work she loved doing. Uncle Charlie had always treated her well, encouraging her like her own father used to. He'd always thought the best of her and expected her to do well. Yes, she would apply for the job and she'd ask Mr Teddington to give her a reference.

Kathleen's future was still undecided some weeks later. She'd applied for the post of agent for the Spitalfields constituency and been called for interview early in December, which meant they were taking her application seriously. But as day succeeded day and still no letter came from headquarters, she began to wonder if it'd been a mistake to try her luck, and whether Uncle Charlie had overrated her chances.

Towards Christmas, when day seemed only the briefest of interludes in winter's perpetual darkness, Kathleen found Robert waiting for her as she left the office. She'd not seen him since their row, and a frisson of surprise and excitement ran through her.

"Kathleen, it's so good to see you." He put out a hand as if to touch her like he used to, but remembered in time and withdrew it. "I've booked a table at The Duke of Cornwall. I was hoping you might care to dine with me this evening." His eyes pleaded with her.

"Yes, that would be nice." She was in an exceptionally good mood, and besides, she wanted to share the news she had just received with somebody, and Robert was just the right person.

"Absolutely marvellous – I'll pick you up about seven."

"Wonderful. I shall look forward to it." She gave a dazzling smile, turned and walked home.

She chose her dress and applied her make-up with the greatest care, and was rewarded by the look Robert gave her as she opened the front door to greet him at seven o'clock.

After he'd parked the car on a bomb site cleared of debris from the raids, they strolled across to The Duke of Cornwall, their breath rising in clouds in the cold air as they talked. Robert was in great spirits and an air of half-suppressed elation hung about him. The table the waiter showed them to already boasted a bottle of champagne in an ice bucket, and Kathleen began to feel slightly uneasy, wondering what all this might mean.

"Tonight, Kathleen, I want to celebrate," said Robert, holding up a glass of champagne and indicating that she should do the same. "Today, my divorce came through. I'm no longer married – I'm a free man; free to be with the woman I love."

She studied his face and wondered how to reply. "I'm very happy for you, Robert. It must be a great relief," she said, and raised her glass.

"I hope you're not still cross with me," he said, meeting her gaze, seeking her reaction. "I hope you might reconsider your decision, and even if you don't – want Jim to divorce you, that is – we might still find a little place together where we could be happy."

"I've had some news too," she replied, ignoring the question implicit in his statement. "Some very good news indeed. I've got a job."

Robert looked puzzled. "I know you've got a job. You've had it a long time."

"This is a new job."

"Congratulations! We'll drink to that too." Robert smiled and raised his glass again.

"It's in London – the job," she said. "I'm working for the Labour Party in Spitalfields, running the constituency office. My Uncle Charlie is going to be the candidate when the election comes."

CHAPTER 28

Robert stared at Kathleen, his expression blank and uncomprehending. "Surely you can't want to live and work in a place like Spitalfields?"

"What's wrong with it?"

"You can't be serious. It's full of dirty slums and gangs and… you just can't."

"How can you say that? It's where I come from."

A gaping chasm opened between them.

"Don't you see?" she continued. "This is just too good to miss. It's something I can do."

"Oh, please don't go. You don't have to, you know. If only you'd let Jim divorce you, we could get married."

She looked down at her hands folded in her lap, trying in vain to find the right words. Robert didn't understand that for Kathleen living the life of a lady of the manor would be like living in a prison of her own making – and in Southwood too, where everyone knew her; knew she'd been Mrs Wilcox. She had to go to London; she had to do this thing for herself.

In the dead space between Christmas and New Year, Kathleen packed her trunk and prepared to leave

Plymouth. Stella's family had been kind and had invited her to spend Christmas Day with them again this year, and she'd been very grateful.

"You don't know how much it meant to Stella, having you stick up for her the way you did," said Stella's mother.

"It was so unfair, expecting her to leave just because she was getting married," replied Kathleen. "And besides, the rest of us would've suffered, because the best person – the person who knew the job inside out – wouldn't have been doing it."

"She's going to miss you." Stella's mother gave Kathleen a warm smile. "She's told me so."

"I'll miss her too," Kathleen replied.

The spare room at Charlie and Mary's was right over the kitchen at the back of the house, and the window looked out over dingy rows of chimney pots, roofs with broken tiles, and cluttered backyards. Kathleen unpacked and shoved her trunk under the bed.

"I do wonder whether you had something to do with my getting this job, Uncle Charlie," she said, when they were gathered round the tea table. "I'd hate to think I'd got it just because I'm your niece."

Charlie put on an expression of feigned offence. "Me? Nothing to do with me. It was that man who gave you a reference – the one you used to work for. That's what clinched it, so I'm told."

"Mr Teddington?"

"That's him."

"He gave me a good reference?"

Charlie let out a bellow of mirth. "Not exactly."

"What, then?"

"He warned us you were a troublemaker. Said you'd organised a strike to stop one of your fellow workers getting the sack." Charlie's body shook with glee and he wiped tears from his eyes. It was a while before he could continue. "And you did it without unionised labour. Now that *really* impressed them. Thought you must be a bleedin' miracle worker, they did." He gasped for breath and a further bout of convulsive hysteria followed.

Mary and Rose joined in and roared with laughter. Kathleen couldn't help herself; she creased up and laughed till her sides ached and the tears ran. If only Mr Teddington knew what he'd done.

Uncle Charlie produced the constituency office keys and on Sunday morning took her along to see the new premises. They walked down Commercial Street, then off to the left, through a narrow alleyway, and across a derelict yard to a ramshackle shed – soot-covered bricks; dirty, rotting paintwork; and windows that hadn't been cleaned for years. Kathleen followed him inside, wondering what she had let herself in for. Admittedly, the building was substantial, but the musty smell and the cobwebs that hung from the rafters did not recommend the place as an office.

Charlie saw the dismay on her face. "Bit of a mess, but nothing that can't be fixed. I've got a few of the men coming along. Reckon you won't recognise the old place by the time they've finished with it."

Scarcely had he stopped speaking when hobnailed boots clattering on the cobbles made her swivel round.

350

Approaching were half a dozen men in collarless, open-necked shirts rolled up to the elbow despite the icy weather. Charlie beckoned and they came in. He shook hands with each in turn, then tossed his head in Kathleen's direction.

"My niece, Miss Wyndham," he said. "She's my agent; going to run the office for us."

Each man wiped a grimy hand on his trousers before offering it to Kathleen with a nod of the head and a mutter of welcome.

Charlie glanced round the filthy room. "Needs a tidy-up, boys, and that's where you come in. I know you'll do a good job for her."

"Right you are, Charlie," said the man who appeared to be the leader of the gang. He tipped his cap at Kathleen. "Be fit for a queen when we've finished with it, miss."

"Thank you," she replied. "It's very kind of you to give up your time like this."

"Ain't nothing more you can do for the time being," Charlie told her. "So you might as well go back home and start looking at the lists I gave you."

In the front room Kathleen sat down with the old shoebox Charlie had given her and tipped its contents onto the table. His 'lists' were scruffy bits of paper containing names and addresses of party members in the constituency. Scribbled against some were notes on who'd offered to do what in the event of a general election – not a single woman among them, she noticed.

She delved further and discovered minutes of meetings that suggested that the executive committee of Spitalfields Labour Party consisted of a chairman, a treasurer and a couple of others. No secretary – no wonder the membership records were in such a state. She made a note of all the things she'd need (besides a first-class secretary and a typewriter), such as a desk, chairs, trestle tables, pencils and paper, and a telephone, and wondered what funds the constituency had and whether there was any hope of getting money from headquarters.

That evening she showed Charlie the notes she'd made. He pulled a face and said he doubted there'd be enough in the kitty, but took her straight away to meet the treasurer, Jack Smith, who lived in a tenement block off Brick Lane. He was a wizened old man with thin, scruffy hair and yellowing teeth; the gap between the front ones making a whistling noise as he spoke. He took Kathleen's hand in his and shook it warmly when Charlie introduced her.

"Pleased to meet the Wyndham who got people wrongly imprisoned out of the internment camps," he said. "Lot of folk round here are grateful to you."

"But I didn't," she protested. "I only asked about someone I knew, and said how unfair and stupid it was to lock him up as if he was a criminal, and I didn't stop until..." She stared. "How do you know?"

"Joseph said it was you; that you knew the right people to ask."

"Joseph?"

"Yes – poor old Joseph."

"Why do you say, 'poor old Joseph'?"

"Back in September one of them V-2s got him." Jack shook his head and gazed into the distance, and after a while he said, "Thought a lot of you, Joseph did."

"Oh no, I'd no idea… I'm so sorry," was all Kathleen could say. Poor Joseph indeed. He'd been so kind to her when she'd needed help. Always wanting to make himself inconspicuous; never wanting to stand out from the crowd. A gentle man who'd harmed no one. It was so unfair.

"Never mind that now," said Charlie. "Kathleen's been asking about money. Any spare dosh for chairs and tables? And she wants a typewriter and a telephone."

Jack sucked through his teeth, producing a high-pitched whistle. "Never kept much money in the kitty; never had an office before. I'll see how much we've got, but I promise you it won't be a lot." He shook his head slowly as he said it.

After that, Charlie took her home, but they hadn't been there very long when the chairman arrived, and much to Kathleen's surprise he turned out to be another Wyndham.

"This here's your Uncle Albert," said Charlie. "Remember Albert? Took over the fruit and veg stall from your dad."

"Good to see you again, Uncle Albert," said Kathleen. "I suppose the last time we met was at my father's funeral."

"You're right there." Albert shook her hand. "Rum do, that was – Ray going like he did. Thought the world of you, he did. Be proud of you coming back here, girl."

"Thanks, Uncle Albert." She gave him a broad smile. "I'll do my best."

"Now, down to business," said Charlie.

"I've got a suggestion to make." Kathleen glanced from one to the other. "Why don't we recruit new members and ask for contributions to a fighting fund?"

Albert looked at her as if she were completely mad. "Don't know what it's like where you've been, but round 'ere folks ain't got two ha'pennies to rub together," he observed.

"I need money and I need volunteers," said Kathleen in a determined tone. "Don't think the constituency office is where you're going to sit and drink bottles of beer, because it isn't." They'd better buck up their ideas, because she meant business.

She could hear Albert muttering under his breath to Charlie, "Well, I never!" and "Who'd have thought it?"

Undaunted, she wrote to Labour Party Headquarters setting out her requirements and an estimate of the cost. She even asked for a regular income to pay for a secretary, and Charlie laughed and said she was too ambitious by half, and it made her wonder whether she had asked for too much. However, within a month she'd everything she wanted, even the telephone, although they offered only enough money to pay for a secretary to work three days a week.

Immediately she wrote to Stella, apologising for the small salary but nevertheless asking if she'd be interested in the job. Mr Teddington's replacement had reverted to the usual practice of not employing married women. He'd given Stella the sack the moment he'd found out that she was married, despite the fact that she was now on her own because Ken had been shot down in a raid over Germany and was a prisoner of war. Stella replied that she'd be delighted – never mind the meagre wages; she'd enjoy the work, and it would help to stop her pining over Ken.

Nobody could say how long the war would go on or when the POWs would get home. Finding Stella somewhere to stay was easier than Kathleen had expected, because a widow a couple of doors down the street from Charlie and Mary wanted a lodger and took to Stella the instant she saw her.

There was still a nip in the morning air, but the lengthening days gave birth to renewed optimism. Kathleen showed Stella the office, now clean and bright, with a square of patterned carpet over the lino, second-hand tables and chairs, an old typewriter, and a telephone.

"How do you think we should go about getting volunteers?" Kathleen asked.

"Same as we did in Plymouth," Stella suggested.

"You mean advertise?" said Kathleen.

"And we could go round knocking on doors," said Stella.

"And leave a leaflet if they're not in," said Kathleen. "At the moment no one even knows we're here; that we've got an office."

"Yes, we've got to let them know where to come," said Stella.

"When we asked for volunteers in Plymouth," said Kathleen, "who were we more likely to get – men or women?"

"Women – at least eight women for every two men," said Stella.

"So let's bear that in mind." Kathleen gave Stella a knowing smile. "And let's find out what women voters really want, while we're at it. Uncle Charlie's explained to me that it's important to find out who your supporters are.

Then you can organise things to get them out to vote on election day. It seems so obvious, doesn't it?"

"Right, let's do it," Stella replied.

It was two or three weeks after Stella's arrival that Kathleen noticed that Rose had grown very quiet and was not her usual chatty self at all. She asked Mary if she knew the reason.

"Mean to say you don't know?" said Mary.

Kathleen shook her head.

"It's that friend of yours from Plymouth."

"Why? What on earth has Stella done to upset Rose?"

"It's not what she's done," replied Mary. "It's what you *ain't* done since she's been here. Looked forward to you coming, Rose did, and now Stella's 'ere she hardly gets a look-in. It's 'Stella this' and 'Stella that', all the time."

"But the two of us work together," said Kathleen.

"And it's Rose's dad what's the candidate, and she wants to help too. Can't blame her, can you? Feels left out, she does, like she's not good enough for the pair of you."

"Really?" Kathleen said, thinking that Mary must be mistaken, but on reflection she began to wonder whether there might be some truth in what she'd said. There was no other reason she could think of that would account for Rose's low spirits.

She asked Stella if there was something Rose could do to help in the office.

"What we really need is another typist/receptionist," Stella replied, "especially in the evenings and at the weekends, because that's when most of the volunteers come in."

"Rose can't type," said Kathleen. "But she could be in charge of the office if I'm out canvassing."

"And I could always teach her to type," suggested Stella.

After supper, Kathleen took Rose to one side and said she had a big favour to ask of her. "I really need another pair of hands down at the office, outside normal working hours, and I was wondering, Rose, whether you'd mind helping out?"

Rose gave her a dubious look. "What kind of help?"

"Receptionist, typist, that kind of thing."

"Having a laugh, ain't you?"

"No. I'm serious. Stella could teach you to type – she taught me. And she could explain the rest of the job – the receptionist bit."

"D'you mean it? Me, a typist?"

"Yes, why not?"

"Cor… that'd be something! That'd really be something to shout about."

"So you'll do it?" Kathleen asked.

"Dad, Dad, guess what I'm going to do!" cried Rose, and ran to tell him.

One morning in May, Kathleen was in the office with Stella, poring over a map of the constituency, when through the open window they heard the sound of calling and cheering. They raced across the yard to see what the commotion was. People were running down the street and leaping about as if they'd gone stark staring mad.

"It's over – it's all over!" a woman called out, waving her arms.

"What's over?" yelled Kathleen.

357

"The war, of course!" the woman shouted back, and dashed off looking for someone else to tell.

The joy she felt was infecting every man, woman and child in sight; the contagion passing like lightning from person to person. So long had everyone waited for this moment that people poured from shops, offices and houses to dance and sing in the streets. A man draped a Union Jack around his shoulders and ran down the road, bellowing at anyone he encountered that the war was over. Without saying a word, Kathleen locked the office and she and Stella ran to see if Mary had heard the news. As they passed The King's Head, the publican was already pinning red, white and blue bunting to the building.

"Heard it on the wireless," said Mary when they told her. "The man said there're crowds outside Buckingham Palace, all cheering and waving."

"Well, what are we waiting for?" replied Kathleen. "Leave a note for Uncle Charlie and Rose and let's get up there."

"Aw, d'you think we should?" Mary's hand went over her mouth.

"Why not?" Kathleen slung her bag over her shoulder and grabbed Mary's hand. "There's never going to be another day like this, ever. Come on, Stella."

It was nearly midnight before they got home.

"Cor! My feet ain't 'alf killing me," croaked Mary, slumping down on the sofa. "Never seen such crowds in all me born days, Charlie. I'm quite worn out with all the cheering and shouting. D'you know the king and queen and the two princesses came onto the balcony and waved to us?"

"They weren't waving at you, you daft thing," said Charlie.

"Yes they was – they was waving at everyone," insisted Mary. "And when it got dark, everything was lit up: all the statues and the columns – everything."

"And then we went on to Whitehall," chipped in Kathleen, "and Mr Churchill came out onto a balcony with Union Jacks all over it, and he waved and gave the victory sign, and we all waved back and people started singing 'For He's a Jolly Good Fellow.'"

"It ain't 'alf gonna be a tough job getting him out," observed Uncle Charlie. "He's done a bloody good job. Country couldn't have done without him."

CHAPTER 29

Two weeks later, Kathleen found herself in Blackpool with Charlie at the Labour Party Conference. The atmosphere was buzzing with hope and expectation, and in the middle of it all, on the 23rd May, came the announcement they'd all been waiting for: Mr Churchill had resigned and called a general election for the 5th July.

All around her people talked, discussed, argued and made speeches. Motions were proposed, voted on, and carried, amended or rejected. Tub-thumping northerners called for the establishment of a Socialist Commonwealth of Great Britain. Some delegates declared that the party's mission was to overturn a class-ridden society, while others claimed that only reform of the system was needed. And what a mixture they were: intellectuals, wartime rebels, civil servants, serving officers from the military, and trade unionists like Charlie. Very few were women.

"For a start, a woman candidate needs a university degree," said a wolfish-looking man, when Kathleen asked the question. "A woman's got to stand out in some way to get noticed." He blew smoke down his nose and regarded her with roving eyes. "Other way is to make yourself agreeable to someone who can support your application. Know what I mean?"

"Make yourself agreeable?"

"You're a very attractive woman," he replied, giving her a wink. "It shouldn't take you long to find a niche for yourself, if you get my drift."

Back in Spitalfields, everything went to plan. Charlie was officially adopted at a party meeting as the Labour candidate for the constituency, and Kathleen prepared his nomination papers, ready to send to the returning officer, but things did not go as expected. The following evening at about seven o'clock, she was briefing a group of volunteer canvassers in the office when Charlie came in. He'd been tramping the streets all day delivering leaflets, and she could see at once that he wasn't well – his face drawn and pale. As he went to put the remaining leaflets on the table they fell from his grasp and scattered on the floor. He slumped down on a chair, clutching his chest.

"Terrible indigestion," he complained. "Can't breathe properly."

"Oh, Uncle Charlie, whatever's the matter?" Kathleen rushed across the room and put an arm around his shoulder. He was white as a sheet and she could see that his breathing was laboured. "We must get you to hospital. You're ill. It's all my fault; I've been making you do too much."

The next day, when she visited Charlie in hospital, he was a sorry sight, unable to move. Mary sat by his side, her face grave, and looked up as Kathleen drew near.

"Doctors say he mustn't talk. They think he's had a heart attack. He's going to have to take it easy."

The lump in Kathleen's throat grew and tears pricked her eyes. Uncle Charlie looked so small and wizened as he lay there; all the fighting spirit, all the energy drained from him. "I don't know what to say," she began. "Have the doctors said whether he'll get better?"

"They're hopeful; very hopeful," said Mary. "You mustn't upset yourself, my dear. Charlie's told me what a marvel you've been, organising things."

Kathleen's eyes overflowed with tears. "And I've so enjoyed working for him. He's a great encourager, just like Daddy..." Unable to say more, she stole away, leaving Mary at Charlie's bedside for a few more precious minutes.

"When I told headquarters what had happened," said Kathleen to Stella, "they said they'd be sending us a new candidate right away."

"*Send* us a new candidate? Can they do that?"

"Emergency measures, apparently," said Kathleen. She glanced at her watch. "They should be here any time now."

"They? How many are there?"

"Just the two: the candidate and the official who's coming with him."

She'd hardly finished speaking when there was a knock at the door.

"Come in!"

The door opened to reveal a middle-aged man of medium height in a crumpled pinstriped suit. He had a deeply lined face; a long nose and pointed chin; beady, darting eyes; and a cigarette between his finger and thumb. Beside him stood a tall youth with stooping shoulders and sleek black hair parted in the middle. He wore round-rimmed spectacles and a Fair Isle pullover beneath a tweed jacket.

"This the Labour Party office?" asked the older man. He looked around as if searching for someone, raised the hand that held the cigarette (leaving a trail of smoke in the process), and pointed at his nervous-looking companion. "I've brought the new candidate," he said. "Name's Hubert Pettigrew. Where's the agent? I was told he'd be here."

"Excuse me—" began Kathleen.

"Get him on the phone. Tell him to shift his backside down here at the double."

"I've been trying to tell you," she said. "I'm the agent."

The man took a drag on his cigarette, looked her up and down in a disparaging fashion, and sighed. "S'pose we've got to make do with what we can get these days. Type well, do you?"

"I do the typing," interrupted Stella. "And if you want our volunteers to support the new candidate, you'll keep a civil tongue in your head when you're speaking to the agent."

"All right, keep your hair on, Miss Hoity-Toity, but there's got to be a candidate in place by the time nominations close or there'll be trouble from on high. And I want you to organise a meeting so the party faithful can meet their man." He pointed a forefinger at Kathleen as if about to prod her into action. "Get on with it!" He turned to Hubert Pettigrew. "Women are fine as long as they do as they're told. Give 'em an inch and they'll take a mile. Remember that, son."

Kathleen hired a hall and sent out emergency leaflets to all party members in Spitalfields, calling them to a meeting.

The leaflets explained that Charlie Wyndham had withdrawn because of ill health, and that at the meeting the executive committee would welcome and endorse the new Labour candidate. He in turn would make a speech saying that he accepted the nomination. She hoped they would all come and give the new candidate their support.

The day of the meeting was dull and miserable. After tea Mary and Rose went off to see Charlie, who was starting to show signs of improvement. Kathleen made up her face with care and put on a clean white blouse and a smart navy suit. By the time she called for Stella the rain had stopped and the pavements were drying out. The hall had been arranged as Kathleen requested, with a trestle table and chairs on stage for the executive committee and, to one side, a separate table for the candidate and his minder, who Kathleen had dubbed 'Rat-Man'. The floor of the hall contained row upon row of chairs flanking a central aisle. It was filling rapidly.

To attract attention and start proceedings, Albert, as chairman, banged the table with his fist three times. "Now then, ladies and gentlemen, I'm sure you're all very sorry that Charlie Wyndham's been taken ill. I'm pleased to say he's going on nicely and it's up to us to do the same. Tonight, we need to adopt our new candidate, sent from headquarters. Polling day's only a little over six weeks away and we mustn't miss the deadline for nominations. I call on our new candidate, Mr Hubert Pettigrew, to make a short speech telling us why he thinks he can do the job for us." He looked around the hall. "A big hand for Mr Pettigrew, ladies and gentlemen."

As Pettigrew rose to his feet a ripple of polite applause came from the audience. Standing to one side at the front,

Kathleen saw how Pettigrew's hands shook as he studied his notes. His face was drained of colour, except for the cheeks, which looked unnaturally flushed. After clearing his throat a couple of times, he began.

"Good evening, comrades." He glanced at a sea of faces through the smoke-laden atmosphere. "I have the benefit of a degree in politics, philosophy and economics from the University of Oxford, and I should like to tell you something of the work in which I am presently engaged."

Kathleen's heart sank. He wore the Labour rosette and therefore stood for the policies in the manifesto, but what else had he to offer? What had he been doing at Oxford, when everyone else had been fighting a war? She looked at the rows of faces turned towards him. Faces she knew so well: the volunteers who walked the streets delivering leaflets, knocking on doors; excited, jubilant, tired faces. In them she saw the glimmer of hope; a kind of expectation that shone through their exhaustion. The people who'd borne the brunt of the war and the years of poverty before that; people who needed doctors, homes and jobs; people who wanted change. Did Hubert Pettigrew know them well enough to share their troubles, fight for them and get them a better deal?

Pettigrew droned on. He talked about ownership of the means of production and distribution, and how the research he was doing for the party proved how much better the working class were going to be when Labour came to power. He presented figures to prove it, and smiled a self-congratulatory smile as he resumed his seat and beamed across at the chairman.

The audience had grown restless as he'd attempted to dazzle them with statistics; yet he appeared oblivious to their inattention. In the subdued light, Kathleen could make out a group of men near the door at the back, talking and joking among themselves. And when Albert asked if there were any questions, one man called out "Why can't we have a Wyndham?" A mutter of approval rose from round about him.

Albert stood up and glowered at him. "Charlie's ill. He's had to retire. That's why we've got Hubert Pettigrew."

"Suppose we don't want him?" the man asked.

"This is an emergency—" said Albert, only to be interrupted by the official sitting beside a nervy-looking Pettigrew.

"Headquarters decided—" began the official.

He got no further, because the whole place erupted in a cacophony of jeers and shouts.

"Ray Wyndham's daughter's here. Why can't we have her?"

"Because you can't," yelled the official. "Under emergency rule number—"

"We don't give a damn for your emergency rules," cried a woman. "Give us Kathleen Wyndham. She's got more guts than that lily-livered specimen sitting up there."

The first of the troublemakers became audacious enough to take a chance and make his presence felt. He careered down the aisle and leaped onto the stage. Intimidated by this turn of events, Pettigrew jumped from his seat and cowered behind his minder.

"Now, you," the troublemaker pointed a grubby finger

at Albert, "ask for a show of hands. Ask whether it should be Kathleen Wyndham or Hubert Pettigrew."

"You can't do that," the official attempted to explain again. "I've already said, under emergency—"

"Oh, shut your gob!" shouted Albert. "I'll do as I like!"

The entire hall exploded in a frenzy of cheers and shouts of encouragement. But before Albert could act, the troublemaker rushed at the official and hit him square on the jaw with a clenched fist. Reeling from the blow, the official lost his balance, his chair toppled backwards, and he landed in a heap on top of the cringing Pettigrew. Terrified out of his wits, Pettigrew extricated himself, made for the safety of the stage curtains, and slipped out of the rear exit with all the speed of a frightened rabbit. Around the hall sporadic skirmishes were breaking out between Wyndham supporters and their detractors. As Kathleen mounted the stage she was shaking from head to foot. Mouth dry as a desert, she swallowed a couple of times, then held up her hands to quell the tumult.

Taking this to be a sign of victory, the crowd began to chant, "Wyndham, Wyndham, we want Wyndham."

"All right, comrades, we'll put it to the vote," Albert shouted. "Now, on a show of hands: who wants Kathleen Wyndham as our candidate?"

Hands shot into the air around the hall.

"Who wants Hubert Pettigrew as our candidate?"

A few brave stalwarts raised their hands amid derisive yells from their neighbours.

"You can't do this, you know." The official, who'd picked himself up from the floor, was shaking his head as though he meant it. "You can't have her as the Labour candidate. It says in the rules—"

"We just have," retorted Albert.

"She can't be the Labour candidate, I tell you." The official was waving the rule book like a demented automaton.

Albert looked him straight in the eye and then turned to the hall. "I say let the Labour Party have Hubert Pettigrew if they like him so much, and we'll have Kathleen Wyndham to take him on. Yes?"

The crowd roared approval.

"I declare Kathleen Wyndham adopted as the Independent candidate for Spitalfields," shouted Albert.

Shouting and cheering broke out again, and the official, spitting with fury, marched down the aisle, jostled by Wyndham supporters. Kathleen stood on the stage, speechless in disbelief.

"You realise I haven't got a job any longer?" she said to Stella the next morning. "But you have, if you'll work for Pettigrew."

"I'm not working for that creep," Stella replied.

"They'll want the key back right away." Kathleen sighed. "We'd better go and hand it over."

By the time they reached the office the official was already there, gingerly fingering the bruise on his jaw. "Don't think you're going to get away with this. You'll be expelled from the party," he said as she handed him the key. He regarded Stella with disdain. "You may as well push off as well."

Kathleen opened her mouth but closed it again without saying anything.

"I'm so sorry, Stella," she said as they sat in Mary's kitchen, drinking tea.

"We'll just have to get on with it," Stella replied. "I've got enough money to keep me going till the election if I'm careful."

"I can't do it – stand as a candidate. It'd be a total disaster – no funds; no agent." Kathleen shook her head and made a face.

"I'll work for nothing," Stella said. "Look, I'm going to fill in your nomination and take it down now."

"You can't. You need signatures, and money for the deposit. I don't have any." Kathleen held up her hands in a gesture of futility.

Thumping on the front door made them both jump. They looked at one another in alarm, and Kathleen went to open it. On the pavement stood a man and a woman. The man was a spivvy sort of character: smartly dressed, neat moustache, with a scar running the length of his right cheek, and the little finger of his left hand was missing. The woman, a few years older than the man, was beautifully made up with manicured hands and bright red nails.

"Mummy! What on earth are you doing here?"

"Aren't you going to invite us in?" said Alexandra.

"Yes, of course, do come in. This is Stella Goodwin; Stella, my mother, Alexandra Wyndham – or is it Devereaux? I heard you'd gone back to the stage."

Alexandra shrugged. "Either – although round here Wyndham seems a popular name."

"Please, sit down. Can I make you a cup of tea?" Kathleen looked at the man, and wondered who he was.

"Cousin of mine," Alexandra said in a rather bored voice, flicking her head in his direction. "No, we're not here for tea." She sat down and signalled to the man to do likewise. "We're here because we've heard you're a candidate and we'd like to do our little bit to help, wouldn't we?" She nudged the man in the ribs, and he grunted his agreement.

"What do you mean, 'help'?" asked Kathleen.

"It's like this," replied Alexandra, eyes fixed on Kathleen. "We – that's the Dobbins – we've got a nice little business going in this patch and we don't want some busybody coming in and spoiling it for us."

"And what's that got to do with me?" enquired Kathleen.

"Don't suppose you've got much in the coffers, and here you are, skint, going to fight an election."

"I don't think I will be fighting the election – there's been a bit of a misunderstanding."

"We could offer you funds," said Alexandra with a feline smile. "Help you on your way, so to speak."

"Why would you do that?" Kathleen asked.

"Do you have to ask?" cooed Alexandra. "I just want to help my little girl. Does a mother need a reason to help her little girl?"

"You've never bothered before," replied Kathleen indignantly.

Ignoring the jibe, Alexandra smiled sweetly. "The first thing you need is money for the deposit. Now, we could help you straight away with that." She opened her handbag to reveal rolls of banknotes. "How much exactly do you need?"

"I don't need any," retorted Kathleen. "I shan't be standing. Last night was a big mistake. Now please go – both of you."

"You'll be sorry about this!" shrieked Alexandra as Kathleen bundled her out of the front door.

"Sorry, that's what you'll be," echoed the man through clenched teeth.

Kathleen shut the door on them, went back to the kitchen and slumped onto a chair, trembling with indignation.

"That was your mother?" asked Stella.

Kathleen nodded miserably and buried her head in her hands.

CHAPTER 30

Half an hour later there was more thumping on the door, and this time it was Albert holding up an old shopping bag and insisting he had enough money for Kathleen's deposit. "Few savings of me own and Charlie's," he said, "and some from other Wyndhams you won't have heard of. And of course we took a collection last night. Wouldn't let 'em leave till we'd relieved 'em of a bit of loose change."

Stella was beside herself with excitement, and insisted they should get on with whatever needed to be done right away. Yet it seemed to Kathleen that everybody, Stella included, had gone completely mad and hadn't thought things through. For instance, only the people who had been at the meeting the evening before would know what had happened, and even if they knew why she was standing, nobody would know what she stood for. When she pointed this out, Albert shook his head in a disappointed way and said he'd thought she had more guts than to give up at the first hurdle. When Albert had left, Stella too observed that it was not like Kathleen to give up so easily. And because Kathleen couldn't quite believe what she was hearing, she told Stella she needed to be alone, to get away and clear her head, and so she was going out for a walk.

She wandered down the street, past the rubble-strewn bomb site, and turned the corner. Already two windows displayed posters: 'VOTE LABOUR: PETTIGREW'. What an enormous task lay ahead if she took on the might of the Labour Party. All the canvass returns, all the lists of volunteers were filed away at the office, and Rat-Man was putting them to use right away. She turned into another street, and not a hundred yards away a man wearing a Labour rosette was knocking on a door. It would be a waste of everyone's time and money if she fought this election.

She went back and told Stella, but Stella only replied that it was totally out of character for Kathleen to not even try. When over supper that evening Rose made a similar remark, Kathleen felt so irritated by the lack of common sense shown by everyone around her that she burst out, "But there's no point in my standing. The names of all the people who might help me or vote for me are at the office."

Instantly, Rose left the table and ran upstairs, and when she returned she was carrying a box containing loose sheets of typewritten paper and looking extremely pleased with herself.

"What's that?" asked Kathleen.

"All the names," said Rose with a smirk.

"How did you get them?"

"Needed typing practice, so I made copies of everything Stella'd already done. Course, there are a few mistakes." Rose screwed up her nose. "But they're not that bad."

"That's wonderful," Kathleen said, but only because Rose was full of pride. "I don't suppose it's a complete list, is it?"

"Pretty near," Rose replied. "Ain't no excuse now."

Kathleen's stomach began to churn in a sickening way as she nodded and looked away. Nobody had actually asked her if she wanted to stand. The mere thought of getting elected scared her half to death. She couldn't do it – go to Parliament and make speeches. She didn't have a university degree; she wasn't clever; she didn't have a party behind her. Her best excuse had gone, and Rose and Albert and the others were sweeping her along on a tide of their own expectations, and she felt desperately alone.

"That's the spirit," Rose replied.

"Ain't no time to lose," chipped in Mary. "Go and see Albert straight away. I'll tell Charlie at visiting. It'll do 'im the world of good to hear you're gonna do it."

Kathleen knocked on Albert's door, hoping it wouldn't take long for him to say he couldn't make out the names. She handed him the badly typed lists and watched him scan the first page.

"Blimey, girl! Like gold dust, this is. How...?"

"Rose – practising." She willed him not to decipher the words.

"Got a way to go yet 'fore she'll get a job as a typist," he observed. "But you can see what she's got here, more or less."

"The thing is, Uncle Albert, it doesn't really change things, does it? We still haven't got enough money, and even if we did scrape some together, Pettigrew's bound to win in the end." Hope that Albert would see sense was draining from her even as she spoke.

"Could put up a hell of a fight, though," he said. "That bastard Pettigrew needs taking down a peg or two, and I reckon you're the one to do it."

"Supposing I won?"

"Supposing you won?" A puzzled look spread over Albert's face. "Well, then you'd go to Parliament and speak up for us, that's what you'd do, girl." He stared at her as if she were barking mad.

"I don't think I can do it." It sounded so feeble, not like her saying the words at all, and she felt ashamed.

"Course you can do it, girl! You're a Wyndham, ain't you?"

There wasn't the remotest chance of her winning, she reminded herself, but at least having a shot at it would stop Albert and the others going on so.

When she got back Stella was making plans to start a poster campaign, and was on the verge of going out to buy paper and paint. So instead of raising any objection, Kathleen told Stella that she was going out to knock on a few doors and would be back later. And it worked, because Stella gave an encouraging smile and left without another word.

In a street not far away, Kathleen knocked on doors she'd knocked on weeks ago, when she was Charlie's agent. Most people were out, because they were at work or shopping or doing other things, but those who answered remembered her and seemed pleased to discover that she was standing in the election. To introduce herself she used the same words each time, and after a while they kept floating around in her head as if they were on a record playing over and over again. It was comforting because it stopped her thinking about what it would be like making a proper speech to a lot of people.

Albert appointed himself her agent, and Auntie Mary's front room became her headquarters. Albert told Kathleen he regretted that in the heat of the moment they hadn't thought to call her 'Independent Labour'. "Point is, we gotta get across that they'll get a better deal from you than from that idiot Pettigrew, because you're a Wyndham and you're local," he told her. And he had Stella turning out posters with the legend:

KATHLEEN WYNDHAM
YOUR LOCAL CANDIDATE
AN INDEPENDENT VOICE

"Someone been looking for you," Albert told Kathleen one morning. "Said his name was Lord Neville and he wanted to help Miss Wyndham. I bumped into him coming away from the old office. Wouldn't have got any joy there, so I told him to get his backside down here and we'd find a job for him. Don't s'pose we'll hear nothing more."

"Robert?"

"Know 'im, do you?"

She nodded. "Yes – very well, actually."

"A toff, working for you? Sure it ain't some kind of wind-up?"

Almost immediately there was a knock at the door, and Stella went to answer it.

"Is this Miss Wyndham's headquarters?" the visitor asked.

"Yes," Kathleen heard Stella say. "Oh, I remember you – at Pilgrim House. You used to leave messages for Kathleen. You're—"

She never got the chance to finish. Sending a sheaf of papers flying, Kathleen dashed to the front door. "Oh, Robert," she cried. "What are you doing here?"

"I heard you were standing in the election and I've come to offer my services," he replied.

"How could you possibly know?"

"I was talking to the political correspondent of the *News Chronicle* and he said something interesting was going on down here: a popular local woman was standing against Labour as an Independent."

"The press knows?"

"You'll probably find a reporter on the doorstep before you know it." He was trying not to smile.

She became aware of Albert standing behind her. "Uncle Albert, I'd like you to meet Robert Neville; Robert, this is Albert Wyndham."

"Pleased to be introduced properly, Mr Wyndham," Robert said, and offered a hand.

Albert closed his mouth and looked at Robert, not quite sure what to make of him, then shook his hand. "Pleased to meet you, sir."

"I'm here to help," Robert said.

Albert recovered his wits and sprang into action. "There's still a deal of canvassing needs doing. You up for it?" he asked.

"Yes, indeed," Robert replied.

"Here you are, then. Here's the streets that need doing." Albert pointed to a list. "Need to take a notepad with you.

Don't spend more than two minutes chinwagging on the doorstep. Your job's to find out whether they're going to vote Wyndham. Make sure they know she's the local candidate, who will fight for people around here. Don't stand there arguing with them – waste of time. Got that?"

Kathleen watched Uncle Albert. He'd never talked to a toff before, let alone barked out orders at one, and she saw his eyes narrow to dubious slits as he wondered if he'd overstepped the mark.

"I think I can manage that, and if I have any problems I'll come back and seek your advice." Robert smiled at Albert.

"I'll come with you, Robert." Kathleen broke in. "For the first few houses, just to see you're all right."

As soon as they were out of sight, she caught his arm and made him stop. "You know I'm doing this – letting my name go forward – because Uncle Charlie was taken ill and there was a big row because no one liked the man who took his place. But he's bound to get in, the Labour man; almost everyone round here votes Labour. So you don't have to try hard, because there's no chance I'll win. Anyway, I don't want to win. I couldn't do it; I just couldn't."

By the time she'd finished she was out of breath and clutching Robert's arm. He stood quite still, and she wondered why he was looking at her that way.

"This doesn't sound like the girl I know," he said. "The girl who's ready to say what she thinks, and who speaks up for people who can't speak for themselves."

"I can't do it – not at meetings, in front of crowds. I couldn't possibly make speeches in debates, like they do at conferences and in Parliament; I just couldn't."

"It's difficult at first," he said. "But it's the kind of thing you can learn, and after a while it isn't nearly as frightening as it was at the beginning."

"You weren't scared, were you?"

"Everyone's scared the first time," he replied.

And when she didn't say anything, he took her hand and held it between his own, just like he used to, and she felt calmer and safer than she'd felt in a long time.

"You don't have to make a speech right away. Some MPs go for years without ever making a speech, and if you wanted to make a speech, I could help you. You wouldn't be on your own."

She saw in his face that he meant it; that if there were things she didn't understand about the way things were done in Parliament, she could ask him. "I… I don't know. I don't know if I can do it. My hands go all clammy just thinking about it, and I feel sick."

"I'll always be there for you, Kathleen, whatever you decide." He squeezed her hand and let it go. "And now I'm going to do what Mr Wyndham told me, and find out who's going to vote for you."

She watched him walk down the street and knock at a house, and the idea of fighting this election – fighting to win the seat – was not as terrifying as it had been. For the first time she wondered if it was possible; if she could do it.

At the end of polling day Kathleen sat in Auntie Mary's kitchen and wondered how she could feel so tired and still keep her eyes open. That night she crawled into bed, too exhausted to care about anything, and fell into a deep sleep.

Robert had been by her side whenever it mattered. He'd been there when the reporter from the *News Chronicle* had come to interview her. He'd helped her prepare a speech for the rally. The hall had been packed; the hubbub almost deafening. She'd sat with Albert behind a table decked with bunting and posters proclaiming that she was the Independent candidate. Although her heart raced and her tongue felt as if it was stuck to the roof of her mouth, she'd made a speech.

There'd been an awkward moment when a man had heckled, and called out that a woman's place was in the home. But it had fired her up and made her angry, and she'd shouted back at him, "A woman's place is where she's needed, and I'll work till I drop to get the things people round here need, like free healthcare, decent houses and proper jobs. And I want a fairer deal for women too." Everyone had cheered and clapped, and afterwards Robert had told her how well she'd done, and she'd been grateful for all his help and had told him so.

Now it was a matter of waiting. They weren't going to count the votes for three weeks, because most of the armed forces were still abroad, and it would take that long to get their ballot boxes home. Stella went back to Plymouth to wait for news of Ken's release, and Robert went off to continue liaising with the American military. Uncle Charlie was allowed home, and Kathleen helped Mary look after him. But after the hurly-burly of the last few weeks, she felt flat and lifeless and didn't know what to do with herself much of the time.

She wrote to Alice to let her know what had happened, and Alice wrote back saying that she couldn't imagine what

Kathleen could possibly get up to next, and refrained from making any comment on Kathleen's political activities.

And I've been keeping a few hens in a corner of the garden – for the eggs, you know – but they're getting on a bit, and Bertie says they're only good for the pot. It's such a dilemma. It would be like killing old friends, and I don't think I can do it. What would you do, Kathleen?

Come and see me soon, and we can chat about old times and perhaps you can help me decide what to do with the hens.

The idea of Alice trying to pluck a hen and get rid of its 'innards', as Edith called them, was so entertaining that Kathleen laughed out loud.

Remembering Edith made her think of Beth and Tom, and that only added to her melancholy. She wondered whether it might've been better after all to let Jim divorce her and get his money. Perhaps, even now, if the court knew that Robert was Beth's father it could make all the difference. Then she recalled how the evidence had been twisted at the trial all those years ago. But if Robert was there and spoke up, surely they'd listen to him. A spark ignited, and a little flame of hope began to burn deep inside her.

When a letter from Edith arrived, she seized it with joy took it into the front room, and sat in an armchair to read it. Edith hoped that Kathleen was well and enjoyed working for her uncle, and that soon he'd have some good news. Kathleen wondered how Edith's face would look if she knew what had actually happened.

We've had some wonderful news down here, and I said to myself, I must write and let Kathleen know right away.

Beth came home with a letter saying she's passed the scholarship and she'll be going to the grammar school come September. She's the first pupil from Southwood School ever to pass for the grammar school, and the headmaster gave them all a half-day's holiday on the strength of it. She's got a clever head on those shoulders of hers, just like her mother. She'll go a long way, you mark my words.

Kathleen read the letter again. It was indeed wonderful news. Then she thought about the divorce and her determination to do battle with Jim for custody of the children. What would happen when the truth came out? How would Beth feel to learn that her mother wasn't dead and the man she'd been brought up to call 'Father' wasn't her father at all? Why, oh why were things always so difficult; so complicated? How could Kathleen suddenly reappear after all this time and expect everything to be all right? It would be the most utterly selfish thing she'd ever done. She couldn't do it, not now; she couldn't hurt Beth. Her tears fell, making Edith's words run in dark streams on the paper.

Charlie was sitting at the kitchen table with Mary when Kathleen and Albert came in from the count on the 26th July.

"You should've been there; you should've heard it!" Albert was waving his arms above his head.

"Goodness' sake, calm down! You know Charlie's not supposed to get excited," Mary reprimanded him.

Albert took no notice. "Victory? I should say so. Total annihilation, that's what it was. I shall see that toffee-nosed git's face till the day I die: Hubert Pettigrew, Labour: 20,460.' He paused for effect. "Kathleen Wyndham, Independent: 25,704."

The kitchen erupted with hysterical cheering.

"Well done, girl!" Charlie looked more alive than he had for weeks. "Your dad would have been proud. We're all proud." His voice shook with emotion.

In the midst of the celebrations there was a knock at the door and Kathleen went to answer it.

"Robert?"

"I came to say congratulations. May I come in?"

"How did you know so soon?"

"I've been at the *Daily Express* offices all morning. They're getting the results as they come in, before the BBC broadcasts them, and I heard yours." He smiled. "And I just had to come and tell you how pleased I am. You're marvellous."

He put his arms around her and kissed her, and she felt as if her heart would break from sheer joy.

"Sounds like it's going to be a landslide," he went on.

"A landslide? What do you mean?"

"Labour's made over a hundred gains so far and it looks like they're going to be the next government. Big changes on the way, and you'll be in the thick of it."

"You will be there for me, won't you?" She put a hand on his arm. "I don't think I can do it without you."

"You won't find it easy to get rid of me." He was smiling as if he knew something she didn't. "I've just taken a flat not ten minutes' walk from Parliament. I'd appreciate your opinion on the furnishings."

"I hope you're not expecting me to clean it for you." Kathleen's expression was one of mock indignation.

"Oh no, oh no, I didn't mean…" Robert's face flushed with embarrassment.

Kathleen laughed. "Dear Robert, the look on your face is priceless. I'd love to dine with you at your flat."

"I'm afraid the flat's not quite ready, but I have taken the liberty of booking a table for two at The Dorchester. Would the Honourable Member for Spitalfields consent to dine with me this evening?"

Kathleen wondered what the future held, and it was clear to her that life would be as difficult and complicated as it always had been, and that there would be no easy answers. And then she thought that, in a way, it wouldn't matter as long as they could be together. She looked up and saw that there was hope and love in Robert's face too, all mixed up, and she put out a hand and stroked his cheek with her finger.

"Thank you, Lord Neville," she replied. "I should be delighted."

This book is printed on paper from sustainable sources managed under the Forest Stewardship Council (FSC) scheme.

It has been printed in the UK to reduce transportation miles and their impact upon the environment.

For every new title that Troubador publishes, we plant a tree to offset CO_2, partnering with the More Trees scheme.

For more about how Troubador offsets its environmental impact, see www.troubador.co.uk/sustainability-and-community